Trails Of Trouble

JACK LAFOUNTAIN

House of Honor Books

House of Honor

ISBN: 978-1-68596-075-9

Printed in the United States of America

Published by House of Honor Books.

Harvest, Alabama

DEDICATION

This book is dedicated to my grandson, Bryan LaFountain whose first attempt at writing set fire to my imagination and gave birth to this book.

FOREWORD

I don't have the best functioning concept of the past. Hannibal crossing the Alps and the American Revolution seem about as immediately in the past as moving to Alabama three years ago. So, when I tell you that I first wrote Trails of Trouble in 2012, you know it's just my best guess based on the date on transferred computer files and my grandson's age.

The inspiration for the story dates back to a time more than five years before that. I had a moving picture in my head of a not-quite-human being racing through trees toward disaster in a distant city with a dominant gold dome. For years, I tried to run with the idea and got nowhere. Though the picture played over in my mind from time to time, I had given up on it as a storyline.

Meanwhile, I self-published a book that became Death Rides the Red River. My grandson, Bryan, ever the imitator of his grandpa, decided to write a story. Proud of his achievement, he brought it home from school and laid it on my desk. I read it and Trails of Trouble was born. I wrote the story one chapter a week and posted it on my blog.

It was later picked up by a small publisher who did some editing on it. It lay dormant there until I reclaimed my rights to it. By that time Ed Landry had claimed my attention. Ed is still full of stories he wants told, but I found time while he was at Mardi Gras to edit Trails of Trouble once more and get it to my new editor at House of Honor Books.

Bryan asked for a share of the royalties and after the long wait it's still a "maybe". What follows is his spark of inspiration for this book and Bryn's adventures yet to come.

This story is about a man named Wingstone. He was a prince with black hair and peach colored skin. His father, King Richard and his three headed hell hound, Krutos lived in the Kingdom of Pryas.

"This is a day to celebrate," King Richard told his son. "The kingdom has had peace since the day the world was created. And son, I have a gift for you, the Sword of Fire. The gods made it themselves to watch over our kingdom. Only the brave of heart can control it."

Later that day, a terrific darkness tarnished the kingdom.

Welcome
To the
World
Of Bryn Bou

CHAPTER 1

General Bou cocked an ear toward a sound that had no place on his parade ground. He knew the sound well and received it with mixed emotions. The excited voices of bystanders cheering on a fight was testimony to the fighting spirit of his cadets. Brawling, however, was a serious break in the discipline and good order of the Academy. The sound grated on the general's ears like claws dragged across a chalkboard. He turned the corner of the mess hall and approached the uniformed figure at the far end of the building who seemed to be absorbed in the illicit proceedings.

"Sergeant Major," he whispered in the sergeant's ear.

The sergeant jumped as if shot. As with any good noncom, he landed at attention. To his credit, his salute trembled only slightly.

"General sir," he said.

"Let me save you an explanation," said the general. "You were just about to break it up, right?"

"No sir. I mean, yes sir, General."

The general stretched his neck to gaze over the sergeant's shoulder at the moving circle of cheering cadets almost lost in a cloud of dust.

"Who's winning?" he asked.

The sergeant turned to look at the mob. Suddenly, the crowd parted and Moryn Del flew from their midst and landed on his back with a thud. A second cadet landed atop Moryn, delivering a series of well-aimed punches.

"I'd say your son seems to be winning, sir."

"Hmmm, so I see. Move over a bit, Sergeant Major," the general said, giving him a gentle nudge. "You're blocking my view."

The circle of cadets shifted to close around the combatants once again. The fight continued for another minute until a shrill whistle abruptly ended the cheering. The cadets snapped to attention as Colonel Ren approached from the far side of the grounds with fire in his eyes. General Bou quickly ducked behind the cover of the mess hall. As he did, he caught the sergeant major by the collar and pulled him along.

"Go and relieve the Colonel," Bou said. "Get the contestants cleaned up and have them report to me."

"Yes, sir."

"Oh, and Sergeant-Major," General Bou said. "Good work on your hand-to-hand instruction."

"Thank you, sir. I'll have them in your office on the double, sir."

Moryn eased the Commandant's door closed as he slunk from the room. His whipped puppy expression lasted only long enough for his eyes to find and skewer his sparring partner. He forked the sign of the evil eye and stormed away. Bryn Bou hung his head. He was next. His classmates assumed times like this were easier for him. Bryn had given up trying to tell them that just the opposite was true. They had no idea how heavy and inescapable the burden of being the son of a legend was.

"Cadet Bou, get in here!" the General's voice barked from the other room.

Bryn jumped from his chair. Long strides carried him through the door to stand front and center. He threw up a crisp salute.

"Cadet Bou reporting as ordered, sir," he announced.

The General returned the salute and fixed Bryn with a withering glare. Sweat coursed in rivulets down Bryn's temples, back and sides. Just as he was convinced, that he would literally melt away, his father sighed and leaned back in his chair.

"What was it this time?" the General asked.

"A difference of opinion, sir."

"About?"

"I respectfully decline to say, sir."

"I see." The corners of the General's beak pulled down even further. "You could not keep your opinion to yourself and simply walk away?"

"I attempted that maneuver sir, without success. The way was blocked by the opposing force, and I was constrained to force my way through."

"Frontal assaults are seldom a wise choice."

"Yes sir, as evidenced by my standing here."

"Then, get out of here. Dismissed."

Bryn saluted, did an about-face, and hurried from the room. He had gotten off easy, the very thing of which Moryn forever accused him.

"Damn my luck." he said softly.

"Well, if you're not glad to see me," a soft feminine voice said. "Perhaps, Moryn…"

"What? Faryn, no. That is, I'm thrilled to see you."

His heart began beating again when she smiled. The cares of the day evaporated; the bruises stayed but he could no longer feel them. Faryn Go was a tall, red-crested, Creator-broke-the-mold, vision of down covered warrior with the power to turn males into quivering swamp jelly. She stepped up to him and gently laid a finger on the cut above Bryn's eye.

"You need to learn to protect that face," she cooed.

"Warriors need a few scars," he said. "Gives them a battle-hardened look."

"If it's scars you want, I'll run my dagger across your arm. You keep that face the way it is."

"I'll do better next time."

"Next time? Next time is not a good idea," she warned.

"No, it's not. It's inevitable though and we both know it."

"Males, honestly."

Bryn stared at the ceiling above his bed. That afternoon's fight with Moryn was only the latest in a series of clashes between the two of them. Faryn lay at the heart of their troubles. It was no secret that Moryn was in love with her. He had been even before they arrived at the Academy. He complained Bryn was interfering with his destiny and trying to steal the wife that was his due.

Thankfully, Faryn didn't agree.

Moryn's recourse was to assail Bryn. He told everyone that Bryn was not cut out to be a warrior, that he was admitted to the Academy on his father's name.

His escape from punishment that day was going to add fuel to the fire. Moryn's focus would be on the special privileges Bryn received. He would fail to mention that he himself was not punished either. It had become a familiar story.

Their confrontations were far from one sided. They were equally matched physically and academically. That too was a thorn in Moryn's side. Moryn's accusations held little truth. Yet many of the cadets were eager to assume Moryn was right despite evidence to the contrary.

What gnawed at Bryn was the knowledge that Moryn, at least in part, was right. He was not a warrior. He had the head for it, but he lacked the heart. His own grandfather had said as much. Still, there was no escaping the fact he was a Bou. The world within the Boubouja expected him to be like his fabled warrior ancestors.

His struggles to fit into the mold cast for him grew more difficult as his graduation approached. Bryn did not doubt his own courage. It was his skill as a leader and his lack of motivation that haunted him. He had a sense of being driven, but no idea where he was going.

The next morning Bryn peered up at the giant trees of his homeland. Their upper reaches were wrapped in a misty shroud. With a deep sigh, he stepped from the sunlit colors of the jungle into the perpetual gray of the Grove of the Dead. He had come to the grove to think about what he would tell his father.

That was true enough, but it was not the whole truth. He had been searching for the words for months. His latest scuffle with Moryn had finally forced him to a decision. Skipping classes to come to the grove set him free from the inertia that held him prisoner. His father would demand to know why he missed his classes. He could not lie to his father. He would be compelled to say the often rehearsed, yet unspoken words.

That would come later in the day. For the moment, he would sit and try to imagine a happy ending to the confrontation. He was already lost in thought, but his feet knew the way. He simply followed them through the fog to the burial tree. His fingers lingered on the letters carved into the trunk that spelled out the name of every soul resting in the branches above him.

Will it ever fit?

Bou was a good name, the name of legends, the name of heroes and warriors. It was his name but, in his heart, he was none of those things. Knowing that weighed like a millstone about his neck. He sighed again and climbed to perch in the crook of the lowest branch. He loved the muted solitude of the grove; it was made for reflection. He could think there.

The Valir people avoided the burial grove. They came when they must and quickly retreated as if chased by unseen spirits. Bryn always lingered. In a way, he was always in the grove looking up at his fathers in their woven burial sacks. There was no escaping it. He was Bryn, son of Byryn of the Bou clan. He was proud of his name, though he wished he were not its prisoner. Bryn closed his eyes and pushed away the image of his father's face.

A hushed shuffle of footfalls on fallen leaves called him from his thoughts. He lifted a single eyelid on an otherwise still face. A silhouette at the edge of his vision wavered in and out of focus. The featureless figure seemed to look up at him. Squinting did not improve his focus. Curiosity eventually won out and Bryn lifted his head for a better look. The gray figure made no move to escape. It stood staring at him until a breath of breeze carried it away like smoke.

Bryn jumped from his perch to the spot where the figure stood. The forest litter was undisturbed. A bright blue orb rested where nothing had been a moment ago. Bryn bent to study it. Sensing no danger, he scooped it up. The ball was warm in his hands. As he lifted it closer, the surface began to move. The movement was followed by a rhythmic pulse that moved from his hands up his arms.

The world around him disappeared.

Bryn blinked back the bright sunlight. Turning in a slow circle told him the world hadn't truly disappeared. It was just no longer the world he knew. The green expanse of bouja trees marshes, swaps and streams were gone. They had been replaced with black sand and crashing waves whose foaming dregs washed his feet.

A blue sea stretched unbroken to the horizon. The air was heavy with the sharp tang of brine. The feathers on his neck ruffled in the breeze blowing in over the water. Unseen was the dark, nagging sense of danger. Bryn shivered and wrapped his coat tighter around his shoulders.

The featureless gray figure he had seen earlier was staring at him from a nearby dune. A fleshless hand emerged from the shifting gray mist and pointed toward the sea.

"Look and see," said a voice that rolled over Bryn's ears like a rushing wind.

Hie eyes returned to the rolling surface of the sea. Though he lived far from the sea, he was not unfamiliar with its undulating surface. He saw nothing worthy of note and certainly nothing to fear. Turning once more, movement caught his eye.

A shimmering mountain of iridescent green rose from the water. A horned head carried on a long, slender neck appeared. Bryn retreated a step. Upon the water dragon's back rode a man in a long purple robe. In his left hand was a sword of sliver; in his right a shining scepter dipped in blood.

At the rider's command the sea monster beached itself. Black clouds built on the horizon and thunder rumbled across the sky. The man slid from the creature's back, rose on the wind, and was gone. Gone too was the gray shadow figure and the dune it stood upon.

In their place was a vast city set upon a plain. A golden dome crowned the highest tower. Beneath the dome Bryn saw creatures of every kind spread out before a high platform where two thrones, white as snow, faced one another. The platform was draped in banners of every color.

Upon the first throne sat a king in a magnificent robe wearing a golden crown upon his head. On the second throne was a man wearing a simple white tunic. The man in white rose, stepped near, and knelt before the king. The king removed his robe and laid it on the kneeling man's shoulders. He put the golden crown upon the man's head. When the crown touched him, a shining sword appeared.

Before the new king's hand touched the sword, the dragon rider appeared and plucked it up. Wielding the sword, the dragon rider slew the two kings and placed the golden crown upon his own head. Then, as he lifted high the shining sword, the crowd bowed down before him.

"Come and see," the gray figure's voice said.

Bryn suddenly found himself standing among the crowd at the feet of the dragon rider. A rumbling sound arose from the east. The sound was like thunder, but not the rolling thunder of a coming storm. It was the thunder of thousands of charging beasts.

The earth trembled as a cloud of dust filled the eastern sky. The thunder built upon itself, blotting out all else. As it closed upon him, Bryn recognized another sound mixed within the first. A blade of ice stabbed his heart. It was the sound of dying—the sound of war. A mounted army of men emerged from the dust. In their panic the retreating army rode down the people of the city trampling underfoot the women and children. The beings gathered there from every kingdom fled in terror.

"Come and see," the gray one's voice rumbled again.

Bryn's world was back. He found himself amid the upper branches of a bouja tree bent over and panting for air. The air around him vibrated with the muffled rumble of a big cat's breathing. Bryn felt it circling just out of sight. He reached for the dagger in his belt.

Gone!

Snapping off a limb, he slipped into the cover of a sapper vine. The cat passed like a silent, black shadow without seeing him. Bryn sprang from cover, driving the broken limb between the cat's shoulders. The cat's scream caught in its throat. It was dead before it hit the ground below.

The feathers on Bryn's neck suddenly stood on end.

"Damn," he whispered, whirling around to meet the charge.

Too late. The second cat's jaws closed around his head and pain exploded.

The pale disc of morning sun hidden in the mist of the Grove filled his eyes. He shook his head and let the dream gradually seep away.

"And that's why you are no warrior," Bryn said to himself. "The General would have known the second cat was there and been ready."

Bryn shook his head once more. Even in his dreams he fell short. It happened every time. He was never quite good enough, always a step behind.

Like right now, the thought blossomed in his mind.

He was sitting there moaning over a dream when his crawling skin was shouting at him that he was being watched. Slowly, so as not to startle the watcher, he turned his head. A pair of large black eyes stared back at him from a nearby branch. Bryn released the breath he was holding. It was only a small, white owl. Owls weren't uncommon in the burial grove, but he had never seen one like this. It was about six inches tall, covered with white feathers and black, heart-shaped spots.

"What are you looking at?" Bryn asked the bird.

The bird swiveled his head and with a silent flap of wings launched into the air. Bryn's flash of anger was gone as quickly as it appeared. Owls couldn't talk and even if they could, how could it possibly know the answer when Bryn had no idea what the answer might be.

Just what am I?

He was no warrior, that much seemed settled. But if not a warrior from a long line of warriors, then what exactly was he? Given the wild dream he just had, crazy was not out of the question. The dream felt so real. The wind on his face, the smell of the sea, it was unlike any dream he'd ever had.

"Too real," he said as though someone could hear.

In the quiet of the Grove, the dream certainly seemed as real as the sound of his voice. Another question sprang suddenly to mind. If it was real, what did that mean?

The Valir believed that dreams were sent by the Creator. Was this one? And, if so, what did it mean? Bryn shrugged and glided to the ground. It was time to go face his father.

Bryn reached the village no more ready to confront his father than when he left home that morning. Students at the Military Academy told the Commandant that they were dropping out every term. There was no shame in it. But then, the Commandant was not their father. His dread might be overcome if he had an idea what he was going to do with his life.

The sun was well past its zenith by the time he reached the outskirts of Vix. He was going through a final rehearsal of his speech when he stumbled into the village square.

"Where you been all day, Bou?" a familiar voice greeted him.

"Don't you know?" a second voice answered. "Anywhere he wants. His daddy is the Commandant."

"Yeah, he can do no wrong," a third voice chimed in.

Bryn cast a quick glance around him. Moryn and his buddy,

Jeryn, stood across Bryn's path. Laryn was circling around Bryn's right side. There was still time to retreat, but the speed that course required didn't sit well with his pride.

"What do you want?" Bryn asked.

"You out of my life would be nice," Moryn said.

"Pack up and go home," Bryn said. "Mission accomplished."

Bryn was moving as he spoke. Moryn's roundhouse punch sailed harmlessly by Bryn's ear. Bryn pistoned his legs, driving his shoulder into Moryn's chest. The blow sent Moryn back on his heels. He regained his balance and launched his whole body at Bryn. Bryn caught his assailant's tunic, side stepped the flying tackle, and sent Moryn sprawling. Unbridled hate flared in Moryn's eyes as he rose from the dust, dagger in his hand.

CHAPTER 2

The old seer was called from a fitful sleep by a voice that was too young and too cheerful. Grumbling a protest, Coryn tossed back the blanket and swung his tired body over the edge of his bed. Gnarled fingers scrubbed his deeply lined face. It seemed unfair to wake up aching and stiff but there was nothing fair about growing old.

"Come in," he croaked, coughed, and tried again with a clearer voice.

"Good day Grandfather," Faryn's voice chimed from the doorway.

"What's so good about it?" Coryn asked. "And quit sounding so darn happy about waking your elders."

"Oh, Grandfather," she chirped and kissed his cheek. "The day is almost gone. You should be out enjoying the sun."

She pulled back the broad leaf curtains opening the room to a stream of blinding sunlight.

"Close that curtain," Coryn growled blinking back the light. "Sunlight is overrated. Where's Catryn?"

"You gave her the day off remember?" Faryn ignored his order and tied back the curtain. "She made me promise to check on you."

"Old busybody," he mumbled.

"What was that?"

"Nothing."

"What was your dream about?" she asked.

"Dream?"

"Yes, dream." she challenged.

"You're too smart for your own good," Coryn told her. "Just like your mother."

"I'll take that as a compliment," she replied. "But not as an answer."

Faryn handed him a steaming cup of fig leaf tea and stared

down at him while he sipped the hot liquid. A quiet unease crept over her. Her grandfather was quick to share his dreams with her. The rare occasions when he hesitated invariably signaled the approach of something bad.

"Well?"

Coryn cleared his throat and sipped his tea once more. A shiver ran down his granddaughter's spine before she heard the words that turned her heart to ice.

"I can't tell you," he said. "Not now. I'm going to have to see the Council."

"Oh," she said, keeping her voice light. "Will the end of the world wait for us to have our walk?"

"I hope so," he replied, but his smile, laced with uncertainty held no warmth. "Help me with my cloak."

Faryn endured the not so playful chiding of her classmates about the time she spent with the old one. It wasn't hard to do; she genuinely enjoyed their walks around the village. She found he exuded a quiet peace that was at odds with his public persona. To everyone else he was Coryn Kel, Seer of the Valir. His reputation as a powerful channel of the Creator was well deserved. The old folks claimed he could work miracles. Miracle or not, his vision and leadership had guided the kingdom safely through a terrible war and an uneasy peace. However, to Faryn, he was simply a kind grandfather from whom friends shied away when she tried to introduce them.

That day, he was unusually quiet. There was little of their usual banter. She thought it was not the best of omens. She could almost hear the wheels turning in his head as he worked over whatever new thing was on his mind. She found it reassuring that the peace she drew from him was undisturbed by whatever occupied his thoughts. She had arrived that afternoon with an agenda. Given his somber mood, she decided it could wait.

As they turned the corner onto the main road through the village, Faryn drew a sharp breath. Her hand tightened on her grandfather's arm. There was a scuffle underway at the edge of the village square.

Three youths in the uniform of the Military Academy circled another boy. She instantly recognized the participants. It was not the first time Bryn and Moryn had squared off in public. Moryn was a bully with a chip on his shoulder. Bryn was the only male she knew who couldn't or wouldn't back down when Moryn pushed. It was all so childish.

Until now.

Daggers had replaced fists. She could see blood on the ground. Instinctively, she moved to intervene as she had done in the past. Her grandfather's hand swiftly barred the way.

"Enough!" Coryn's voice boomed.

The force in his voice startled her. It seemed to have the same effect on Moryn and his buddies. They tucked their daggers into their belts and ran leaving Bryn to face the prophet's rebuke alone.

Coryn shook his granddaughter's hand from his arm and walked quickly to the boy intending to administer the expected tongue lashing. Before he could say a word, the boy looked up. At the same moment Faryn's arm wound a restraining hold on him. The seer sighed.

"Bryn Bou," Coryn's voice was almost a whisper.

"Forgive me," Bryn said.

"You're bleeding," Faryn said, touching his arm.

"Come with us," Coryn ordered. "We'll look after that and speak in private. There's been enough brawling in the street for today."

Bryn followed them to the seer's house, sitting quietly while his arm was bandaged. Faryn tied off the dressing and carried away the basin of water. Coryn waited until she was out of earshot and turned to Bryn.

"Want to tell me what that was all about?" the seer asked.

"A misunderstanding, sir," Bryn replied.

"A potentially deadly misunderstanding it would seem."

"Yes, sir. Sorry sir."

"Who started it?"

"It just sort of happened," Bryn said.

Coryn's eyes fastened on Bryn who struggled in vain to look away. After an eternity, Faryn returned to the room, and he was able to escape.

"Yes," Coryn said. "I think I see the answer now. In any case, your father will want to hear what you have to say sooner rather than later."

"Grandfather," Faryn said, "Is that really necessary?"

"I'm not speaking of this little altercation." His eyes returned to Bryn's. "You know that don't you?"

"I was on my way there when...." his voice trailed away into a shrug of his shoulders.

"Good," the seer replied. "I want you to come see me after the Council meets. We'll talk about the future."

"Sir, I don't think the Council—" Bryn began.

"They don't know it yet," Coryn interrupted and smiled. "But they will meet soon. Promise me you will come."

"If that's your wish," Bryn said. "I will come."

"Good," the seer patted Bryn's arm. "Go see your father and speak your heart."

"Yes, sir, I will."

"As for you, young lady." Coryn pointed at the chair Bryn vacated. "Sit."

Faryn smiled at him and did as she was told. With a delicate toss of her head, she squared her shoulders as her eyes rose to the challenge.

"Have you no shame?" he asked, but there was no real reproof in his voice.

A slight tilt of her head was the only answer she offered.

"Look at you," he moaned. "Sitting there mocking your poor old grandfather."

"You are neither poor nor old," she said. "At least not as old as you pretend."

"You're in love with that boy," Coryn replied. "The way ahead will not be the romantic lark you imagine. As we speak, he is on his way to quit the Academy."

Faryn's protest was stopped by his raised palm.

"Oh, but he is," Coryn said with a nod of his head.

"You have seen something," she said. "Please, tell me."

Her grandfather took her hand, closed his eyes, and sat back in his chair with a sigh.

"Young Bryn Bou is searching for direction," he began. "The Council will meet very soon. If they act according to their character, he will find his place at the end of a long trail filled with trouble. When that happens, the world will not be the same again."

***

The eyes of the seer were not easily dismissed. Bryn lay on his bed and tried to shake off the feeling that his soul had been laid bare by the old man's stare. He attended the gatherings that honored the Creator like everyone else in his family, but he was not overly religious. As in all things, not the man his father was.

He hinted to no one, not even Faryn, about his decision to leave the Academy. He had not been certain he'd find the courage to do it until that day. Yet, the seer looked at him and knew his heart. Coryn hadn't guessed—he knew. What else did he see? Bryn had no doubt there was more.

There was a time for everything, that's what his father always said. Whatever Coryn knew would have to wait. He had heard his father come in nearly an hour ago. The time to speak could not be put off any longer. He heaved himself onto the side of the bed and to his feet. Without thinking, he stopped at the mirror to see that his dress was in order. He found his father sitting alone in the parlor sipping a cup of tea. He motioned for Bryn to join him.

He was waiting. Damn it, he knows.

"You were not in class today," his father said.

"No," Bryn admitted.

His father sipped his tea and studied the fire on the hearth.

"I was out at the Grove," Bryn began. "I go there to think sometimes."

"And today thinking was more important than your studies?"

"No sir," Bryn shook his head. "I mean, yes sir. The term is nearly done. I've been thinking for some time about my future.

"A wise course. And what have you decided?"

"I want to leave the Academy," Bryn blurted out. "But you know that already, don't you?"

"No, I didn't know," the general said. "You seemed unhappy. I thought it was trouble with that girl of yours. I was just waiting for you to tell me what the trouble was."

"Oh, hell." Bryn buried his face in his hands for a moment before looking up. "I sure screwed that up. I didn't want to say it like that. I had a whole speech planned. When I saw you sitting there, I thought you must know. I'm sorry. I just don't think I'm cut out to be a soldier."

"I understand."

"You understand?" Bryn shock-laced voice asked. "You're not disappointed?"

"Maybe, a little," he said with a shrug. "I suppose every father wants his son to follow in his footsteps. However, the right path is better than the expected one. I sometimes wished that I had the courage to tell your grandfather what you just told me."

"But you're General Bou. You're a hero—a legend."

"A hero who wonders what else he could have been," Byryn sighed. "You may not be a soldier, son, but never let anyone tell you that you are not brave. What you've just done took more courage than charging the fiercest enemy."

"Can I come in now?" a voice asked from the other room.

"Yes, dear," Byryn said. "Come meet a remarkable young man."

The rising moon flitted between the branches throwing shafts of glowing silver light across his path. The night wind, heavy with the scent of blooming jasmine, blew soft and gentle against Bryn's face. The burden gone from his shoulders; his light step kept time to the distant beat of the music floating on the night. The Fete of the Full Moon was underway. He was on his way to meet Faryn at the celebration on the village square and he was running late. That morning being half an hour late would have filled him with anxiety, but he was a soldier then. He wasn't sure what he was at the moment, but whatever it was, he was his own.

A half mile ahead, the village square was alight with flickering torches. Long shadows played over the surrounding walls in imitation of those gathered beneath their glow. The fact that the festival came every forty days never seemed to diminish the Valir's enthusiasm for it. The children wearing masks of coconut husks chased one another around the tables and between the booths playing gotcha and myball. The chase continued as the players grew older, but the games changed.

The game was on for Bryn and Moryn. The object of their pursuit lingered near the band sipping mango wine and inflaming the passions of every young male at the festival. Faryn's sweeping red crest flowed onto slender wings that wrapped seductively around her. Every subtle curve was created to stand out in any crowd.

Faryn was more than beautiful. She was a warrior; untamed, wild, and more than a match for any ordinary male. Moreover, she was the granddaughter of Raryn Tog, the Valir's Minister of Justice, and by some perfect the alignment of fate, also the granddaughter of Coryn the Seer. Her lineage assured wealth, social prominence, and political power for whoever she chose for a mate.

As in childhood, Moryn arrived first. She and Moryn had played together as children. He sat beside her through ten years of school. He loved her; shared her laughter; held her when she cried; defended her. He had been the one to savor her first kiss. After graduation, they left Brz together to enroll in the military academy at Vix.

Then, came Bryn Bou. Bou the sniveling, weakling whose only claim to a place at the Academy was his father's reputation. What Faryn saw in him was beyond Moryn's comprehension. Bou was a paper warrior. His abilities stopped at the classroom door. Moryn had availed himself of every opportunity to try and expose the general's son's weakness.

He looked down at the bandage wrapped around his hand and promised himself that next time he would put an end to Bryn Bou for good, seer or no seer. He opened another bottle of beer and jerked his head in Faryn's direction.

"See you later, boys." He gave Laryn's arm a soft punch.

"Aw, give it up," Laryn said.

"Never," he shot back over his shoulder.

Faryn pretended not to see him coming. She knew it was no use trying to run or hide. He had pursued her since they were children, he would only follow.

"Curse you, Bryn Bou for being late," she mumbled and put on a smile for her old beau. "Moryn, how nice to see you."

"You're beautiful, as always," he bowed and kissed her offered hand. "Don't worry, Bou is not around. He's probably at home crying over his scratches. I would never be late to see you."

"He will be here," Faryn said. "And you should be ashamed."

"What for?"

"Brawling in the street for one thing," she replied. "Your continuous fighting with him for another."

"Bou needs to learn that not everyone will bow at the sound of his name."

Faryn froze him with a cock of her head and ice in her eyes. He caught her arm as she turned to go.

"Okay, okay. I'm sorry," he said. Over her shoulder he caught the attention of the band and patted the air. "One dance, that's all."

Faryn took his hand as the band slipped softly into a slow rhythm. She wasn't sure she believed he would be satisfied with one dance, but it was worth a try. She didn't want a repeat of the afternoon when Bryn finally decided to show up.

His father's acceptance was too easy. Had Coryn gotten word to him somehow? That would mean his father lied to him and that was a road he didn't want to go down. He had better things to think about, Faryn foremost among them.

Bryn loved her and believed she shared his feelings. He was a realist. His decision to quit the Academy would not go over well with Faryn. She wanted to be a warrior. Unlike him, she chose the Academy over other prospects. She wanted the military life he rejected. Would she understand his decision? More importantly, would she accept his uncertain future? He would soon know.

"Damn," the word escaped his beak unbridled.

The cost of being late to the festival suddenly unfolded before his eyes. Faryn was in the arms of Moryn. His hand clutched at the empty place in his waistband.

"Damn," this time he meant to say it.

Bryn pushed down the rising anger. Willing the muscles of his face and hands to relax, he walked into the village square. He gave Laryn and Jeryn a curt nod as he passed. Aryn Bas, playing bartender for the night, plopped a dark brew in front of him.

"Easy," Aryn said. "Only their first dance. She'd been waiting for you. He cornered her."

"How lucky for me, she's so damned polite," Bryn snarled.

"You're damn lucky," Aryn said. "Never forget it."

"You're right." Bryn felt the anger drain from him.

"Now, get over there."

Bryn let his friend's gentle push propel him off the stool. A lazy saunter carried him toward the dance floor and the next step in his future. He gave Faryn a casual wave as the music ended.

"Moryn," Bryn said. "Thanks for standing in for me."

"Don't start," Faryn demanded, pushing Moryn back a step.

Moryn's hand fell to his side. He bowed to Faryn.

"As you wish," he told her and turned his eyes on Bryn. "Should you ever step from behind her, never do it unarmed."

"That was unnecessary," Faryn told Bryn after Moryn had shouldered his way passed him.

"You're right," he admitted. "But don't expect me to apologize."

"I'm not sure what to expect of you anymore."

"What's that supposed to mean?" he said, following her through the dancers.

Faryn found a table just off the dance floor. Bryn left her and returned with glasses of mango wine. He tried a sip of the sweet liquid, grimaced, but kept it in front of him. Faryn's face melted into a smile. She pulled the glass of discarded wine to her.

"Go get a beer," she said with a laugh. "I promise not to run away with Moryn while you are gone."

Bryn kissed her forehead and vanished into the growing crowd. True to her word she was still at the table when he returned and sat beside her.

"Well?" he said.

"Well, what?"

"What did you mean you don't know what to expect of me anymore?"

"Grandfather told me that you were leaving the Academy."

"First, my father, now you. Does everybody know?"

"Your father knew?"

"He said he didn't, but he sure seemed ready for the news."

"Maybe you're not the Valir of mystery you think you are," Faryn gave him a fresh smile. "As far as I know, grandfather told no one except me and he swore me to secrecy."

"What else did he say?" He gathered her hands in his. "Because I'd sure like to know what I'm going to do now."

"He isn't saying," she told him. "And, no, I won't try to get it from him."

"You've already tried, haven't you?"

"Of course."

"And you?" Bryn asked. "What are you going to do?"

CHAPTER 3

Still unanswered, Bryn's question chased sleep from her. Since her grandfather told her about Bryn's decision, everything seemed to be spinning out of control. Her life had been snatched from her. The future had turned to smoke hanging low over her head; waiting for the storm she knew was coming to blow it away. Haunted by the ghost of yesterday, Faryn tossed and turned, searching for a place of comfort and found none. She kicked aside the blanket and went to sit in the open window. The moon sinking into the west would soon vanish behind the treetops. Morning would come to push her into a day she didn't want to face. It would be the first day in four years without Bryn sitting beside her and marching by her side. No one would understand his decision to walk away. She wasn't sure she understood.

One thing was clear. He would be labeled a weakling, a coward from a line of heroes, and a quitter who would not do his duty. Moryn would see to it. She knew Bryn was none of those things. She also knew the same labels would stick to everyone who stood by him. Her career would be over before it started.

Her grandfather was the Seer of the Valir. He was a wise and talented man But was he really in touch with the Creator? According to her other grandfather, that was too much to swallow. She walked a thin line between them. She offered up a prayer to the Creator much as a general lined up his reserves against a coming battle—just in case.

Her half-hearted prayer brought her a half-hearted answer. Word came that Bryn had taken ill and would not be mustering with the class for a few days. His father may have understood, but obviously was giving him time to change his mind and still save face. She had her answer. She would talk him out of this folly.

***

Bryn woke to the sound of a heavy fist against the front door. A decidedly deep voice asked to see the General. The footsteps that followed led to the door of his father's study. He heard his mother's soft knock.

"A messenger to see you, dear," she said.

"General Bou." Bryn could almost see the crisp salute. "A message from the king."

"Come in, Captain," his father replied.

The door closed and the conversation was lost.

Bryn quickly dressed. Avoiding the creaking tread midway, he crept downstairs. His mother was sweeping the hall just outside the study. She lifted a finger to her lips as he approached. Bryn arched the brow above his right eye, and she responded with a shrug. When a minute had passed without a sound from inside the study, she waved for Bryn to follow her to the kitchen.

"Not a word," she whispered. "Whatever the message was, it must be written."

"Yeah," Bryn agreed. "No door could hold back that guy's voice."

"That will be all, Captain," the general's voice carried to the kitchen. "Tell the king that I will attend."

"Yes, sir," the captain's voice heralded another salute.

The general ushered the messenger out before joining his family in the kitchen.

"You always do that," his wife said. "Oh, don't give me that puzzled look. You know what I mean. You always use that loud command voice of yours before leaving the study like you think we were listening or something."

"You were listening, weren't you?" he replied with a smile.

"Well, yes, but it might be more fun if you would try to catch us."

"I'll try to remember that," he said. "As for the message, it's no secret. The king has called for a meeting of the High Council. It's to be held in Vix tomorrow."

"Wow," Bryn said. "He was right."

"How's that?" His father asked.

"The seer," Bryn said. "He told me yesterday the Council would be meeting soon. I told him it wasn't, but he insisted that it was."

"Oh, he did, did he?" The general rubbed his beak. "That's very interesting."

***

Faryn turned toward the voice calling her name. Moryn waved and jogged to catch her. She meant to brush him off quickly and be on her way, but the excitement dancing in his eyes changed her plans.

"Did you hear?" he asked. "Classes are suspended tomorrow for the Council meeting and Colonel Res is accepting volunteers to act as a security detail for the meeting."

"I didn't know about the detail forming," she told him. "You're volunteering, I suppose."

"Of course, it will look good on our record when we graduate," he said. "Come with me."

"I'm going to pass," she said. "My family's involved. It wouldn't be right."

"Yeah, guess so," he said, a sharp edge coming to his voice. "Well, I need it."

That shift in his voice always came between them. She was born to influence. His parents were shopkeepers. He tried to hide it, but she sensed that he resented her for it. While he was with her, he succeeded in repressing the anger that was never far from the surface. It was that constant boiling anger, not Bryn Bou, that came between them. Moryn could never see that.

"Run along after Bou," he snarled as if reading her thoughts. "It's what you do best."

He left her standing there and joined his friends headed for the colonel's office. She wrapped her arms around her chest to ward off a sudden chill. Moryn Del was dangerous. She touched the dagger at her waist and hurried on her way. Perhaps Bryn would listen to reason.

She found him propped in his window, back against the frame, one foot against the other side, and one foot dangling in the air. It was not quite the picture of illness one expected. She hoped no one from the Academy happened by. He waved when he saw her. Pivoting in the window, he dangled both feet over the edge and patted the place beside him. She didn't bother with the door.

Climbing along the creepers she reached his room on the lowest branch of the bouja tree that was his home.

The Valir built their villages on the dry, high ground where they could find it. Homes near the villages generally had a ground level entrance. Private family rooms, like bedrooms, occupied the branches of the bouja tree to which the entrance was anchored. Away from the villages, every home was entirely arboreal. Highway branches through the dense jungle of the Boubouja region were the preferred method of foot travel, saving the ground paths for carts and caravans.

Faryn dropped down beside him. Their beaks met; this was how her life was supposed to turn out. The view from the window looked out over infinite shades of green, broken here and there by brightly colored homes leading to the village about a mile away. Above them, wildflowers soaking up the bright sunshine in the treetops lent their scent to the air. She had traveled to the cities built by men. She marveled at their great buildings, but even the golden dome in Shiloh could not compare to the land she called home.

The Boubouja was a land to itself. In the time before memory, a shift in the landmass of Tettias sent the Boubouja plunging to the sea. A thousand-foot-high wall of rock now separated it from the rest of the world. Then came the rains. A green explosion followed, covering the land; waters flowed through the jungle and flooded the lowlands. From the perpetual mists of the great river, Hiddekel, that flowed along the base of the cliffs, emerged the Valir.

"It's beautiful," she said as much to herself as to him.

Bryn nodded in silent agreement.

"Keeping it for our people hasn't been easy." She glanced at him and smiled. "It demands strict adherence to duty and sacrifice. We are known throughout all Tettias as the guardians of this land and respected as warriors."

Bryn sighed deeply.

"Nicely said," he told her. "At least as well as my father put it, maybe better."

"I love you, Bryn." She pecked him on the cheek. "I'm worried that you haven't thought this through or considered how it will affect those around you."

A wan smile lifted the corners of his beak. This was it, the supreme test of his resolve. Bryn took her in arms and kissed her deeply. When he finally let her go, he stepped inside the room. She turned but did not follow.

"I hope you don't believe that," he said. "I have known from the start that this decision would cost me more than I wanted to pay. You have chosen to be a warrior. I love that about you. It is not the easy life you might have."

The words filled the space between them with an almost physical presence that slowly pushed them apart. Tears stood in Bryn's eyes in a kind of reflection of those that rolled down her face.

"Take a place in the guard for the Council meeting," his broken voice urged. "Be the warrior you must be. I don't know what will become of me, but it can only hurt you to be part of it. Go, live the life you must."

Faryn began to speak, closed her mouth without a word and slid from the window to the path below. She felt his eyes watch her walk away.

***

Bryn was vaguely aware of time passing. He wasn't sure where the hours went or what happened while they passed by. A dark hole had opened inside him swallowing his hopes and dreams and leaving an empty husk behind. The emptiness that followed Faryn's departure was slowly being replaced by an unrelenting ache.

He knew her leaving would hurt. He told himself that he was ready for it. That was a lie. He was completely unprepared for the physical pain that accompanied the emotional wounds. The hurt in his chest was testimony to the reality of the word heartbreak.

He crawled out of his inner darkness to find night had fallen. Outside his window the stars were shining through the breaks in the canopy. His room closed in on him until he felt he was suffocating. He had to get out into the open air of the forest. He stepped from the window into the night at once unsure and quite certain of his destination.

His classmates had often poked fun of his traditionalism. Bryn met their ribbing with silence. He held to the traditions of the elders. That is, as far as his conscience allowed. Bryn Bou's beliefs were handed down from his heart, not his ancestors. The Valir, including his liberal classmates, believed the dead slept lightly and they took great care not to disturb them. His departure from that belief was fueled, in part, by the ever-present haunting pressed upon him by his name.

The way to the Grove of the Dead was firmly etched into his mind. He needed neither light nor the signs along the path. He climbed the gnarled branch of a joba tree onto the highway branch going south from the village. The Valir avoided the jungle floor at night. Leopards ate in the trees, but they hunted on the ground. Even the bravest warrior did not invite that kind of trouble. Although Bryn came to the grove often, he rarely came at night. The dark held no terror for him, but he was not completely free of taboos surrounding the dead. Since his last visit, the Grove of the Dead was no longer a place where he was completely comfortable.

The great wall of the grove just ahead rose above the branch he travelled on. Bryn dropped to the ground. No leopards ventured here. The forest of the grove was as forbidding as it was forbidden. Sounds were swallowed up here; light lost its sharpness becoming a soft glow where it reached at all. The weight of the darkness was a physical presence. The night air was full of unseen tendrils that brushed those who ventured there.

Bryn passed rank upon rank of smooth skinned tree trunks, some as wide as a small house and towering three hundred feet into the sky. Unlike the surrounding jungle, nothing grew between the trees of the grove; few vines wound up their trunks, no leaves grew on the branches. The forest floor was hard, black clay devoid of litter and creepy crawlers. Having neither shelter nor forage, animals avoided the trees that grew here. Mourning was the grove's only fruit. From these branches, great and small, hung large teardrop sacks of woven leaves suspended from silken fibers that are the burial pods of the Valir.

Bryn wound his way between the trees brushing away the silken threads that clung to him. His eyes were irresistibly drawn to the pods that glowed in fleeting snatches of moonlight. Less than a quarter mile into the forest, he stopped before a giant bouja tree. Gently rubbing his hand over the carvings in the tree, his fingers read the name—Bou. This was the place where his clan rested in silvery shrouds. Under their watchful eyes, he sank down against the cool bark.

The last time he was there a dream led him down the path to decision. He wasn't a warrior, that he knew. The dream had been reinforcement of that knowledge and his decision. Yet, he sensed it had been more than that, much more. All those things about kings and dragons were a mystery he kept to himself. He could tell no one about that because those things made no sense. He could ill afford to appear delusional while quitting the Academy. He wasn't crazy. At least, he didn't think so.

The seer looked into him and saw his plans for confronting his father. Did he know of the dream too? Coryn had pulled a Council meeting out of the air. Thoughts of what else the seer was capable of sent a shiver down his spine. What did the seer want to see him about? He was plain old Bryn Bou. He trained as a warrior but was untested in battle. He did well in school, yet he was no scholar. He was not the strongest, fastest, or toughest. He had always felt small, but he could feel himself shrinking. While pondering the peculiarities of dreams and seers, his legs slowly stretched out in front of him, and his head came to rest on his chest.

The hoot of an owl interrupted his soft snores. He listened for a moment without opening his eyes and trying to convince himself what he was hearing was real. Owls were uncommon, but not unheard-of visitors to the grove. This one had a particularly doleful voice that struck a chord in Bryn. He went in search of the noisy bird. Sounds were deceiving in the grove, and it took some time to locate his quarry. He found a snow-white owl no more than six inches tall perched in the lowest fork of a burial tree. Swiveling its head this way and that, the owl watched him draw closer. It did not fly away as Bryn expected. He had seen this owl before.

"You're a bold one," Bryn said.

"Not really," replied the owl.

A gasp escaped Bryn's beak. He stumbled back a step; shook his head and stared at the bird. This could not be happening.

"You're not that intimidating," the owl said by way of explanation. "Kind of ordinary looking really."

Bryn took another step back. He lifted a trembling finger in the owl's direction. "You spoke," he said.

"No, you did," answered the owl.

"But owls can't talk," Bryn protested.

"They can't?" The owl ruffled his feathers and scratched his head with a tiny foot. "Maybe, you're dreaming. Pinch yourself and see."

"Ouch," Bryn cried.

"No, not dreaming," said the owl.

Without another word, the owl flapped his wings and flew into the darkness. Pinch or no pinch he had to be dreaming. He reached back to feel for his family's tree, but it was not there. The night drew in around him. He watched as a softly creeping mist spread itself along the forest floor around him. He could see only a few feet in any direction. A chill ran up his spine and the feathers on his neck stood on end. Someone was watching. Bryn strained to see through the blanket of fog. He saw no one; heard no sound, but someone was there, he was sure of it. He tried to step away from whatever was out there, caught his own foot and crashed to the ground. This was no dream. There was nothing but the mist and the watcher.

"Who's there?" he called out.

No one answered. Bryn fought the growing urge to get up and run. He had only a vague idea of where he was. Where would he go? He slipped the knife from his belt. The sound of footsteps behind him brought him to his feet, waving his dagger in front of him. Slowly, the curtain of mist parted. Bryn's mouth fell open, but no sound came. His grandfather stood before him wrapped in an eldritch glow. His face was as it had been when Bryn helped wrap the death shroud over it.

"Beware the dragon rider," the apparition spoke through unmoving lips.

Bryn's world went black.

When his eyes opened again, the mist was gone. He was lying on the hard ground beneath the Bou tree staring up at the treetops. The faint glimmer of a new day was spread across the sky. He was not sure how he got here or if he had really ever left the spot. His head swam with lingering dreams of dragons, blood, talking birds, and dead grandfathers. There was no time to worry over that now. The Council would be meeting soon, and he had an appointment to keep. Bryn struggled to his feet and started out in the direction of his village.

CHAPTER 4

The village was abuzz. Rumors rippled through its houses and shops. The news that the High Council was going to meet was on everyone's tongue. The reasons given for the meeting grew more fantastic with every telling. The General Council could be called together for any cause by petition. Summoning the High Council to a private session, like the upcoming one, was a privilege reserved for the king.

Two days of speculation had passed. The High Council meeting was set to begin. The Councilors had arrived. The curious filled the streets. In doorways and on street corners knots of people gathered to share the latest mumbled rumors. Others strained to get a glimpse of the participants as they filed into the meetinghouse. An undercurrent of muffled boos greeted the arrival of Raryn of Zelph as he marched to the meeting flanked on either side by military guards in blue and gold dress uniforms. He didn't seem to notice their dislike.

"The gods forgot to put a heart in that one when he was made," a scarred old soldier leaning on a post outside the blacksmith's shop told those standing nearby.

"He just does his job," a uniformed policeman said from the back of the crowd. "Everybody hates the police until they need us."

"Minister of Justice, ha," the soldier replied. "Rather have one of you coppers off the street than the likes of him."

The conversation shifted when a cheer went up a couple of streets away. Some of the crowd stepped out into the street trying to see what was happening.

"What is it?" asked the old soldier standing on tiptoe.

"I can't tell," came the answer from one of those in the street.

"It's General Bou," a deep voice supplied the answer.

The voice drew the attention of the little crowd. They turned to disapproving, schoolmaster eyes held the crowd in check. His smooth skin and plumage were testimony to his lack of warrior service. Nevertheless, no one present questioned his courage or his capabilities. Magryn had a tongue every bit as sharp as his beak and he was not afraid to use it.

"We will come to order," Magryn commanded.

The crowd expelled its pent-up breath releasing a flood of voices. Magryn pounded the table.

"I said, order!" he shouted above the din. "That doesn't mean everyone start talking. Now, be quiet or I'll clear this hall."

Magryn's scowl ensured no one dared mention that he had no authority to make anyone leave. Silence reigned where his eyes went. Enjoying the moment, he cleared his throat and pounded the table once more.

"This meeting of the High Council will come to order," he announced. "I remind the members of the full Council in attendance that they may speak if they wish, but only the members of the High Council have a vote during this session."

Magryn looked around the chamber and sensing no objections, pressed on to the business at hand.

"Today's attendance suggests that somehow word leaked out that this meeting was called by the king in response to the request of Coryn, son of Sethryn, Seer of the Valir." He pushed on over the murmur. "So, we will get right to the business at hand. Seer, you have the floor."

The old prophet used his staff to leverage up his right side and then the left to the sound of popping, creaking joints, and a soft groan. His hands trembled with the effort. Through half closed eyes, he fixed his gaze somewhere above the heads of the Council. Byryn Bou smiled back at the seer. He was one of the few present who knew Coryn for the showman he truly was. There was not an arthritic joint in the prophet's body. He had perfect vision and was still as strong as a young warrior. However, he found a certain pleasure in perpetuating the popular image of a wise old sage. He gave the Council a labored bow.

"It has been a long time since I have addressed this Council. In fact, I don't believe I have ever addressed this particular Council. No matter. It is true that we have disagreed over the years. However, I find disagreements make for good government. That said, I wish you all to know that I hold you in the highest regard. That is why I am here today. I have had a dream," he paused to let the words work their magic.

As expected, a buzz of voices filled the room. Coryn delighted at the word "dream" as it echoed from row to row.

"Order, order!" Magryn shouted.

The president nodded for Coryn to continue. The seer offered a slight bow before pressing on.

"This was no ordinary dream. As you all know, we live in troubled times. Relations with the other kingdoms, especially the kingdom of men are strained nearly to breaking. I believe this dream is a warning of things to come. Trouble is coming for our people."

Coryn let his eyes wander slowly over the Councilors before him. One or two shifted in their seats but offered no comment.

"In my dream, I stood in the mist on the banks of Hiddekel near the place from which our people came to life. All around me death held sway…"

Coryn went on to weave a tale of war, pestilence, and death into a tapestry of awe and fear. The crowd listened in rapt amazement. No one moved; no one spoke; no one interrupted the rise and fall of his voice. When he finished speaking, Coryn looked over the Councilors once more before turning to the audience behind him. A smile touched his face as he struggled to lower himself into his seat.

Conversation exploded throughout the longhouse. Magryn made no move to try and contain it. He knew the majority of the Valir trusted visions and dreams as omens of the future. His own belief told him that one neglected such omens at great personal peril. There were those among the elders, including some on the High Council, who believed dreams superseded law and duty. The seer's tale flowed from the windows and doors in ripples through the village.

After several minutes, Magryn's gavel restored order. Raryn was the first on his feet seeking recognition. Magryn granted him the floor after issuing a warning to the crowd that regular order would be preserved.

"That's it?" Raryn asked, his voice honed to a sharp edge. "You troubled the king to call us together and caused all this commotion because you had a bad dream? Has all reason abandoned this chamber? Please tell me there's more to this meeting than an old one's fantasies."

Order vanished.

It was replaced by a swirling cyclone of "here, here" and "Raryn's right" mixed with cries of "heretic", and "blasphemy" that erupted from the crowd. A scuffle began in the street outside. The police moved in to restore order while Magryn gaveled for the same. Calryn of Dei was on his feet; he wasn't waiting for order or recognition.

"Raryn's denial of the Creator and his hatred of religion is as well known," Calryn shouted over the crowd, "as is his personal hatred of the seer. Surely, even a faithless degenerate can see this is more than someone's bad dream. Men have been encroaching on our freedom for years. The Councilor is well aware of the reports of our citizens being detained in Shiloh without cause. This dream is a warning of calamity for our people. It's a sign from the Creator that cannot be ignored."

"A sign?" Raryn was incredulous. "Signs? Brethren, are we reduced to this? How long are we to continue to live bound by ignorance and superstition, scattering runes and gazing at entails? I was under the impression the Valir are beyond relying on this kind of religious nonsense and fear mongering."

"It's only nonsense to those who have abandoned faith in the Creator," Calryn shot back.

"Faith in a Creator is not the question here," Raryn countered. "Whatever Coryn's beliefs, his integrity is without reproach among our people. However, in all honesty, they are *his* beliefs, not mine and certainly not universal among the Valir. His nightmares are not a governmental crisis. If there is a crisis in what he says, it is a crisis of the world of men. The Valir have no interest in the affairs of men or dreams about men. To ensure our wellbeing, we have only to continue in our present determination to avoid humans."

Cheers and boos turned into pushing and shoving among some of those inside the longhouse. Scuffles broke out all along the street as the word spread. The police were helpless, unable to reach the trouble spots because of the crowd. Magryn's calls for order were ignored.

"Brethren," a booming voice, experienced in battlefield

command brought instant order.

Byryn Bou was on his feet, hands raised above his head. The crowd inside settled back into their seats to listen to the general.

"Have we forgotten our duty? We are the Valir. We are ruled by law. Decency and order are supposed to be our way of life, yet here we are acting like humans."

Quiet in the longhouse became complete. The fighting outside subsided.

"At the request of the king, Coryn has come to this Council to advise us of his dream. No matter what one believes, this is the right and proper course according to the law and traditions of the Valir. The Boubouja is not an island. Whatever affects the kingdom of men, will eventually affect us as well. This Council was called to hear the seer's concerns for the safety of the kingdom. This we have done. However, we are arguing as if he made demands of us. Coryn has made no request of us except to hear him."

The silence in the longhouse held. Raryn and Calryn glared at each other but said nothing. Magryn looked over the room daring someone to disturb the proceedings.

"Byryn is right, of course," Magryn said at last. "We have heard no request. No one has proposed any action. No one on the Council has even asked the seer if he has a word for us beyond what he has shared. Let me rectify that. Coryn, in light of this dream, do you have a request to make of us?"

A smile brushed the seer's face and wrinkled the corners of his eyes. He did not rise. He leaned forward on his staff and spoke softly.

"A small favor." Coryn cleared his throat and looked up. "I wish the High Council's permission to send a personal envoy to Eeryn, son of Enoryn in Shiloh."

Several Council members started to rise. Magryn waved at them to remain seated.

"To what end?" Magryn asked. "The seer knows travel to the kingdom of men is banned by the Council's decree and has been for some time. He also knows Eeryn is part of the reason that ban exists. Why a personal messenger, why will a letter sent in the diplomatic pouch not suffice?"

"It is in respect to the Council's ban that I am here," Coryn said. "I wish a one-time exemption to consult Eeryn. I do not wish to consult the Ambassador."

"Do you presume to be above the Council?" Raryn was on his feet. "We are not in the habit of suspending our rulings for personal privilege. If this dream concerns our relations with the Kingdom of Salem, as you say it does, then Ambassador Dorryn needs to know the details."

"I'm sure the ambassador knows the workings of the Council well in advance of the arrival of the diplomatic pouch." Coryn offered the Council a wry smile. "It is not my intention to inform the ambassador of my thoughts. My envoy seeks Eeryn's advice on my personal thoughts about the vision. Though it may surprise you, I'm looking for direction as is everyone else."

A murmur rumbled through the hall. The Seer of Valir seeking advice? Coryn was renowned for his wisdom. How can this be?

"I must protest," Raryn said. "Advice concerning our relations with Salem is the purview of the ambassador. Eeryn no longer holds that position. He has no access to King Zedek nor the palace in Shiloh. Moreover, he is a disgrace to the Valir."

The seer snapped to his feet. The old man image evaporated in an instant. He rapped the floor twice with his staff. Thunder shook the hall with each blow. Outside, the clouds grew dark and menacing. The show the crowd came to see was suddenly more than they imagined; they cowered as if the sky might fall in upon them. Coryn's frame reverberated with fury. White knuckled fists wrapped around his staff and fire lit the prophet's eyes.

"I do not wish to consult King Zedek," Coryn's voice crackled with electricity, filling the chamber with the scent of ozone. "I do not wish to consult Ambassador Dorryn, nor do I wish to debate with you the trustworthiness and abilities of either of them. It is only from an exaggerated sense of civic duty that I have sought this Council's permission. I have made my request; the Council will be so kind as to answer yea or nay without further slander of my friend."

The collective intake of breath was audible. The High Council looked on in shock. Magryn staggered back a step, his wide eyes and blinked as if he had been punched. Several of those in the windows dropped from their perches and melted into the crowd. There was no immediate rush to occupy their abandoned seats. Silent moments passed; every eye was locked on the seer who still trembled with rage. Byryn broke the spell.

"Whom do you wish to send?" The steel in his voice restored firmness to the ground beneath them all.

Blood rushed back into Coryn's hands. His grip on the staff relaxed. He took a deep breath and let it out. His voice steadied.

"One of my own choosing." He paused a heartbeat, "Someone known only to me."

"Absolutely not," shouted Raryn. "We will not be bullied by you. You cannot have a free hand to meddle in affairs of state. I vote, Nay."

"I concur," Bowryn spoke up for the first time. "Eeryn is a traitor. He's lucky King Zedek didn't take his head. This Council will not condone secret communications with him. Nay."

"Nay," Shuryn and Peryn said in unison.

"I don't remember a vote being called for," Byryn pointed out. "However, the best course may be to have it and be done. Without knowing the envoy or what protection he will be given; I have no choice but to abstain."

"I vote Aye." Calryn cast a disappointed look at Byryn. "May the Creator be merciful to us."

"I must add my voice in opposition," Magryn said. "Eeryn still has the ear of Prince Luz. It is not beyond reason to believe the prince may be plotting a bloodbath. The High Council cannot tolerate even a hint of impropriety in this situation. I too vote Nay. Request denied. Do others wish to speak?"

"I did not invite this dream," Coryn said when no one spoke. "I did not conjure it from my imagination as some of you suppose. Nevertheless, the dream has come. I am responsible for what it says to me as are every one of you here today. I have heard your decision. So be it. You may deny me that is your right. You cannot deny the will of the Creator."

"I resent your arrogant tantrum and I warn you not to defy this Council." Raryn shook a long slender finger at the seer. "We have a duty too. Defy us and your reputation will not save you."

Coryn gave a curt bow and, without a word, turned slowly on his heels. He made his way to the door ahead of the rumbling voices within the longhouse and did not look back. The big blacksmith pushed aside the crowd in the doorway to let the seer pass. Coryn paused; looked up at the big blacksmith and smiled.

He held up a finger while he rummaged inside his robe. Finding what he sought, Coryn pulled a small, craved figure of a female from his robe and handed it to Vulryn.

"For your wife," the seer whispered and passed through the crowd.

CHAPTER 5

Vulryn shuffled through the crowd, side-stepping slow-moving elders and dodging careless youths. He held the tiny figure the seer gave him in his big, calloused hands. He had dropped it in the crowded street once and was not taking any chances on it happening again.

"For your wife." That's what the seer told him.

His world was wrapped up in those words as tightly as he held the idol. Vulryn was convinced the words were the promise of a brighter tomorrow. He had to get home before the magic wore off his prize. Stepping over his carelessly abandoned hammer, he rushed through the shop without so much as a glance at the forge. Long stiff legged strides carried him across the overgrown garden to his front door. He paused outside the door to collect his breath before gently turning the knob. The Creator be thanked for well-oiled hinges. The big blacksmith stole silently over the room with catlike grace to peer through the open door of his wife's room.

It took him a moment for the slow rise and fall of her chest to register. She was so frail. He was not surprised to find her sleeping. Tiptoeing to her bedside, he slipped the tiny talisman beneath her pillow and backed quietly from the room. Slipping back into his shop once more, he reclaimed his hammer and stoked the forge to a bright red glow.

The song of the hammer on the anvil played while Vulryn's mind drifted through fantasies in which love triumphed over the predictions of physicians. There he remained until the lengthening shadows of evening fell across his doorway. Leaving his anvil, he closed up the shop and latched the door behind him. He drew a bucket of cold water from the well in the little garden between the shop and home then dropped into his chair. The quiet flower-filled place was a refuge between worlds in which to savor a drink of cold water and let the exertions of the day melt away.

There were days Maryn didn't acknowledge his return home. Those were the bad days. On the good days, she would sit up and talk with him. Sometimes, she even smiled. Whether it was a good day or bad, he tried to enter their home with a mind free from the day. He wanted to be completely there for her. The weight of her rapid decline from bride to invalid was almost too much for his big shoulders to bear. While he could bear it, he would be wholly hers.

Vulryn's stomach rumbled with a sudden embarrassing vigor. He took a sip of water trying to quiet it. His effort was greeted by another rumble, this one louder than the first. The unmistakable smell of grilling fish filled his nostrils. It was rell cooking on planks of bouja wood if memory served. Yes, it definitely was rell with, maybe, a hint of dill. Cursing under his breath whichever neighbor was responsible for this culinary torture, he retreated inside to escape the mouthwatering aroma.

The smell that burst through the door as he opened it hit him like an epicurean fist. An instant later all thoughts of food were gone. Thunder boomed inside his head. A bolt of lightning bolt struck his chest, crackling with electric impossibility. The cursed cook was his own wife. Maryn looked up at him from the grill. She stopped singing to smile at him. His knees couldn't hold him, and he crumpled to the floor.

"Get up silly," she chirped. "You're way too big for me to lift."

"How…what…when?" he sputtered.

She shrugged and smiled. Vulryn jumped to his feet; ran into the bedroom. He began throwing the blankets and pillows around the room.

"What are you doing?" she asked from the doorway.

"There was a talisman—from the seer," he explained.

"You mean this?" She held up the little wooden figure. "This is just a toy. I had one just like it when I was a little girl."

"It's a miracle," he whispered though his tears.

***

Bryn looked up at the sun. There was something pulling at his conscious mind. It was something important; something he should know.

The Council!

No, no, no, it couldn't be as late as he thought it was. It mustn't be. He was on his feet and racing for the village. The door to his future was opening at that meeting and damn it, he just slept through it.

The crowd around the longhouse was trickling away as folks returned to their homes and businesses. Bryn whirled and weaved through the knots of lingering gossipers who clogged the streets. He searched frantically for the familiar face of someone he could trust to tell him the news. At last, he spotted Aryn. He was picking his way around the final obstacle between him and his friend when a red-crested face appeared beyond Aryn's shoulder. He turned on his heels hoping to slip away unnoticed and collided with a wall.

"Hey," the wall said. "Watch where you're going."

"Sorry," Bryn said scrambling to his feet.

"Hey, where's my talisman?" Vulryn said looking at his empty hand. "You knocked it out of my hand. Help me find it. Come on be quick about it."

"Is this what you're looking for?" Bryn held up the little figure whose profile was imprinted on his knee.

A meaty hand closed over Bryn's; a second one snatched the carving from him. The blacksmith crushed the figure to his chest and lumbered into the crowd leaving Bryn standing alone in the street with a confused look on his face. A quick shake of his head cleared the cobwebs and Bryn hustled off toward the seer's house hoping he had escaped Faryn's notice.

***

"Are you coming, Byryn?" Magryn laid a hand on the shoulder of his fellow Councilor.

"No." Byryn heaved a sigh. "I'm going to sit here a while and think this over."

"Don't brood too long," Magryn told him. "We did the right thing. I have great confidence in our seer. I know you do too. However, we must put our personal feelings aside in this case. The High Council could not go on record as granting him a free hand to meddle in the affairs of men. We both know that is what he is planning."

“Here,” Byryn tapped his head. “I know you’re right. In my heart, I’m not so sure. Losing his temper didn’t help his case, but that doesn’t mean he is wrong. There are those on the Council who want normal relations with men restored. To Valir like Coryn and I, they seem too willing to forget those who died at the hands of man the last time this was tried.”

“The times are changing, Bou.” Magryn shook his head. “We are slipping into the minority. If we don’t change, we’ll soon be irrelevant. You did the right thing. *We* did the right thing.”

Did we, Magryn?”

“Of course, we did,” Magryn answered. “Go home. Find a little peace while you can. I fear this affair is far from over.”

Magryn looked back from the longhouse door, Byryn’s chin was in his hands; his elbows propped on the table. There was a faraway look in his eyes. The Chairman of the Council closed the door leaving the general to his thoughts.

Byryn didn’t tarry long. His thoughts were too dark for that. He pulled the longhouse door closed behind him. The warm, humid air felt good on his face. Orchids bloomed on the branches overhead. It was a beautiful day, but not for much longer. In the east, a wall of clouds was building, turning the horizon black. Storms this time of year were not unusual. Still Byryn couldn’t help thinking how this one matched the events of the day. Conversations stopped as he passed. Calryn, standing with a small group at the edge of the square, gave him a quick wave and hurried on without a word.

Guess I’m not the only one troubled by the path I’ve chosen.

For the first time in a long time, he felt old. Byryn ambled aimlessly across the square and started slowly for home. At least that is how it looked to those who followed his movements from behind their curtains or peered around corners. The General kept a trained eye on his back trail. He had a destination in mind. He wanted to keep it a private destination.

He was sure Magryn was right about one thing. This affair was not finished, not if he knew the seer as well as he thought he did. Thunder rolled in the distance. Byryn quickened his pace. He ducked inside a weaver’s shop and quickly out the back door putting the village behind him. Where the shops disappeared and the homes grew further apart, he came to a thick wall of liana that grew along the path. He squeezed through a small opening. Long strides took him through the maze of vines to the entrance of a ramshackle house. The branches supporting its upper rooms were strong and healthy as were the beams that held the rooms. The wooden walls surrounding the base of the tree told a different story. Moss grew in the sagging wood and patches of it dotted the walls. The doorframe was askew. There were no carvings on the doorposts as was the fashion. The owner had not even bothered to carve his name into the door. The banana fronds that covered the lattice overhanging the door were brown at the edges. Byryn knocked on the door and went inside without waiting for an invitation.

Once inside, the appearance of wear and neglect vanished. The interior was a world of simple, but exquisite, furnishings. A fire crackled on an ancient stone hearth flanked by a pair of carved chairs made of bouja wood and covered in thick, rich red linen. On one wall hung a tapestry in blues and greens depicting the creation of the Boubouja. The rug underfoot was cloud soft. A bright red centerpiece of orchids decorated an ironwood table that was older than its owner. Flickering coconut candles graced the table. At one end, a silver platter held slices of mango and a steaming cup of tea.

"You were that sure I'd come?" Byryn said pointing at the tea.

"Rumor has it I'm a seer," Coryn replied with a smile.

"What confused soul told you that?"

"I believe." Coryn scratched his beak, searching his memory. "It was your father. Yes, yes, I'm sure of it."

"So it was." Byryn chuckled and took a sip of tea. "He was senile at the end you know."

Coryn waved the comment away and motioned for Byryn to take the empty chair beside him. The two drank tea watching the fire in silence.

"I'm sorry about the Council's vote," Byryn broke the silence.

"Don't be," Coryn replied with another wave of his hand. "It went exactly as I expected."

"You expected to be denied?"

"Of course." Coryn looked at him. "The High Council was in no position to reverse the ban on travel to Shiloh for my sake. Besides, they would never agree to some cockeyed mission of which they knew nothing."

"Then, why…?" Byryn voice trailed away.

"The High Council deserved to be consulted if for no other reason than that they are the High Council. Honor to whom honor is due. Have you forgotten, that is our way?"

"No, I have not forgotten." Byryn cocked his head to look at his friend. "Magryn is right. You are going to do it, anyway, aren't you?"

"Yes, of course I am."

"I knew it," Byryn said. "Raryn and his cronies have to suspect it too. They will be watching. If he catches you defying the Council, he will throw you under the prison."

"I'd wager he is salivating with anticipation right now." Coryn leaned closer to his guest. "I promise, they will not succeed. That is why I am glad you are here."

"You think I'm going to go?" Byryn was on his feet. "Coryn, you are crazy."

Coryn laughed and slapped his knees. "Sit down, dear boy. It's not you. You would be missed. I'm not sure why, but you'd be missed just the same. No, I have someone else in mind."

"I cannot openly help you," Byryn said.

"I would not ask it," Coryn said. "However, since you showed an interest in my intentions, perhaps you would do me the favor of contacting the chosen envoy on my behalf. He seems to have gone missing. You have only to say that I'd like to see him."

***

Concealed amid the upper branches of a giant bouja, Bryn Bou watched his father enter the house of the seer. While trying to elude Faryn's notice, he almost collided with his father as he had the blacksmith. Thankfully, the general was too preoccupied to notice. That sort of preoccupation struck Bryn as out of character for his father. It was therefore reason enough to follow him. His father's subsequent attempts to elude anyone following him was confirmation that following him was definitely in Bryn's best interest.

His trip through the streets in pursuit of his father had garnered enough snatches of conversation for him to know the seer exploded when the Council denied his petition. Trouble of some sort was brewing. His father and the seer were friends, and he thought perhaps his father was going to see Coryn to sooth ruffled feathers. Whatever was going on in the house below him, he would wait until his father left before keeping his own appointment with the seer.

The approach of a bobbing red-crest marching along the path from the village proved the wisdom of this course. The sight of Faryn in her dress uniform set his heart racing. The gnawing ache to call out to her, to hold her and tell her that he would surrender to her wishes came close to pulling him down from the tree.

He shook it off as a mirage, a trick of the heart brought on by the passion of the moment. They were walking different paths, and neither could go back. That was to embrace the lie that they could live happily ever after having abandoned their dreams. She would never truly be happy as anything but a warrior. He would never be happy as a warrior.

***

Byryn leaned back in his chair and turned his attention to his old friend, the seer of the Valir.

"Okay," Byryn agreed. "Who is this daring soul that you've recruited to defy the Council with you?"

A knock on the door prevented the seer from answering.

"One moment," Coryn called to the visitor. "Catryn?"

Catryn, the seer's ancient housekeeper, appeared from the kitchen and shuffled slowly towards the door.

"If that is your messenger," Byryn said. "I don't want to see him."

"Catryn, would you see who it is before letting them in?"

The housekeeper's arthritic hand worked the knob to the sound of a muted groan. The door cracked open just far enough for her to slide her eye into the opening.

"Your granddaughter," she announced.

"Let her in," Coryn told her. "Come in child. You know the Commandant, I take it?"

"General." Her greeting was accompanied by a brisk salute.

"Be at ease, cadet." He returned the salute. "This is your family home. I am a guest. No need for formality."

"Sit with us," Coryn said and went to get another chair. "This concerns you too."

"Coryn?" Byryn cautioned.

"No, no, she's not the one," he said with a shake of his head. "The general and I were just discussing the ramifications of the Council's decision."

"And by 'she's not the one' you mean there is one and you will ignore the Council's order not to send a messenger to Shiloh?"

"She's very bright," Coryn told the general with a smile. "Make a great staff officer."

Byryn laughed and Faryn flushed as red as her bright crest.

"I'm sure she will," Byryn answered. "But, to repeat myself, who is it you plan to send?"

"Plans sometimes go awry," the seer said. "I have no commitment from anyone. You understand what I am saying? I would, however, be very grateful if you would ask you son to come visit me."

CHAPTER 6

Faryn and his father left the house together looking like the seer had spiked their tea with bitter alum. They paused beneath the branch where Bryn was perched out of sight.

"I have to leave you here, sir," she said.

"I hoped you would have tea with my wife and I," the general said. "Maybe visit a bit while we waited for Bryn."

"Please, excuse me this once, General. I have an urgent errand."

"Give him our love." The general returned her salute.

They had not gone far when Bryn spotted a pair of uniformed police officers fall in behind his father. He was right. He was being followed.

Is the seer being watched too?

Bryn worked his way through the trees making a complete circuit of the house. No one was lurking outside. He needed to get inside before anyone else showed up. He had jogged all the way from town to keep the appointment and now his legs did not seem to want to go any closer.

His mouth was too dry to spit. Which was more than could be said for the rest of him. Sweat beaded on his forehead and trickled down his back. His hands trembled. He rubbed them against his thighs. A summons to the seer's house was not the kind of thing one looked forward to receiving. He had played it off as so much swamp gas. The gas had suddenly become very real. A parade of possible curses and predictions of doom played in his head. What lonely fate worse than death awaited him inside that house? His stomach rolled and tumbled. He took a few steps toward home promising to return tomorrow when he reminded himself that the only thing worse than being summoned by the seer was failing to show up.

"Creator, be merciful," he whispered and dropped from his

perch to the ground outside the seer's door.

He reached for the door and snatched back his hand from the knob. If only he could stop shaking. He tried again to swallow.

"For the love of the Creator," the seer's voice said from within. "Come in here Bryn Bou and be quick about it."

Bryn slowly twisted the knob and pushed the door open enough to peek inside.

"Get in here," Coryn snapped.

Bryn jumped, ducked inside, and slammed the door behind him. The room was not the diabolical realm of torture he had imagined. There were no shelves lined with disgusting ingredients for magic potions or books of spells. He felt oddly disappointed. The room looked like most of those in the village. The table was arranged with fruit and tea and looked almost welcoming. Coryn motioned him toward the table.

"Have something to eat," he said. "Then, come sit here by me."

Bryn helped himself to some figs and tea. He crossed the room sure he was being measured once again by Coryn's piercing green eyes.

"Are you frightened?" the old one asked when Bryn settled into a chair.

Bryn drew himself up and straightened his shoulders. His first thought was to deny the charge, but he found himself confessing.

"Almost out of my mind," he said. "I had a long night."

The seer chuckled and nodded. He patted Bryn's arm. "Relax, once you get to know me you may feel differently. Familiarity breeds contempt, you know. Who knows, you may leave here feeling about me as does our Council."

"I'm afraid I missed the Council meeting," Bryn confessed.

"Yes, I know. No matter," the seer replied. "That was just a bit of formality to be taken care of before we talked. You are well spoken of by my granddaughter, you know."

Bryn could feel the heat rising in face. He shifted uncomfortably in his seat.

"Don't be embarrassed, my boy." Coryn smiled. "She's a very discerning young one. I trust her feelings about people. Besides, I know your father as I knew his father before him. I see them in you. I suppose that is why you were chosen."

"What do you mean chosen? Chosen for what?"

"Chosen, selected, picked from a group," Coryn said. "It's an easy concept. The Creator has chosen you to carry a message to Eeryn the Prophet in Shiloh."

"I don't remember choosing anything," he protested. "I'm not even especially religious."

"My boy, the Creator chooses." The seer drew his chair closer. "We obey or refuse and live forever with our decision. Now, tell me about your dream."

"But, why me?" Bryn asked.

"A good question," Coryn said. "I've asked it of the Creator at least a thousand times myself. The best I've come up with is that the Creator is the Creator. He does as he wishes and chooses whom he wills. The dream?"

"I was in the Grove of the Dead..." Bryn began.

He recounted the dream and the events of the last few days while Coryn listened with only a nod here and there. Occasionally the seer closed his eyes and seemed to Bryn to drift on the words as if living them with him. When Bryn finished his story, he melted into the chair. Coryn leaned closer and laid his hand on Bryn's arm. A subtle thrumming began along Bryn's arm. Tiny vibrations danced over his body as the seer spoke in soft conspiratorial tones.

"Do you still question what your future holds?" Coryn asked.

Bryn searched his heart and surprised himself with the answer. "No."

"Then, my boy, what is your answer to the Creator?"

"I will do all you ask." Bryn met the seer's eyes. "I will carry the message."

A tear pooled at the corner of the seer's eye. He cleared his throat before trying to speak. "My faith in our kingdom is restored. I hope you do not come to regret your decision Bryn Bou. You do understand that we are about to defy the orders of the High Council."

Bryn nodded.

"You have discerned the task is not an easy one; that's good. Once you leave here my life and that of your father are in your hands. There is little we can do to help you. You must trust only in the help the Creator may give and in no other. You asked His help outside my door, keep asking and trust He will answer."

"Has my father agreed to this?" Bryn asked when the seer finished speaking.

"Your father knows that I asked to see you," Coryn said. "He knows of my intention to defy the Council. Anything else he may know he has deduced from those two facts. If we are found out, you and I will be tried as traitors. It will be embarrassing for your father, but he can truthfully deny knowing any of it."

"No one will believe him," Bryn said.

"You're right about that." Coryn agreed. "However, believing it and proving it are very different things. He will survive it. Secrecy is our best defense."

"How do I find Eeryn?"

"Ah, there's the trouble," Coryn cautioned. "You must not ask after him in Shiloh. Eeryn is banned from the palace. He is also unwelcome at the Embassy so you must stay away from the ambassador. Finding Eeryn, even being in his company, is dangerous. Do not worry too much. Eeryn is resourceful. *He* will very likely find *you*."

The two silently stared into the fire with their tea growing cold. They were held captive by a myriad of unanswered questions and future possibilities. When their thoughts had taken them as far as they could go and there was nothing else to say, Coryn reached into his robe and removed a neat packet of folded paper tied with coarse twine.

"This is only an introduction." Coryn handed the paper to Bryn. He tapped the boy's head. "The message is the dream, guard it well."

Bryn slipped the paper into his tunic as he headed for the door.

"One last detail," Coryn's words stopped him. "Delay your departure until sunrise. I have arranged what help I can to see you underway without detection."

"May I ask a favor?" Bryn asked.

Coryn cocked his head to study Bryn's face. Satisfied with what he saw, the seer spread his hands inviting Bryn to continue.

"I spent last night away from home in my private place. I didn't say goodbye." Bryn's voice cracked, but his eyes never left the seer. "It's best I don't go back. That way they can say I ran away."

"I will send your love," the seer assured him.

Coryn watched Bryn move through the branches as he headed away from the village. Bryn did not look back. That was good. As the seer turned to go inside, a flash of sunlight on metal caught his eye. Someone on the Council wasted no time setting a watch on his house. With only a slight pause in his step, he spotted the sentry hidden in the branches at the far side of his dooryard.

You need a rabbit to chase, he thought and smiled to himself. *You shall have one.*

The wheels were in motion. Coryn knew the boy would not disappoint him. What bothered him was his own role. Had he just stopped an apocalypse or started one? Only the Creator knew, and He was keeping the answer to Himself.

In the shadows above the seer's house a pair of village deputies watched Bryn leave his meeting with Coryn.

"It's just a kid," the short one said.

"Do you want me to follow him?" the other asked.

The short fellow scratched his head. "No, let him go. He's not who we're looking for."

"Well, who are we looking for then?"

"You heard the captain. We're looking for someone whom the seer might send to Shiloh." He pointed at the path below. "Someone like that."

Vulryn bounced through the branches toward the seer's house. His big heart was light as a feather. His long legs stepped smartly to the tune he whistled.

"I remember him," the short one said. "He was at the Council meeting."

"Everyone was at the Council meeting, but he is hard to miss," the other replied. "My wife's cousin was standing in the doorway with him. She said the seer passed something to him."

"What was it?"

"She couldn't see clearly," he said. "But she thought it was some kind of talisman."

"He's the one then."

Vulryn knocked on the seer's door and was surprised when the seer hurried him inside. Coryn looked left and right as if making sure no one was watching and then disappeared inside. The big blacksmith fell on his knees and through his tears kissed the seer's robe. Coryn strained trying to lift him, but the blacksmith was too heavy.

"Please stop that," Coryn commanded when his efforts to pull his robe from the blacksmith's hands proved as futile as trying to lift him.

Vulryn obeyed. Still wiping tears from his eyes, he rose to tower over the seer.

"My Maryn, she's healed," he said. "You healed her."

"No," Coryn corrected before the blacksmith could go on. "The Creator healed her. I was only the messenger. A messenger with an agenda, I might add. I need a favor."

"Anything," Vulryn said.

"Don't be too hasty," Coryn cautioned. "I might ask for your first-born son."

"But I don't have a first-born son," Vulryn answered.

"You will," the seer assured him. "But, for now, I'd like you to go home as quickly as you can, get your fishing pole and go down to the Hiddekel. Camp north of the lift, fish, enjoy yourself, and return in two days. Oh, and bring me some fish."

"That's it? A fishing trip?" Vulryn asked.

"That's all," Coryn said with a shrug of his shoulders. "That, and trust that everything will work out for the best no matter how it seems at any given moment."

Coryn steered the blacksmith toward the door and the two stepped out into the morning sun.

"Now," Coryn said loudly with another sly look left and right. "Go quickly and don't let anyone see you."

Back inside, Coryn rested against the door to catch his breath.

"That should satisfy Raryn," he said and settled into his favorite chair. It had been a busy day and Coryn was sure he deserved a nap.

Vulryn was almost home when it occurred to him that the seer said he would have a son. He doubled his pace eager to tell Maryn the news. The one thing that never occurred to the blacksmith or Raryn's spies was that they had been expertly played.

CHAPTER 7

A thin faced clerk with a green crest stuck her head into Raryn's office. "Minister? There's a Captain Zee to see you. Something about a surveillance."

"Send him right in." Raryn left the captain at attention while he rifled through the papers on the desk in front of him. "You have something for me?"

"Yes sir, I think so."

"Well?"

"The blacksmith of Vix, the one named Vulryn, called on the seer about an hour ago," the captain explained. "He left in quite a hurry and the seer told him not to let anyone see him. My deputies also reported that the seer was seen passing something to this blacksmith following the Council meeting."

"Was anyone else seen leaving there?"

"Yes, Byryn Bou and the seer's granddaughter. They arrived separately but left together. Later, there was a boy from the Academy."

"The boy's name?" Raryn looked up into the captain's face. "Find out, Captain. While you are doing that, send someone to call on this blacksmith."

If there was something sinister going on, the police captain knew the blacksmith would never willingly admit it to him. However, there was someone on the force this Vulryn might talk to. Zee went in search of the deputy he had in mind.

Tomryn knocked on the door of tiny house behind the blacksmith's shop. The house looked like every other house in the neighborhood except for the door. The heavy bouja wood door was framed about the edges in series of elaborate, engraved loops and whorls. The engravings were words from the Valirian Book of Prayer. Large iron hinges held the door to a similarly wrought casement of iron. The name Pey was inlaid in copper.

When no answer came, Tomryn knocked a bit harder careful to avoid the usual pounding that was the trademark of police. He was rewarded with the sounds of someone moving inside. To his surprise, the blacksmith's wife answered.

"Oh, hello Tomryn." She smiled up at the uniformed cousin of her husband. "It's so good to see you again."

"Is Vulryn in?" he asked.

"I'm afraid not. He's gone fishing," she said. "Is there anything I can do for you?"

"You mean he left you all alone?" he said in a voice laced with concern. "Are you sure you're well enough?"

"Don't fret Tom." She smiled and turned a neat pirouette. "As you can see, I'm perfectly fine. Please, come in."

Tomryn followed her inside to a small nook tucked into a corner of the kitchen. A small table simply furnished with a pair of pewter candlesticks took up most of the room. A single cup was set before one of the chairs.

"Can I get you some tea?" she asked.

"That would be nice."

He shifted uncomfortably as she busied herself with the tea. Her light and effortless movements followed the tune she hummed. Though he was in a hurry to report Vulryn's absence to the captain, he thought her sudden good health might be important to his mission. The last time he saw Maryn Pey she couldn't get out of bed without help.

"How is it you're feeling so well?" he asked when she returned to the table.

"Isn't it wonderful?" a musical lilt filled her voice. "The seer gave Vulryn a talisman. As soon as I took it in my hands I was whole again. It's a miracle."

"It is amazing," he admitted. "Did Vulryn say how it happened that the seer gave it to him? Did he do some work for Coryn recently?"

"I don't think so." She thought a moment. "No, he said the seer just handed it to him and said it was for me."

"How strange," Tomryn said. "Seers don't usually do things like that without a reason."

"But, Tom, it made me well."

"Oh, I didn't mean it like that," he said. "I meant only that seers often want something in return, something for their own profit. Did Vulryn say if the seer asked for anything in return?"

"Come to think of it he did," she answered. "He asked Vulryn to go fishing and bring him some fish."

"When did this happen?"

"Why, just a little while ago," she said. "Vulryn went to thank him for the talisman. When he came back, he was in a big hurry. He gathered up his things and rushed right out."

"Did he say where he was going or when he would be back?"

"He said he was going to the river, but he didn't say when he would be back," she said with a shake of her head. "And that's not like Vulryn at all."

"I've got to go," he said. Tomryn pushed his cup away and stood to go.

"But you haven't finished your tea," she called after him.

"When he gets home," Tomryn said from the doorway. "Tell Vulryn he must come see me right away."

"Males," she huffed at the closed door. "Always rushing about."

Tomryn hurried away from the blacksmith's house torn between two emotions. He was proud to do his duty, but the excitement he ought to feel was missing. A heaviness lay on his heart. His duty might be about to destroy the life of his kinsman. There was no hiding what he knew from his superiors. They knew Vulryn met with the seer before leaving the village. Even if they didn't, Vulryn was too big and the village too small to mask his absence. His job was to find out where the blacksmith was going. His success was rewarded with a nagging sense of betrayal. Captain Zee waved him into a clearing where a small knot of soldiers and police waited.

"Something wrong, deputy?" the captain asked as he approached the group. "You look like you have a beakful of sour fruit."

"As you suspected, he's headed for the river," Tomryn said. "He left almost immediately after leaving the seer."

"Did she say why?"

"No," he replied. "She gave me a story about the seer sending him on a fishing trip. But there is something going on. Vulryn's wife has been sick for more than a year. Most of the time, she can't even get out of bed. Today she's dancing around like it never happened. She told me the seer gave Vulryn a healing talisman."

"Sounds like the blacksmith owes the seer a favor," Zee said. "We have to get this information to the captain."

"Good job, Captain," Raryn said when Zee relayed the information. "I have here a signed order from the High Council for the apprehension of Vulryn Pey. He is to be apprehended before he can cross the river and brought back immediately for trial."

"Yes sir," the captain replied. "What is the charge?"

"You need not concern yourself with that," Raryn snapped. "Just do your duty and bring him back. You will also post a guard on the home of the seer. I want to know his every move. Do you understand me?"

"It will be done Councilor."

Vulryn, unaware of the trouble rushing to meet him, felt more alive than he had for a long time. Maryn's illness weighed more heavily on him than he realized. He didn't like leaving her and the shop. However, now that he was away, the idea was beginning to grow on him. A little vacation would do him good. Surely, the seer knew it before he did. He skimmed over the branches with long easy strides.

It seemed strange that the seer sent him fishing. Then again, seers were strange creatures. Their world had its own odd set of rules that nobody really understood. Maryn was healed. If the seer had asked for one of the moons of Tettias, Vulryn would have given it. What was a few fish but blessing on top of blessing?

He made camp for the night in the crook of a bouja tree. He unwrapped the fish Maryn had packed for him and settled in for a cold dinner. The fish had a slightly tart taste that played well with the mangoes he gathered while building his nest. He especially liked the crunch of the gold and red scales. Vulryn patted his stomach producing a resounding belch and settled down to listen to the lullaby the jungle sang just for him.

Falling quickly to sleep was never a problem for Vulryn. That night was no exception. For all his great size and strength, Vulryn was an innocent. He had borne the heartbreak of seeing his bride stricken by disease and yet, like a child, his optimistic faith in ultimate goodness remained as strong as ever.

The Valir say that the Creator gives His beloved sleep. Sated with a good meal, the blacksmith slept the sleep of the blessed It was that rare rest reserved for those from whom the weight of the world has suddenly been lifted. He was alive again and joy permeated his dreams. The blacksmith turned in his sleep and snored in absolute contentment. In Vulryn's world seers did not scheme nor plot; Councilor's served only the good of the people; and faith was rewarded with good.

The Valir also believe that there is a time and a season for all things. Vulryn's season of innocent sleep was done. It was time to awaken to the Creator's service in the real world; the world where seers do scheme, and Councilors do plot.

***

Bryn Bou left his meeting with the seer to spend the day fishing in Bonaire Bayou. He'd had enough of the Grove of the Dead for a while. There was little chance of meeting anyone on the bayou, at its best, the fishing there was poor. Bryn had not caught a fish all day which was fine by him. He only wanted to look busy while doing nothing more than thinking.

Now that he had time to think, he was not sure the seer hadn't put a curse on him after all. Although he was an only child, he had never been truly alone. Growing up in the house of a general, he did not lack for discipline. Yet, there was always a deep layer of friendship in his relationship with his parents, especially his father. His fellow cadets envied his being the son of the one who shepherded them all like a father. That envy put off those like Moryn who chose to believe Bryn was privileged. Such was not the case with everyone. Bryn enjoyed a mutual comradery with most of his classmates.

Then, there was Faryn.

He could not let his mind go there—not now. He forced his thoughts elsewhere, wandering back to the immediate problem of escaping the Boubouja. Between him and the kingdom of men lay the great river, Hiddekel. Beyond the river, the Edge of the World rose up into the clouds. A system of cars on cables had been constructed to allow passage between the two lands. None but diplomats had used it since the Council banned travel to Shiloh.

Lost in the mists of time there existed another way across. The great warriors of old once tested their prowess by leaping the river. More than a few fell to their deaths in the river. Even if he could conquer the crossing, there was still the wall. If real warriors failed, what chance did he have? Coryn told him to go. He said nothing about how. There was no trial and error with leaping the river. It was more do or die.

There has to be a way.

His cane pole began to tap out a message. Dinner was on the line. With practiced hands he worked the fish onto the bank. A three pound shirk usually generated more excitement in him. That day, neither his heart nor his head cared much about fish or dinner. He worked the hook out of the fish's mouth meaning to throw it back. A sudden rumbling in his stomach changed his mind. He had not eaten since he left Coryn's house. His belly remembered even if his mind did not. The fish was soon turning over a small fire and filling the air with a scent that screamed, "Aren't you glad you didn't throw it back?" The shirk's flakey orange flesh tasted like buttered cashews. He found a comfortable branch above the bayou on which to savor his catch and watch the sky turn from gold to violet.

Darkness brought a visitor. A small white owl glided on silent wings to perch on the branch next to Bryn. The owl's head swiveled right, then left studying him briefly from every angle. It reminded him of the little owl he saw in the Grove.

"You look familiar," Bryn said. "Of course, you all look the same to me."

"I was just thinking the same thing," replied the owl.

Bryn's smile vanished. He slapped his cheek. He was definitely awake.

"This is crazy," he said.

"You're telling me," the owl answered. "I was hoping to work with someone a bit more....well, just a bit more."

"Go away," Bryn tried to brush it away.

The owl didn't move. It cocked its head ninety degrees giving Bryn a sideways stare. The big eyes sparkled. The owl ruffled his feathers and squared his head over his shoulders.

"You're making this harder than it has to be," said the owl.

"Work with me, here."

"What do you mean 'work' with?" Bryn asked.

"W-w-w-o-o-o-r-r-k w-w-w-i-i-i-th," the bird slowly drawled. "As in cooperate, join forces, labor together."

"I know what it means," Bryn snapped. "Just what do you think we are going to work on together?"

"Life in general," the owl replied. "And your mission in particular."

"I don't know what you're talking about," Bryn said.

"Very good," the owl replied. "You have playing dumb down pat."

"Who *are* you?" Bryn glared at the bird. "How is it you can talk?"

"Calm down," the owl said. "My name is Oto and I'm on your side. It seems we have a mutual friend."

"Coryn," Bryn said. "Coryn has a hand in this. So, I'm not crazy."

"Crazy is yet to be decided," Oto replied. "After all, you were just sitting here thinking about leaping the river. Not exactly the stuff of sound minds."

Bryn slowly nodded. His head snapped up, eyes bright with hope. "You know another way, don't you?"

"No," Oto answered. "You'll have to leap. It really is the only way."

Bryn's shoulders fell along with his hopes. "You're no help," he said without looking up.

"I do what I can," Oto told him. "It's best we get underway. I get the feeling there's someplace you want to go before the river?"

"Yes, there is."

A short while later Bryn gazed down at the firelight playing in the windows of his home. What were his mother and father doing? He shook his head to chase the thought away. It was best not to think such thoughts. He wanted to kiss his mother goodbye. It was selfish, but there it was. To go down there would only endanger his parents. Besides, if he went home now, he might never leave. He had a job to do. There was no going back on that; not now. Oto fluttered down onto Bryn's shoulder. Bryn made no move to chase him away. It occurred to him that more than a small bird now rested on his shoulders.

"It's time to go," Oto whispered in his ear.

Bryn nodded. He climbed up to the high branches and started east toward the river. Bryn knew the way well enough, but a mistaken handhold in the dark might end his mission before it began. There would be a late rising moon. He would make better time after moonrise. He knew a place with trees heavy with ripe fruit. He would wait there until the moon was up.

A mile before reaching his destination, Bryn caught sight of a firelight flickering in the dark ahead. Bryn climbed higher and moved away from the highway into the shelter of a banyan tree. Voices drifted in on the night breeze, but he was too far away to make out the words. He hunkered down to watch and wait. The fire wasn't moving. Deciding that whoever it was had probably made camp for the night, he moved in for a closer look.

Soldiers were spread across the highway. Bryn's heart leaped into his throat. It was hammering so hard he was sure the soldiers would hear.

So much for Coryn's diversion.

"Damn," he whispered.

His academy training that battles never go as planned was small comfort. Two thoughts ran together. First, that he would have to push for the river tonight. They were camped for the night, and he had to put as much distance between him and the soldiers as possible. The second thought was the bigger blow to his plans. He really was alone. He could not count on help from Coryn.

He recognized two of the soldiers. They had been two years ahead of him at the academy. They were recent graduates out to make a name for themselves. If he was caught, they would not be reasonable or swayed by the seer's having sent him. The four old guard enlisted soldiers with them would be more agreeable, but they were out ranked. The other two were village deputies. Their presence removed all doubt that they were looking for him. This was an arrest detail.

CHAPTER 8

The flesh on the back of his neck began to crawl. Bryn slipped a hand over the handle of his dagger. He had been sure there was no sentry, and it didn't make sense for the soldiers to post one this far into the Boubouja. Still, someone was creeping up behind him. A soft rustle of leaves to his right told him where that someone was hiding. In one fluid movement, he pulled the dagger from his belt and wheeled on the ambusher.

Faryn greeted him with a single finger pressed to the center of a huge smile. Taking his head in her hands, she kissed him lightly. She waved for him to follow and moved away from the soldiers below before he could respond. He followed the sway of her hips through the branches. Ardor quickly overcame trepidation. She came to a halt safely out of the soldiers' earshot.

"I browbeat Grandfather into telling me," she explained. "But I think he let me win. It was too easy."

"Why? What could you possibly gain by following me?"

"Because I love you more than being a warrior. Unless you're willing to say that you don't feel the same way, you're stuck with me."

"There's no future in it," he said.

"I'll take what I can get," she answered and fell into his arms.

His arms closed around exquisite softness and he was helpless. It might be wanton selfishness, but he could never turn her away again. He closed his eyes and pulled her closer. Her head tucked into his shoulder. He could feel her breath on his bare arm and wished the moment would never end. The sensation of movement made Bryn open his eyes. On a branch above them, Oto ruffled his feathers.

"We don't have time for this," Oto said.

Faryn didn't move. He looked down at her nestled in the hollow of his shoulder.

"Did you hear something?" he asked.

"Only the beating of your heart, why?"

Oto shook his head and flew away.

"Oh, nothing," he said. "I thought I heard an owl."

"The old ones say that's good luck."

"Maybe," Bryn said. "Come on I want to make it to the river before dawn."

Bryn led them through the higher branches in a wide arc before returning to the highway. Keeping the moon at their backs, he and Faryn followed the highway branch to within a half mile of the river before stopping to rest.

"We'll stay here until the sun is up," he said.

Faryn nodded and they began gathering leaves for a bed. They looked at their work a few minutes later and laughed. They had built two beds on two different branches.

"For now," she said.

It was his turn to nod in agreement. They settled into their collections of leaves and soft twigs. The distant sounds of the river drifted to them on the breeze. Peepers sang their songs accompanied by the croaks of alligators and deep bass groans of the giant viaths. The symphony of the Boubouja combined with physical exhaustion carried them away into silent slumber.

***

Byryn and Galryn climbed the stairs to their bed knowing that neither would be able to sleep. Their future, which always seemed so secure, was coming apart like the morning mist in a gale. They had prayed for so long for a child. When Bryn came, he filled up their lives. He was strong, intelligent, and mature beyond his years. They lived with an abiding sense that he was destined for great things. When he fooled everyone and went to the military academy, they were sure of it. Before turning in, Galryn paused to look in on his empty bed.

"Will he ever come back?" she asked.

Byryn, unable to trust his voice, simply nodded. It wasn't a lie exactly. But she knew how to read his face. Steel crept into his eyes; his chin lifted just a little bit. The set of his jaw pushed the wrinkles deeper. Galryn buried her face in her husband's shoulder and wept. A single rebellious tear crept down Byryn's face.

"God speed, my son," he whispered.

***

The sacredness the Valir attached to duty was built upon their belief that there was a time to every purpose under heaven. Bryn's life was changed by Coryn's call. A hint of purpose was displacing the aimlessness he felt. The call imparted a sense that his time was coming. He glided between the branches with Destiny stalking him like a shadow.

His errand was simple. True, there were dangers, but life was dangerous. The road east was long and filled with creatures he had only read about. The veil of youth, sewn of immortality, excitement and naivete, hung over his eyes blinding him to its difficulties. He knew that if he were caught, he would be thrown in prison. He ignored even the possibility of being apprehended. He would do his duty to deliver a message and return home—simple.

High above him fleeting patches of dark sky were sprinkled with the dust of a million stars. The soothing song of the river softly played against its banks. The breeze tumbled through the branches ruffling the feathers of his crest without disturbing his sleep.

He awoke with the first gray light on the eastern horizon. Minding his step among the smaller branches, he climbed into the canopy above. Bryn watched the eastern sky, barely breathing, waiting. A red crescent peeked over the cliffs and grew into the sun. The new day touched his skin chasing away the morning chill. Somewhere nearby a poct shook its emerald wings and launched into song. Bryn breathed in the fresh, clean, and cool morning. He dropped from his perch, caught a branch, and let his weight carry him to the next. Hand over hand he passed through the branches until he reached the sleeping figure below.

Faryn smiled at him. "You're awake early."

Her arms flew around him. Her beak touched his. The kiss was quick and sweet. Bryn forgot where he was. He forgot why he was there; forgot about missions and duty; forgot everything. The feel of her hand on his face; the deep, soft, golden pools of her eyes; and her face next to his was intoxicating. He swallowed hard. His mouth was so dry his words became hopelessly tangled.

"We will be the talk of the village tonight." Her voice was soothing as the streams of the deep Boubouja. "And if we don't get moving the talk will be about our capture."

His jaws closed with an audible click. He nodded. At the moment, it was all he was capable of doing. Bryn picked up his pack and began stuffing it with fruit.

"Have you thought about how to cross the river?" she asked.

"I have given considerable thought to how *I* will cross," he said. "Your appearance has complicated the matter considerably. So, no, not really."

Faryn froze him with an icy stare.

"Er…I mean...that is to say," he stammered. "Oh hell. I was going to leap."

"And you are thinking that I am not capable of doing the same, is that it?"

"No," he said squaring his shoulders. "I think I love you too much to risk your life."

"That's the sweetest bunch of poct manure anyone has ever said to me," she said with a warming smile. "Let's go."

The highway was too dangerous. Bryn led the way, threading through crisscrossing limbs, keeping the highway on their right and below them. He continuously scanned the trees as they moved east. Once across the river, the safety of the branches would be gone. They would be forced to travel through open spaces amid strange, untrustworthy men.

Once we cross?" Bryn laughed at the thought. *More like if we cross*.

The Hiddekel was no forest stream swollen by rain or the finger of a bayou winding between the bouja trees. There was nothing like it in the western world. The Hiddekel was the great divide between the jungle and swamps of the Boubouja and a sheer granite wall called the Edge of the World. Atop the Edge lay the kingdom of men.

They reached the Hiddekel in less than an hour. Under the cover of the canopy, they watched the river flow on its way to the Great Sea. They both knew the glassy surface was a lie. The only peace those waters carried was whatever peace lay beyond this life. Below the still surface, lurked the viath, armor plated cousin to the dragon. Its bone crushing jaws were lined with rows of teeth propelled by a thick, powerful tail. The river carried death just as it brought life.

"Two things are never full," Bryn recited. "The Great Sea and the beast within the waters."

Faryn nodded in silent agreement.

The forest stretched its arms over the river seeking those of the far shore and never finding them. Less than a mile downstream from where Bryn stood was the tram that carried travelers over the river and to the top of the Edge.

Ages ago, the bravest warriors dared to leap to the far side of the river. Only the strongest lived to look back from the far shore. Bryn looked out across the river. He felt neither brave nor strong. He felt trapped, a prisoner of his words. It was better to die in the jaws of a viath or drown in the waters than to fail his oath.

He looked at Faryn beside him and fresh doubt stole over him. It was one thing for him to die. But, to succeed and see her lost to the river was worse than death. For all her fire and independence, she was not physically his equal. He inhaled deeply and blew out a long, slow breath. He was oath bound to leap no matter how he felt. He had no choice but to dare the leap. Faryn was not. She could go back.

Her voice intruded on his thoughts.

"A patrol," Faryn whispered and pointed to a small group approaching from their left.

"Those are not the ones from last night," Bryn said using his arm to gently push her back.

From the cover of hanging vines, they watched in silence as the patrol passed beneath them moving in the direction of the tram. The Council maintained regular patrols on both sides of the river to enforce the ban on travel and prevent smuggling.

"Move it, you dinks," an angry voice below ordered. "We're gonna be late."

"No worries, Sarge," came an answer. "We'll take him and be home for dinner."

"I hear he's a giant," another said.

High above them, Bryn looked at Faryn and shrugged.

"Obviously, they're not looking for me," he said when the patrol was gone.

"Obviously." She gave him a sidelong look and smiled. "Let's see what they're up to."

"Why?"

"Humor me," she replied. "We can't cross and scale the Edge today anyway."

"Okay," Bryn said. "But it sounds like tempting fate to me."

Faryn didn't wait for his answer. She set off in pursuit of the patrol. They caught up to the soldiers where the highway met the river. A moment later, they were joined by the soldiers they had seen camped the night before.

***

Sharp pain stabbed his chest. Vulryn's eyes flew open, and his hand closed on sharpened iron. There were soldiers everywhere. An angry soldier held a lance to his chest. He tried to squirm away from the blade that kept him pinned to the ground while uniformed shapes pressed in around him.

"Are you Vulryn Pey, son of Tarryn?" a soldier asked.

"Let's see your hands," another ordered.

Vulryn slowly raised his hands. He had nothing to hide. He had broken no laws and had done no one wrong. He innocently believed that was enough.

"Get up," a soldier ordered.

The voice sounded like Zaryn Kul. Vulryn told himself that could not be. What would the village Sergeant of the Guard be doing here?

"Stand up," the voice commanded again. It *was* Zaryn. "Are you Vulryn Zee?"

"You know I am," Vulryn answered. "We've lived in the same village all our lives."

The soldiers circled the blacksmith wary of his size.

"Just keep quiet and do as you're told," Zaryn ordered.

"What's this all about?" Vulryn asked disregarding the command.

"Just slowly turn around," Zaryn demanded. "Private, tie his hands."

A loop of rope was thrown around Vulryn's right wrist. A sudden jerk brought his hands together behind his back. A moment later, his hands were fastened to his waist. The soldier put a hand in the middle of Vulryn's back and shoved him toward the village. The blacksmith didn't move. The soldier tried again, harder this time. The giant still didn't move.

"Let's go Vulryn," Zaryn ordered. "Don't fight us on this."

"I'm not moving until somebody tells me what this is all about," Vulryn insisted.

"Treason," Zaryn's voice was flat and hard.

"Treason? That's crazy," Vulryn said. "Since when is fishing treason?"

"Stop resisting," Zaryn shouted and brought the handle of his dagger down on Vulryn's head.

The dazed blacksmith stumbled but stayed on his feet. A second soldier drove the blunt end of his lance into Vulryn's abdomen.

"Kill the damn traitor," a deputy shouted and threw his lance.

The blade buried itself between Vulryn's chest and biceps. Blood spread over his tunic as Vulryn staggered and fell. Lances and daggers rose all around him.

Bryn and Faryn hit the bunched-up soldiers at a run scattering bodies and weapons over the ground before them. Bryn landed a straight right hand on the jaw of a soldier sending him to the ground. Faryn ducked under a roundhouse punch and kicked the soldier's feet from under him. Springing up, she planted her foot on the soldier's throat and brought her weight down—hard.

She pulled the lance from Vulryn's arm and cut his bonds. The freed blacksmith brought both fists down on the head of a soldier about to skewer Bryn from behind. The soldier collapsed in a heap and Vulryn grabbed his lance and spun around to fend off the rush of two others. One opted for the better part of valor. The other was impaled on Vulryn's lance and hoisted skyward. The dying soldier's screams brought a lull in the battle.

"Put him down, please," Bryn said.

Vulryn dropped the dead soldier and stood over the body panting and holding his wounded side. With a mechanical movement, he turned to look at Bryn. The big Valir's wide eyes filled his slack face. Faryn took him by the arm.

"Sit down," she said. "You'll feel better."

"They were going to kill me," Vulryn said in a faraway voice.

"I know," Faryn whispered in his ear.

"Alright," Bryn said, pointing a lance at the soldiers. "You two, get over here. Move!"

The soldiers joined their companions on the ground. Faryn and Bryn bound them all together hand and foot.

"One's missing," Faryn said.

"That way," said Vulryn with a jerk of his head.

"I'll get him," Bryn said and disappeared into the jungle.

Bryn returned a half hour later with the frightened soldier. Faryn tied him to the rest while Bryn helped himself to a long drink of the soldier's water.

"How is he?" Bryn pointed at Vulryn.

"Skin wounds," she pronounced. "He'll heal in a few days."

"Meanwhile, what do we do with him?" Bryn asked.

"Am I your prisoner now?" Vulryn said. "Isn't that up to me?"

"He has a point," Faryn said.

"Yes," Bryn said. "And he put that point through the heart of a soldier sent to arrest him for treason."

"They were going to kill me," Vulryn protested.

"Says who? You?" Bryn bent his head toward the soldiers. "Or them? Who will the judge believe?"

"Bryn?" Faryn said. "There's something you should know."

CHAPTER 9

The lift station materialized out of the mist. The silhouetted figures of sentries, depot buildings, a cable car, and towering pylons took on color and detail as Faryn and her escort approached. In the distance a poct called to its mate. Faryn gasped, startled by the sound. A few soldiers were huddled together at the gate. One of them detached himself from the group to receive the newcomers.

Years ago Edge Station bustled with activity. Valir and humans flowed over the Edge like one of the many waterfalls. Things improved for a time after the war, then, a sudden chill in the political atmosphere froze travel once again. On the Valirian side, the reason remained obscure. The High Council banned travel; that was reason enough. For Faryn, with one grandfather on the Council and another a revered seer, a decree from the Council had never been enough. She insisted on the whole truth.

She had traveled to Shiloh as a girl and was fascinated by the tall buildings and the mechanical wonders of men. The smooth skinned creatures were rather hard on the eye but seemed pleasing enough company. Their world was loud and crowded and infected with a general abrasiveness and ingrown sense of superiority. Though it filled her with anger, the recent human decree reported to the Council that the outlying species were inferior and available as chattel didn't come as a complete surprise.

The soldier at the gate signaled for them to stop. Faryn smiled at him and pulled a golden bag from beneath her cloak. The soldier snapped to attention; gave her a crisp salute and swung open the gate.

"You're early today," he said. "Afraid you'll have to wait for the mist to lift before the car arrives."

"Yes, I'm aware of that. Thank you, Sergeant," Faryn said.

"You're welcome to wait in the Captain's office," he said.

"He's away, but I'm sure he wouldn't mind."

"You're very kind." Faryn nodded and smiled.

The sergeant led them to a shack set back from the boarding area. The single room was dominated by a wide desk which faced the door. The walls were lined with tall shelves that were home to hundreds of books. Faryn noticed that none of the books had anything to do with laws, military regulations, or martial procedures. Most bore the titles of popular novels. A large volume of crosswords puzzles on the desk lay open to a half-finished puzzle.

"Not a very busy bunch," Vulryn observed.

"No, I suppose there's not much to do anymore," she said. "Have you ever been to the top?"

"Never," he answered. "My father never strayed far from Vix. I think we visited the Grove once or twice when I was growing up."

"You're in for quite a shock," Faryn warned. "Are you okay?"

"I think so," he replied checking to see that no blood showed. "Feels like someone's scrubbing my insides on a washboard."

"Think happy thoughts," she answered.

"That's easy for you to say." Vulryn went on rubbing his angry middle.

Faryn walked to the window and looked out at the empty grounds. The old depot building just across the way wore a thick covering of moss. Small ferns sprouted haphazardly up and down the pitch of the roof and clogged the gutters. Choker vines wound their way up one wall and a bouja seedling worked its way skyward beside the stone chimney.

"It wasn't always like this," Faryn said with a sigh.

"No, I suppose not," he said.

Faryn settled into a chair behind the desk and stared silently out the window. This was not the way it was supposed to go. She had stolen the golden diplomatic bag from her grandfather's office. She and Bryn were to use it to get across the river and into Shiloh. Then, came Vulryn. They couldn't leave him behind. Though he was innocent of treason, he was a murderer. Besides, in true Valirian style, he refused to abandon those who saved him. There was no changing it now and time was short. Vulryn would pose as her bodyguard and Bryn would have to leap after all.

She was called from her thoughts by a rap on the door. The sergeant stuck his head inside.

"Car is coming down, Miss," he announced. "Be here in a few minutes."

"We'll wait outside, if that's alright with you," Faryn said.

"As you like," he said and disappeared outside.

"Last chance to back out." She laid a hand on the blacksmith's arm.

Vulryn shook his head. "Duty calls. No turning back."

Faryn watched the gondola drift down through the clouds. Gears and chains ground in accompaniment to the whirl of spinning wheels. Vulryn was absorbed with the conglomeration of turning gears and wheels that moved the car from cliff top to riverbank. Power for the lift came from solar powered motors atop the Edge.

She offered a silent prayer that the ride be without incident. The specter of deception she manufactured at the bottom lacked substance. Once the gondola began to rise again, Faryn would have to rely on her wits and the intimidating size of her companion to cover up her lies. She hoped it would be enough to secure their passage before the theft and their subsequent deadly encounter with the soldiers caught up with her.

They boarded as the last of the morning mists burned off and rose into the clear sky. Above the canopy, they looked over the breathtaking ribbon of blue that wound through endless shades of green along the base of the granite wall. Vulryn's grip on the rail turned his knuckles white. He tried not to look down, but the view was as amazing as it was terrifying.

Passing through a thin layer of white clouds, they reached the top in time to see the human lift operator in animated conversation with a small box affixed to the top of a shiny pole.

Faryn grabbed Vulryn's sleeve. She tried to pull him quickly through the gate. A mosquito may have gotten more movement from him. She snapped her fingers in front of his face and motioned him to hurry. They were the only passengers and Vulryn was hard to miss. They had to get away from the station and into the waiting human hovercraft before the operator finished his discussion. She prodded the blacksmith onward, putting her shoulder into his back and pushing with all her might.

"The Valirian Embassy," she said and lifted the pouch so the driver could see the diplomatic seal. "Please hurry."

"Yeah, yeah, yeah," the driver snarled. "It's always hurry up with you birds."

Vulryn started to his feet. She stopped him with an outstretched hand and a shake of her head. The motion was not lost on the driver. He decided it was a good time to get started and pushed the accelerator forward. He didn't notice the lift operator chasing after them.

"Try to ignore their insults," she whispered to Vulryn. "At least until we get where we're going."

Vulryn smiled and nodded. The hovercraft moved faster than anything he had ever seen or imagined was possible. He soon overcame his fear and leaned over the rail to let the wind blow against his face. The rapt look on his face brought a smile to hers.

Simple pleasures, she thought.

As the sun set behind them, the hovercraft came to rest in front of a small inn. A sign over the door bore the mark of a four-pointed star painted in purple and gold.

"The royal crest of Shiloh," Faryn explained as they stepped beneath the sign.

The inn was simply furnished. Large, hand-crafted chairs fashioned from the local wood were gathered around scattered tables of the same material. A long, polished wooden bar covered one wall. At the end of the bar nearest the door a plump woman in a homespun dress dropped her towel and walked over to them.

"You seem a might unprepared," the woman said. "Didn't they tell you? The pouch takes a week to reach Shiloh."

"Yes ma'am," Faryn replied. "We're just traveling light."

"Mmm-hmm." The woman shrugged her shoulders. "As you like it then. The room is upstairs on the left. Dinner is in an hour."

Faryn started for the stairs with Vulryn in tow. She stopped suddenly and the blacksmith lifted her off her feet to keep from running over her. Faryn peeked around him at the woman.

"Oh, by the way," she said. "Do many Valir stop here?"

"The only one's like you that stop here are carrying that pouch." She pointed at the bag Faryn held. "The legal ones that is."

"Legal ones?" Faryn asked.

"There are more ways to Shiloh than this one, luv," she said. "Most not so public if you get my meaning."

"Thank you again," Faryn said and looked up at Vulryn. "You can put me down now."

"What was that all about?" Vulryn asked when they were alone.

"She's suspicious," Faryn said. "We're not the typical couriers."

"What do we do now?"

"We stick to the plan," she told him. "For now."

The room was furnished as befitted a neglected way station on the edge of civilization. Cast offs from richer stations, government residences, and the palace itself filled the room with frayed elegance. Beneath the nicks and scars, the ornately carved furniture clung to a faded shadow of its former splendor.

"How come there's only one bed?" Vulryn asked. "Don't couriers always travel in pairs?"

"One is supposed to be awake at all times." She pointed at a high back chair with a chest built under a pillowed top. "One sits there; the pouch goes in the chest."

Vulryn groaned.

Dinner was a tasteless collection of bread, cheese and highly questionable fruit hauled up from the Boubouja. Feigning exhaustion, they wasted little time in conversation with the humans before rushing back to their room. Faryn settled into the bed. Vulryn was marginally successful at wedging his bulk into the guard's chair. He was more successful at ignoring his discomfort and was soon snoring loudly.

"Oh, great," Faryn said and folded her pillow to cover both ears.

Her expectation of a sleepless night evaporated quickly. Her soft snores joined Vulryn's buzzsaw imitation. The restful scene was superficial. All was not quiet within. Faryn's dreams were haunted by images of death and destruction.

She was home again, standing in the smoldering ruins of Vix. The stench of burning flesh scorched her nostrils. Something warm trickled down her face. She touched her forehead, and her hand came away a sticky red. Faryn stepped over broken bodies weaving her way through the village.

"Bryn Bou," she cried.

Her only answers were moans of the dying who littered the street. Exhausted and discouraged, she dropped down with her head between her knees. The beating of wings made her look up. A small white owl flew out of the carnage and circled Faryn. An involuntary shudder went through her. The owl seemed to be whispering her name urging her to follow. She struggled to her feet following the bird and found Bryn buried beneath the rubble of the Academy.

"Run," he shouted at her. "Run and don't look back."

Darkness blacker than the night overshadowed them. Faryn began to run in the slow motion reserved for dreams. A dragon, iridescent scales glowing green against the blackness, descended catching Bryn in its talons. Leather wings beat the air. Faryn caught hold of Bryn's feet and they were lifted into the air. She struggled to hang on and failed. She watched him borne aloft by the beast as walls of granite flew by.

She jolted awake, safe in her bed at the inn amid the sonorous breathing of her guard.

CHAPTER 10

Bryn knew the strength and feel of the branch beneath his feet was more important than how high it was or how far it reached out over the river. He resolved not to take unnecessary risks. He still hunted for the highest and farthest-reaching branch but with an eye to strength and flexibility. Gingerly sliding one foot in front of the other, he felt his way forward from the trunk.

If he went too far the branch might not bear his weight, it might snap and dump him in the river. Fail to go far enough and he would not have the recoil to reach the safety of the branches on the other side. The branch began to sway beneath him. It had a slight give, a feeling of a soft spring beneath his feet. A few steps further and the branch began to bounce with each step. He made a few practice bounces and found the spot with the most recoil. He measured the distance with both his eyes and his heart.

He began to coil and release the muscles in his powerful legs. The branch moved in a growing arc beneath him. Satisfied the branch had given its all, Bryn launched himself into the air. Propelled by the upward swing of the branch, he climbed high above the river. At the peak of his climb, he opened his wings, and an updraft carried him higher. The wind under his wings brought a sigh of relief to Bryn's lips and renewed hope to his heart.

All the Valir had wings, but none could truly fly. Relying on winds and thermal currents, they glided on transparent wings that were too weak and fragile for flight. Yet they were strong enough to carry their muscled bodies short distances.

Why, in the name of the Creator, there existed winged creatures who could not fly made no sense to Bryn. Then again, neither did the sightless guides of Deutero who led pilgrims across the lava fields of the Pietra.

"Accept the world as it is," Grandfather always said. "Rather than weep that it is not how you would have it."

His flight took on an ominous feel. Something below him was not right. He had acquired a shadow that did not belong to him. It was not on the water, but under it. The surface rippled as a row of black armor plates broke the surface and quickly disappeared again, turning Bryn's blood to ice. His momentum and the strength of the updraft were spent. He was descending. The branches reaching out from the far shore were still thirty yards away. He pulled his legs and tail tight against his body trying to decrease drag. Trembling lips whispered a desperate prayer to the Creator for a few more feet.

He glanced down and the surface of the river exploded. Huge jaws with teeth the size of daggers rocketed up to meet him. The viath's entire body rose from the river. The monster was standing on its tail high above the surface.

Bryn screamed. His bladder let go. Inches from his feet, huge jaws came together with the sound of snapping tree trunks. The sound reverberated in his ears and echoed through the woods along the river. Strangely, there was no pain until he hit the branches. The jolt vibrated the length of his legs. He swayed but hung on. Steady again, he rushed along the branch to lock the trunk in a fervent embrace. He locked himself around a branch and did not let go until the tremors of unspent adrenaline were past.

Steadier, he dared to look down again. The shadow still circled beneath the surface of the water.

"Creator be praised." He held a hand to his thundering heart. "I made it."

He didn't yet quite believe the words. He, Bryn Bou, failed warrior disappointment to his ancestors, had actually leaped the Hiddekel. He climbed through the branches for a better look at this new world. The sight that greeted him brought an involuntary gasp. Since childhood, he heard the stories of the land across the river. However, words could not describe the sight of the sheer granite wall rising upward and blocking out the world beyond. The old stories called it the Edge of the World. The name paled in comparison to the sight. The unseen world beyond the wall was as alien to him as one of the moons. It was a world full of men and, as the old folks told it, countless evils.

His sense of wonder was short lived. He heard someone or

something moving in his direction. Bryn jumped to a branch on the north side of the tree and climbed away from the approaching footsteps. From behind the shelter of the leaves, he could make out the red tunics of soldiers. It was the border patrol that prowled the narrow eastern bank. Had they heard the fate of their fellows from the other shore?

"It was near here," a lean Valir wearing sergeant stripes told the pair of soldiers following him. "Sounded like a big one too."

The patrol came to rest on the branch vacated by Bryn moments earlier.

"Look at that, would ya," one of the soldiers said pointing at the shadow in the water. "I've never seen one that big before."

"They're out there," the sergeant assured him. "Now spread out and check for signs of a leaper. That thing didn't just decide to jump out of the water. It was after something."

"A leaper? You can't be serious. No one has leaped the river in a generation."

"Humor me, Corporal," the sergeant growled. "Check anyway."

The patrol split up and scoured the nearby trees. After a fruitless search, they returned the way they came. Bryn watched from the safety of his hiding place until they were out of sight. Then, as quietly as possible, he moved east through the trees toward the escarpment.

The granite wall loomed up from the forest floor and climbed two thousand feet into the sky. Most Valir had seen The Edge from the western shore. On holidays they brought their children to the river just to stand and stare at the imposing sight. Up close words lost all power to describe the geographical wonder. Stones the size of houses littered the base of the cliff that ran the length of the horizon.

Bryn imagined that this massive wall of stone was the Creator's way of saying to the Valir and their beloved Boubouja, "this far and no farther." The sentiment was echoed by those who had dared to venture beyond it into the world of men. While the wall held the Valir back, it also served as a defense against the encroachment of the world beyond. The abrupt uplift kept the Boubouja covered with clouds. The tall tropical forest blocked out most of the sunlight needed by man's war machines.

Those same thick clouds blocked his view of the top. Coryn assured him there was a series of steps and handholds cut into the stone a holdover from the days before the lift. According to the seer, the staircase was hidden in a horseshoe shaped bend in the wall. To Bryn, a five-foot-tall Valir, accustomed to life in the trees all that stone looked the same. There seemed to be neither projections nor hidden valleys. He was sure a closer look would not be any more revealing but set out to explore it anyway.

"What I need," Bryn said. "Is a sign saying, 'This way to the secret path'."

His attempt to be lighthearted failed. The truth, hard as the granite wall, hit home. He was alone in a strange land that could only get stranger. He could not call for help, there was no one to hear. The enthusiasm nurtured by the prophet's faith and his own recent accomplishment withered away leaving a dark hole of dread in its place.

"Send me a sign," he pleaded to no one in particular.

No one answered. No one at all seemed to hear. No sign appeared in the heavens to save him. He was alone.

So be it.

"The lift is to the south," he said to himself and started moving north.

The trees nearest the wall were either broken by giant stones calved from the wall or stunted by the nearly perpetual darkness of its shadow. It made travel difficult and slow. Bryn retreated to the line of tall trees keeping as close to the wall as possible. No staircase appeared.

Night came quickly in the Boubouja. Bryn found it fell quicker still in the shadow of the Edge. The sun was inching down the sky behind him. He would have to stop soon and wait out the night.

"What kept you?" A small white owl said from the branch a bouja tree.

Bryn missed his step and nearly fell.

"Oto?" he gasped. "Don't do that."

"I'm small and you weren't paying attention," Oto said in his own defense. "Now, that I have your attention, follow me."

Oto flapped his wings and seemed to disappear into the stone. Bryn scrambled to the place where Oto had been sitting. His former perch was the edge of a sharp salient in the wall. He had flown into a depression in the escarpment.

"Coryn's horseshoe," he whispered.

Bryn followed the curve of the stone for about a half hour stopping only when darkness hid the way. Working by feel and instinct, he put together a rough, shelter of small branches, palm fronds and large waxy leaves. He crawled inside moments before it began to rain. The patter of the rain on his shelter lulled Bryn to sleep. As he drifted off, his thoughts turned toward home. It was there that his dreams carried him.

The clamor of a passing band of pocts welcomed Bryn to a new day. He slept longer than he had planned, but the time was well spent having washed away the weariness from his mind and muscles. Nearby bouja leaves provided a cool drink of water saved from last night's rain. He splashed some on his face. Light was creeping into the sky. Somewhere to the east the sun was up, but it would be hours before the sun reached the shadows beneath the Edge. Bryn didn't need the sun to tell him it was time for breakfast; his rumbling stomach did that job. The sweet, golden pulp of a large mango from his pack quieted his belly. He licked up the juices running down his fingers savoring every drop and finished by rolling the pit in his beak to clean away the remaining bits of fruit. His plans for a second mango were interrupted by a sound moving through the trees. Bryn moved off the path and climbed out of sight.

These travelers were not the border patrol. They wore no uniforms and there was no talking in their ranks. They were moving quietly and with purpose into the horseshoe. In the lead was a big Valir. He was not as big as Vulryn, but it was close. He wore no pack, which was odd for someone so far from any village.

A second look told Bryn the leader was armed better than most soldiers. A crossbow was slung over his right shoulder. The quiver at this waist was full of short Valirian bolts cocked with poct feathers. A pair of daggers were tucked into his belt alongside a wicked leather cord studded with sharp pieces of bone. His equally sharp eyes swept the trees ahead.

Ten paces behind him, a string of a half dozen smaller Valir roped together at the waist and loaded down with huge baskets of woven bamboo followed. Dust puffed from the packs that bounced against their backs. As they passed under Bryn, a noxious odor wafted up from the packs. The smell caused his stomach to involuntarily lurch. Bryn began to breathe through his mouth trying to hold down his breakfast. Walking in the wake of the stench were two more armed Valir.

Only one kind of merchant avoids the lift. Smugglers.

They were headed for the old staircase. Bryn smiled, looked skyward and nodded; he had a guide.

He fell into line behind them keeping their rear guard in sight and below him. He kept to the large branches. A branch cracking underfoot now would be dangerous. Near the deepest part of the horseshoe, the smugglers left the trees and moved along a well-packed dirt track that wound through the mountains of debris. Bryn followed as closely as he dared. Once, he stepped on a sharp stone buried in the track and clamped a hand over his mouth to stifle a curse.

The smugglers called a halt protected from prying eyes by a circle of large stones. Bryn ducked behind a boulder well behind his newfound guides. If they didn't move on soon, he would retreat back into the trees and better cover. The decision came a moment too late. A vise closed on his shoulder.

"Well, well, what have we here?" a deep voice asked.

Bryn struggled to break free, but the fingers dug deeper into his flesh. He turned to face his attacker and was thrown back against the boulder. His head met the stone with a dull thud. The white pain of impact slowly washed away leaving spots that danced before his eyes. When his vision cleared, a single bloodshot eye glared back at him. Over the smuggler's shoulder he saw a second band of smugglers passing by. Bryn was lifted off his feet.

"What are you up to boy?" the one-eyed smuggler growled. "Don't you dare lie to me."

"Nothing," Bryn said.

"Nothing?" One Eye drove an iron right hand into Bryn's midsection.

Bryn's breath exploded from him with a loud whoosh. He fell to the ground gasping for air. One Eye followed the blow with a kick to Bryn's stomach. Breakfast exited Bryn in a hot, golden stream and his world began to lose focus. Before darkness swallowed him, Bryn was hoisted onto his feet again. He was almost thankful for One Eye's iron grip. He was certain his own legs could no longer hold him. Bryn was relieved of his dagger.

"Let's try this again," One Eye said. "What are you doing here?"

"I…I…I." Bryn gulped down air. "I ran away."

"That's more like it," One Eye's voice took on a congenial tone. "Now, another easy one. Why are you following my partners?"

"The stairway." Bryn took another deep breath. "I was hoping they would lead me to the stairway."

"Well why didn't you say so." One Eye shoved him along the path. "Right this way."

Bryn stumbled into the clearing behind One Eye's team of smugglers. His presence brought the trio of armed smugglers in the clearing to their feet with hands on their daggers. Standing amid these rough edged Valir, Bryn felt small and alone.

"Codryn, you had a shadow," One Eye told his companions. "Says he's a runaway but take a look at this."

Codryn, the big leader of the gang Bryn was following, looked at the dagger that One Eye handed to him. He lumbered closer to Bryn and bent over until they were beak to beak. His sharp eyes burned into Bryn.

"Bou is it?" Codryn's breath stunk of rotten fruit. "How long have you been following us?"

"Since early this morning."

"Says he wants to climb the stairs," One Eye said.

"The stairway?" Codryn rubbed his beak. "How does a little pinger like you know about the stairway?"

Bryn's mind raced for an answer. He needed the confident sound of the truth, but not too much truth.

"I heard the village seer speak of it," he said.

Codryn looked at One Eye who shrugged and smiled. Codryn cocked his head and stared at Bryn trying to read the truth. Bryn refused to look away. His face remained a mask of indifference. Codryn backed away a few moments later making it easier for Bryn to breathe.

"Could be he's telling the truth," Codryn said. "Bou is a big name in Vix. He probably rates with the seer. Our little pinger here must like to listen at doorways. Tie him to the gimp. We'll grant his wish to climb with us. I have the feeling he's worth a ransom."

One Eye lashed Bryn to the last member of his gang, a small Valir with a withered left leg. Bryn helped his new companion struggle out of his pack and get settled against the stone to rest.

"Fedryn Rad, son of Bedryn," he whispered to Bryn and held out a calloused hand.

"Bryn Bou, son of Byryn."

Bryn looked his new companion over. Fedryn had the light skin of the northern Boubouja villagers. His beak lacked the sharp hook characteristic of most Valir. Bryn wondered if this, like the withered leg, was a happenstance of birth. Fedryn's most remarkable feature was his eyes. They sparkled with intelligence and strength of spirit. Despite his small size, he carried the same pack as the others.

"What are you carrying?" Bryn asked with a nod toward the packs.

"Not so loud," Fedryn warned. "Codryn doesn't like a lot of talk among the slaves."

"Slaves? But…but you're Valir," Bryn whispered.

"Captured Valir," Fedryn corrected. "Captured by Codryn and his band and destined to be sold in Shiloh along with the rest of the goods."

"Sold to who?"

"Men. I've heard them talking. Apparently, there's a big market for outland slaves in Shiloh. At first it was just the purple mills buying workers. Better pray you don't end up there. Now, everyone in Shiloh is buying slaves. That's the real reason the king has banned travel to Shiloh."

"I've got to get out of here," Bryn said.

"Good luck with that," Fedryn countered. "I haven't seen a way yet. They keep a sharp watch on the merchandise day and night."

Codryn let the second gang rest for a half hour before getting them all started again. Fedryn's waddling gait and bobbing head in his line of sight played havoc with Bryn's queasy stomach. He tried to focus instead on the ground in front of him. Small stones strewn along the path gouged at his feet. Soon Bryn was limping in time with his companion. They reached the stairway a few minutes later and began to climb.

The stairway was wider than Bryn imagined. He guessed it was about three feet wide; each step rising nine inches to the next section of stone. The steps, worn smooth by many travelers, wound in series of switchbacks up the face of the cliff. Each set of stairs was identical to the one before, but headed in the opposite direction and upward, always upward. The sun appeared over the rim just ahead of midday. For the first time in his life Bryn groaned at its arrival. The muscles in his legs were on fire. A stitch of pain bit into his side with every step. The rising heat on his back added greatly to his misery. Still, they climbed.

Bryn lost track of time. Every movement, every thought centered on taking one more step. Somewhere amid countless steps, Codryn signaled for a halt. Porters and guards alike collapsed onto the steps in a chorus of huffing, puffing, and gasping for breath. Bryn sat with his head between his knees forcing air through his burning lungs.

CHAPTER 11

While Bryn Bou sat on the stairway dripping sweat and trying hard to breathe, Maryn Pey, tears streaming down her face, knocked at the door of Coryn the Seer pleading for someone, anyone, to answer. The soldier standing watch grew tired of listening to her cries.

"For the Creator's sake," he called down from his post. "Quit that caterwauling and go home."

Marshalling the last of her faith, she rapped harder.

"Please," she whispered and laid her head on the door.

The knob turned with a faint click. The door fell away. Maryn looked down into a heavily lined face beneath a snow-white crest. A black shawl worked with silver thread was draped over hunched shoulders. The maid's gnarled hand dropped from the door and beaconed Maryn enter.

"Come in dear," the maid's voice shared none of the feebleness her body bore. "Master Coryn will see you. He is just over by the fire."

Maryn dabbed the tears from her eyes with the hem of her apron and followed the maid across the dark room. Her steps were as unsteady as those of the maid she followed. She had heard stories of the seer. Neighbors told her not to go, but how could she refrain. She would brave jaguar or viath for her Vulryn. Her first actual glimpse of the mysterious prophet of the Boubouja was a disappointment. He wasn't much to look at. He certainly wasn't the giant of lore. Coryn was a male, no more. A small one compared to her Vulryn. His chestnut plumage was marked by a single patch of white just above one eye as if touched by the glancing stroke of a small paint brush. A scar ran down the right side of his beak, the tip of which was missing. She couldn't help but wonder if the rumors about his age were false. The feathers above the cut of his cloak were the bright, smooth green of a young male.

The maid steered Maryn into a chair beside her host before hobbling from the room. Maryn sank into the offered chair. Now that she was face to face with her benefactor, she could think of nothing to say.

"You've been crying," his voice rescuing her from the lengthening silence. "Are you ill?"

She searched for her voice, but a small croak was all that came. The maid saved her. The old one reappeared clutching a cup between her twisted claws. Maryn accepted the cup. A sip of the hot brew helped the words to flow.

"Police came to see me," she said. The tears were back, but her voice remained steady. "They say Vulryn is a traitor."

Coryn leaned close to her. His eyes were on her face, but she felt he was looking through her. A chill shot down her spine. She shivered involuntarily but held his gaze.

"What would you have me to do?" Coryn asked his voice soft as down. "I'm just a seer."

"Please, save him from the prison," she pleaded. "Tell them he's done nothing wrong. They'll believe you. Oh, please, please help him."

"Do you trust me?" He cocked his head; eyes still on her.

"Yes, my Lord," she whispered.

"My Lord, is it?" His brow rose and he gently patted her arm with a weathered hand. "I've not been addressed like that in many years. You have my word all will be well."

"Please hurry, my poor Vulryn..."

"Hurry is the one thing I cannot do, my dear." Coryn leaned back in his chair. "Dry your eyes."

"But I don't understand," she replied.

"The authorities believe Vulryn was carrying a message from me to a seer in Shiloh," he began. "Of course, he wasn't. Nevertheless, I need them to go on believing it is true a little longer. Your husband will be free in due time. Now, finish your tea and go make ready for his return."

"You're sure he will be alright?"

"Absolutely," he said. A wry smile touched his face. "I have given my word."

"Forgive my doubts," she replied.

“Go, do not be afraid,” he said. “All will be well.”

Coryn’s maid led Maryn out. At the door, the maid waved at the soldier before shuffling back across the room to claim the seat Maryn vacated.

“What are you going to do now?” the maid asked.

“The hardest thing of all,” Coryn said with a sigh. “Wait.”

The best laid plans, even those wrought by faith in a mighty Creator, are subject to the grand design. There is a time to gather stones together and a time to scatter them abroad. When a thing is scattered, that which may be is multiplied on the winds of creation. Prophets “see” when the Creator opens a small window. Rarely do they see all the Creator sees.

Maryn was only moments gone away from his door when came another knock. Coryn sprang from his chair. Long, quick strides carried him swiftly across the room. Uniformed soldiers filled his doorway.

“I am mere steps ahead of your arrest,” General Bou announced.

“Come in and sit there.” Coryn pointed at a tall chair near the fire. “Tell me what has happened?”

“You sent a decoy?”

“I did,” replied Coryn.

“Well, he killed one of the soldiers Raryn sent to arrest him,” the general said. “It gets worse. The blacksmith you sent was aided by two young Valir said to be cadets at the Academy.”

The door, thrown open by a well-placed boot, slammed against its hinges. A half dozen police officers flooded into the room.

“Coryn Kel,” their captain announced. “You are under arrest. You will come with us.”

“What is the meaning of this?” General Bou rose to face the officers. He folded his arms across his chest, fixing them with a glare.

“General,” Raryn said as he stepped inside. “I thought I would find you here. Coryn is under arrest for defying the Council’s order to refrain from sending a representative to Shiloh—an order you signed, General. It is only because I am still gathering evidence that you are not joining the seer. Do not interfere. You may accompany us and make a statement if you wish."

"I shall just get my cloak," Coryn said.

"Step softly, sir," the police captain cautioned.

Coryn gave him a friendly nod and went to gather his cloak from a peg by the window. He threw his cloak around his shoulders before shooing a small white owl from his windowsill.

"Stop lurking around my door," Coryn shouted up to the trees as they stepped outside. "Come out and walk with us like Valir."

Coryn waved for the soldiers to follow. Head high, he led the way to the magistrate.

Deep inside the Ministry of Justice, the offices of Raryn Go were a kind of luxurious intimidation. At one end of the room, atop a thick carpet, sat desk of polished mahogany adorned with golden tools of the minister's trade: pens, quills, and the ministry's golden seal. The decree of the king appointing him Minister of Justice graced the wall behind his chair. The walls were covered with intricately woven tapestries depicting the legends of Valir in the blue and green dyes that came from beyond the Gishon. They were suspended from carved serpentine branches inlaid with silver and blue.

Magryn, the President of the High Council, occupied a chair beside the desk. Coryn gave the president a wave and settled into one of the chairs opposite Raryn without waiting for an invitation. He then closed his eyes and let go a long cleansing breath.

"Well," Coryn said. "I've caused a stir once again."

"I'm glad this amuses you." Raryn glanced at Magryn and back to Coryn. "Are you arrogant enough to think you can ignore the Council with impunity? No, wait, of course you are. But you will not get away with it this time, seer."

"You make 'seer' sound like a dirty word," Coryn replied with a smile that drew an involuntary snicker from his friend."

"You would do well to walk softly Byryn Bou," Raryn snarled. "Your involvement in this requires some explanation too."

"Let us get to the heart of the matter," Coryn interrupted. "I confess that, of my own free will, I sent the village blacksmith on a fishing expedition. Vulryn has no message for Eeryn. Should he be in your custody, please release him to his wife."

"The blacksmith is not in custody." Raryn leaned back in his chair and laced his fingers together on his desk. "I'm sure you know that. A border patrol soldier aiding in his arrest was killed and at present Vulryn's whereabouts are unknown."

"That is very unfortunate for everyone," Coryn answered. "However, I fail to see how that involves me in anything illegal or in violation of the Council's orders."

"Do you deny that you sent a messenger to Shiloh?" Raryn said.

"I neither confirm nor deny." Coryn met the challenge in Raryn's eyes. "I only claim to have done duty."

"Duty?" Raryn roared, jumping to his feet. "Your duty is to obey the rulings of this High Council."

"Since when has duty been dependent on any council, but that of one's own heart?" Coryn rose to meet him. "You are not the Creator. You decide no one's duty but your own. And while we are on the subject, the innocent Valir you pushed to violence is guilty of nothing except returning a favor for a friend. I asked him to catch some fish. That is all."

"Who did you send?" Raryn demanded.

A sly smile spread over the seer's face. His eyes danced with the smug pleasure of secret knowledge. He turned to the captain of the guard.

"You may convey me to my cell now, Captain. I have nothing more to say to Minister Raryn."

"This is just beginning," Raryn told his fellow Councilors. "We all know he violated the Council's order. If he did not send the blacksmith, then the persons who freed him are Coryn's messengers."

"If they are not found by tomorrow," Magryn said. "You must release the seer. Your accusations and our assumptions are not reason enough to imprison him."

"If the General will form all his cadets at the Academy," Raryn said. "A roll call will reveal the guilty. Two of the soldiers recognized the others as cadets. Let us see who fails to appear."

"Minister," a voice called from the door. "Pardon the interruption. There is news."

CHAPTER 12

The crack of Codryn's whip announced vacation was over. The porters leaped to their feet. It was time to move, time to climb.

Bryn ignored the protests of his aching muscles. Free or tied to a string of slaves, he had to move. He was committed to the climb, there was no choice but to reach the top before dark. Better to suffer his aching muscles than the pain of one misstep in the dark. Above him Fedryn started to shoulder his pack. His right arm missed the strap and the weight swung free pulling Fedryn with it. His left knee gave way and Fedryn stumbled toward the precipice. Bryn caught the pack in his left hand and Fedryn in his right. Eyes still wide with terror, Fedryn looked over his shoulder at his savior.

"Here let me," Bryn said.

Bryn worked his arms through the straps and bounced it on his back to distribute the weight. Ready to go, he pointed upward with his beak, and they began to climb. Fedryn gave him a grateful smile and led the way. A few steps with the pack tugging on his shoulders gave Bryn a new respect for the little guy.

The pace slowed to a crawl; the exhausted climbers struggled with each step. When Codryn finally called a halt, the porters fell down with the packs still on their backs. Fedryn offered to take the pack, but Bryn refused to give it up. Water was passed up and down the line. Then came the order to move. As hard as it had been to restart the climb after the last rest, this was worse. Bryn prayed for his trembling legs to hold him. After a brief argument, they obeyed. The band of smugglers began their push for the top. They climbed for another hour to a chorus of groans and whispered prayers for the ability to take just one more step.

"Almost there," Codryn shouted from the lead. "Make the top and we rest for the night."

No one cheered. The spirit was willing, but the flesh was weak. Nevertheless, Codryn's words had the desired effect. A spark of hope ran through the line of climbers. The belief that they would make it ignited a spark in them. One foot at a time, one step at a time, Bryn climbed on. He was too exhausted to be amazed at his strength.

"Rocks," a voice shouted. "Lookout below."

Rocks the size of fists ricocheted off the cliff wall and tumbled down the steps. Cries of pain followed the stones down the line as tumbling stones collided with heads and barked shins. Unable to see anything but the climber in front of him, Fedryn hands went up to shield his head. He pressed his back against the cliff and glanced up through his fingers. A stone hit his lead foot. Fedryn jumped at the sudden pain and came down on a loose stone. His ankle rolled sending a bolt of pain up his leg. Fedryn fell to his knees, over balanced, groped for a handhold, missed, and tumbled over the edge. Fedryn's weight ate up the slack between him and Bryn in less than a second. The rope snapped taunt snatching Bryn off his feet. Bryn's fingers dug at the unyielding stone step vainly seeking purchase and failing. His fingertips dug wildly at the stone surface but refused to hold. He was pulled steadily toward the precipice.

One Eye dove to catch Bryn's hands. Bryn's hands, bleeding from efforts to dig into the stone, slipped through his grip. One Eye scrambled forward on his belly and caught Bryn's tunic. One Eye's face twisted into a mask of pain as he strained to arrest the slide. Releasing his grip with one hand, One Eye grabbed Bryn's hand in his. He gained a good grip, but One Eye was being carried to the edge by the combined weight of Fedryn and Bryn dangling over the edge. Two of the porters shed their packs and fell across the smuggler's body. Their combined weight stopped the slide.

"Hold on," Codryn yelled as he shouldered his way by the porters on the stairs. "I'm coming, hold on."

One Eye looked over Bryn's shoulder at the floor a thousand feet below. Vertigo sent his head spinning. He shut his good eye and dug his fingers deeper into Bryn's collar. Farther below, Fedryn's feet windmilled desperately trying to gain a hold on the cliff face.

"I can't hold on," One Eye groaned.

Codryn reached over him and seized Bryn with both hands easing the strain on One Eye. The two partners in crime pulled in synch. Bryn rose half a foot and could go no further. There was no room on the step for more hands and the ones that held the fallen porters were fading fast.

"I'll hold them," Codryn said. "Cut the gimp loose."

"No," Bryn yelled up at One eye. "We can do it."

Bryn pushed against the stone with his lower body. Codryn and One Eye pulled harder.

"Cut it," Codryn ordered when the second attempt failed. "Cut it or we lose everything."

One Eye drew his knife and wiggled closer to the edge. The knife flicked across the rope just below Bryn's waist. Fedryn's wide eyes locked on Bryn's face as the rope came apart and he dropped into empty space. His wings snapped open, but instead of catching the air and slowing his descent, Fedryn began to spin. He hit the rock face with a sickening snap of bone. His right wing crumpled. Clawing at the sky, he tumbled over in midair and dropped headlong onto the rocks below.

One Eye vomited down Bryn's back at the sight of the impact. The hot liquid ran down Bryn's body and dripped in a vile rain on Fedryn's broken corpse. Codryn and One Eye hauled the lighter load back to the safety of the stairs before collapsing in a panting heap. Bryn scurried over the stairs and pasted himself to the rock face. He wrapped both arms around his knees to combat the violent tremors that followed.

"Get up kid," One Eye ordered. "The sun ain't going to stay up extra on our account. We got to move."

Bryn knew he was right. He levered himself onto his feet and the line began to move again. He passed the rest of the climb in a mental fog.

There was no celebration when the column reached the top. No one looked back over the edge to see how far they climbed. No one took in the spectacular view afforded from atop the Edge of the World. They fell exhausted on the coarse, brown, grass without a word. Bryn tried to close his eyes. The result was the same every time. He saw Fedryn drop away, saw the lost look of horror on his face, and heard him hit the ground.

It took several minutes for the realization that they weren't alone to sink in. About forty yards from where the tired porters lay, two rows of armed men stood in front of a circle of white tents. On either side of the soldiers, great horned beasts wearing armor pawed the ground and strained at their reins. A human voice barked, and the ranks of soldiers parted.

A tall man in a black uniform trimmed in gold stepped from one of the tents. He wore a sash of purple tied around his narrow waist and moved easily with flowing strides. Head erect, shoulders squared, his long, dark hair fluttered on the breeze as he moved through the ranks of soldiers. His thin face and angular features were crowned with a pair of piercing black eyes. He was no soldier, but clearly commanded all he saw.

An icy fist closed on Bryn's heart. Tremors spread over his body. He stared thunderstruck.

It was the dragon rider.

The clothes were different, but it was him. The sudden reality of his dream took Bryn's breath. It was easy to speak of dreams sitting in the seer's house where they lacked substance. There, dragons, men, and blood were symbols, they weren't real. In that moment, Bryn found the dream wasn't over, it was just beginning.

Codryn rose and went to meet the dragon rider. Bryn stifled the urge to shout a warning.

"Lord Zett." Codryn raised a hand in salute.

"Welcome Codryn." A smile creased the man's regal face. A manicured hand returned the salute. "I trust all went well."

"As always," Codryn replied.

"Good, good," Zett said with a nod. "Come with me and you will receive your reward."

Codryn left his crew of smugglers and the slaves with the soldiers. He fell into step with Zett, and they disappeared into one of two large tents.

After a short rest, the soldiers ordered all the others to their feet. Packs were shouldered and the weary porters escorted into the tent adjacent to the one occupied by Codryn and Zett. The tent into which Bryn and the others were taken was empty except for two tables piled high with fruit, stacks of smoked fish and pitchers of water. The weary travelers' empty stomachs pushed aside weariness with a newfound strength. They snatched up armfuls of food and dropped down on the hard packed ground to eat. Bryn shoveled handfuls of overripe fruit into his mouth; swallowing huge chunks and chasing them down with gulps of water. He told himself that he would chew later.

Full bellies soon presented a new misery. One by one the smugglers dashed outside to relieve themselves under the watchful eyes of the soldiers. When the last Valir returned to the tent, a new group of soldiers arrived bearing iron shackles. The band of porters officially became slaves. Their legs were bound together by a long chain that wound through the iron shackle on each Valir's right leg.

"He's with us," One Eye said when the soldiers came to Bryn. "Fresh meat."

The soldiers laughed and passed by. When the chain was secure around each slave the ends were fastened to the ground by a heavy iron spike.

The smugglers were only slightly better off than the slaves. They remained free to move about, however, they were told that they would not be allowed to leave the tent until Codryn came for them. With little else to do, soldiers and smugglers settled down to wait. The new slaves, their situation largely unchanged, fell instantly asleep.

"You lot keep alert," One Eye cautioned in a hushed voice.

Bryn moved to take a seat next to the smuggler.

"Thanks for saving my life," Bryn said.

"Forget it," the smuggler said with a wave of his hand. "You had the goods on your back."

"Yeah, well, thanks anyway. And thanks for," Bryn pointed to his right ankle.

"Don't flatter yourself," he replied. "I haven't given up on the ransom idea. Are you really General Bou's kid?"

Bryn wasn't sure how to answer. The smuggler had been a forceful proponent of honesty before the climb. Bryn was unsure of his own status with the law and didn't want to give too much away.

"Yeah, you are." The smuggler decided for him.

"Bryn Bou," he confessed. "What do I call you?"

The smuggler pointed at his face and laughed. "They call me One Eye, but I'm at a loss to say why."

One Eye pulled a pipe from his tunic; stuffed it with brown leaves from a hide pouch and lit it. He leaned back and closed his eye as a wreath of blue smoke swirled about his head. Some of the other smugglers did the same. The tent rapidly filled with smoke and the sweet scent of burning banana leaves. The soldiers retreated outside coughing and holding their noses.

"Seems our hosts don't appreciate a good smoke," One Eye said.

Laughter broke out among the tiny group of Valir. It was to be short lived.

The moon had passed its zenith when the guards gradually filtered back inside. An uneasy peace ensued in which the two sides glared at one another while they slept in shifts until morning.

An hour after dawn, the tent flap flew open, and the guards were called to attention. A platoon of lancers marched inside and formed up in the center of the tent. Their officer pointed to One Eye's little group. Lances dropped to the ready and the smugglers were prodded to their feet. A tall, thin silhouette backlit by the morning sun appeared in the door. Lord Zett strolled into the tent followed by even more soldiers.

"There's been a change of plans," Zett announced with a casual wave of his hand. "You have made your last delivery. Captain, chain these...these... creatures with the others."

One of the smugglers drew a knife. A blue arc jumped from a lance, and he fell to the ground twitching and jerking uncontrollably.

"Codryn will have something to say about this," One Eye said.

"Oh, yes Codryn." Zett smiled at them. "Bring him in."

Two soldiers dragged Codryn into the tent. His face was a mass of lumps and bruises. His right eye was swollen closed, and the feathers of his crest gone. He seemed to be bleeding everywhere. The soldiers dropped his body on the ground at Zett's feet.

"As you can see," Zett said. "Codryn has agreed to join you in the marketplace. I'm not sure he will fetch as much as he once would have, but we shall see."

Zett shrugged; turned on his heels and strolled from the tent. The soldiers dragged Codryn into the line of prisoners and fixed his shackle to the chain. The still twitching smuggler was chained beside him. One Eye and the rest offered no resistance as they were added to the chain.

CHAPTER 13

Coryn Kel strolled along the highway branch. It felt good to stretch his legs. He didn't need to glance over his shoulder to know he was being followed. They were soldiers; subtilty was not their strong suit. He left the highway, pushed through a curtain of liana, and dropped into his yard where Byryn Bou leaned against his doorpost. He took a deep breath; straightened his shoulders and cleared his mind.

"Old friend," he hailed the waiting Councilor with upraised hand. "Your formation was a success?"

"Raryn was surprised with the results." Byryn rubbed his beak. "Did you know your granddaughter would be absent?"

"No, but I suspected that might be the case. Come inside, we'll drink tea and commiserate."

Byryn followed the seer inside. The table was spread with bouja fruit and cups of steaming tea. Byryn slowly shook his head.

"Trouble?" Coryn cocked his head, an amused look in his eyes.

Byryn pointed to the table. "Will I ever find you unprepared?"

"When you find me dead, know I was not prepared," Coryn said. "Sit here with me."

The two friends sat silently sipping tea. One knew the other would speak in time. The other pondered over what he must say. Coryn turned to his friend.

"It is my duty to inform you," Coryn began. "That Bryn, has chosen to become my envoy to Eeryn."

"No," Byryn feigned shock. "How can this be? He is only a boy."

"I know you truly believe that." Coryn laid a hand on his friend's arm. "Believe me, he is more of a warrior than anyone knows. I suspect even more than he himself realizes."

"Is he safe? Have you seen a vision?"

"I have not seen it. However, I know it is so."

"How?"

"Let's say a little bird told me." Coryn smiled. "It is both the truth and protects my source. Bryn has left the Boubouja and travels in the company of men toward Shiloh."

"Thank the Creator." Byryn sighed. "His mother worries."

"Yes, I'm sure she does." The seer smiled again.

"You old swamp rat," Byryn scolded. "I'm in this as deeply as you. A little worry on your part would ease my mind."

"I have the master of tactical improvisation on one hand," he said motioning toward Byryn. "And the strategy of the Creator on the other. Worry could be seen as blasphemy."

"Humor me. The blacksmith that you sent to the river as a decoy did kill a soldier. He has since disappeared along with Bryn and Faryn. Who, by the way, have been positively identified as aiding his escape."

"Without Bryn's testimony, no one can prove I sent him. Vulryn was sent to fish, not to kill."

"Did you sent Faryn to steal a diplomatic pouch?"

"What? No." Coryn's face lit up. "Ho ho, Raryn must be beside himself. I shall likely resume my place in prison for that bit of youthful ingenuity."

"You knew nothing about it?"

"Absolutely nothing, not that Raryn will believe that."

"A young female carrying a diplomatic pouch accompanied by a very large bodyguard rode the lift to Shiloh yesterday morning." The General's eyes narrowed. "If the pouch was not your idea, how did you advise Bryn to cross the—oh, no. Don't tell me you told him to leap."

Coryn held his palms up and shrugged.

"He made it, if that's any comfort."

Byryn nodded. "It will have to be. Maybe, in time, it will be something to boast about."

"Exactly so," Coryn agreed. "We must have faith that what we have purchased will outweigh the cost. Is that a summons in your pocket?"

"Yes," Byryn's shoulders fell. "May I walk beside you?"

Coryn nodded, set down his cup, and stood to go. "Together into the furnace, eh? I am honored."

***

Raryn sat behind his ironwood desk flanked by members of the High Council. Coryn studied each face and without waiting for an invitation sat in the lone empty chair. He closed his eyes long enough for a cleansing breath.

"Well," he said. "I see Councilor Calryn is absent. No matter, you have a quorum. Let's proceed."

"Because you are not in shackles, do not suppose yourself free." Raryn glanced left and right.

Coryn trained his eyes on Raryn. "Let us get to the heart of the matter then. I, Coryn Kel, of my own free will, did send an envoy to my fellow seer in direct violation of the Council's order. I further state that no one knowingly shared in either the planning or execution of my duty."

"Duty?" Raryn jumped from his seat. "Duty is it! Your duty is to obey the rulings of this High Council."

Coryn slowly rose to meet Raryn's glare. When he finally spoke, the softness in his voice came with great effort.

"A Valir's duty is not dependent upon any council, but that of his own heart in obedience to the Creator. My dear Minister of Justice, despite the high opinion you have of yourself, you decide no one's duty save your own. If you wish to speak of duty, High Councilor, you have failed miserably in your own. While you were chasing a blacksmith on a fishing trip, my envoy eluded you. He is now well on his way to Shiloh."

Gasps escaped the Councilors. Raryn dropped back into his seat to stare at his desktop for several moments. Byryn broke the silence.

"Brethren, since the beginning of time the Valir have held duty as the highest virtue. Duty to our Creator and duty to our fellow, this is the creed we have lived by for a thousand generations. Do we now wholly abandon that belief to judge one who has confessed his devotion to duty? I cannot judge him harshly."

"Hollow words," Raryn said. "Since your son is guilty of the same.

"If Bryn is guilty of doing his duty," Byryn replied. "Count me a proud father."

"Councilor Raryn spoke of impunity," Coryn said. "Duty knows no impunity. I ask no mercy from you. I am ready to accept the consequences of my actions. I hope the Council is as ready."

"Are you threatening the Council?" Magryn asked.

"The Council is threatened," Coryn replied. "But not by me."

"Go home and stay there," Magryn ordered. "A soldier will accompany you. The Council will send word as to what shall be done with you."

CHAPTER 14

Zett sealed Codryn's fate with a parting kick to the ribs. The smuggler was past feeling. A blast of breath forced from his lungs was his only response. Zett turned on his heels, the guards snapped to attention, and Zett stalked from the tent. Outside the open tent flap, a sleek, wheelless wagon awaited. Zett ascended a set of steps that followed him aboard the wagon and was whisked away leaving a cloud of dust.

Soldiers silhouetted against the blazing horizon were busy breaking camp. A few handfuls of hardtack were thrown at the prisoners who scrambled for the bread. Bryn ignored his hunger and stuffed the hardtack into his tunic. When the bread on the ground disappeared, the prisoners went to work folding tents and stacking them atop the rigging.

The long chain linking the prisoners together was removed. The packs laden with crushed shells were hoisted onto their backs; and the march to Shiloh began. The column stretched out for a half mile. The foot soldiers led the way followed by the wagons and captives. The armored cavalry plodded along at the rear of the column.

Bryn gazed with awe at the treeless plain of this new world. It was a scene better suited to one of the moons than anything his imagination conjured for his world. Baked red clay stretched out to the horizon in every direction. It was broken only by the occasional patch of scrub grass or sagebrush that dotted the roadside depressions where rain collected before rapidly evaporating. Desolation filled his eyes and seeped into his soul.

"The humans call this place the Sawnone," One Eye said with a wide sweep of his hand. "Their legends say that long ago men pushed off their farms came here seeking hope. But they saw none."

"How can so much emptiness exist?" Bryn asked.

“I have traveled this way to Shiloh only once before,” One Eye said. “However, you will find the world of men is filled with emptiness of one kind or another.”

Bryn returned his eyes to the distant horizon. He was not sure what to make of his companion. The smuggler turned slave struck him as a hard pragmatist one moment and a cryptic sage the next. One thing he was sure of, One Eye was the one person he dared trust.

“I saw you saving the hardtack,” One Eye told him. “Good lad.”

The soldiers were content not to add to the trials of the march. As long as the column kept moving, the Valir were allowed to talk among themselves and move about within the column. The shared misfortune of the smugglers and the slaves was not enough to bridge the old gap between them. The one-time smugglers were forced to carry packs, but they remained aloof. Those originally bound for the auction block kept to themselves and left the smugglers to bear the burden of caring for Codryn. The chief smuggler was not faring well. His right eye was swollen completely closed. The left was no more than a slit. For all practical purposes, Codryn was blind. He stumbled along holding to the arms of his old crewmates for support. At times, he grew so weak from the cruel effects of the sun he collapsed in the dirt and was dragged along by his arms.

The Sawnone was without mercy offering the marchers three constants, the sun, the dust, and the unbroken horizon that never seemed to draw closer. The soldiers did what they could to protect the Valir from the first two. It wasn't that they cared for the slaves. Their reason was more practical. The Valir needed to fetch the best price possible on the auction block. Lord Zett demanded it. The soldier’s fortunes and their shield from the wrath of their lord was the health of the slaves. Even Lord Zett could do nothing about the elusive horizon. The only solution was to keep marching.

At the end of the first day, One Eye estimated they marched about thirty miles. If he was anywhere close to correct, they wouldn't reach Shiloh for a month. This intrusion of reality weighed on Bryn's heart. He never imagined his trek involved so much time and distance. The further the column marched the more he realized how unprepared he was for this mission. Laboring under the scorching sun, he wondered if his lack of preparation was intentional.

Did Coryn hide the hardships and accent the glory of duty?

Faith in his ability to meet the demands of delivering the message waned with the relentless plodding through this barren world. His feet ached. His tongue spent hours glued to the roof of his mouth. It was sometimes an entire day between water holes. All the while the sun beat down like a hammer. Climbing the Edge of the World no longer seemed the monumental task he thought it was. Like that climb, he would do this or die. Daily, the latter grew more likely. On the tenth day his spirit lifted. Silhouetted on the horizon was a town.

Concho Flats was a collection of adobe huts arranged in two rows on either side of the road. Compared to the rest of the Sawnone, it was a busy metropolis. Squat, square shouldered men with leathery skin the color of the hard baked ground and thick black hair on their face lined the road to stare at the column.

In Vix a caravan of such size would generate a celebration. Save for the icy stares, the townspeople of Concho Flats went sullenly about their business as if the column didn't exist. The soldiers steered the caravan to a well on the eastern edge of town where a hovercraft waited with fresh supplies.

They made camp in a circle around the well. The campsite's saving grace was the stand of cottonwood trees that crowded the well. There was shade, glorious shade at last. The Valir dropped their packs. For a moment soldiers, slaves, and smugglers were one. They fell upon the well smiling, clapping one another on the back and drank until they could drink no more.

The moment did not last. The tents were erected. A meal of hardtack and dried fish eaten and the Valir were returned to their chains. The soldiers took up their weapons once more and life went on.

Bryn found himself chained next to One Eye. He had discovered the smuggler possessed the talent to sleep anywhere at a moment's notice. However, for the last two days, One Eye was not making use of his gift. He never seemed to sleep. He was the first to rise and the last to rest. Even now, with those around him sleeping, he was busy. Bryn pretended to sleep, while through half closed eyes maintained a watch on One Eye.

"What are you doing?" Bryn whispered.

One Eye jumped like he'd been shot. His eyes shot daggers at Bryn while he quietly stuffed something inside his tunic.

"Go to sleep, boy."

"I want to help."

"Then, shut up."

One Eye turned toward Bryn and lifted the chain that joined them into the moonlight. Two of the links in the long chain were scarred. One Eye retrieved a small, serrated blade from its hiding place in his tunic. He handed it to Bryn with a sawing motion. While One Eye pretended to snore, Bryn sawed away.

The next morning Bryn's arms were lead. He tried to scrub the sleep from his eyes, but his hands didn't go where he told them. One Eye was looking at him and smiling.

"Hurts, don't it?"

Bryn nodded. It hurt, but it was a good kind of hurt. His father called it freedom pain. He said it was the pain that beings of conscience suffered in order to be free to face a mirror. A dawn of understanding lit Bryn's mind. His estimation of his father took on new dimensions.

Yeah, he told himself. *It's a good hurt.*

A cheer went up when the captain announced they would be staying in Concho Flats another day, maybe two. Their good fortune was owed to the cavalry. Their mounts, worn out by the harsh conditions of the Sawnone, needed rest and fresh feed to renew their strength.

The camp guard was light, only a few scattered sentries. There was nowhere for the prisoners to go. The soldiers napped in the shade; played cards or spent time lying about their exploits. The prisoners lounged in the shade of the cottonwood trees. Bryn wandered over to sit beside One Eye.

"Tonight," One Eye said. "Find a place on the chain away from me."

Bryn's sidelong glance brought a chuckle from the smuggler.

"Look around, boy," he said. "I'm not going to desert you. If we tried to escape now, we'd die out there."

"When?"

"Soon enough." One Eye looked to the east. "Another day and the march starts downhill to the sea. There's plenty of bumps in the road, but it gets easier. We'll find a place where there's food and shelter."

"Some of the others are in bad shape," Bryn said.

"So?"

"So, how will they keep up?"

"They won't," One Eye said. "This is just you and me boy. They'll chase us for a while. But in the end, they'll settle for the small loss as long as they have the rest. We try to take everybody, and we'll all end up like Codryn. You keep your beak shut; you hear?"

"I hear."

Bryn didn't like the idea of leaving his companions behind to be sold. He liked the idea of failing in his mission even less. One Eye was right, they could not all escape, but two might get away. For now, he would follow One Eye's advice.

For the rest of the day he avoided One Eye's company choosing to lounge in the shade of a cottonwood tree and eavesdropping on the soldiers. One Eye's prediction was accurate; they would soon leave the barren, parched, Sawnone behind. It was good news indeed. That night he picked out a spot in the middle of the chain away from One Eye. Sleep came quickly.

Touched by the mist, his clothes damp with dew, Bryn shivered. He walked as if on a cloud. His feet tread upon soft nothingness and everywhere he looked the swirling vapor held him. Drawn by a voice he did not know; he wandered a land he could not see.

A howling rush of wind parted the clouds. A wall of rock flashed before his eyes and Bryn's face collided with the cold stone. The wind ripped away the mist. Above him the wall rock reached into the empty blue of the sky. He dug his hands into the stone to keep from being blown away. The frozen wind bit his face and stung his hands. He could see a familiar sea of broken boulders below.

He was clinging to the Edge of the World, and he was not alone. A short youth with a withered leg was beside him. Fedryn had one hand wedged into a small crevice. The other hand was twisted in Bryn's tunic.

"I can't hold on much longer!" Fedryn shouted; his words

whisked quickly away on the wind.

Bryn tore his hand from the wall. He caught Fedryn's coat between the shoulders.

"I've got you. Hold on!" Bryn screamed.

"Don't let go," Fedryn pleaded.

He inched his feet closer to Bryn. His arm remained tight against the stone, but the movement stretched his reach weakening his hold. The wind snatched Fedryn's left arm free. His body followed twisting away from the rock as he was carried from the step. His free hand clutched at Bryn's back, missed, and flailed the air. Bryn fell to his knees. He blindly tried to grab Fedryn with his right hand.

The sound of ripping fabric heralded his friend's cry.

"Bryn, save meeeee!" Fedryn's face dropped away, the cry following his descent to the rocks.

"Noooooo!" Bryn screamed.

Bryn jolted upright. Around him the Valir lay quietly in the chain. Guards paced a short distance away. He had not screamed after all. Slowly he drew his knees to his chest. The rattle of his chains caught the attention of a guard who wandered over.

"Bad dream," Bryn whispered and lay down.

Sunrise brought a return to the familiar routine of breaking camp, cold hardtack and water followed by taking down the tents. The Valir loaded the wagons and the plodding march into the rising sun resumed. Near mid-morning the first gnarled cedar tree appeared along the road. The dark green cone shapes multiplied as the day wore on.

The track tipped gradually downhill. The soldiers claimed the worst was behind them. The Valir knew better. Their steps were lighter, however their future remained unchanged. A few lucky ones might avoid the purple mills and the salt flats, but at the end of the journey, they were to be bought and sold. Although they would still walk and talk, their lives were over. No one in the Boubouja would ever know what became of them and they would never rest in a woven shroud in the grove of their ancestors.

Any remaining hopes for freedom were crushed the next day. The Sawnone gave way to rolling hills covered with oaks and tall grass. The countryside came alive. Fields of golden grain swayed in the breeze. As the land grew richer, tension among the soldiers increased. One Eye called Bryn to him at the noonday halt.

"Stick close," he whispered. "The chains are coming."

Bryn gave him a quizzical look.

"Look around. If we got free, we could live here. The soldiers know it too. We have to get chained to the weak links."

"When do you think it will happen?"

One Eye suddenly frowned and pointed over Bryn's shoulder. The soldiers were stretching out the chain.

"That soon, huh?"

The next two nights, Bryn and One Eye spent hours watching the guards make their rounds. Every time they thought they had the riddle solved, the guards changed routines.

"This isn't their first march," One Eye observed. "But our chance is coming. There's a place up ahead where the woods move in close to the road. We will probably make camp near there."

"How will we get back across the Sawnone?" Bryn asked.

One Eye crossed his arms and sighed. "We don't. There's no going back now."

CHAPTER 15

The palace towers cast long shadows down the Avenue of Kings. Their hovercraft dodged the slower horse traffic as they wove their way into the city. The driver swore as he swerved around a platoon of the night watch who were on their way to the palace. Tourists milled about the crowded sidewalks dotted with vendors and packed themselves into cafes. Closer to the palace, others jostled for position to watch the changing of the guard.

Faryn ignored the commotion. She had seen it all before. Beside her, Vulryn was mesmerized by all the human activity. He'd fallen into a state of perpetual wide-eyed amazement the moment they began the descent from the highlands.

Shiloh *was* an impressive sight. The city leapt from the backdrop of a pale blue sea. The glistening, white towers of the palace overlooked a massive ring of granite that formed the city walls. Rising above it all was the Temple, its golden dome reflected in the calm waters. Rows of embassies lined the Avenue of Kings just outside the palace.

Vulryn's breath caught in his throat at his first glimpse of the massive treehouse rising above the walls of the Valirian embassy. The gates swung open to admit the hovercraft. The portly figure of Ambassador Dorryn stood at the doors, his arms folded across his chest. His stance was perfectly complemented by the scowl he wore under tightly knit brows. These were replaced by his best diplomatic smile as Faryn stepped from the hovercraft to greet him.

"Faryn Go, what a surprise." He took her hand. "My how you've grown."

"Ambassador Dorryn, how nice to see you again," Faryn said.

"You have placed me in a difficult position, young lady," he replied. "A very difficult position."

"I ask your pardon, Ambassador," she responded, a note of

worry in her voice. “It was truly unintentional.”

"Come inside." He took her arm and guided her along. “We’ll have tea."

Vulryn followed them into a wide lobby. Like a long house it was hung with richly colored tapestries depicting the history of the Valir. The warm bamboo floor was a delight to his feet. Tucked into a semi-circle of bouja trees planted in green pots, was a small ironwood table staffed by two secretaries. A small detachment of soldiers on the other side of the room were seated before a fireplace.

They followed the ambassador across the room and entered an open-air atrium built around the bouja tree that supported the entire embassy structure. Small banana palms interlaced with miniature banyans grew along the walls. Two bouja trees dripping with orchids flanked the great tree and lent their fragrance to the air. They climbed a spiraling staircase of branches into an upper floor. Passing through a curtain of woven silk, they came to the Ambassador's private office.

Dorryn made no secret of his taste for the finer things his position offered. His desk was inlaid with polished dragon bone and silver. The floors were covered with thick woven rugs that softly cradled each step. The Ambassador steered them to a cluster of armchairs away from the desk where there was a view of the sun dissolving in reds and oranges into the sea. Higher in the sky, stars twinkled across the descending dark. Without a word from their host, a waiter appeared with a silver tea service.

"Ah, our tea has arrived." Dorryn motioned for them to sit. "Dear Faryn, you haven't introduced me to your companion."

“My apologies, Ambassador Dorryn," she said. "This is my bodyguard, Vulryn.”

“I take it this is your first escort duty to Shiloh?” Dorryn turned to Vulryn with a smile. “I haven’t seen you before.”

“Y…y…yes sir,” the blacksmith stammered.

“Welcome.” Dorryn said with a bow of his head. Then, turning back to Faryn. “As I said, you have me at a disadvantage. I was not expecting your arrival and so have not made arrangements for your stay.”

“I must apologize. Our departure was hastily arranged.”

“You have a pouch for me I see.” Dorryn held out a hand. “Do you know it's contents?"

"Yes sir, a communique from my grandfather."

Dorryn pulled a paper from the pouch. Faryn watched the ambassador's face as he read. His eyebrows raised in surprise as he finished the message.

"A spy?" he asked. "I am assuming a spy would not have access to the lift and the king's highway, So, we have some weeks before he will arrive."

"Yes sir," Faryn said. "However, it is imperative that I find Eeryn the Seer immediately."

The ambassador's cup stalled halfway to his mouth. An expression like he'd just bitten into rotten fruit clouded his face. Dorryn's hand began to tremble as he placed his teacup on a nearby table. He rose from his seat and walked to the window without a word. He stood silently looking out for a moment before returning to his chair.

"You don't know what you're asking," his voice was unsteady. "Eeryn is sure to be implicated in this matter. You must not go anywhere near him. You could wind up in a human prison or worse."

"I appreciate your concern," she answered. "All the more reason I must find him. As the message said, Coryn has already sent his spy to Eeryn. The High Council forbade it, but the seer did it anyway. I am to try and intercept that messenger before he gets to Eeryn. Grandfather said lives hang in the balance."

"Well, yes. I can see that," Dorryn said. "Let me make inquiries. Even with your bodyguard, you must not wander around Shiloh searching for him. Tensions here are running high in opposition to outlanders. Moreover, Eeryn is known to frequent some rather undesirable parts of the city."

"Speed is of the utmost importance," she insisted.

"It has been a long trip," Dorryn said, his smile back. "I will have rooms made ready. Meanwhile, I will make inquiries about the seer."

"Your assistance is very appreciated. I know this is a great inconvenience for you, but our needs are small. I'm certain my grandfather will see you are amply rewarded."

"I doubt anything connected to your bodyguard is ever small. Nevertheless, we shall accommodate your needs as best we can. I can arrange a room for you here, but I'm afraid your companion will have to be housed in the barracks with the soldiers."

"That should do nicely," Faryn said and winked at Vulryn.

"That will do nicely," Vulryn mimicked her voice as he threw his bag on an empty bunk.

Faryn was right though, the barracks suited him just fine. He wanted no part of the finery inside the embassy, but she didn't have to toss him out without asking. He decided to try out his bunk before exploring the grounds. He stretched out his tired limbs. His feet dangled over the end, but otherwise the bed was soft and comfortable. Vulryn began to snore.

Back inside the embassy, Dorryn pulled a cord hidden beneath his desk. A secretary poked her head through the door.

"Yes, Ambassador."

"I want Davryn and Samryn in my office immediately."

The secretary nodded acknowledgment and disappeared. Ten minutes later she announced the arrival of the Embassy liaison officers. Davryn Mar was a weather-beaten ex-soldier. His angular face looked as though it was cut from stone. His scarred crest was a dull green that matched his plain suit. His partner, Samryn Lo, was a soft spoken, impeccably dressed, ex-college professor. Their methods were as different as their appearance, but both were never-fail information gatherers.

"Sit down," the Ambassador said. "We have a situation tailor made for you. Faryn Go arrived a while ago bearing a diplomatic pouch and message from her grandfather, Minister Raryn. The pouch was stolen. The message is factual enough. However, it was not written by the Minister."

"What's the message?" Davryn asked.

"It seems that Coryn the Seer, in defiance of the High Council, has smuggled a messenger out of the Boubouja with a word for Eeryn. Faryn says she is here to stop delivery of the message and wishes to contact Eeryn. I want you two to ensure that she never sees Eeryn. Find him and bring him to me quietly. The Minister will be extremely grateful if you know what I mean."

"Just like that, you want us to find Eeryn and bring him in?" Davryn said.

"Exactly like that," Dorryn demanded. "Do it. Do it quietly

and do it now or you will take his place in the palace dungeon."

Vulryn was awakened by a steady tapping on his shoulder. Stars dotted the night sky visible through the window. As he rubbed the sleep from his eyes, a soldier sat on a stool beside his bunk. Vulryn looked up with fire in his eyes. The soldier threw up his palms.

"Steady big guy," he said.

"Who are you?"

"Name's Elvryn. I'm in charge of the house guard. I hear you and your friend are looking for Eeryn."

"Wow, word gets around fast," Vulryn swung his legs off the bed to sit facing his visitor. "You heard right though."

"Rumors are our business." Elvryn shrugged. "I know what you're here for. What puzzles me is why. No one from Valir, or anywhere else outside Shiloh, has come looking for Eeryn in years. Why now? What's your interest in the seer?"

Chapter 16

Moonlight washed the neat row of tents tucked into the tree ringed meadow. Silent sentries walked their posts. Shiloh was still a week's march to the east. Approaching the end of their mission seemed to put some of the soldiers on edge. A bright half-moon watched the warm breeze sway the treetops, dance in the grass, and lull the sentry in the doorway to sleep.

One Eye worked open a link and soundlessly fed the chain through the shackle on his right leg. He was free. A nudge of his elbow told Bryn to do the same. Bryn slid free and, on hands and knees, followed One Eye until they were directly behind the snoring sentry.

One Eye pressed a finger to his beak. A sliver of moonlight glinted on the sharpened tent peg drawn from his tunic. One Eye rose to a crouch. The strike was swift and sure. His right hand closed over the human's mouth; his left drove the stake upward in a single powerful thrust, severing his spine where it met the base of his skull.

One Eye pushed the body off him. Bryn closed his eyes to the image of the man's lips still working to take air into lungs that no longer moved. It didn't work. The image was tattooed on his memory.

One Eye returned the sentry to his position in the doorway. He stripped him of weapons and signaled Bryn to follow. Bryn avoided contact with the body, sure it would jump to life if he touched it. Sightless eyes watched him pass into the empty compound. Bryn knew two more sentries were walking the perimeter. He and One Eye stayed close to the tents taking advantage of what little cover the canvas afforded.

They stopped at the northern edge of the camp and One Eye pointed across the meadow to a line of trees. Twenty yards of open ground separated them from freedom. On the far side of the camp a match flared briefly silhouetting the guards. One Eye dropped into a low crouch and with a jerk of his head launched himself into the open. At his side, Bryn's legs churned furiously for the safety of the trees. The youngster's foot hung in a tuft of grass, and he went down. One Eye hauled him back onto his feet and shoved Bryn toward the trees.

"Halt!" a human voice shattered the quiet.

The warning was punctuated by the sizzle of an atlatl dart passing inches from Bryn's ear. Behind him, One Eye grunted in pain as a dart hit his wing with a loud crunch. He stumbled but kept running.

The alarm echoed through the camp. Soldiers poured from their beds. There was no time to check One Eye's wound. Bryn let him take the lead, pausing to snap a small branch from an oak. He threaded the branch through his belt letting it drag the ground behind them hoping to cover their trail.

The voices behind them had faded into the distance when One Eye stumbled and fell to his knees. Bryn wedged his shoulder under the old smuggler and lifted him to his feet.

"Stop fighting me," Bryn scolded.

"Leave me," One Eye's voice was reduced to a harsh whisper.

"I'm not leaving you," Bryn told him. "Now, come on."

"Don't be a fool, boy," One Eye said, but he was moving again.

"Too late for that."

About a mile further along they picked up a game trail and followed it until they heard running water. Bryn steered them toward the sound. They found a narrow stream and Bryn waded out to test the depth. It was shallow enough to wade. Bryn helped his wounded companion walk against the current until they came to a downed tree lying on the near bank.

Leaving One Eye in the shelter of the tree, he worked the smuggler's bloody tunic over his head. Curses escaped from One Eye's beak with each tremor of the dart in his shoulder. Bryn carried the tunic back where they entered the stream, waded out into the water, and released the bloody rag. His prayer to the Creator was answered when the cloth snagged on an overhanging branch. He crossed the stream and climbed the bank. Walking backwards he re-crossed the stream and headed for his downed partner.

"We've got to move," he told One Eye.

One Eye struggled to his feet. This time he let Bryn support him. The two pushed upstream for another two hours before they dropped to the ground exhausted.

"I can't go on," One Eye said when he caught his breath. "You've got to leave me."

"We've been through that already," Bryn said. "I'm not leaving you. But you're right, you can't go much further. I've got to find us someplace to hide while I see about that shoulder."

"Go," One Eye told him.

"Don't you try and run out on me," Bryn warned, moving off away from the stream.

They had to rest. One Eye wouldn't be able to go on for at least a day, maybe two. Bryn longed for the dense forests of home and the safety of the giant bouja trees. Finding a refuge from their pursuers among these rocks and scattered trees wasn't going to be easy.

The feathers of his crest suddenly stood on end. Bryn ducked. A white blur streaked over his head. It circled a large oak tree and started back.

"Hoot, hoot," the owl said.

"Oto? Bryn blinked, trying to focus. "Is that you?"

"How many strikingly handsome white owls do you know? Oto replied. "Of course, it's me."

"Must you always be a pain in the tail feathers?" Bryn asked.

"No, not always," he replied. "It's simply more amusing that way. I've found what you are looking for. Follow me."

"Wait," Bryn said. "I have to go back and get One Eye."

"Leave him," Oto said. "He'll never make it."

"Then leave," Bryn snapped. "I'm not going on without him."

"Just checking," Oto replied. "Calm down and go get him. I'll wait for you here."

Later, half dragging, half carrying the larger Valir, Bryn collapsed beneath Oto's perch. He tore a piece of cloth from his tunic and replaced the one he'd packed into One Eye's wound before they had started up the hill. When his muscles quit screaming and he could breathe again, Bryn followed Oto. The owl led him along a path that weaved through the woods.

They stopped at the foot of an immense boulder flanked by two others of roughly equal size. The rocks formed a triangle of solid stone. Bryn found a small opening and dragged One Eye into the shelter. Blood still oozed from his wound, but One Eye no longer seemed to care. Bryn checked and found a strong pulse. He whispered a prayer for the Creator's protection. There was nothing more he could do. He stretched out beside his companion and fell asleep.

He was clinging to the Edge of the World.

"I can't hold on much longer." Fedryn shouted.

Bryn reached for him. He caught Fedryn's coat just between the shoulders.

"I've got you. Hold on."

"Don't let go," Fedryn pleaded.

The wind snatched Fedryn's left arm free. His body followed; twisted by the wind and carried from the step. His free hand clutched at Bryn's back; missed Bryn's tunic and flailed the air. Bryn fell to his knees. His right hand groped blindly for Fedryn. The sound of ripping fabric broke through the wind.

"Bryn, save meeeee." Fedryn's face fell away. His cry following him to the rocks below.

"Noooooo." Bryn cried.

Bryn awoke to stars shining in a clear night sky. Beside him, One Eye's chest rose and fell in a steady rhythm. Leaves rustled overhead; the song of peepers floated up from the stream, but there was no sound of pursuit. Shuffling movement and ruffled feathers overhead drew his eyes up. Oto was perched atop the boulders keeping watch. Bryn closed his eyes and let sleep reclaim him.

He opened his eyes again to a washed-out gray sky. Bryn shook off the heavy dew and stretched the knots from his tired muscles. He was unfamiliar with the oaks and pine trees that surrounded their shelter. Here and there along the way, he passed plants that looked like those of his homeland, but he couldn't be sure. One Eye needed to rest, but rest would not be enough. If he didn't act soon, One Eye would die. He would have to take a chance on the plants at hand.

That dart had to come out. The bleeding needed to be stopped and the wound closed. Bryn's mouth was dry, and his eyes felt like they were packed with sand. His stomach rumbled and everything hurt. There was no time to waste on complaints about how bad he felt. His friend needed help. Bryn squeezed through the cleft in the rocks and crawled out into a dense stand of pines. He started downhill through the dim light. If his luck held, he would find what he needed.

Searching through the litter and the branches, Bryn gathered leaves and pulled up roots. He followed the stream to a stagnant bit of backwater surrounded by cattails that looked promising. Bryn dug his hands into the mud working his fingers through the mire until they brushed a cluster of soft round objects. Burrowing deeper, he felt the stalk securing them to the rock beneath. He wrapped a finger around the fibrous stalk and pulled. The cluster of seraphim eggs came free in his hand. He wrapped the gelatinous eggs in the burr-bush leaves he had found earlier and tucked them inside his tunic.

Now to get back before he bleeds to death.

Why he felt duty bound to save a felon who planned to sell him into slavery, Bryn couldn't say. But there it was. Duty, the supreme virtue of the Valirian cosmos was as much a part of him as his arms and legs. The duty to do right to others ran in his veins and held together every joint and sinew of his being. He would no more neglect his duty than cut off his right hand.

Granted there were Valir like One Eye who had turned away from the true faith and lived for selfish consumption. That One Eye had abandoned his sense of duty did not permit Bryn to do so. Nor did it permit him to leave One Eye to die alone. Bryn willed his weary legs to keep moving. The sun had passed overhead some time ago and the fading light threatened to disorient him in the unfamiliar woods. There was no time to rest. He had to keep going; their lives depended on him.

Bryn reached their refuge as twilight gave way to the dark. Hidden away in the shelter of the rocks, he kindled a small fire and dragged One Eye close. The wound had clotted off stopping the bleeding. That would last only until the dart moved again. Of course, removing the bandage and the dart would have One Eye bleeding again anyway. If One Eye tried to walk, the result would be the same. Better to have it done with. They were safe for now, but he didn't think that would last long either.

“This is going to hurt,” Bryn said.

One Eye’s single eye flickered. His beak moved without a sound.

Bryn worked the cloth from the wound. The smuggler groaned as the dried material stuck to the wound tore away the clot and debris below. Blood began to flow. There was not as much bleeding as Bryn expected. He hoped that wasn't because One Eye had lost too much already. He simply did not know. Bryn was a...

He wasn’t sure what he was, but he was no healer. Bryn poured water from a burr leaf pouch over the open wound. The dart had pierced One Eye's right wing and was buried deep in the flesh of his shoulder. Bryn decided a Valir who managed to live with one eye could probably get along with one good wing, but he was going to need that shoulder. The dart had to come out without ruining the muscles around it. The sooner that happened the better.

Unfortunately, there was no time for delicacy. Bryn pulled away broken bits of feathers and flesh from around the dart. One Eye hardly stirred. Encouraged by the muted reaction, Bryn grabbed the dart and pulled. The smuggler's good eye flew open. So did his mouth, but the sound that escaped was more a loud grunt than a scream.

Blood poured from the open wound. Bryn washed the area once more and quickly pressed the seraphim eggs into the wet hole in the shoulder. He covered the eggs with a layer of crushed roots. A thick bandage of burr leaves went over the poultice. Sweat dripped from Bryn’s brow. He propped his back against a stone wall and laid both his legs over One Eye's shoulder to add pressure to the dressing. Only two things remained for Bryn to do.

Wait, and see.

The washed-out gray of morning was back too soon. Bryn felt something cold, wet, and slimy crawling on his right leg. He tried to scurry away, but his feet found no purchase. He swatted at the offending sensation. One Eye shifted beneath him, and Bryn remembered where he was. He lifted his legs from his companion's shoulder.

"Get those damn things out of me," One Eye ordered.

The command lacked strength. Nevertheless, One Eye was speaking coherently. That was definitely a good sign. Bryn pulled off the bandage releasing a small army of tiny six-winged slugs that promptly flew off in the direction of the stream from which they came.

"Where are we?" One Eye asked.

"You're welcome," Bryn said. "If it helps, we are about a quarter mile south of the stream and a mile or so east of where we struck it."

"East?" One Eye turned his good eye on Bryn. "You're going the wrong way, kid."

"Not wrong; unexpected," Bryn corrected. "I'd like to keep free of human chains if that's all right with you. That, and I still mean to go to Shiloh."

"You cannot be serious."

"Oath bound serious," Bryn replied. "Although I don't expect you to understand."

"Don't get all uppity with me, boy," One Eye said. "Don't forget who pulled you back from the Edge."

"To save the pack on my back and a slave to sell," Bryn replied. "It's not the same."

"Keep telling yourself that," One Eye told him. "I gave an eye for duty, honor. I'm paid up. I don't owe anyone; not anymore."

Bryn's eyes rolled skyward. The feathers of his crest stood on end. The words seemed to come from the trembling dark hole in his middle that was shaking his entire body.

"You're wrong about that."

"Don't go betting your life on that," One Eye told him. "My duty is to myself."

Bryn didn't seem to hear. He dropped his head to study the ground between them. The strained silence that stretched out left each lost in his own thoughts. The spell was broken by the hoot of an owl. One Eye picked up a stone and threw it in the direction of the sound. The owl hooted louder in retaliation.

"Get out of here." He threw a second stone in the bird's direction. "Damn you *and* your master."

"Take it easy," Bryn cautioned. "Be still and let that shoulder heal."

"Get that death bird out of here," One Eye said. "Owls are a bad omen. They'll call the death angel right down on you if you let them."

"I'm going out for a look," Bryn said from far away. "Be still. I'll try to find something to eat."

"Just make sure and chase that owl off," One Eye said. "Mind what I say it's bad luck."

Bryn shrugged off the suggestion. The traditional Valir shunned owls, ravens too for that matter. They were considered consorts of spirits. Bryn was not satisfied with the idea that good and evil could be determined by species.

Oto said he was sent to help. That proved true—so far. It was also true that Oto never said exactly who sent him. The little owl was waiting outside the hideout.

“What cheek,” Oto said with a ruffle of his feathers. “I ought to leave the both of you right here.”

“But you won’t,” Bryn said.

“No,” Oto admitted. “I won’t. But don’t push it.”

“Where are the soldiers?”

“Following the stream back towards the Boubouja,” Oto said.

“Do you think they will call off the search soon?” Bryn asked.

“From the sound of things around the camp, probably tonight,” Oto told him. “They think One Eye is damaged goods and even if he lives, not worth the trouble. Their opinion of you is only slightly higher.”

“Thanks.”

“Just repeating what I hear.”

“How about making yourself useful," Bryn said. “See if you can find a way to Shiloh that doesn’t involve my being in chains.”

“Oto do this. Oto do that. Never a word of thanks." The bird ruffled his feathers, shrugged his shoulders, and with a twist of his head, flew off to the east leaving Bryn alone and hungry.

CHAPTER 17

Bryn shivered in the cool morning air. Blowing into his hands, he set out along a nearby game trail in search of food. He missed the Boubouja most on mornings like this. Home was warm; the trees were full of fruit and the waters teemed with fish. In the Boubouja he would spend an entire morning gathering food, instead of searching for it.

He topped a small rise and climbed an oak tree for a better look at his surroundings. A stand of trees about a quarter mile to his left looked promising. He dropped to the ground and headed in that direction. At the edge of the grove, he came across three sets of footprints. The poorly shod tracks did not belong to soldiers. These had to be humans foraging for food. A shift in the wind brought a scent Bryn knew well. He left the trail, pushed through some second growth, and followed his nose to a wild tangle of darberry vines. Ripe clusters of the smooth black berries hung scattered amid the thorns waiting to be plucked. Bryn went to work and in short order had a pouch full. His fingers stained black by the berries ached from careless touches, but he had food for the day and a smile for the walk back.

He found One Eye huddled over a tiny fire inside their little stone sanctuary. For the first time in days, Bryn thought he looked stronger. One Eye smiled up at him.

"Yeah, I'm okay," One Eye said. He pointed to the pouch tied on Bryn's hip. "Looks like you hit the jackpot."

"Enough to keep us going for now." Bryn settled next to him.

"And you're still set on going to Shiloh?" One Eye asked.

Bryn nodded slowly.

"You're a fool." One Eye held out his hand. "But I'm with you kid. Damned if I know why."

"Because somewhere under that rough exterior," Bryn began. "You're a Valir at heart."

“Well, let’s just keep that between us, shall we?”

“The soldiers are still searching west of where we hit the stream. I think they’re sold on the idea that we’re headed for home.”

One Eye opened his beak to speak, closed it again, and stared at Bryn for a moment. “Never mind,” he said at last. “I don’t want to know.”

After a meal of berries, One Eye announced he was fit enough to move. Bryn thought the words were more bravado than a true assessment of ability. Whatever the case, they did need to move. Bryn agreed and led the way for a second sweep of the darberry patch to replenish what they ate for breakfast and fill a second pouch.

Hoping to confuse any pursuers, they followed in the tracks left by the humans. Whenever possible they moved through the trees to avoid leaving tracks of their own. It was slow going. There was nothing here to compare with the smooth steady run of highway branches that interlaced the forests of the Boubouja.

They heard the men before they saw them. The trail below widened and turned down a steep hill. The men were gathered in a small clearing at the bottom. Bryn and One Eye climbed higher in hopes of seeing the commotion below without getting any closer. A pair of wagons made of rough-cut wood sat unattended at the edge of the clearing. In the middle of it a dozen ragged men of various ages danced around a cart Bryn thought looked very familiar.

One Eye tapped Bryn on the shoulder and pointed to their left. A lone sentry stood at the base of an oak tree with his back to them. He was young and more interested in the proceedings below than standing watch. Bryn worked his way closer to the guard.

He opened his wings to soften the landing and silently dropped down on the sentry. One hand closed over the kid's mouth; the other held a sharpened stone knife he’d made to the soft skin of the sentry's neck.

"Make a sound and die," Bryn whispered in his ear. For emphasis, he pushed the knife edge until a small red dot of blood appeared.

Bryn walked the sentry back into the trees before removing his hand from the boy's mouth. The knife blade didn't move. The boy remained silent as One Eye trotted over. The smuggler leaned in, his beak almost touched the boy's nose, and his one good eye focused on the boy.

"What's your name boy?" One Eye rested his blade on the boy's cheek.

"W…W…Wynn," the boy stammered.

"Well, W…W…Wynn," One Eye mocked him. "What are you and your lot up to?"

"Looking for food is all," Wynn replied.

Bryn took the boy's head in his hand and turned his face to look into his eyes.

"That cart you're looking for food in belongs to Lord Zett," Bryn said. "Don't you think he will want it back?"

"I didn't want to steal it," the boy cried. "Fargo made us do it. We were hungry, that's all."

"Damn thieves," One Eye snatched the boy's head back in his direction. "And stupid ones at that. Let's get out of here."

"We've got to warn them," Bryn said, watching One Eye roll his single eye.

Bryn marched the boy down the hill without waiting for One Eye to protest further. He kept Wynn between them and the foolhardy revelers. The laughter and shouts died when the men caught sight of their sentry being forced into their midst. A squat, heavily built man came around the captured cart and lumbered in their direction.

"Let that boy go," he demanded.

"Are you the one called Fargo?" Bryn asked.

"I am," the man replied. "What's it to you?"

"The boy tells me you were stealing food," Bryn stepped closer to the wagon keeping Wynn in front of him. "How much did you get?"

"We ain't looked yet," Fargo lied. "Not enough to share with the likes of you."

"Take a look," Bryn told his partner.

One Eye leaped on the wagon. He loosened the rope tied around the neck of one of the sacks and tilted it for all to see.

"What the hell is that?" Fargo said.

"Crushed snail shells, millions of them," One Eye explained. "They are being taken to Shiloh to make royal purple dye. This stuff is worth a fortune."

"Hear that boys," Fargo cheered. "We're rich."

"You're idiots," Bryn corrected. "Right now, every soldier assigned to that caravan is on his way here. If I were you, I'd send that wagon back to where you found it and run while you still can."

"Too late," One Eye said, his head cocked to the south. "They're coming."

One Eye threw a small bag over his shoulder and jumped from the wagon. He hit the ground as the first disrupter blast hit one of the men in the midsection ripping him in two. Bryn snatched a weapon from the dead man.

"I know what you're thinking," One Eye told Bryn. "Forget it. Save the boy. Come on."

Bryn nodded, grabbed hold of the boy, and followed One Eye toward the cover of the trees. Human disrupter fire sizzled over their heads. Beyond them trees exploded. Bryn, still holding the boy, cut a zig-zag pattern through the woods chasing after One Eye and away from the blasts and human screams. When the sound of slaughter died behind them, One Eye signaled a stop. He bounded up the nearest tree taking cover in the upper branches. Bryn followed, carrying their charge.

"Will they follow?" Bryn asked between huffs and puffs.

One Eye shook his head and waited until he was breathing easier. He blew one last long breath and looked at Bryn.

"Not right away. They got what they wanted," he said. "They'll probably tell their captain that they killed everyone."

"What's in the bag?" Bryn asked.

"A little something you might like." One Eye opened the bag and poured out a half dozen Valirian daggers. "Bet one has your name on it."

It so happened one did have Bryn's name on it. He tucked it into his belt. His eye caught on another name. He tucked Fedryn's dagger in the other side and whispered a promise to his dead friend.

"Here kid." With a wink, he handed the boy a dagger. "Just in case."

"You mean I'm not a prisoner?" Wynn asked.

"Of course not," Bryn said. "What would we do with a prisoner?"

"Feed me?" Wynn eyed the pack on Bryn's back.

"All we have is darberries," Bryn pointed at the boy's hands. "Looks to me like you've had some of those already."

"Where are you from?" One Eye wanted to know.

"Gotebo." Wynn pointed a skinny finger to the east. "That way, about a day's walk."

"Any soldiers there?" One Eye asked.

"No," Wynn said. "Just hungry people."

It was well after dark when they neared Gotebo. They decided it was safer to spend the night in the woods and wait until it got light. They each ate a handful of darberries, and Bryn and One Eye bedded down in the lower branches of nearby oak. Wynn curled up against the trunk of the same tree.

The Valir awakened the next morning to find their makeshift packs gone along with their entire store of darberries.

"Damn little thief," One Eye growled.

Wynn's tracks led them to the little town less than a mile away. The boy was wrong. His town wasn't hungry; it was starving. Hollow eyes followed Bryn as he made his way to the square where children with bloated bellies lay against the stones. A withered hand caught Bryn's sleeve.

"Please sir," an old woman pleaded. "Do you have a crumb for my baby?"

Bryn looked at the wrinkled, brown body cradled in her arms. The child had been dead for days. Bryn shook his head and kept walking. He tried to turn his face away from the suffering, but there was no safe place to focus his eyes in Gotebo. The town was inhabited by living skeletons with large hungry eyes that followed the strangers to the village center. The empty houses, full of furnishings, were left to the ghosts that skulked in doorways and peeped out of windows.

"You think they eat Valir?" One Eye asked.

"I think they'd eat anything," Bryn whispered back.

CHAPTER 18

Wynn sat on the edge of the well surrounded by his people. The stolen packs, as yet unopened rested beside him. Bryn shook his head and gave the boy a smile. Duty to his people; Bryn could not condemn it. He untied the woven edges of the pouches and spread darberries over the leaves. The sight of food might have caused a stampede. Sadly, there wasn't enough strength in all the town for that.

"What are you doing?" One Eye said. "You want to starve too? This is crazy. I won't do it."

But, slowly, hesitantly, he nodded agreement. A score of women and children crowded closer to the open packs, yet none of the starving reached for the offered food.

"It's alright," Bryn said. "Take all you want."

"No, it's not alright," a woman's voice answered.

A tall woman passed through the crowd. Her emaciated legs and halting stride gave Bryn the impression of a rather large stork. The ragged hem of her tattered dress ended just above her bare feet. She came to stand beside Bryn and turned to face the villagers. Her hand shook as she raised it to the crowd.

"We will not eat until we give thanks," she announced. Long thin arms reached skyward. Her chin followed. "Thank you, God, for these You have sent to save us. Bless them with strength and guidance. Amen."

The congregation croaked a corporate "Amen" and surged forward. They crammed darberries into empty stomachs as fast as hands could deliver and mouths could swallow.

"Where are all the men?" Bryn asked.

"Where we left them," Wynn replied. "Dying back in the clearing."

"All of them?"

Wynn answered with a lazy nod.

"All that were left. Iko is in charge now." He pointed to the tall woman.

Bryn sat on the low stone wall of the well. The darberries vanished with miraculous speed leaving nothing except stained faces and fingers.

What have we done? Give our all to win another day, maybe two, of more suffering?

Bryn was full of questions and certain he was empty when it came to answers.

"Come with me," Iko said when the feast ended.

Bryn and One Eye followed her to a mud-covered house a few rows from the village center. The mother who had pleaded with them to help her dead baby had joined the infant in eternal sleep.

"Her name was Agra," she said. "There was nothing you could do to help either of them."

The interior of Iko's home was cool and dark. Sunlight filtered in through a hole in the roof above an earthen oven. She seated them at a wooden table with stone legs and bustled about a small pot.

"Willow bark tea," she said, setting cups before them. "It keeps the stomach from rumbling and deadens the pain."

The hot liquid was bitter and strong. Bryn sipped slowly. One Eye caught Bryn's grimace and casually pushed his untouched cup away with the back of his hand. Iko set her cup down with a sigh.

"Gotebo was a happy place," she said. "Before the Ferals came."

"Ferals?" Bryn asked.

"Wild people pushed down from the north by the Wolven," Iko explained. "The King of the Wolves drove them out. Ferals don't hunt or plant, they steal from those who do and devour all they can. They took everything—our food, our children, anything they wanted."

"How long has this been going on?" Bryn asked.

"Five growing seasons," Iko said. "The last time they came was two months ago. They took everything. They made our men strip the woods and the hills of food. Then, they took that and the men too. A few hid in the woods. The boy Wynn was with them. Tell me, what has happened to those who were with him?"

"They robbed the wrong caravan," One Eye said. "Instead of

food they stole Lord Zett's shipment of purple. He made an example of them. Their heads are probably decorating the cart they stole."

"But you got away?" Her voice dripped venom. "How fortunate for you."

"We warned them to leave the cart and flee," Bryn said. "They wouldn't listen. It was their decision to die."

"They were our last hope." Iko bowed her head to hide her tears.

"I hope you're better at taking advice than your men," One Eye told her. "Because this isn't over yet."

Iko's head snapped, tears on her cheeks.

"That's right," One Eye continued. "Lord Zett is that evil. The slaughter of your men will not be enough. He won't take the chance someone escaped. His soldiers will follow their tracks back to this village. When he has killed everyone here, he will make sure word of his treatment of thieves is spread."

"Come with us," Bryn said. "We'll find a safe place for you."

"You've seen these people," Iko said. "They are in no condition to travel and there is no food to be found for at least two days in any direction."

"Starvation or disrupters," One Eye replied. "Either way they are dead. They will probably die on the road, but at least they will die fighting for life."

"And if the soldiers should overtake us? What will you do then?"

"We did not abandon your men as you suppose," Bryn said. "They died because they refused to heed our advice. Is that your choice too?"

"Where will we go?"

"We are going to Shiloh," Bryn said. "You may go or stop anywhere along the way."

Iko led them back to the well where the townsfolk waited. Her voice raw with emotion, she explained they must flee or die. Those who choose to go must be ready leave in minutes.

One Eye found a few wooden carts in the village. He, Bryn, and Wynn harnessed themselves to the carts. A handful of the villagers were strong enough to walk, the rest were loaded into the carts. Wynn carried some of the lighter children. Bryn and One Eye divided the remaining villagers between them. Iko told them of a village three days walk from Gotebo. However, she warned Bryn that they would not be welcomed in Manitou. The people of that village had been turning away immigrants from Gotebo for two seasons.

The little caravan started out through vacant fields that wore the signs of plundered harvest. Broken plows, uprooted stalks of corn, wasted, empty harvest sacks littered the ground where crops once grew. The outlying woods looked little better. The trees were stripped of leaves and bark. Broken branches lay strewn about the bare trunks. Wynn groaned under the weight of his cart but continued to pull. Two of the older children jumped out and ran alongside to lighten his burden.

Travel was slow. Exhaustion and debility forced them to make frequent stops to rest. Things were further complicated when half the children developed diarrhea from the darberries.

Bryn led the way with Iko as his guide. He looked back over his shoulder every few minutes to make sure everyone was still moving. He pushed Wynn as hard as he thought possible. He needed to keep the boy on his feet and that third cart moving. Instinct told him the soldiers were not only coming but closing in on them.

At twilight, he called a halt in a meadow of tall grass that bordered the road. The forest hugged the road opposite them. The humans piled from the carts and stretched themselves on the cool grass glad to be free of the carts that bumped and bruised their thin frames. Bryn kindled a fire while Iko made tea from a supply of willow bark she carried in her pack. One Eye set about scouring the woods for anything that appeared edible.

The group huddled in a circle around a small fire clutching their ragged clothes tightly about them to keep warm. Iko passed cups of tea to everyone reminding the little ones to blow on it to cool the hot liquid. Before the first sip, she offered another prayer of thanks for what they had and for their saviors.

Bryn disliked Iko's notion that he and One Eye were somehow saviors. He was about to protest but was stopped by a sudden thought. Arguing about the title would discourage them further and they didn't need any more blows to their faith. Faith was all that kept them going. Nevertheless, he wished their God had seen fit to provide his people with better saviors.

One Eye returned to camp just after dark. Moonrise was still an hour away. By the firelight, Bryn could see his companion was smiling. One Eye knelt and unfolded his tunic. Within the folds of the garment was a smorgasbord of beetles and grubs.

"Every single one edible," he promised. "I like mine toasted."

He picked up a small twig and showed the little ones how to skewer grubs and hold them over the fire. The adults followed his lead and were soon crunching roasted grubs without a single complaint about taste. The children were still licking their fingers when a noise from the woods sent them scurrying to their mothers.

"It's just an owl," Bryn announced. "I'll go chase it away."

"Don't count on that," One Eye whispered to Iko. "That owl's been following us for days."

"Is that bad?" she asked.

He answered with a deep sigh and a shrug of his shoulders. One Eye had given up trying to convince the unlearned that owls were a bad omen. He considered telling everyone roasted owl was even more delicious than grubs but decided instead to find a soft spot to lie down.

Had One Eye heard a conversation going on just beyond the firelight, he might have spoken up.

"How many?" Bryn asked.

"A twenty-man squad," Oto said. "One of the poor bastards back there lived long enough to name his village and point the way. They'll catch up by midday tomorrow."

"We've got to stall them somehow," Bryn said. "Iko says it is another two days to Manitou. And I'll need some time to convince those in Manitou to shelter these people."

"I suppose it's useless to suggest you leave these people here," Oto said.

"Completely useless," Bryn assured him.

"That's what I thought," Oto replied. "I'll scout ahead. Tell that woman to keep praying. I'm afraid you're going to need it real soon."

"Well?" One Eye asked when Bryn returned to the fire.

"Well, what?" Bryn asked.

"Did you chase it away?'

"It's gone."

"That's not what I asked," One Eye said. "I asked if you chased it away."

"Not exactly," Bryn answered.

"I didn't think so." One Eye shook his head. "It's bad luck to consort with that type."

"Are you a witch?" Iko asked Bryn.

"Answer the lady." One Eye prodded him with an elbow. "I'd love to know the answer myself."

"No," said Bryn. "I'm not a witch. Owls see things; know things."

"Witch," the others said in unison.

Bryn jumped to his feet and with a loud huff walked out into the night. His anger lasted only long enough for him to look at this from their side. He spoke to a bird. Worse, the bird spoke back. He was no witch; he was sure of that.

But what am I?

The question was never far from the front of his mind. Seers often had birds. He couldn't remember Coryn having one. But Coryn also had no apprentice as seers were wont to do. What did he really know of Coryn and seers? His family were warriors. No one ever had the gift of seeing. He was trained as a warrior.

And you don't want to be a warrior, he reminded himself.

If Coryn, who had no apprentice, had chosen him for this mission. Did that make him a seer's apprentice? Impossible.

Right, you've always talked to owls, he chided himself.

Whatever he was, if he didn't come up with a plan to get away from the soldiers, he would be a dead one. He laced his fingers behind his head. Less than a minute later, he was asleep.

He stared into the rock face of the Edge of the World once more.

"I can't hold on much longer," Fedryn shouted.

"I've got you. Hold on."

"Don't let go," Fedryn pleaded. "Bryn, save meeeee!"

As Fedryn's terror filled eyes fell away, his face began to melt. Then, it was Faryn's face falling. Her cry silenced on the rocks, her body twisted and mangled. Her dead eyes stared up at Bryn.

"No!" Bryn screamed, sitting bolt upright, drenched in sweat, and his heart hammering in his chest. He reminded himself it was only a dream.

Only a dream?

Was it figurative? Fact or fantasy? Bryn didn't know. He was not completely sure he wanted to know. One Eye looked at him from across the camp; shook his head; and lay down again.

***

"Vulryn Pey to see Faryn Go, please."

The embassy secretary looked up at the towering blacksmith and nodded. The papers dropped from her trembling hands. She gathered herself together and rose from her seat.

"I'll just go and..." her voice trailed away. "And, um...announce you."

Vulryn smiled as she scurried away into the atrium. He could almost hear Maryn laugh. She was always amused by people's reaction to his size. With a heavy sigh, he remembered again how much he missed her. He ran his hand over a tapestry depicting the creation of the Valir in the grove of Ryn.

"Fine work," he said.

"Yes, it is," a voice replied.

Vulryn turned to find a tall male in a somber gray coat embroidered with golden thread in abstract leaf patterns at the collar and cuffs. A fine gold stripe ran down the side of the gray pants he wore. Vulryn's eyes were drawn to the dagger at his waist. The handle was a double spiral of polished iron with bold silver filigree.

"Almost as fine as your dagger," Vulryn said with a nod at the weapon.

"You must be the smith I heard about," he said and extended a hand to Vulryn. "Samryn Lo."

"Vulryn Pey."

"Will you and Faryn be staying with us long?"

"Only long enough to complete our business," Faryn answered for him.

"Which is?" Samryn asked.

"Confidential I'm afraid," Faryn took Vulryn by the arm. "Let's step outside."

"Nice to meet you," Samryn called after them. A smile lit his face as he waved to them.

"The Ambassador will be glad to hear his suspicions are correct," he muttered under his breath.

Faryn led the way to a large firepit tucked into a grove of bouja trees. The pit was flanked by wide benches cut from bouja wood. After the traditional fashion, the benches were set back from the pit allowing room to dance. She steered Vulryn to a bench that allowed them to see the entrance to the embassy.

"I've made a contact," he said when they were seated. A guard by the name of Elvryn. He says he was here when Eeryn was ambassador. He may be useful."

"We must be careful who we trust within these walls."

"I got that impression. Elvryn seemed to already know our business."

"Does he still have contact with Eeryn?"

"He didn't come right out and say so. But I got the impression he at least knew where to begin looking."

"Find out."

Ambassador Dorryn gazed out over the grounds. He watched Faryn and Vulryn's walk to the fire pit. She must have inherited some of her grandfather's canniness; she knew better than to talk inside the embassy walls. No matter, her intentions would soon be known. His thoughts were interrupted by a knock on his door.

"Enter."

Samryn pushed open the door and with a wave from Dorryn, came to stand beside him at the window.

"She's careful," he said.

"Thankfully," Samryn said. "Her friend is not. He is the blacksmith."

"Which confirms her complicity in the death of the policemen," Dorryn added.

"So it would seem. She took him out before I could learn anymore."

"And Eeryn?"

"I shall join Davryn shortly in search of the prophet. However, the prospects of locating him today are poor at best."

"Very well, but speed is of the essence."

Vulryn left Faryn sitting on the bench. He needed to stretch his legs and a reconnaissance of the ground would make him feel better about being walled in. The compound's wall was too high to scale. There was no structure high enough to allow him to glide over the wall. Exit was going to be by one of two gates, and both were guarded around the clock. He considered that another reason to try and befriend Elvryn.

He was sure Faryn shared his lack of patience. She would be eager to go looking for the seer long before the ambassador was ready to give his blessing to the effort. They had to find a way to slip out.

He had slept little the night before. Guards came and went at all hours. Getting out of the barracks did not pose a problem. Although his size made him hard to forget, most of the guards paid no attention to him. Getting out of the embassy unnoticed was going to be harder, especially for Faryn; she turned every head in the place.

This new life of intrigue was exciting. However, he knew the excitement came at a price. It was costing him time with his wife; time that he had only recently won back. How were they to have a son with him chasing after seers so far from home? He couldn't think about that now. The seer promised him a son. He would make it through this and so would Maryn. He had to believe that. Meanwhile, he needed to find Elvryn.

Elvryn was, at that moment, leaving the embassy compound. He made a left turn outside the gate moving down the Avenue of Kings and away from the palace. A few blocks along the way, he crossed the wide avenue and headed for the crowded northwest quarter of the city that was home to most of the city's outland species population.

He turned the corner at Olas and Pine and, from the corner of his eye, caught sight of a face that changed his plans. The driver of a cart made an obscene sign when Elvryn suddenly jumped in front of his horses. He ran up the middle of the street, cut in front of another cart going in the opposite direction and across Olas. Down the block, he ducked into a cafe; pushed his way to the back door and into the alley. He doubled back to Pine Street and headed toward the embassy.

Two blocks later, he slipped into a corner shop. He pretended to admire the oranges while he watched the street outside. He didn't have to wait long. Samryn Lo's slender, bespectacled face and expense gray suit were unmistakable. The ambassador's stooge was checking the shops across the street. Elvryn let him work his way down the block before slipping from his hiding spot and heading off to a pub a few blocks away.

Elvryn waved at the barman and made his way to a table near the back. He slid into a chair next to a Valir wearing a hack driver's coat. The barman laid a beer down in front of him.

"Thought you couldn't make it," the driver said.

Elvryn took a long pull of his beer. His hand trembled slightly as he wiped foam from his beak and checked the door.

"Change of plans," he said.

"You okay? You look a little green to me."

"Sure, I'm fine," Elvryn told him.

"Look, I know lies are a part of where you work," the driver leaned closer. "Don't try that stuff with me brother. You keep checking the door, expecting someone?"

"I was followed from work."

"What the hell? Where were you going?"

"I'd tell you," Elvryn ruffled the feathers of his brother's crest. "But you're better off not knowing.

CHAPTER 19

Fatigue rescued Bryn from visions of dying friends about the time the moon dipped behind the trees. He drifted off into dreamless sleep in the shelter of an oak tree. Throughout the camp a gentle night wind caressed the little band of travelers. Peace for a night was all they could hope for.

"Bryn," a voice called to him.

He stirred, turning from the voice in hopes of escape into deeper sleep.

"Bryn wake up," the voice called again.

"Go away," Bryn mumbled.

A sharp pinch tore at his arm. Bryn yelped and jumped to his feet searching for his assailant through bleary eyes still heavy with sleep. A white smudge slowly crystallized into a familiar figure.

"You bit me," Bryn said rubbing his arm.

"You need to wake up," Oto told him. "Get these people moving."

"How far behind are the soldiers?" Bryn asked.

"A couple of hours at most," Oto warned. The way is clear ahead, but..."

"But we'll never make it," Bryn finished for him.

Oto bobbed his head. A twig snapped in the trees behind them. The owl flapped his wings and sailed silently out of sight. One Eye stepped from the cover of the woods. He looked at Bryn for a moment, his single eye searching the boy's face.

"You know we should leave them?" One Eye held up a hand to forestall the answer he knew was coming. "I'm just saying. How bad is it?"

"They will be on us before midday," Bryn said.

"Maybe," One Eye said rubbing his chin. "We can slow them down."

"How?"

"I know a few tricks," One Eye said. "I was once a smuggler, you know."

"So I've heard," Bryn said with a smile. "Let's get to it."

After redistributing the loads, Iko took on the job of pulling One Eye's cart. Bryn led the way as they trudged through a countryside steadily becoming less sterile, but still stripped of edibles. Neither flower, seed nor edible root could be seen. After two hours of marching, they came to a tiny creek. A quick search for food came up empty. There was no time to fish. The band of refugees pressed on ignoring their cramping muscles and rumbling bellies as best they could. A few of the humans began plucking up the grass that grew between the wagon ruts. It quieted their restless stomachs but provided little in the way of nourishment.

Bryn's hopes sank with each step. They were moving slower than the previous day. He watched the sun climb ever higher in the sky and wondered how long these people could go on without food. He could not hear the pursuing soldiers, not yet. Nevertheless, he knew they were growing ever closer. Atop a small hill he called a stop. His muscles were on fire. Iko and Wynn had to be suffering even worse. They had to rest.

At the bottom, he told himself and urged the little caravan down the hill.

True to the promise he made to himself, at the base of the hill, Bryn dropped the traces and sat down in the grass beside the road to rest. Iko and Wynn collapsed where they stood. The rest of the humans piled out of the carts to join them on the ground near the wagons. Bryn fought the urge to sleep. The silence that settled over the group was broken by an insistent sound from the woods behind them.

"Do you hear that?" Wynn sat up, excitement in his voice.

Bryn's heart leaped. He recognized that sound. It was not the muffled thump of marching soldiers, but a deep-throated humming. His mind made the connection Wynn had already come to.

"Bees!" cried Wynn. "Honey!"

All order vanished in the stampede that followed.

***

One Eye watched the carts disappear around a bend in the road.

Bryn was gone. He was alone. He was free of Bryn's warped sense of loyalty and duty. He was free of the whole affair. He could save himself. All he had to do was melt into the woods.

Only he knew it wasn't Bryn's sense of duty that held him. It was his own. He had thrown in with the kid, the Creator alone knew why, but there it was. Somewhere this whole mess had gotten out of hand. Bryn had not left him. He would not leave the kid. He owed the kid his life. A week ago he would have called things even. He'd risked his neck to pull the kid off the Edge. Or was it his own skin he had really saved? He wasn't sure it mattered anymore. He owed the human soldiers a hurting for the dart he took from them. That was something within his ability to control. He went to work.

There was not a lot to work with, but he thought he could delay the pursuit for several hours. Hopefully, that would be long enough. He gathered up stout bits of broken branches as he searched for clumps of briar vines. As he walked, he sharpened each end of the sticks he picked up. It didn't take long to find the briars. They were hardy parasitic vines that flourished on the oaks in the area. Their bitter taste, sharp thorns and emetic reaction discouraged human contact, even from starving humans. He gingerly untangled the vines and cut them to suitable lengths. When he finished braiding the vines his hands were a bloody mess. He wrapped his hands in scraps of his tattered shirt to avoid leaving a trail for the soldiers to follow. Then, he went looking for a suitable place to put it all to use.

He remembered a place about a mile further down the road where the woods closed in on the road. The road was flanked by rock outcroppings that funneled traffic between them. Their pursuers had to pass through here or take a wide detour. Either way they would lose time on their march. Using his dagger, he planted the sticks in the ground leaving only an inch or two and the sharpened point above the surface of the road. He worked the sticks into a pattern around a triangle of larger points. He slipped a vine around a tree branch, pulled it tight, threaded it through the planted points and secured the snare to the ground. He covered the entire thing with a bed of leaves before moving on in search of his next location.

He returned the way he had come and found the next spot for

an ambush. Several willows grew near a low spot at the bottom of a hill. One Eye fastened a vine across the road about four inches off the ground. He piled leaves near the vine but left the vine itself visible to a watchful eye. He climbed into the neighboring trees and secured a vine with a stone tied to the end of it to the nearby branches. Then, with a big smile on his face, he dropped to the ground and went in search of a perch from which to wait.

The human kingdoms had fought a war or two with every other species on Tettias. They had also fought several wars between themselves. It had been a long time since the Kingdom of Shiloh tangled with the Valir though. The old human soldiers who told stories of the war were long dead. The forgotten battles provided a tactical advantage that One Eye thought to make use of. Confident in the power of their disrupters, the soldiers might get careless.

Disrupters came to the ready as the soldiers approached the narrow section of road. Starving villagers and two Valir didn't pose much a danger, but they weren't totally abandoning their training. The point man went into a crouch making himself a smaller target as he crept forward toward the narrow gap in the trees. His eyes scanned the trees and the underbrush. His one mistake materialized in an instant. His feet flew out from under him with a sudden jerk that snapped his ankles. His warning shout caught in his throat. He bumped over the road until he hit the buried spikes. He came to a sudden stop with a scream. Blood gushed from his impaled crotch and the spike that broke through his right thigh.

The soldiers following him were thunderstruck for a moment, unable to believe what happened.

"Go!" their captain shouted.

Four of the soldiers broke into a run to rescue their downed comrade. Two of the oncoming soldiers shouted in pain and went down. The soles of their boots leaked blood as they writhed in pain. The remaining two froze in place.

"Medic!" one of the trapped soldiers shouted.

It took two hours to clear the way and pry the dying point man off the spikes. Another hour was spent digging a grave. The two who could no longer walk were loaded onto a makeshift travois. Their bleeding had stopped, but their cries of pain continued as the stretchers dragged along the ground at the rear of the column. They underestimated their enemy and swore not to do that again.

The new point man saw the vine across the road well in advance. The patrol fanned out avoiding the trap and working their way through the willows. The point man stooped to examine the trip wire. He traced it along its length to the base of one of the willows. It was tied to the tree and nothing else. He was still trying to figure out the trap mechanism when the screams began. A half dozen soldiers flew into the air, feet ensnared. As they swung forward, a stone tied to the other end of the vine swung to meet them. A few were able to ward off the blows with their hands and arms. A couple weren't so lucky. The swinging stones met their heads with a loud, hollow thud and the lights went out for good. After splinting a few broken limbs, burial for the less fortunate took place alongside the road.

Their number had been cut in half and twilight was on them. They made camp and settled in to eat. The captain announced he was planning to leave the wounded to push on at their own pace. He would take a squad and go after the fleeing caravan the next morning.

His plan was spoiled as soon as darkness settled over the camp. The quiet peace of the camp was broken by a sharp cry. One of the sentries staggered into the camp. An arrow protruded from his chest. The triggers clicked harmlessly on the soldier's sun deprived disrupters.

One Eye slung his bow across his back. With a satisfied smile, he hurried through the branches for a half mile before dropping to the ground and returning to the road. One Eye set a steady pace. He hoped to catch up with Bryn and the refugees from Gotebo by midday. According to Wynn, it would take another day's travel after that to reach Manitou. He had reduced the size and pace of the soldiers, but they would continue to follow. They had no reason not to. Manitou was the shortest route to their main body. For the first time One Eye held out hope the refugees would get to Manitou first.

He topped a small hill as the sun was coming up. Remnants of a campfire glowed in the shallow valley below. One Eye moved away from the road keeping just below the crest of the hill. He worked through the cover of the woods to a point just above the camp. A hissed curse slipped from his lips. He dropped from the tree.

That's it? His heart sank at the thought. *That's as far as they got*?

His disappointment grew when he walked into the camp. The humans covered with angry red welts lay scattered about the camp and refused his efforts to get them up. Bryn Bou was nowhere to be found.

CHAPTER 20

One Eye flew into a rage. He stomped through the camp looking for Bryn.

"Bou!" One Eye bellowed.

He pulled Wynn up by the collar and shook him. "Where's Bryn?" He growled. "Damn it boy, where is he?"

"I...I...I…" Wynn stammered.

"He's right here." Bryn slipped his dagger into his belt as he stepped from the woods.

"What are you doing?" One Eye waved a hand over the camp. "Did I just risk my neck for nothing?"

"You tell me," Bryn snapped back. "Take a look at them. Are you blind?"

"What happened?" One Eye's grip on Wynn relaxed, leaving the boy's face a dusky red.

"Bees," Bryn said with a sigh.

One Eye stared at him as if Bryn had just sprouted a third eye. Bryn sighed again.

"We heard bees. They thought there would be honey and there was no stopping them," he explained. "They ate well but are paying the price for it now."

"So I see," One Eye said. "It will just be the down payment if we don't get moving."

Bryn's head bobbed in agreement sure that One Eye could see the strain on his face and read his thoughts.

"It's not your fault," One Eye said. "It ain't even their fault, starving dinks. That doesn't change our situation. Those soldiers are licking their wounds right now. In an hour or two, they will be up and coming again looking for payback and carrying disrupters. Let's break the news. Wynn, I apologize."

One Eye, still holding the boy's collar slapped him across a bloated cheek. Wynn screamed and heads came up around the camp. Satisfied that he had their attention, One Eye hauled Wynn around the fire to where Iko stirred from a fitful slumber. He grabbed the human leader with his free hand and hauled her upright. He pulled her and Wynn to within an inch of his beak.

"Damn humans," he growled. Their heads swung in time to his shaking. "Now, you two listen like your miserable lives depended on it, because they do. Get these people on their feet and move up that road. And do it now!"

He dropped the moaning humans to the ground, looming over them with a glare.

"Move!" he shouted when they didn't immediately follow his order.

"We will not!" Iko shouted back at him.

"You will," One Eye said his voice cold steel. "I just risked my life for you worthless humans. By the Creator, if you don't do exactly as I say we will leave you here alone to deal with your own kind."

"You would just leave us here?" Iko returned his glare.

Bryn stepped between the two of them. It was Iko he looked in the eye.

"In a heartbeat," he assured her. "One Eye is right. We have done our duty by you. You were starving; I get it. That does not change a thing. Maybe you are ready to sell your lives for a mouthful of honey, but we are not selling ours that cheaply."

"Now, get these miserable dinks on the road," One Eye ordered. "We'll try to hold off the soldiers. That, or lay back down by the fire and let us be on our way."

Bryn nodded agreement. Iko's eyes held his for a moment longer. Bryn refused to look away. The moment stretched out and One Eye shifted uneasily. Finally, Iko blinked.

"Everyone up," she announced. "We must be on the move."

"They are weak and hurting," Bryn told her. "I understand, but if you don't keep them moving, they will be dead. Do you understand that?"

"Yessss," she hissed at him.

"Good," Bryn said. "Wait for us in Manitou. If we don't arrive a day behind you, we didn't survive. Do what you must for your people."

"I'm staying with you," Wynn spoke up. "Iko can care for

them without me. She's done it before."

Bryn looked at One Eye and back to Wynn. His own image clouded over the boy's face for just a moment. He could not refuse.

"Do your duty as you see it," Bryn pronounced.

The soldiers were still in camp when the people of Gotebo started down the road. There was no sign the soldiers planned to move soon. The litters of wounded were arranged close to the fire. Two of the men were standing watch. One was positioned where the trees met the road. The other paced around the periphery. Bryn took silent inventory. One Eye assured him that five were dead. He counted another six wounded. That left nine able bodied soldiers.

"Three to one not the best odds," he whispered.

One Eye pointed at the nearby sentry. He then motioned for Wynn to follow him. When they were about twenty yards from the guard, One Eye left Wynn in the shelter of a thick oak tree and worked his way through the branches to a position above the sentry.

One Eye pounced, dropping without a sound. His blade found the human's throat. He pushed the man's jaw against the blade as he drew it across the human's neck severing jugulars and trachea. Blood splattered and bubbled covering One Eye's face and hands. He kept a tight hold on the sputtering, dancing human until the sentry was still before dropping him into a spreading patch of his own blood. One Eye stripped off the sentry's coat and hat, wiped away as much blood as possible and signaled for Wynn to join him.

Wynn slipped into the stained coat and pulled the hat low on his head. One Eye positioned the boy in the sentry's place. After a quick explanation, he left Wynn under the tree and returned to Bryn's side. The two exchanged nods. Bryn went left; One Eye went right taking up positions opposite each other.

Bryn searched the trees on the far side of the camp until a flash of movement caught his eye. He could see One Eye was in position and whistled the call of a night hawk. The tang of One Eye's bow answered. Bryn's fingers released their grip on his taut bowstring and an arrow sprouted from the back of the sentry walking the perimeter. One Eye's arrow landed in the road near Wynn.

"Attack! Attack!" Wynn sounded the alarm.

Soldiers scrambled from their tents fumbling for weapons. Wynn screamed and fell to the ground with an arrow tucked securely in his armpit. Soldiers fanned out around their captain and rushed to the aid of their downed companions. Bryn and One Eye picked off those that attended the dead sentry in the middle of the camp. Except for the captain, the soldiers forgot their orders and ran for cover. The captain continued to the spot where Wynn had fallen. He bent down to check on his wounded soldier. Wynn plunged a dagger into the man's chest.

Wynn was up and running from the camp before the soldiers realized what had happened to their leader. Except for a few arrows fired as the Valir retreated, the battle was over. Bryn's muscles ached. Twice he slowed to a limping gait trying to massage the cramps away. The others fared no better, but they kept going. One Eye carried Wynn the last quarter mile.

They need not have pushed themselves so hard. The humans lost their taste for blood. They retreated into their camp after a short pursuit. The trio of attackers caught up to the refugees that afternoon. The road to Manitou was theirs.

CHAPTER 21

Faryn elbowed Vulryn in the ribs and jerked her head toward the embassy guards headed their way.

"Looks like trouble," she told him.

"Think they're on to us?"

"Probably. Follow my lead."

Faryn stood to meet the guards. Her smile momentarily softened the captain's scowl.

"May I help you, Captain?" she asked.

"The Ambassador wishes to see you both in his office," the captain announced. "If you will follow me, please."

Vulryn stood and followed a pace or two behind Faryn. The guard at his back was a crawling pressure between his shoulders. Over his shoulder he kept an uneasy watch on the guard and resisted the urge to drag him up alongside. In doing so, he failed to see Faryn pull up short. His chest collided with her back, and she tumbled to the ground.

"You clumsy oaf!" she screamed and punched him in the leg.

Her words stung far more than the blow. Vulryn bent to help her up. Faryn held her ankle and writhed in pain. Vulryn caught her under the arms and lifted her.

"I'm so sorry, my lady," he apologized.

"Help me walk," Faryn ordered.

She leaned heavily on his arm. The scowls of the guards and Faryn's limp became more pronounced as they neared the building. Faced with the stairs to Dorryn's office, Vulryn scooped her up in his arms and carried her to the Ambassador's door.

Dorryn was seated at his desk. Standing at the window behind the Ambassador, Faryn recognized the Valir she found speaking with Vulryn the week before. Next to him stood a rough-looking Valir with hard black eyes.

"Please, sit," Dorryn gestured toward the empty chairs at his desk. "I have news."

"You have found Eeryn?" Faryn asked.

"Unfortunately, no. That particular task has proved to be beyond the ability of my investigators." He nodded at the pair by the window. "My news is of a more personal note. It seems that before beginning his career as a diplomatic escort our large friend here was a blacksmith. It happens that a blacksmith is being sought in the murder of police officers sent to arrest him. Coincidentally, he was aided in his crime by a stunning female and the son of none other than General Byryn Bou."

Dorryn shook his head and held up a hand to stave off Faryn's denial.

"There's more I'm afraid. I have given the two of you the freedom of the embassy. You posed no threat and, well dear Faryn, you are the granddaughter of the Minister of Justice. However, your real value is bait for young master Bou. I had hopes of capturing the three of you and handing you over to the Minister in exchange for his undying favor. Alas, that is not to be."

"Where's Bryn?" Faryn said. "What's happened to him?"

"I'm afraid your beau has fallen in with thieves. Valirian smugglers to be precise. This bunch attacked a royal caravan. Lord Zett's goods were recovered, but the thieves escaped. What's worse is that in their flight they destroyed two outlying villages and killed at least ten of Lord Zett's soldiers. They are still counting the human dead in the villages."

"Bryn would never be party to anything like that," Faryn assured him.

"We shall know soon enough," Dorryn countered. "Most of the smugglers have been taken prisoner. Those still living are being brought to Shiloh for execution. Knowing Lord Zett, the heads of the others will accompany the caravan."

Dorryn leaned back in his seat. He watched the news spread over their faces. Putting on his best diplomatic smile, he leaned forward resting his elbows on the desk.

"News of the atrocity reached Shiloh this morning," he said over tented fingers. "As you can imagine, relations between us and the humans are precarious to say the least. The city is a powder keg waiting to explode. For your own safety, you will remain under guard here on the embassy grounds."

"You said most of the smugglers were taken." Faryn looked at Vulryn.

"Two of the leaders are said to have escaped. But it's just a matter of time," Dorryn said. "The army or some human out for a reward will get them soon. Slaughtered villages tend to make human tempers run high. I shall be busy for days trying to keep the humans from killing every Valir they come across. So, you see, you are safer here. Do not try to leave the embassy."

“We will honor your wishes,” Faryn said.

“He’s going to be very angry when he finds out you lied to him,” Vulryn whispered to Faryn as he deposited her on her bed.

“Dorryn is a diplomat, he deals in lies,” she said after the guards withdrew. “We have to go tonight. See what you can find out.”

Vulryn found the barracks empty of gossiping guards. It was just as well, he had to get outside before he smothered. His space was no smaller, the guards on the grounds no larger, the single guard assigned to him gave him a wide berth, but the knowledge he was being held was somehow suffocating. He made his way to the outer court and strolled along the walls. The air there was full of foreign smells. Most of them were pleasant enough though none smelled like home. He could almost feel the crush of people moving on the other side of the walls. Nevertheless, it felt better to be out in the open air.

On his second circuit of the grounds, raised voices drew him to the embassy’s main gate. Vulryn followed a pair of soldiers rushing to reinforce the pair stationed at the gate. An angry crowd of humans was gathered on the other side of the high iron gates.

“Murdering birds,” a tall, thin man with straw colored hair shouted. “Open those gates and we’ll see how you do with real men.”

“I’ll pluck the freaking feathers of your head,” another man yelled and lunged against the bars.

His hand closed on empty air, but his comrades had a solution. Rocks began to fly. One of the guards received a glancing blow to the head as the Valir scrambled for the cover of their shack and the inner gates. Blood streaming through his fingers, the wounded guard swayed uncertainly on his feet. Vulryn lifted the guard’s dagger from his waist as he helped him to a seat in the guard shack. A second guard held out a cloth torn from his shirt.

"Here put this on his head," he said.

"You're going to be okay," Vulryn assured the wounded guard. "Just keep that cloth on there and stay down."

More embassy guards arrived armed with bows as rocks and garbage flew over the iron gates. A sergeant notched an arrow and drew back his bow. Elvryn knocked the bow toward the ground and slowly shook his head at the sergeant.

"Take him to the doc," Elvryn ordered the bowman. "The rest of you help me close the inner gates."

The sergeant helped the wounded guard to his feet while Vulryn joined Elvryn and the rest of the guards to push the massive inner gates closed. A large crossbar was slid into the lock to secure the gates. Rocks continued to beat against the top of the solid iron walls for several minutes before the humans gave up and contented themselves with hurling obscenities.

Vulryn produced a pipe from his tunic and one of the guards offered him a light.

"The Ambassador said it would be safer in here," Vulryn said. "Guess he was right. What's the uproar all about?"

"A human army detachment on patrol," a hint of a smile touched Elvryn's face. "Out near the Edge happened upon the tracks of a band of purple smugglers. They trailed the smugglers to a village. Every human in the place was dead. Valirian arrows were found in some of the bodies. The captain sent out a detachment to track them down. Long story, short, the patrol wound up dead. The main body caught up to the smugglers at a place called Manitou. Most of the town was dead by the time they got there. The rest died during the capture of the smugglers. The army is bringing them here for execution."

"They should be here in the next day or two," another guard added. "The Ambassador has been called to the palace twice to get an earful from Prince Melchiz."

"Doesn't make a lot of sense to me," Vulryn said. "Why would Valir want to kill those people? I mean, if they were smugglers, wouldn't they want to avoid attention?"

"Beats the heck out of me," the guard answered. "But, if you go out there, be careful. I swear, humans don't mind killing. It's what they do best."

"Our friend here is restricted to the embassy," Elvryn said. "There will be no going outside for him."

"Yes, sir."

"I'll keep that in mind," Vulryn said. "Maybe, I'll just go get some sleep."

"You do that," Elvryn said. "Oh, by the way, I heard a couple of the smugglers escaped."

After a late dinner with the ambassador and his investigators, Faryn joined Vulryn for a stroll through the gardens. She leaned heavily on his arm. Her very pronounced limp allowed their guards to relax and smoke at a distance.

"Do you think Bryn is mixed up in what happened?" Faryn asked.

"The timing's right," he answered with a shrug. "The Captain of the Guard hinted as much this afternoon. He implied Bryn might be among the escapees."

"I've heard the same thing whispered around the offices. Dorryn still thinks Bryn will come here. That's why he has not sent us home. We have to get out and find Eeryn."

"Any ideas about how we do that?"

"Take this." She reached across Vulryn and dropped a neatly folded kerchief. "Return it to me in an hour,"

Faryn turned and motioned for the guards. One knocked out his pipe against a nearby tree trunk; tapped his fellow on the shoulder and headed her way.

"I'm ready to return to my room," she said. "Could you help me back. My friend wishes to sit a while longer."

The guard gave her his arm and Vulryn watched her hobble across the garden. He smiled at her struggles before reaching into his tunic and drawing out his pipe. He extended the pouch to the remaining guard who accepted with a smile. While they smoked in silence, Vulryn let his mind wander to the future he was building in his mind for himself, Maryn, and their children.

The wreath of smoke shielding him from the present trouble cleared as the embers in his pipe died. Time for Faryn's game to begin. Vulryn tapped out his pipe. He bent forward, discovered a kerchief, and held it up for his companion.

"Oh my," he said. "Faryn dropped her kerchief. Do you mind following me to return it?"

"I go where you do," he answered with a shrug.

After a brief debate with the guard at Faryn's door, Vulryn was admitted with a warning to keep the visit short. He found Faryn in bed covers pulled to her beak.

"Get in here" she whispered as he started to back out of the door.

"Ma'am, I brought your kerchief." Vulryn dangled the cloth before her face.

"Oh, thank you," she said as the door closed behind Vulryn."

A quick smile lit her face. Faryn threw back the blankets. She was dressed in the uniform of an embassy guard.

"We're going."

Faryn pulled a cloak from a chest drawer and threw it at him. Vulryn managed to get his shoulders inside the garment. There was no way it was going to wrap around his bulk. He gave her a sheepish smile and a wink. Faryn was not finished with her surprise. Reaching back into the chest she hauled out a length of rope. She tied one end to the railing of her balcony and threw the other end over the side.

"You first," she said.

Vulryn gave the rope a couple of stout tugs. "Are you sure about this?"

"Get going," she told him.

He closed his eyes and slipped over the railing. When the rope held, he opened his eyes again and began to work his way to the ground. He had to stifle a scream when a hand touched his leg. He looked down between his arms to see the guard he was smoking with earlier holding the end of the rope. The guard held a finger to his beak signaling for quiet. Faryn was already making her way down. The guard helped her to the ground, and she motioned Vulryn toward the barracks. Halfway across the grounds, she changed direction. They took shelter in the shadow of the wall while the guard checked the activity at the gate. He waved a hand at Faryn.

"Okay," she whispered. "Keep your head down."

As she passed, she laid a hand on the guard's arm and mouthed a "thank you" before slipping through the gate. Vulryn followed her onto the street. This female was nothing if not resourceful. He would have to remind himself not to underestimate her. Faryn led the way down ever narrowing streets weaving from street to street. Vulryn thought they were headed north but with all the twists and turns, he could not be sure. Eventually, they came to a tangle of passageways barely wide enough for foot traffic. Vulryn noticed she made frequent checks of the doors and roofs.

Please Creator, don't let her be lost, he prayed to himself.

As if in answer to prayer, a gasp caught in Faryn's throat. She pulled him into a doorway. The entry hid enough of him that he remained unseen by a group of humans passing on a crossing path. They made their way to the end of the passage and made one more right turn. Faryn stopped to study the way ahead. Something moved above one of the doors in the middle of the block. She nodded and moved toward it.

Candlelight spilled through the open door. It was followed closely by the smell of Valirian smoke and beer. Vulryn was suddenly homesick. Faryn straightened her clothes and walked inside as though she belonged there. He stopped to see what was above the door that first caught her eye. A large black bird was perched on the remnants of an old sign post suspended above the door. The raven eyed the big blacksmith warily before making a loud croaking sound. Vulryn stabbed a single finger in the bird's direction. Faryn stopped just inside to look around.

The Raven and Owl was a single room of tightly packed tables and chairs. While furnishings looked to be the cast offs of seedy dives, the bar itself was a wonder of polished bouja wood. It occupied an entire wall to the right of the door. Bottles of every shape and color crammed the shelves in front of three large mirrors. A blue haze hung above the patrons wedged into the tables. The long bar was packed elbow to elbow. The crowd included every species know to Tettias but was dominated by Valir. A table in the far corner was an exception. It was occupied by a double ring of a wolf-like species known as Wolven. There did not appear to be an empty seat anywhere in the place. Bar maids twirled this way and that swinging trays over the heads of seated customers in a spinning dance between the bar and the tables.

"Nice place," Vulryn said his hand resting on the hilt of his dagger.

Faryn waved for him to follow. She sidestepped a neat weaving pattern through the crowd that Vulryn found impossible.

He bulled a path behind her to complaints from both sides of the path. Their destination soon became obvious. In one corner sat a thin figure nearly swallowed up by a cloak of leaves. A seer for sure; Eeryn by conjecture. Those sitting with the seer rose and disappeared out a nearby door.

"Faryn Kel, granddaughter of both my old friend and my old enemy," the cloaked figure said without looking up. "I trust that I wasn't too hard to find. Who is this giant who follows you?"

"This is Vulryn the blacksmith of Vix," she said.

"Sit, my friends," Eeryn pointed to a pair of empty chairs. "Tell me why you have stolen, lied, and defied the High Council to come see me."

CHAPTER 22

Vulryn wedged himself into a chair. Faryn took the seat next to the seer. Eeryn wasn't as old as her grandfather, but he had the reputation of being Coryn's equal. A reputation quickly on the way to being discredited, in her eyes, by his cocksure attitude. He had rubbed shoulders with human royalty, and it showed. She hoped he was as full of information as he was of himself.

"We are looking for a young Valir," she said. "He was sent to you with a message from my grandfather."

"Does this Valir have a name?" Eeryn answered through an exhaled cloud of smoke.

"He does." Faryn waved the smoke away from her blazing eyes. "But, as my grandfather defied the Council to send him, you can use your powers to discern it. Has he found you?"

A smile tugged at the edges of his beak and spread over his face, lighting his eyes. Eeryn lay down his pipe and forsook the posture shared by the drunken and the broken in the bar. He sat upright and shook the cloak from his shoulders.

"Ah," he said with a chuckle. "I see you share the fire of both your grandfathers. Well done. I am Eeryn, son of Enoryn.

She took his offered hand. His face looked younger and his eyes brighter somehow.

"I have a certain image to uphold," he explained. "Down and out prophet banned from the palace and all that. I have not seen your messenger. However, I would still like to know his name."

"Bryn Bou," she replied.

"The son of Byryn," he cut her short. "It must be some message to send the son of a Councilor. You must not tell anyone else his name. Do you understand? The army is looking for him. They say he is involved in the massacre of humans."

"The villages," Faryn said. "The Ambassador told us about that. Surely you don't believe Bryn was responsible?"

"If it's any consolation," Eeryn said. "No, I don't believe Bryn is involved. However, you must remember that very few people care what I believe."

A low croaking call rolled through the pub's open door followed by flapping wings. The raven skimmed over the heads of ducking, dodging patrons. Faryn sought shelter behind the seer. Vulryn's arms flew from his sides trying to keep from tipping his chair as the bird landed in the middle of the table. The seer held out his arm and the raven jumped from the table onto the offered perch. A series of croaks accompanied by twists and turns of the bird's head removed the smile from the seer's face. With a quick upward thrust of his arm, he launched the raven which returned the way it had come.

"Quickly," Eeryn said. "We have to get out of here. This way."

Turning over the table and chairs in his haste the blacksmith followed Faryn without hesitation. Eeryn pushed through the crowd toward an exit near the rear of the building. Customers parted to make way. All, that is, except a large, heavily muscled Wolven. The seer hit the wolf-like creature's body and stumbled back into Faryn. Vulryn caught them both in one arm. and deposited them behind him. He stepped forward with a smooth twist of his body and sent a huge right hand into the Wolven's face. The wolf staggered, blood streaming from his lips. A nearby table kept him from going to the floor. The wolf steadied himself and slowly advanced on Vulryn.

"I'll kill you for that bird man," the Woven growled. Sharp claws shot from its fingers.

"No time for that," Vulryn said.

The blacksmith caught the advancing wolf by the throat and lifted him from the floor. Claws raked Vulryn's back, but his free hand found the Wolven's shirt just above the waist. Vulryn threw the creature over a table of stunned humans into the bottles lined up behind the bar. A cloud of shattered glass and liquor materialized behind the Wolven's sudden stop. The smell of alcohol in the room tripled. The bartender pulled his club from under the bar, but it was too late. Eeryn and his guests were gone.

The seer led the way across a narrow alley behind the pub and into a cleft between two of the adjacent buildings. Vulryn turned sideways to negotiate the cramped space that gave out onto a street a couple hundred feet beyond. Eeryn turned left keeping to the shadows. A mile further on he ducked inside a dark building and closed the door behind them. The dark within was complete. Faryn could feel Vulryn at her side but could not see him. She waved a hand before her eyes—nothing. No, that wasn't quite right, there was something, a presence was in the room with them.

"Vulryn," she whispered.

"I feel it," he whispered back.

A familiar low croak was followed by the flare of a match. Eeryn lit a candle and placed it on a small table. The raven flapped through the dark to land on the back of a tall wooden chair.

"Want to tell us what that was all about?" Vulryn said.

"Thanks to you my friend," Eeryn replied. "We got out of there seconds before the army raided the place. My guess is that they were looking Bryn Bou. However, they are just as likely hunting the two of you. I thought it best not to hang around and find out."

The raven uttered another of its croaking calls.

"Yes." Eeryn stroked the black bird's head. "You helped too my friend."

The raven bounced into the air and flapped its wings.

"Yes, I know," Eeryn said. "It's not safe here, so we mustn't stay long. I want to check the valiant blacksmith's wounds before we move on."

"It's nothing," Vulryn protested, but allowed himself to be turned around and inspected.

Four deep gouges ran between his wings. Two small lacerations marked the skin of his right shoulder. The blood had dried quickly on all the wounds. Eeryn ran practiced fingers over the blacksmith's skin.

"You'll heal well enough," he said. "Now we had better—"

The seer stopped mid-sentence and cocked an ear toward the street. The raven did the same. Voices in sharp, clipped commands were moving closer. Eeryn picked up the candle and led the others through a maze of dusty rooms and short hallways. He slipped into a room near the rear of the building. In the dim light Faryn could make out a broken-down bed with a bare mattress next to a worn chest of drawers. Eeryn stood listening for a moment before moving to the far corner of the room. He knelt and held a finger to his beak for quiet. Gingerly, he pried open a door concealed in the planking and motioned Faryn into the space below. The blacksmith squeezed himself through the opening and the seer followed.

Beneath the floor was a room with walls of earth furnished with a table and two chairs. A pitcher of clear liquid flanked by a pair of wooden mugs sat in the middle of the table. The room was just large enough for the table and the three of them. Vulryn took up a seat on the floor; wincing as he propped his back against the wall.

Somewhere overhead hinges protested. Eeryn blew out the candle and darkness swallowed them. Heavy boots moved across the floor above them. Faryn found the still blackness an uncertain refuge from the danger above. She told herself that the humans wouldn't dare harm her because she was the granddaughter of a Valirian High Councilor. It was a lie she no longer believed. She had stolen a diplomatic pouch and crossed the border under false pretenses. She had escaped house arrest and deportation. Although her crimes were more against her homeland than Shiloh, she didn't think that would make much difference to the soldiers searching for them.

Muffled voices directly above them sent a shiver down her spine. Footsteps moved in separate directions. They were searching the room above. The bed was dragged away from its place. They were searching the floor, tapping random places, searching for a hidden space. Footsteps stopped directly overhead. Boot heels stomped on the door; stopped and began again. In the dark, no one moved; no one breathed.

"Come on, Slick," a voice called from above. "They're not here."

"But, Sarge," Slick protested. "I think..."

"You're not paid to think," Sarge snapped. "Now, move it."

Below the receding footsteps, breathing began again. After a few moments of silence in the building, Eeryn lit his candle. He held a palm up. Faryn and Vulryn waited. A sharp rapping sounded on the floor above. Faryn gasped. Eeryn smiled at her and stood to open the door. The raven was perched on the bed. It watched them climb up through the floor.

"Now," said the seer. "What to do with the two of you."

CHAPTER 23

They would reach Shiloh soon, not soon enough to suit Bryn, but the end was in sight. They had been traveling downhill for days. According to One Eye, the city was on a plain not far beyond these hills.

After depositing the Gotebo refugees in Manitou, they spent the next two days tramping up and down rolling hills. One Eye thought avoiding the roads and human contact was unnecessary. He didn't think many soldiers would be committed to looking for them, they were old news. Bryn wasn't willing to take unnecessary chances this close to their goal.

The sun was settling with a golden glow into the treetops behind them. To prevent being silhouetted against the sky, they kept below the crest of the hill, watching the village from the cover of huckleberry vines. They needed water. A hot meal would be a welcome relief. They scanned the village while weighing the risks of entering it ran through their minds.

Nestled in the trough between two hills, terra cotta tile and redwood shingled rooftops radiated from a central square. A fountain bubbling in the square was a powerful lure.

"We'll wait until dark," Bryn said.

One Eye nodded in silent agreement and crawled back through the huckleberries into the shelter of a tall oak. He climbed to a wide fork in the trunk and closed his eyes. It was still two hours until dark. Bryn found a comfortable spot in an adjacent tree. He thought One Eye had a real talent for sleep. He, on the other hand, found sleep increasingly elusive. Once, he mentioned the dreams that haunted him to his companion. One Eye told him that such dreams were the price he paid for having a conscience.

Bryn shrugged off the assessment. There were worse things than having a conscience. He let his mind wander to the problem of finding Eeryn when they reached Shiloh. The tales he heard of the size of the city defied his imagination. Coryn hinted that Eeryn might find him. He hoped it would be that simple.

Twilight crept toward them and the dark followed. There would be a late rising moon. Bryn tapped his friend on the shoulder and with a jerk of his head in the direction of the village, dropped from the tree. One Eye did the same. They moved silently among the trees using the tangle of undergrowth for cover. When that played out, they abandoned any pretext of stealth. Moving onto the road they became two wearying travelers looking for a place to spend the night.

The square was deserted. Bryn saw a few fires burning inside homes, but the town was dark and empty. They passed two pubs that were closed. That seemed odd for humans. So too did the lack of foot traffic around the town. One Eye sat beside the well. Bryn drew up the bucket and filled their water bags.

"Let's get out of here," One Eye said after a drink of water. "It's too quiet. It's giving me the creeps."

"Okay," Bryn agreed. "We'll find a place to make camp on the other side of town."

They found a street leading east that they hoped would join the highway outside of the town. Away from the square, a few people scurried by in the dark. None of them paid much attention to the hooded strangers. One Eye suddenly stopped. He cocked his head straining to hear. A moment later Bryn heard it too. Tramping feet moving in unison toward them.

Soldiers.

They ducked into the shadow between two dark houses and knelt behind a stack of firewood. Bryn peered over One Eye's shoulder to catch a glimpse as troops passed. He counted at least a dozen. A short while later, he heard the officer call a halt.

"In the square," One Eye whispered to him pointing back the way they had come.

Bryn followed him moving away from the soldiers. It was not long until a much different sound drew their attention, one they expected and appreciated—music. The sound was coming from an isle of light on the edge of town. It had to be a highway tavern. There was life in this place after all.

The sign above the door declared this oasis of merriment was the Travelers Rest. Bryn chanced a look in one of the windows.

There were plenty of travelers inside. However, only one appeared to be resting. A smallish man sat face down at the far end of the bar. Bryn turned to One Eye, but the old smuggler was already stepping through the doorway.

"Let's go in," Bryn said.

He nodded to himself and headed for the door. A cloud of blue smoke welcomed him. He could feel the beat of the music on his skin. To his left, couples gyrated on a wooden dance floor. Beyond them the band rocked on about the value of three steps. Bryn found that especially fitting. One Eye absentmindedly bumped into one of the dancers drawing a sour look. He smiled and continued on to take a position at the bar near the resting patron. He motioned Bryn over. Bryn joined him at the bar where beer magically appeared.

"I don't mean to be a drudge," Bryn said. "But don't we need money for this?"

Just below the top of the bar, One Eye dangled a small pouch. Seems the smuggler was also a talented pick pocket. He smiled at Bryn's surprise and took a long pull on the drink in his hand. Bryn tossed his hood back on his shoulders. The move caught the barman's attention. He stepped close pretending to wipe up a spill.

"Put that back up," he whispered to Bryn. "I don't care who drinks here. Money is all the same to me, but your kind ain't good for business right now. I don't want any trouble. Drink that and get out of here."

"What? Right now?" One Eye asked.

"Damn right, right now. Have you been hiding under a rock?" the barman asked. "Valirian smugglers wiped out two villages back up the road. They would probably still be at it if the army hadn't caught them."

"What villages?" Bryn asked, pulling his hood back in place. "Where?"

"Place called Gotebo," he answered. "Another one called Manitou."

"That's a lie," Bryn said. "We were just—"

One Eye was hauling him for the doorway before he could say more. Bryn resisted until his words echoed in his mind, then pushed ahead of his partner.

"Stop them!" the barman shouted.

He had a strong voice, but not strong enough to overcome the band. Unfortunately for Bryn and One Eye, their sudden bolting for the door and the barman's gestures were enough for a pair of very large men sitting near the door. They filled the doorway with a speed and agility men that large should not possess. Bryn pulled up short while One Eye turned to face the advancing barman who had armed himself with a club. The appearance of One Eye's dagger slowed the barman's advance.

The music stopped. Every eye in the bar was fixed on them. This wasn't good. The room felt too small and was rapidly shrinking. One of the big men guarding the door reached for Bryn. The man's eyes grew wide, his hand froze in midair.

"That's right," the small man said. "Everyone just stand still."

"I'll be damned," One Eye said.

"This way." Wynn motioned for them to follow.

One Eye pulled Bryn's cloak. They backed out of the bar followed closely by their savior.

The flickering string of lights winding its way down the hill opposite them began to slow. Midway down the slope, the lights came together. A circle flame formed on the hillside. Then, one by one the lights started back up the hill. Bryn smiled at One Eye, who returned a knowing smile of his own.

"Officially, it's too dark to track us any further," One Eye said. "That's what they will tell their superiors anyway."

"Unofficially?" Bryn asked. "How did you know?"

"We're armed," One Eye said. "It's dark and they could easily be picked off one by one. Men are not cowards, neither are they stupid."

"Okay," Bryn said. "But you said they would give up when they reached Manitou."

"They couldn't," Wynn spoke up. "Not after what happened. They have orders to kill you both."

Bryn and One Eye stared at him. Their blank expressions confirmed Wynn's suspicions.

"You don't know, do you?" he said. "You really don't know."

"Know what?" One Eye snapped at him.

"The day you left us at Manitou," Wynn began. "Soldiers came, lots of soldiers. They tortured people there until they told them where Iko and the others were hiding. The soldiers rounded up everyone; those from Gotebo and the villagers in Manitou, herded them into the center of the town and killed them all. Then, they burned the village. I was on my way to join you. I saw the smoke and turned back, but there was nothing left."

"What's that have to do with us?" Bryn asked.

"The army is saying renegade Valir smugglers did the killing," Wynn explained. "The heads of your friends that were still held by the column are already on the way to Shiloh. Now, the army wants yours."

Bryn and One Eye sat in stunned silence. The story was absurd, but Bryn had to admit it played to human prejudice. From the stories he had heard, wanton slaughter by outlanders was delicious fodder for human consumption. True the Valir had killed men, but soldiers, not innocents. That wouldn't matter now. No one would ever hear it. The army obviously did not plan on there being any story but their own. Bryn noticed the tear on Wynn's cheek.

"It's not your fault," he told the boy. "You couldn't have stopped what happened."

"I could have died with my people," Wynn said.

"Pardon me for being a practical fellow," One Eye said. "But, to what end? Your dying would not have saved them. It wouldn't have done you a great deal of good either."

"He's right," Bryn added. "But by living, you saved us tonight."

"We'll fight on together," One Eye offered. "Who knows you may still get a chance to die."

"Any idea where we are?" Bryn asked.

"None," One Eye said.

Wynn shook his head.

"I'm not sure which direction we've been running," Bryn confessed.

"Away," One Eye said. He slid from his perch to the ground where he stretched out with his hands locked behind his head.

Bryn and Wynn dropped to the ground to join him. Bryn bit back the urge to tell One Eye it wasn't nap time. They needed to think, not argue. They sat in silence studying the landscape. It was still the same coastal forest of firs, oak and laurel they traveled through all day. The shape of the land held no clues. No lights shone in the distance. There was nothing but a dark forest. The idea of waiting for dawn ate at Bryn's gut like acid. As bad as that was, the idea of wandering around aimlessly in the dark was worse.

"We go that way," One Eye suddenly announced. He pointed over Bryn's shoulder. "I've been watching the moon. It's moving this direction; that's west. We put it to our backs. Let's go."

Choosing the right direction was not their greatest challenge. Traveling at night was dangerous. Moving itself was dangerous. Obstacles hidden in the dark could break a leg. If they avoided physical injury, without a fixed landmark, there was still the natural tendency to wander in a circle. They could travel all night and go nowhere. The heavily forested hills provided only occasional glimpses of the moon, making for slow going and increasing the chance of getting lost all over again. However, staying in one place was deadly. They had to keep moving. Daylight would power the human's technical wonders. Disruptors, hovercraft, and communicators would give their pursuers a huge advantage, especially now that they had the scent.

Moving air rushed along Bryn's cheek. Ahead, an overhead branch dipped. Bryn rolled his eyes up searching for whatever was moving in the dark. A pair of large eyes dropped down from the branch to meet his.

"Oto?" he said.

The owl hopped onto Bryn's shoulder, giving them eyes in the dark. He guided the trio through the trees at a steady pace. For the moment, no one was actively pursuing them, nevertheless a sense of urgency drove them on. They stopped only when exhausted and returned to the trail when they could force their bodies to stand again.

The eastern horizon melted through a deep indigo to a dusty blue. Bryn's legs were on fire. He dropped down against the trunk of a tall pine, and the others followed. It took a few minutes before they became aware of the wet briny tang hanging in the air. They were near the coast. Oto flew to the top of the tree. A moment later he lit upon Bryn's shoulder.

"Get some rest," he whispered. "What is ahead is far more deadly than what is behind. Take a look through those bushes."

Bryn crawled through a thick mass of huckleberry bushes to find himself on the edge of a steep cliff. Below him a wide highway stretched to the walls of a city that spread across the horizon seemingly as vast as the sea that lay beyond. At the center of the city, like a jewel in a field of azure, an enormous golden dome glistened in the rising sun.

Shiloh. At last.

CHAPTER 24

One Eye crawled through the vines to lay beside Bryn. Wynn materialized on his other side a minute later. The spectacle of a new day dawning behind the city held them captive. The sky burning with orange, red, and gold was reflected in the distant sea. The dome of the temple sparkled in the sun casting brilliant kaleidoscopic images on the palace towers. The city was still a day's journey away, but the sight lifted their dampened spirits and tired bodies. As the sun climbed higher, their wonder faded into thoughts of troubles ahead. The others followed Bryn's gaze over the edge of the precipice.

"Long way down," Wynn said.

"Any ideas?" Bryn asked.

"Two," One Eye answered. "And neither is a good one."

"Let's hear them anyway," Bryn said.

"We climb down," One Eye began. "In which case, we risk a fall and die in the sudden stop at the bottom. Two, we make our way to the highway and march into the city like we haven't got a care in the world."

"Which gets us arrested and hanged or worse," Wynn finished for him.

"Right," One Eye agreed. He gave Bryn a pat on the shoulder. "Show us that determined will to reach Shiloh you possess."

"Let's take a walk," Bryn said.

***

Inside the city walls another trio struggled with a decision. Following Faryn's escape, the Valirian Embassy became a fortress under siege. The soldiers of King Zedek lined the street outside the walls. Inside, guards, hands on their weapons, stood tall behind iron bars. Their bravado was real. Though outnumbered, they would die if the men outside tried to storm the gates. No one inside or out doubted that. From across the street, two figures watched the posturing of the soldiers on both sides of the wall.

"Trust me on this," Eeryn said with a sly smile. "I am a prophet, you know. I have a feeling that going back to the embassy is no longer an option."

"You really think so?" Faryn gibed.

"Oh, yeah, almost certain," Eeryn answered. "Come, I have one last idea."

They moved away from the window and down the stairs where Vulryn waited. The story was written on their long faces. Faryn shook her head and motioned him to follow them into the parlor.

The house belonged to a man named Roque, an old friend of the seer. Rich fabrics of blue covered carved chairs grouped for quiet conversation. Gold and blue draperies hung from a series of tall windows that opened onto the wide avenue just beyond. Roque had taken care to close the drapes and provide candlelight.

"What will you do?" Roque asked.

Eeryn, aware of the eyes on him, took a long, deep breath. Until now, this had been a little game of cat and mouse. Eeryn knew the soldiers had no chance of finding him in this city. He had been dodging them for two years with the aid of friends like Roque who were more loyal to him than their own king. Faryn and Vulryn presented a logistical problem. Every Valir and human in the city would be looking for the missing granddaughter of a member of Valir's High Council. If that weren't problem enough, she was accompanied by a giant and neither were the kind to sit by and do nothing. Their very presence here in Shiloh was testament to that.

Desperate times call for desperate measures.

"I'm going to see the prince," Eeryn said at last. "Can you hide us until tonight, my friend?"

"Of course," Roque answered. "My home is yours."

"Just so we're clear," Eeryn said, turning to the others. "You two will stay inside and out of sight until I tell you to do otherwise. I must have your word on that."

***

Shielded by a stand of pines, Bryn watched the surge of men and species from the outer kingdoms move along the highway. This was the King's Highway, the thoroughfare into Shiloh. The road lacked just one thing—Valir. He and One Eye were going to stand out no matter how they tried to avoid it.

So much for hiding in plain sight.

The thought of stepping out of the trees made Bryn cringe. A small detail of soldiers, laughing and joking, passed by, seemingly oblivious to their fellow travelers. Bryn moved back further into the trees and watched until they disappeared. Anger flashed in him.

Valir do not cower in the shadows.

"Well, boys," he said. "Shall we go?"

The little band of felons stepped out onto the highway. No shouts of alarm were raised. No soldiers charged toward them. One or two heads turned slightly before ignoring the newcomers altogether. As they walked on, Bryn began to relax. He had not completely banished the cold finger of fear and realized he was slouching in a vain attempt to hide. He quickly squared his shoulders. He hoped the others hadn't seen his fear. He shook the lingering remnants away and picked up his pace.

The walls of the city seemed to grow as the road leveled out onto a plain. Small businesses crowded the highway pushing back the woodlands and the fields. Farmers with makeshift stalls appeared first. Melons, apples, wild berries, and vegetables of every sort decorated the beds of hand carts and small wagons. Legions of ragged children dodged in and out among the travelers hawking their parents' wares and picking pockets.

A family of Wolven sold ironware beneath a blazing red awning that stretched from the top of their wagon. Nearby a human woman nursed twins as her man offered passersby the "finest hemp rope in the kingdom." Opposite them a cloven footed Orrus with powerful arms and tawny fur beneath its dark mane showed his wheat and corn to a dwarf with a single eye in the middle of his forehead. Bryn punched One Eye on the shoulder and pointed out the dwarf.

"Friend of yours?" he asked.

"Very funny," One Eye said and pointed down the road. "Now, that is interesting."

Bryn eyes followed his friend's finger. He was pretty sure he knew what had attracted his partner's attention. A second later, he saw it; a low-slung building of rough cut pine logs set back from the road. In front of the building a mismatched collection of unoccupied tables and chairs called travelers to stop, rest, and drink.

"That didn't go so well the last time," Bryn reminded him.

"All the more reason to try again," One Eye shot back. "You're not a quitter, are you?"

"No," said Bryn. "I'm not dumb enough to be baited either, but I am thirsty."

One Eye beamed and slapped him on the back. "You have potential, son."

"We stay outside though," Bryn shouted after him, jogging to catch up.

They sat at the table furthest from the road on the east side of the inn just in case they needed to make another quick getaway. The pub door was open to the warm day. There was no sign above the door, only the carved image of a large black bird. No music or barmaid chanced to venture outside. Bryn decided the tavern was not yet open for business. One Eye did not give up so easily. He disappeared inside emerging moments later with a scarlet crested Valir maiden of impressive proportions.

"Look what I found," he said. "This is Elryn. Her father owns the place."

"Please, come inside," she said.

Without waiting for Bryn's reply, One Eye caught her by the hand and started for the door with the giggling female in tow. Wynn and Bryn exchanged glances, shrugged, and followed One Eye inside. The pub was empty saved for a short, bowlegged Valir in a spotless white apron who came around the bar to greet them.

"Jaryn, son of Eldryn," he stretched out a hand to Bryn.

"Bryn Bou, son of...," he didn't finish.

"It's alright here," the barman said. "But be careful among men. I'm glad to see you whoever you are."

"How is it a Valir runs a pub on the king's highway?" Bryn asked. "Not many of our kind travel through here."

"None of our kind," Jaryn corrected him. "Not for a long time."

"It looks like business is off today," Bryn said.

"I like this kid," he said with a wink at One Eye. "Doesn't miss trick."

Jaryn pointed them to the bar and took up his place behind it. He poured tall glasses of beer from the tap and set it before them. Bryn sipped, started to set down his glass, and returned for a second taste. The dark liquid was cold and smacked faintly of boubouja, a little taste of home for weary travelers. The barman smiled and gave Bryn a knowing wink.

"Now that we've discussed my folly," Jaryn said. "Let's talk about you. What sort of foolishness has brought you to Shiloh?"

"What makes you think us foolish?" Bryn said.

"You don't clack when you walk," Jaryn replied.

Bryn gave One Eye a puzzled look. The smuggler shook his head. Wynn shrugged. Bryn turned his eyes back to the barman.

"You either have balls of iron," he explained. "Or you're the world's biggest fools. The entire king's army is looking for you and you're marching straight down the king's highway. Since I didn't hear them clack together, well..."

One Eye exploded with laughter sending beer from his nostrils. Wynn fell on the floor holding his stomach and roaring with laughter. Bryn smiled and flushed for a moment.

"Clack, clack," he said, gesturing at his crotch.

Jaryn couldn't hold back. He burst into laughter of his own. Bryn joined in. It was one of those golden moments when all the cares of the world are rolled back. Like all such moments, this one ended with a crash. A long shadow fell over the bar. Silhouetted in the doorway stood a large man with a weapon in his hand.

CHAPTER 25

The old barman was fast. His dagger was in his hand and on its way before Bryn could turn to face the threat. Unfortunately, for Jaryn the man in the door had reflexes just as quick. Even as the dagger buried itself in his chest, his finger closed on the trigger of his disrupter. The air sizzled. Bryn smelled ozone. Jaryn spun with the force of the impact and landed face down behind the bar twitching.

Bryn caught the gasping human by the neck and threw him inside the bar. Blood sprayed from the soldier's chest enveloping Bryn in a red mist. It was too late to escape. The soldiers outside were converging on the door. Bryn turned to warn One Eye.

The smuggler was already moving out the back door, bow in hand and Wynn at his heels. Elryn took a step toward her father. Wynn grabbed her collar and dragged her out the door. The soldiers covering the rear entrance were still moving into position when One Eye kicked open the door. His first shot caught one of the soldiers in the neck. As the soldier went down, One Eye heard the snap of Wynn's bow over his left shoulder. An arrow sprouted from a soldier's abdomen. The soldier dropped his disrupter, clutched his bleeding belly, and staggered away. One Eye sent a second arrow that hit the man between the shoulder blades. He went down in a heap.

One Eye led them out of the pub at a run. No one looked back until they reached the safety of the woods. The smuggler's heart sank. Bryn was nowhere in sight.

Bryn dropped down beside the barman. A quick glance told him there was no saving Jaryn. Soldiers burst through the door. It was too late to run. Bryn threw his bow over the bar and stood with his hands held high. The soldiers crowded around him. One greeted him with the blunt end of a disrupter to the right side of his head.

Two men dragged Jaryn's body from the pub. His blood mixed with the dirt leaving a damp trail leading from the tavern. The blackness slowly receded from Bryn's head. It was replaced with a dull roar that throbbed with his pulse. He looked up at the soldiers through the slit that was his right eye. He could hear glass breaking inside the pub.

Moments later, he saw a soldier with a torch pass by. A huge whoosh was followed by waves of heat that rolled across his face. Rough hands stripped him of his weapons and yanked him to his feet. The world began to spin, and darkness closed in again. Somehow his legs held. The same could not be said for his stomach. Beer and breakfast spewed from him.

Bryn's arms were pulled behind him where ropes bit into his wrists. He suppressed the instinct to fight back. He slowed his breathing and swallowed the rage building inside him. He closed his eyes withdrawing from the destructive edge of his emotions.

Save it for a fight you can win, he told himself.

As he was led to a waiting transport, each step brought a strange peace. The feeling was like nothing he had experienced before. The heat of outrage succumbed to cold, hard determination. He could not help Jaryn, but he would live to deliver his message and see havoc wrecked upon his enemies.

A crowd gathered to watch the bloodied Bryn as he was led from the tavern. Whispered words traveled, mouth to ear, through the watchers. This is the one responsible for the Manitou Massacre. Bryn was stuffed into a six foot by four-foot metal cage atop a wagon. His hands were fastened to an O ring bolted to the floor forcing him into a slumped, posture of defeat.

Satisfied the bonds were secure, the soldiers backed out of the cage. The wagon, pulled by a single ceros, began lumbering down the highway drawing a growing crowd in its wake. Anticipation of a gruesome spectacle at the end of their journey seemed to lighten the mood of the travelers. Laughter and dancing chased after Bryn's misery.

One Eye and company watched flames climb up the walls of the tavern and through the roof. The sight brought a fresh round of tears from Elryn. One Eye knew from experience that age was no barrier against the pain of being orphaned and homeless. Elryn would replace the pain with something. Revenge was the most likely replacement. On her own, that course would get her killed. One Eye decided to channel her pain. He decided to take her with them.

The decision turned out to be a good one. As the tears ebbed away, the strength he knew was buried inside emerged from her. Her steps grew stronger, more determined. Best of all, she knew a way through the woods and into the city of Shiloh. As One Eye suspected, Jaryn didn't get all his supplies from legitimate sources. Elryn knew not only the routes; she knew his contacts including a bar owner in the city who liked to brag about the seer that frequented his establishment. Beautiful, resourceful, and mad as hell at mankind; he liked the combination. Shiloh awaited.

They reached the city walls as the sun set behind them. Elryn offered a subdued wave to a couple of the soldiers on duty who pretended not to see the gesture or the trio of strangers passing through the gate. The houses near the city walls leaned against one another for support. The constant attacks of salt air long ago convinced the peeling paint to abandon the rotten wood. The creatures shuffling along the filthy streets wore matching suits of neglect. They clung to life buoyed by the knowledge that they lived inside the walls. Outside of the city wall, miserable wretches wiped at flowing sores, dragged twisted limbs, and begged at the gates for their continued existence.

Elryn led them through a maze of streets without misstep. She turned down a dark street where they splashed through puddles in the cobblestone until they came to an open door. The smell of stale beer, smoke, and unwashed patrons drifted to them. On a beam with no sign a raven perched above the door. Elryn led them inside.

One Eye ignored his guide's suggestion that he wait at the door. He waded through the crowd with Wynn to belly up to the bar. The barman cast a sidelong glance at One Eye's choice of companions. The barman's we-don't-like-his-kind look was not lost on One Eye. The smuggler let his hand drop to the hilt of his dagger as he returned the barman's look. Two pints of beer promptly appeared, and the barman retreated. Elryn waved the barman to the far end of the bar and more congenial conversation. Their huddle broke up quickly and Elryn moved down the bar to join the others.

"Eeryn hasn't been here in a couple of days," she said. "He was last seen with an attractive young female with a giant bodyguard. The bodyguard got into a scuffle with that big Wolven over in the corner. The barman doesn't know what the fight was about, but Eeryn hasn't been in since."

"Does he have any idea where Eeryn might be now?" One Eye asked.

"No, but there's an embassy guard who frequents the place who might know."

"Is he here now?" One Eye looked around the room.

"Not yet, but the barman expects him soon."

"Well, I suppose there are worse places to wait," One Eye pointed to a table. "Shall we?"

They had not been seated long when the tall Wolven the barman had pointed out pressed through the crowd to their table. One Eye saw him coming and pushed a chair out for him.

"Sit, my friend," he told the Wolven. "What can we do for you?"

"Name's Cross," the Wolven said. "We'll see about being friends later."

"Okay, Cross. What's on your mind?"

"I haven't seen you around before," he nodded toward Elryn. "I was wondering just what are you doing here with her?

"If you must know," One Eye said. "She asked us along."

"If you were there when her father died," Cross leaned closer. "You need to keep the hell out of here. You'll bring the army down on everyone."

"We're looking for a friend," One Eye replied. "Help us and we're on our way."

"You can go back to your business now, Cross," a voice from behind One Eye said. "I'll help them from here."

Cross' lips curled back revealing sharp canines. A low growl rumbled in his throat, but he said nothing. Cross slowly rose from his seat and backed away. The embassy guard, Elvryn, dropped down in the vacant seat.

"Cross is a hothead, but he's okay," Elvryn said. "Hello, Elryn. Sorry to hear about your father. I was told you were looking for me."

The mention of her father brought fresh tears to her eyes. She quickly wiped them away with the back of her hand.

"We must find Eeryn," she said.

"He's sort of expecting us," One Eye added.

"So are Zett's soldiers," Elvryn replied. "Cross was right about that. Zett has your friend, and he wants to complete the set."

"So, Bryn's still alive?" One Eye asked.

"Yes, but not for long. Tomorrow he is to ride the wheel to the chop block." Elvryn motioned them closer. "If you were to loiter near the old slaughterhouse about a mile from here, perhaps you would stumble upon the one you seek. Take Cross' advice and get out of here."

Elvryn left them for the bar without another word. One Eye gave a quick nod toward Cross as he got up to leave.

CHAPTER 26

The steady thumping of the cart's wooden wheels hammered up Bryn's spine and reverberated inside his wounded head.

Human prison carts were designed to inflict pain. Floor mounted chains kept the prisoner slumped over. The screaming pain this posture produced was intensified by jolts of fresh agony as the cart's wheels pounded over uneven roadways and delivered every bump to the base of the passenger's spine. To ensure sufficient pain was delivered, the wheels were made slightly out of round. After what seemed an eternity, Bryn Bou's thumping torture came to a halt. Forcing his head up against the knotted muscles in his shoulders, he could see the walls of Shiloh looming in the distance.

Three soldiers wearing gold braid barred the road. The leader of the group approached the soldier leading the cart while the other two chased away the crowd. The officer and the driver entered into an animated discussion. Bryn could not make out what they were saying but there was vigorous head shaking and pointing in opposing directions. The driver soon threw up his hands and steered the wagon off the highway. The cart bounced through a narrow gap between a rug merchant and tobacco shop into a clearing ringed with soldiers.

Rolling over potholes had made Bryn's body throb with pain. Bouncing across the open field behind the shops was sheer torture. Bryn clamped his hands against the sides of his head in a vain attempt to ward off the lightning bolts shooting into his brain. About twenty yards into the clearing, they came to a merciful stop. The guards were pitching camp.

"I don't see what difference it makes," one of the soldiers groused. "Whether we throw him in the dungeon now or in the morning."

"Yeah," said a tall, thin man wearing corporal strips. "I could be snuggling up against my wife in my own bed tonight. How come we got to wait until morning anyhow?"

"Because Lord Zett says so," their sergeant answered. "I'll write you out a pass if you want to go discuss it with him. If not, keep your yaps shut."

“Ah Sarge, the first man said. "We was just complaining like good soldiers do."

"Well, you lot may want to wash behind your ears tonight," the sergeant said. "We're gonna be part of a big show tomorrow."

"Zat so?" the first soldier replied. "Well, la-di-da. I'd rather have a cold beer. Hell, I'd settle for a warm one."

"You go looking for one tonight," the sergeant said. "And you're liable to end up sitting next to this one the rest of the way. You mind what I say."

The soldiers built up the fire and cooked dinner with a minimum of complaints. They were doing what they were told. In the end that’s what they always did. Their complaining was but a brief bit of autonomy that made following orders more palatable. After dinner they settled in around the fire swapping lies that grew bigger as the night wore on. Bryn was given a sip of water, but no food and no opportunity to lie down. There was nothing to do but listen, choke back the pain, and sleep in spurts when exhaustion won out.

Moonlight brought snores from around the campfire. The dark hours seemed without end. Bryn longed to look up at the stars, but the pain of doing so far outweighed any comfort the sight afforded. Beaten, condemned, and shackled to the bed of a prison wagon was not the future he imagined when he left the Academy. Coryn said he was chosen by the Creator. Did the Creator not see? Did he not hear? Didn’t the Creator know how weak he was? The crushing weight of being abandoned was the worst pain of all. His tears mixed with the blood that covered his face. Was One Eye right? Was his trust in the Creator, his elders, and his duty a pipe dream?

To Bryn’s surprise, the feelings of shame his tears brought dried them. His loneliness and pain abated, replaced with a kind of numbness. This journey wasn’t just about him. Somehow it was about the vision. His duty to the people of his village remained, but in a faraway sense that made it seem less urgent. One Eye, Wynn, and Elryn escaped capture, that was important. As much as he wanted to be free, he prayed One Eye wouldn't do anything as foolish as try to rescue him. They must get to Eeryn and tell him what happened. His mind occupied with the safety of his friends; he slept. And dreamed.

A river of blood bubbling from a headless body flowed down the sides of a huge wooden block. The blood ran along the floor of a raised platform to drip onto a churning mass of humanity. Men and women jostled one another fighting for position; wanting to see the blood, to bathe in it, to taste it. Against a wall at the edge of the crowd a pile of leaves stirred. Whirling upon themselves the leaves rose in a funnel-shaped column until a bow appeared within the leaves and launched a flock of arrows. One Eye glided onto the blood-stained platform. He snatched up the severed head and jumped into the crowd waving his dagger. Screaming spectators opened a path for the smuggler brandishing the severed head. The leaves followed him, arrows flying in their wake. Wynn met them at the edge of the square. The whirlwind, Wynn, and One Eye came to rest in the smoking ruins of Jaryn's tavern. Faryn and Elryn were seated among the ashes at a table with a headless body. One Eye put the head on the table and turned it to face the body. Bryn's own slack, lifeless face looked up at him---and smiled.

Bryn awoke with a scream. Pain flared in his arms and shoulders as his body slammed against the restraints. The chains around his wrists rattled but held. Angry faces and glaring eyes held a pair of lances to his throat. The sergeant stepped between the guards for a look at Bryn.

"That's nothing compared with what's waiting for you tomorrow," he said. "It will be here soon enough. Let's all go back to sleep."

"What happens tomorrow?" Bryn asked.

The sergeant's smile disappeared. "Tomorrow, you ride the wheel."

CHAPTER 27

Shiloh slept beneath a swaddling of moonlight that painted the Temple's dome and the empty streets a soft silver. Atop the palace walls, the sergeant-at-arms nodded wordless greetings to the sentries as he passed. A breeze carried the scent of jasmine from the Royal Gardens through the open windows of the palace bedchambers.

Eli, Prince of Salem, his soft breathing the only sound, turned beneath silk coverings. Near the window, a single candle flickered atop a carved ironwood table as the air fluttered the delicate purple curtains. A scuff of leather on flagstone announced the arrival of a long black shadow that stole over the sleeping prince. A second brush of leather brought the prince to wakefulness. Unmoving, eyes closed, he waited, more curious than frightened. The brave of heart are cautious. The prince's hand slid beneath his pillow and closed on his knife.

"No need for that, my Lord," a voice spoke from the foot of the bed.

"Says one banned from this palace," Eli answered with a smile and sat up. "Good even, Eeryn old friend."

"Add this to my many sins." Eeryn shrugged.

"Sin is the usual business of this hour, But I doubt that is what's on your mind."

"You'd do well not to be so sure, my Lord," Eeryn replied. "Sin is only the beginning of troubles I bring."

Eli waved a hand for him to continue.

"I don't know all that the future holds, but all I see is evil and death," Eeryn said. "I pray you find an excuse to leave Shiloh as soon as possible."

"You know that's impossible," Eli protested. "My brother is to become king next full moon I cannot be absent."

"Very well," Eeryn's voice dropped to a whisper. "But, be

prepared. I fear for your life."

"Melchiz would never harm me," Eli said. "I know such things happen, but I cannot accept my brother acting in such fashion. He knows only too well that I have no desire to rule."

"In that you say true, my Lord," Eeryn told him. "You need not fear your brother. I tell you a darkness is coming that even kings cannot resist."

A subtle, yet insistent knock sounded on the chamber door. The prince held a finger to his lips. Bare feet slipped from the bed. Soundless steps carried him to the door. Before answering, he glanced back at his friend. Eeryn was gone.

"Enter," the prince said.

"Forgive me, my Lord," said a short, powerfully built soldier. "I thought I heard voices."

Luther Silas, captain of Prince Eli's personal guard, swept the room with his steely gray eyes before his beefy hand dropped from the hilt of his sword.

"A dream, Captain" Eli replied. "All is well."

"As you say." Luther gave a quick nod of his head and backed away pulling the heavy door closed behind him.

"For now," the prince whispered.

He went to retrieve a small slip of paper from the table near the window. Three words were scrawled in a familiar script, "Our place, tomorrow."

Eli shredded the paper as he moved to stand at the rail of his balcony. He let the paper fall into the cool night air that brushed his face and stirred his long dark hair. It was a handsome face. The soft lines of his mother's beauty dampening the harsh angles of his father. The prince shunned the beard made popular among the people by his father and older brother. His eyes, a deep rich brown, looked out over the gardens to the city square beyond. The gardens were empty, but not so the city square. Construction of the coronation stage continued as it had day and night for the last week. Preparations of one kind or another would go on until the morning of the ceremony. In accord with tradition, his father Zedek, King of Salem was about to transfer the crown to his eldest son, Prince Melchiz.

Zedek would retire to a life of ease as the king's councilor. Melchiz would reign as king. Eli's future eluded him. He did not anticipate a position in Melchiz's council. It was not because Melchiz feared Eli as a rival. His elder brother thought Eli lacked the bearing and self confidence that flowed in the veins of the rest of the royal house. It was this perceived inner weakness that would keep him from the affairs of state.

It was Eli's skill with weapons and tactics that saved him in his father's eyes. Eli believed his future lay in the military defense of the kingdom. He hoped to steer his brother in that direction and away from his reliance on Zett. Meanwhile, Eli spent his days with the soldiers, gaining their confidence and growing admiration for him as a warrior.

There was not a soul living in all the kingdom who doubted the favor Eli held with the queen. It was she who introduced Eli to Eeryn. At the queen's urging, the seer sent as the ambassador from Valir, befriended young Eli. His trailing after the seer worried the king. He feared the youngster's attachment to Eeryn and Eli's interest in the Valir's religion. It was the queen who pointed out that Valirian devotion to duty was shaping Eli into a staunch defender of the kingdom and his father.

Later, Eeryn was banished from the palace for his criticism of Melchiz's bride and her brother Zett's entrance into palace affairs. Eli secretly remained loyal to Eeryn and continued to seek his council. The seer's wisdom and visions were unerringly accurate, and Eli trusted the old Valir's word.

His trust in Eeryn now vexed him. Whatever danger the prophet saw, it had to be serious to warrant his coming to the palace. It meant lives were at stake. Eli could not escape Shiloh during preparation for his brother's coronation. It would be disloyal. To stay might be to gamble his life and maybe the lives of others.

"You look ill, my son," the queen said at breakfast. "Did you not sleep well?"

"A bad dream," he said, hoping that was enough.

The queen waited for him to explain. When she saw no answer was forthcoming, she let the subject drop. She knew her youngest son. He was strong, independent, and stubborn. She knew from experience that he would come to her with any problem that was beyond him. His willingness to seek counsel when overwhelmed by troubles was a trait neither his father nor his brother possessed.

"I think I shall go for a ride this morning," Eli announced.

"Without breakfast?" Her eyebrow arched with the question. "Yes, well, take Luther if you are going outside the city. Do it for me; please."

Eli nodded and kissed her cheek. "I will," he promised.

"And say hello to Eeryn for me," she whispered and smiled that mother's smile.

Eli blushed at how well she knew him and how much she cared. He gave her a quick nod and quickly left.

***

Prince Eli found his captain waiting at the stables. Luther's official title, Minister to the Prince, was deceptive. While he attended Eli's personal needs, he was much more than a valet. Luther Silas held the rank of commander in the elite King's Guard. It was a rank he earned on the battlefield and carried on his face where a Maran arrow plowed a jagged, white furrow from his right cheek and took half his ear. He was a short man with heavy gnarled limbs and a torso solid as a tree trunk. For all his powerful bulk, Luther moved as swiftly and silently as the spotted cats of the Boubouja.

During Eli's military training, Luther found a true warrior's spirit lived in the youth. The prince was an enthusiastic student and quickly won his mentor's confidence. Since that time, he was convinced service to Eli was more capable of honor than a dozen battlefields. His oath to die for his prince gave Luther a renewed reason to live.

In his hands, Luther held the reins for a pair of saddled ceroses. The naturally armored beasts strained against the leather straps eager for the open spaces. Tri-hoofed feet pawed the ground raising small clouds of dust from the stable floor. Royal purple blankets bearing the king's crest and saddles laden with silver covered the beast's massive, thick, gray hides. Blunt covers of sliver adorned the row of pointed horns that ran up of the middle of the creature's forehead.

"Are we going to battle, Luther?" Eli asked.

"The Queen wasn't happy to find me in the stables," Luther answered. "I thought I ought to be prepared for anything."

"The Queen? How did she…?" Eli threw up a hand in resignation. "Is there anything she does not know?"

"It's always best to proceed believing she knows all," Luther said with a smile.

The Prince took the reins and swung into the saddle. The ceros bolted a step. Eli hauled back on the reins to hold him. Holding these snorting beasts to a walk while navigating the streets of Shiloh required skill and strength. Although Eli preferred them to the horses of the light cavalry units, their use seemed a bit too much for the occasion.

"You haven't asked where we are going," the Prince said when they were clear of the stable.

"No sir," the captain said. "You see, the Queen…"

"Say no more." Eli smiled at his companion.

The prince's smile faded when they reached the street. A half dozen mounted riders armed with disrupters and lances fell into step on either side of them. Eli cast a sharp glance at his captain.

"No troops," he ordered. "Crowd or no crowd you're all the protection I need. Send them back."

"But, Highness," Luther protested. "The Queen insisted. Perhaps just until we reach the city gates."

"Very well," Eli relented. "But then, they return to the palace. There's to be no following at a distance no matter what the queen said, understood?"

A smile flashed across Luther's face. "Yes, sir."

The crowd was already three deep along the main throughfare. As Eli approached, men lifted their young ones to get a look at the prince. Eli smiled and waved. The prince knew he was not what the people came to see and felt free to hurry by without fanfare.

Lord Zett's spectacle is well attended.

The thought disappointed rather than surprised Eli. The crowd loved nothing better than public bloodletting and humiliation. Eli had no taste for it. He had attended an execution once and never again. He was a soldier. Violent death between combatants held neither terror nor revulsion for him. However, watching a beaten foe paraded through the streets, shoved to his knees, and slaughtered like an animal sickened him. Even if this Valir led an assault on human troops and two villages, he deserved a better death than riding the wheel to the chopping block.

"Zett will be pleased," Eli said with a jerk of his head toward the crowd.

"As much as Zett can be pleased by anything, I suppose," Luther observed. "How will we find the seer?"

"I have an idea; he will find us."

Eli continued to smile and wave. Luther's eyes swept the throng, for signs of danger. His actions were largely habit. There was little actual risk. The prince was well loved in the city. As they made a left turn into the city square, the captain's eyes came to rest on a pair of Valir, a young female and a very large male. Strange, they would risk being among the blood thirsty mob. There was something hard about the female's face. Her stance was casual, yet her eyes were studying the troops managing the crowd. He could almost hear her mentally counting them and marking their positions. The big fellow, obviously a bodyguard, was doing a discreet job watching her back. He considered warning the prince but decided to let Zett care for his own problems.

Eli's entourage took a direct route through town eager to gain the open countryside and avoid Zett's spectacle. Free of the city, Eli let the ceros have its head. Grain fields flew by in a golden blur as the riders urged their mounts on. After about a mile, the beasts slowed of their own accord. The ceros were unmatched in the power of their charge, but they could not maintain that speed long. Eli turned his ceros off the road onto a footpath barely wide enough to accommodate the beast. Luther pulled his bow and adjusted the position of his quiver. Their destination was silhouetted against the horizon, a single giant oak on a rocky cliff overlooking the sea. The prince thought the half hour it would take to reach the tree was worth the journey.

He was right. Sitting relaxed at the base of the tree was Eeryn. Luther hobbled the ceroses and sent them to graze. Eli unfolded a campstool and dropped it beside the Valirian to look out over the blue expanse. He came to meet his old friend, but the view was worth the trip. To his right a dozen streams cascaded over the cliffs in a series of long white tails that disappeared into the waves. Heavy mist covered the pools where the falls joined the blue arch of the bay.

"Do you miss the Boubouja?" Eli asked.

Eeryn sighed and looked up at the prince. "Only when I

breathe."

"Why not return?" Eli drew his stool closer to the seer. "Why suffer for my family's thin skin?"

"The king has the right to ban me from the palace," Eeryn began. "However, he cannot erase my oath to serve him. My oath is not just to the king. It is also to my people. I am their sworn ambassador to the house of Zedek."

"The Valir have appointed a new ambassador," Eli protested.

"My oath ends when I die or with the destruction of the royal house," Eeryn explained. "I will go home wrapped in my burial robe."

Luther joined their watch over the sea. Neither prince nor seer spoke. Luther was accustomed to the two of them sharing silence. He admired the prince's ability to draw and be drawn by the strong of heart. His intensity, not his position kept the prince from casual friendships. A glance at the pair beside him was evidence enough of that. On one hand was the tall, dark prince. His youthful face disguised an old soul. His long arms hung lazily from wide, square shoulders. Eli shunned the elaborate tattooing of the day. His skin knew the sun, but he escaped the leathery appearance of his bodyguard.

Then, there was Eeryn. The seer was a Valir. Luther wondered what could be more different than the Valir's crested avian heads, feather covered shoulders, gossamer wings, and the bare green flesh of their bodies. Of course, he held a similar opinion of all the inhabitants of the outer kingdoms.

Luther called the Valir green-skinned birds, but he was not sure they were covered with skin at all. It looked like human skin but to touch it was as cold and hard as he imagined their hearts to be. They swore oaths to their own hurt and never relented. They had a fierce loyalty and sense of duty to their Creator god. To this they added speed and agility. and an almost supernatural skill with their foot long daggers that made them formidable foes. King Zedek's great grandfather once crossed the Hiddekel to conquer the Valir and their Boubouja. It is said that a mountain of bones still marks the place where the invaders died.

"Tell me all your heart," Eli said at last.

CHAPTER 28

Bryn heard the soldiers stir. The rising sun reflected off the temple's dome giving the morning a golden glow. His back to the camp, it was impossible to see what the soldiers were doing. He recognized the sounds of making a meal and dismantling a tent. Below these were others he knew but which seemed out of place; rope and chain passing over wood.

The morning glow faded, replaced by the warmth of the climbing sun. The sergeant appeared at the wagon to unlock the barred door. A soldier with a pole then pushed Bryn as far away as the chain allowed. The sergeant opened the padlock and threaded the chain through the ring in the floor.

"Get out," he ordered. "Slowly."

Bryn kept his eyes locked on the sergeant as he scooted from the wagon. The muscles in his back screamed in protest as he forced himself to sit upright. His knees buckled when his feet hit the ground. He held to the wagon until his wobbly legs steadied themselves. Soldiers with disrupters closed around him while the sergeant removed his shackles. It felt good to be free of the chains though Bryn was certain the feeling wouldn't last long. The sergeant's next command sealed his certainty.

"Strip those clothes off," he ordered.

"No." Bryn answered.

"What the hell did you say?" the sergeant snarled.

"No." Bryn tried to keep his voice flat and emotionless.

Bryn squared his shoulders. A soldier countered, driving the tip of his lance into Bryn's right shoulder. Skewered by the lance, a stream of bright blood flowed down Bryn's arm.

"We won't kill you," the sergeant told him. "But we can make you wish you were dead. Take off the clothes."

"No," Bryn repeated. "I'm afraid if you want them, you will have to come and take them."

"Suits me." The sergeant motioned for the soldier to pull the lance from Bryn's arm.

Bryn flexed his knees, widened his stance, and waved the sergeant closer. There was only one possible outcome. Bryn was going to get the crap kicked out of him and lose his clothes. So, be it. He wasn't going quietly. The sergeant circled to Bryn's left. Bryn fainted with his wounded right hand then caught the soldier with a left to the temple. The sergeant's head snapped back. He went down but managed to grab Bryn's leg. Before Bryn could shake free, a soldier hit him with a flying tackle that carried them both to the ground atop the sergeant. Air exploded from the sergeant's lungs when their weight hit him. Gasping for breath, he struggled to get out from under the punching, kicking tangle of limbs.

Bryn rolled free, gained his feet, and was almost upright again. The blunt side of a lance hit him across the shoulders knocking him back to the ground. A soldier piled atop him and drove his thumb into Bryn's wounded shoulder. White light burst behind Bryn's eyes; curses flew from his beak. Bryn shot an upward looping left hand that struck home with a loud crack. He wasn't sure if the sound came from the bones in his hand or from the soldier's jaw. He didn't wait to find out. He kicked an advancing soldier in the groin before being swallowed up by a mass of humanity. Crushed beneath the combined weight of the soldiers he was unable to move.

"Hold him," the sergeant shouted.

The order was followed by a sharp pain in Bryn's middle. He stopped struggling.

"That's my knife," the sergeant informed him. "I'm going to cut those clothes off you. The more you struggle, the deeper it goes."

"Gut him, Sarge," one of the soldiers shouted.

"The knife moved steadily up to Bryn's throat cutting through his tunic and leaving a spreading red furrow from groin to chest. He was rolled to his stomach; his hands pulled behind his back and chains fastened to his wrists.

"Stand up," the sergeant ordered.

Bryn was yanked to his feet just to make sure he understood. The command was punctuated by a fist driven into his face that ripped open a cut above his left eye. Bryn's knees buckled but the soldiers kept him propped up. He was dragged away from the wagon naked and bleeding. Blood filled his rapidly swelling left eye. Though he tried to blink back the blood, he was now blind. As the soldiers held him, the sergeant buried his fist in Bryn's guts. The breath exploded from him. Pain rippled from the impact to his extremities and back again.

Then, he was falling. His head thudded against something hard. Stars danced in the black world behind his eyes. His arms and legs were spread wide. He couldn't see, but he knew he was being tied to the spokes of the large wagon wheel delivered from town last night. The hub bit into his back; ropes chewed his wrists and ankles. A chain was pulled across his chest.

"Well done, Sergeant," an oddly familiar voice said.

Zett, the name echoed in Bryn's mind.

"Sergeant, I want you to take your time on the drive in," Zett instructed. "We're in no hurry here. Let everyone get a good look."

"Yes, Lord Zett."

"On my signal," Zett said and walked away.

***

The gates of Shiloh opened to the flourish of trumpets. The cavalry escort abandoned by the prince and still at the gates was ordered to fall in with the procession. Triumphant, sword held high, Lord Zett led the column into the city. Far behind the Lord of the Army, a lowly sergeant in a disheveled uniform spurred his ceros on and the large wooden wheel began its bouncing journey into the city.

Bryn tried not to think about what was happening. He concentrated instead on a prayer to the Creator. It was not a prayer for the deliverance of escape. The time for escape had passed. Bryn prayed for strength to endure whatever lay ahead.

The sergeant kept the ceros under tight rein, wanting a slow plodding trip. Lord Zett wanted the crowd to have plenty of time and opportunity to inflict their torture. The sergeant was intent on pleasing Zett while savoring a bit of personal satisfaction with every indignity the Valir suffered.

Lord Zett waved to the crowd from atop his prancing black charger. He had defeated the butchering Valir and had brought their leader to justice. He welcomed the crowd's adoration, reveled in it, soaked up their wild cheers. The smile upon Zett's face was a rare genuine one.

He was the brother of the next queen, son of the King of Mara, Lord of the Army of Shiloh and, in his mind, that was just the beginning. The execution of this bird was but a small step on the way.

The cheers rose as he held out a hand toward the arrival of his prize. The roar of the crowd doubled and doubled again as the wheel finally entered the gates. The figure on the wheel writhed in agony with each jolt as it bounced over the cobblestones. Blood flowed from the bare chest of the wheel rider and ran down his arms and legs. His face was a swollen, misshapen mass of bruises and blood. That was not enough for the crowd; their cries welded into a shriek for blood. Zett waved a hand and the soldiers holding back the citizens of Shiloh melted away. It was time for the people to vent their righteous indignation.

A man with a large stone in his hand broke from the crowd and hurled it at the wheel. The stone crashed into Bryn's ribs with a loud crack. Restraint evaporated. The punching, kicking, throng rushed on Bryn shouting obscenities, throwing stones, rotten vegetables, and animal dung at him. A woman jumped up on the wheel, lifted her skirts and urinated in his face. Children beat his body with bamboo canes. A hotel owner poured the reeking contents of a chamber pot over him before bashing him over the head with the empty pot.

Bryn lost track of time and distance, but never a moment of consciousness. Strapped to the wheel, covered in blood, garbage, and excrement, he was dragged through the city until the procession finally reached a raised platform near the city center. Soldiers stood the wheel up. Bryn's weight fell against ropes that held him and fresh pain ripped through his wounded arms and shoulders. The soldiers slowly rolled the wheel end over end to the top of the platform. There, for all to see, the wheel was fastened to a raised post. The crowd was forced back beyond range of thrown garbage and human waste. The occasional stone that reached the platform was discouraged by the guards only because the aim was poor. The wheel set, a soldier came to see if the prisoner was still alive. When he signaled Bryn was alive, the mob began to slowly dissipate. There was little more to see until the ax man arrived in the morning.

Bryn Bou was alive. Every part of his body screamed confirmation to him. Standing upright, the sagging weight of his body provided sufficient pressure to stop most of his bleeding. Every movement sent waves of white-hot pain rippling over his chest and down his extremities. It hurt to breathe. It hurt to think. The smell of human waste infested his nostrils. Tears leaked from his battered eyes, squeezing through swollen lids to wash tracks through the filth that covered his face. Deeper within, a cold stone had replaced his aching heart, and that frigid numbness was the worst hurt of all. Without natural feelings he might as well be dead and for the first time in his short life, he wished he was.

Time ceased to exist on the wheel. Pain had stolen it. There was eternal and unrelenting pain and nothing else. Bryn welcomed the blackness that overflowed him. For a moment it seemed his wish had come true.

He awakened to another world. Through the slits that were his eyes he saw soldiers standing under the dim light of ebbing torches. He was being guarded. Lord Zett would not be cheated of his spectacle by an over eager citizen. Bryn forced his head up against the pain. There was a waning moon above, its light and life draining away into the vast darkness. The moon would be reborn not many days hence. He would die with the dawn.

Behind the flashes of pain, came a rumbling sound. Bryn tried to focus on the new sound hoping to discover its meaning. It was the sound of a wheel turning, but not his wheel. The sound came from everywhere. Its rumbling filled his head, spread out over the sky, and swallowed up the universe. Then, it was gone, swallowed up by an all-pervading silence as if the wheel of all creation suddenly stood still. The stars held their breath. The world stopped spinning.

Bryn's world fell away. He stood alone on the vast emptiness of space looking down at a small blue-green orb of his world. The great sea began to boil. The head of a crimson dragon rose from the foaming waters and the monster's thrashing tail beat the sea.

Bryn sensed he was no longer alone. A presence, powerful and dreadful, stood beside him. He feared to look and yet could not resist turning his head. At Bryn's shoulder bright green fire folded in upon itself; at once consuming and renewing the fabric of creation. He didn't know how he knew; only that he knew. The light was alive. A flame from the living fire became a sword. Bryn reached for the weapon.

"I will," the words sprang unbidden from his soul.

Pain shot through his limbs. The wheel upon which he hung began to turn. The city square and the moon changed places.

Was it a dream? It had to be a dream. The pain has driven me mad.

That made sense, but it didn't ring true. He was struggling for a firm grip on consciousness. The soldiers began to stir. Weapons snapped up to the ready. Bryn could just make out a blurry figure weaving a path toward the platform. Two soldiers moved to intercept it.

"Stop right there," one of the soldiers ordered.

"Wassah matta, gener'l. I wass jes lookin."

"Well, that's close enough," the soldier said. "Look and move along."

"You're drunk," a second soldier chimed in. "Go home and sleep it off."

"Aw gener'l, I only had a few, honest," the drunk held up his hands, but continued to move closer.

One of the soldiers stretched out a hand to hold the man back. The drunk bounced off the soldier's hand; stumbled and fell. As the soldier moved to catch him, the stranger's head jerked up and caught the soldier on the chin with a loud thud. The soldier's head snapped back. The stranger followed it with a hard right hand sending the soldier sprawling. The second soldier stared in frozen surprise at the drunk's sudden sobriety. His shock lasted just long enough to get hit by a spinning kick to the groin. He collapsed in a heap.

Moonlight reflected off the blade that leaped into the stranger's hand. He jumped onto the platform and slid toward Bryn. The slicing blow to the throat Bryn expected never arrived. The stranger deftly cut the ropes holding Bryn's hands and feet. Bryn crashed down onto the platform planking.

"It's me," Wynn said. "We're getting you out of here."

A bolt from a crossbow hit the spoke beside Bryn's ear sending waves of pain through his head. The soldiers were closing fast. Wynn pulled Bryn to his feet, but his legs refused to hold him, and Bryn crashed to the ground.

"Sorry," Wynn said, moving to meet the oncoming soldiers.

Bryn's blood was up. His eyes, fueled by the surge of adrenalin, blazed, pushing back the pain. He pushed his chest off the ground, working his knees under him. Through the slits that were once his eyes he saw Wynn and One Eye grappling with the guards. With a determined push, Bryn gained his feet and immediately collapsed. Soldiers were pouring into the square from all sides. The newcomers were no guard detail. Even with his limited vision, Bryn could see these were real warriors.

"Everyone stand down," a voice boomed across the square with an authority that brooked no disobedience.

Though he could do little else, Bryn froze in place along with everyone within hearing. His hands were bound once more. Two soldiers lifted him and held him propped between them. Wynn and One Eye were shackled together beside him. A solidly built officer with a scar across his cheek grabbed Bryn by the crest and lifted his head to glare at him. Bryn's vision blurred, dimmed, and went out.

"Sir," the captain of the guard detail said. "This man and his Valir accomplice tried to free the prisoner. We were about to take them into custody, sir."

"Yes," the officer sneered. "So, I see. It's a good thing we happened along. Much more of your custody and your Lord Zett would have been without a show tomorrow."

"Yes, sir," the captain said.

"I'm taking charge of these prisoners," Luther Silas said. "They will be transferred to the palace dungeon."

"But sir, Lord Zett..." the captain's voice was chased away by the glare of the prince's bodyguard. "Yes, sir. As you wish, sir."

"They need no longer concern you," Luther said. "You may tell your master they are now prisoners of the royal house."

"Yes sir. As you say, sir."

With a snort of disapproval, Luther turned away from the trembling captain to the three prisoners. They weren't much to look at. Nevertheless, they were set to take on the best Zett had.

They had balls, not much in the way of brains, but damn, they had balls. Maybe the prince wasn't completely mistaken after all.

"Major Frye," Luther commanded. "Take these three to the palace dungeon and secure them. And, for God's sake, clean that one up and put some clothes on him."

CHAPTER 29

The dank nether region of Shiloh palace breathed sorrow. Its stone walls wept over the forsaken moans that echoed through the halls. Despite the clinging darkness, Bryn Bou found the dungeon preferable to the wheel. He had been half walked half dragged from the wheel. The pain was immense, but the march through prison by the Prince's Guard felt like salvation. Bryn was shoved into a small antechamber. His face hit the stone wall on his way to a rough stop on the floor. He was ordered to stand still. Through a fog of pain, Bryn found soldierly humor in the command. His legs could not hold him, and he was told to stand still.

"Okay, now Louie," the officer shouted.

Icy water pounded Bryn's back. The sudden shock forced the breath from his lungs. A knife of pain shot through his chest. Bryn gulped air as his body shivered uncontrollably.

"Turn over."

Bryn obeyed, but not fast enough to suit his tormentors. Hands caught his feet and arms. He was flipped over and dropped to the floor. Fresh pain ignited his chest with fire. Water pelted his wounded face and burned trails down the cuts in his body. A wooden bucket was pushed next to him.

"Wash yourself," a voice commanded.

Bryn sponged water from the bucket to his face. It hurt like hell, but he knew infection from the vile things thrown on him would be worse and scrubbed his body as best he could. When the soldiers saw that the water lost its ability to torture, they decided Bryn was clean enough. A bundle of clean rags was thrown his way.

I smell better anyway.

The cold water actually eased the bleeding and the swelling in his face. His vision was improved. It still hurt to breathe, but he was breathing and thankful for it. All in all, he felt blessed.

Still clinging to the clothes he was given he was dragged down a long hall lined with cells. The soldiers stopped before a tall oak door fastened to the stone with iron hinges. The two soldiers holding him up were met by a pair of prison guards stationed at the door. Three of the men joined to push open the heavy door while the other held Bryn upright. A few steps inside the outer door, was a second door of iron bars. A jailer worked the key in the iron door and swung it open to reveal mildew covered stone walls and a straw strewn floor. A hand in the middle of his back shoved him inside. Bryn stumbled forward. He found enough strength to use his arms to break the crash to the floor. Iron bars clanged closed, and he heard the outer door scraped across the stone.

It took a minute for his eyes to adjust to the dark inside the cell. He needed no time to know that he was not alone. His cell mate was his old friend and would be rescuer. One Eye bent over him and offered a smile. The smuggler looked none the worse for wear. He wasn't bleeding anywhere Bryn could see. Bryn had the impression his companion was awakened by the commotion at the door.

"Come in, come in," One Eye welcomed him. "Make yourself at home. My cell is your cell. Can you stand?"

"Not so far, but let's try it—slowly, please."

One Eye scooped his hands under Bryn's shoulders and lifted him to a sitting position. Bryn held up a hand and One Eye stopped there.

"Okay," Bryn said when his head cleared.

One Eye shifted his grip catching Bryn under the arms. He pistoned with his legs and Bryn slowly rose from the floor. One Eye held Bryn to him until the nausea passed. He loosened his grip but remained close behind Bryn.

"Try to walk," he said.

Bryn slid one foot across the cobblestones, shifted his weight forward and repeated the procedure with the other foot. His legs held. The shuffle walk continued until they reached the wall opposite the door. One Eye eased Bryn to the floor and went to gather the bundle of rags.

"By the way," he said. "You will never speak of me holding your naked ass to anyone. Let's get these clothes on you."

Bryn struggled into a moth-eaten pair of gray pants. One Eye studied the shirt for a moment before ripping the bottom half of the garment. He pulled the bottom portion tightly across Bryn's chest and tied the band of cloth in place. That done, Bryn slipped his arms through the remainder of the shirt.

"Not perfect," One Eye said. "But it will make it easier to move and breathe. What's left covers most of the wounds."

"You sound awful cheerful for a prisoner," Bryn replied.

"We're alive," One Eye said. Then his voice dropped to a whisper. "And not without resources. We found your prophet."

"You found Eeryn?"

"We did. Wynn and the girl are with me…er…*were* with me." One Eye corrected himself. "Jaryn, the tavern owner was part of an underground network. Eeryn is tied up in it somehow, at least he knows its workings. From what I've learned so far, Valir and outland species being sold as slaves is only the tip of a corrupt mountain of human evils. The humans are filling work camps everywhere with what they call "lesser" species."

"What happened to Wynn?"

"Released. He's been under the Valirian spell you cast on him at Gotebo. He didn't know what he was doing until he was rescued tonight. At least that's the story Eeryn gave him, and he must be telling it well."

"What? There's no such thing as a Valirian spell," Bryn said.

"Humans are gullible creatures," he said with a shrug. "They believe creatures from the outer regions are capable of anything. There seems to be a special paranoia right now."

"Well, played, Wynn. Do you know who brought us here?" Bryn asked. "That officer who broke up our escape was not one of guards left in the square. He looked capable of putting us to the sword on the spot."

"Yeah, I don't know about that," One Eye said. "I do know that he is the Captain of Prince Eli's personal guard."

"Really?" Bryn rubbed his chin. "That's interesting. I've heard my father say that Eeryn was friends with the prince."

***

Far above the whispered dungeon conversation, Luther Silas

rapped on the door of his prince interrupting yet another whispered conversation. Eeryn slipped noiselessly onto the balcony.

"Enter," Eli called.

Luther stepped inside and closed the heavy door behind him. "It's done, Your Highness."

"Thank you," Eli said and turned toward the balcony. "Come in Eeryn. Your young messenger is safe for the moment. Pull up a chair and join us, Captain."

"As long as I'm in this up to my neck," Luther said, drawing up a chair.

"Well," the prince began. "What now? Zett will be livid you know. He will demand they be turned over to him for immediate execution. Whatever respite I managed to buy them won't last long. My father will not let the sun go down on his reign without a resolution of this problem. We are going to have to act quickly."

"Leave that to me." Eeryn caught the prince's puzzled look. "Better for you not to know. Zett will try to implicate you. This way your denial is the truth."

"I don't want anyone killed," Eli said.

"I can't promise that," Eeryn said. "See if you can you get the execution delayed until the ceremony."

"I don't know," Eli nervously tugged at his chin. "I'll try, but that's a long time."

"You're planning to use the ceremony as a distraction to work an escape, I assume," Luther chimed in.

"I am," Eeryn admitted.

"It might work," Luther said.

"It better," Eeryn said. "Or we may all wind up on the wheel.

The prophet sprang to his feet, head cocked to one side. Without a word he dashed to the balcony and disappeared. The prince looked at his bodyguard and shrugged. A moment later, Luther touched a finger to his lips and pointed it at the door. A loud knock followed his cue.

"Enter," Eli called.

The door swung open to reveal a tall, thin figure wrapped in a black cloak. His raven hair combed straight back on his head gave a clear view of close-set black eyes. Zett's long straight nose added to the sharpness to his narrow face. Parchment hued skin stretched smoothly from his brow to a narrow, beardless chin.

"Lord Zett." Eli fabricated a smile for the visitor. "How good of you to come. I was about to call on you."

"Truly," Zett said with a slight bow of his head. "You have been busy then?"

"Indeed," Eli replied. "The captain here was just reporting to me how he came upon your men under attack. It seems someone was trying to free your prisoner. You can rest at ease. The prisoner and his accomplice are secured. I've taken the liberty of having them held in the palace dungeon to await the King's pleasure."

"Well done, Your Highness." Zett looked at the now empty seat between the prince and his captain. A small smile brushed his lips. "How fortunate for me he happened along at such an odd hour."

"Yes, wasn't it?" Eli said. "What's the story with this Valirian?"

"He is the leader of the smugglers who massacred the villagers in Gotebo and Manitou," Zett explained. "My men captured him as he approached the city. He was hiding out in a well-known resistance way station. Given the severity of the crime, I hoped for his speedy execution."

"I trust a short delay for the King's blessing on his death will not be too much of an inconvenience?"

"Of course not, Your Highness." Zett bowed. "I will address the King on the matter in due course. Good night, my Lord."

"Good night, Lord Zett." Eli waved a hand in dismissal.

The Lord Minister of the Army's clenched fists and stiff march out of the room betrayed his inner rage. Eli watched him go with equally restrained amusement. The initial clash was over. The war was on.

***

Zett shoved his way by the fawning captains who served as his aides. His cloak billowed behind him riding the storm of anger that powered his steps. He climbed into his carriage, slammed the door closed, and fell into the cushions, arms folded tightly across his chest.

The guards outside his home, already at attention, drew themselves up a little taller as their master exploded from the carriage and stalked inside. No one dared speak; no one looked up; no one moved. The door to Zett's office slammed to a collective exhale of breath and sudden scurrying for cover outside.

The sound of smashing furniture and shattering glass slowly subsided behind the massive double doors. Still, no one ventured to ask after the master's welfare. A solitary figure, sweat dripping from his brow, paced just outside the office doors.

"Balfour!" Zett screamed.

The lonely figure hunched his shoulders in preparation for the onslaught and opened the door.

"Yes, Lord Zett," Balfour whimpered.

"Get me that dink of an ambassador in here now," Zett commanded.

"Yes, my Lord," Balfour bowed. "Which ambassador, my Lord?"

"The Valirian Ambassador, you sniveling, brainless, dink."

"Right now, Lord?"

"If Balfour would like to keep breathing." Zett said, pointing a long finger at the servant. "Of course, right now."

Balfour ducked a crystal statuette that flew by his ear and shattered against the wall.

"Get moving," Zett shrieked. "And send that bumbling captain and his men in here."

Zett's minister didn't bother to ask which captain he was to send. He'd find one to sacrifice. However, the task proved easier than he imagined. On the steps outside stood a quaking officer and a handful of miserable looking men held under the watchful eye of General Ergen.

"Lord Zett wants them inside," he said over his shoulder as he passed. "I'd hurry if I were you."

The general signaled to his troops and the guards turned prisoners were pushed inside. Following the string of shouted profanity still hanging in the air, they approached Lord Zett. He was standing behind an empty desk staring down at it as if measuring how far he could throw it. General Ergen saluted but said nothing.

"Do you incompetent dinks have any idea of how you have interfered with my plans? Plans, mind you, more than a year in the works." Zett began to pace. "No, of course you don't. To know that would require you to be able to think."

Zett came around the desk. His black eyes studied his prey as he drew closer, stopping in front of the man whose face bore the marks of Wynn's head butt. Zett leaned in, his nose almost touching that of the soldier. Zett drew a deep breath. The tirade everyone expected never came. Zett cut the man's throat with a smooth flick of his hand. The soldier's bladder let go and he fell twitching into a puddle of his own blood and urine.

"You," Zett pointed at one of the soldiers. "Would you like to live?"

"Yes, Lord," the man croaked.

"Your sword, General."

Zett held out a hand. The General gently handed him the scabbard. Zett drew the blade and handed it to the soldier.

"Then, kill the rest of these idiots," he commanded.

CHAPTER 30

The cell was exactly forty stones wide and twenty stones deep. Bryn counted every one of them. Worry kept his mind racing. Pain kept his eyes open. Neither seemed to affect his companion in the least. One Eye spent the night snoring and occasionally searching for a more comfortable position. That he could sleep at all on the cobblestone floor was a mystery to Bryn.

Two locked doors barred the way to freedom. The outer door was made of four-inch-thick oak beams strapped together with wide iron bands. Opening the door was a full-time job for one person which meant guards showed up in pairs. The inner door was a hinged latticework of iron bars secured with a lock of its own. The weave of bars was reinforced with welds wherever they touched. The walls were granite blocks two feet thick. The only light that entered came through two small windows. One was in the outer door and another impossibly high up on the east wall. Unaided escape was impossible. They would have to have help. Eeryn was banned from the palace, just how he might help was a mystery to Bryn.

His pacing didn't generate solutions. However, it did pass the time and help restore flexibility to his bruised, aching muscles. One Eye had tightly bound Bryn's chest with a cloth that made breathing and pacing with broken ribs a bit easier. It was no help at all in reconciling his dream in those last hours on the wheel. He felt so awake; his senses so sharp, but it had to be a dream. Seers sometimes told of waking visions.

But he was no seer. He was a leaf carried on a stream swept along on a current not of his own making. He couldn't tell a vision from a dream or a hallucination. In other words, he was at sea about his destiny as he was that morning in the Grove of the Dead.

An hour before dawn, Bryn heard the lock turn in the cell's outer door. He stopped pacing. It was not mealtime, something was happening. The big outer door opened. Two guards drug a blood covered man inside. One of the soldiers balanced the prisoner against the wall while the other worked the lock. The inner iron door swung open, and the soldiers threw the wounded man onto the stone floor. The man landed with a thud and a groan. The soldiers left him sprawled on the stone and signaled for the outer door to be opened.

The newcomer lay unmoving while Bryn and One Eye studied him. As far as Bryn could tell, he was bruised, but the blood on his clothes was not his own. A short time later, the man groaned and rolled slowly on to his side facing Bryn and One Eye. Intrigued by the man's face, Bryn started over for a closer look.

"He's okay," One Eye said from where he lay curled up against the wall. "I can hear him breathing. He'll come around. Come sit down."

Bryn returned to his place beside One Eye and spent the next few minutes watching their new cell mate. Gradually, the man *did* come around and returned their curious looks.

"What are you birds looking at?" he asked when his eyes focused.

"A blood covered turd," One Eye said. "That would be my guess. How about you Bryn? You ever see anything like that?"

"I'm not sure," Bryn said. "Maybe once; stuck to the bottom of my shoe."

The smile starting on Bryn's face suddenly faded. He worked his way to his feet; his eyes never leaving the human. Fire burned in his face.

"Actually, I do recognize this human garbage," Bryn said. "He was one of the guards at the wheel."

Ignoring his aching muscles, Bryn kicked the downed man in the gut. The blow sent the breath rushing from him. Gasping and coughing, the man tried to crawl away. Bryn followed, landing sharp kicks to any spot left unprotected.

"Are you planning to kill him?" One Eye interrupted from across the cell.

"Maybe," Bryn said. "Does it matter?"

"It might," One Eye replied. "He might know something we ought to know. We could ask him, but you'd have to let him live awhile longer."

"Damn you," Bryn said, grabbing the man by the collar and dragging him to where One Eye sat.

One Eye leaned over the wounded man and flashed an innocent looking smile. He took the man by the shoulders and propped him against the wall. When the former guard's breathing returned to normal One Eye gave him a friendly pat on the shoulder and nodded toward Bryn.

"He really wants to kill you," One Eye said. "He's crazy like that. They say he killed everyone in a whole human village. You might be able to talk your way out of this."

"Go to hell," the man answered.

One Eye twisted his upper body and sent a looping left hand into the man's face. His head snapped back into the stone wall with a thud. Blood began to pour from the man's lips.

"You might as well kill him," One Eye said.

"No wait," the man mumbled through smashed lips. "What do you want to know?"

"What's your name?" Bryn asked.

"That hardly seems worth knowing." One Eye caught Bryn's look from the corner of his eye. "Just saying."

"Joel," the man answered before Bryn could ask again. "Joel Sens."

"How well do you know this place, Joel Sens?" Bryn asked.

"Not very well," Joel said. "I'm regular army."

"What's that got to do with it?" One Eye jumped in.

"This is the royal dungeon," Joel explained. "The army has its own prison. It's across the city. We don't come here."

"Who does come here?" Bryn said.

"The Royal Guard."

"So, the soldiers that came last night..."

"Royal Guard," Joel cut him short. "They belonged to Prince Eli. Every royal has his own personal guard."

"How do you know who they belonged to?"

"The badges on their uniforms," Joel said. "They belonged to Eli alright."

"And the army belongs to Zett," One Eye said.

"Yes."

"Why did the prince's men step in?" Bryn asked.

"I don't know," Joel answered. "But Lord Zett was in a rage

about it. He had my captain and some of the others executed for letting you get away. He ordered me beaten and thrown in the dungeon."

"Bryn." One Eye jerked his head away from where Joel sat.

The two moved as far away from the human as the cell allowed. One Eye held a cupped hand close to Bryn's ear.

"Why would they..." One Eye began to whisper.

"Yeah, why here?" Bryn's voice grew dreamlike, his eyes focused far away.

"Do you think Eeryn might have convinced the prince to send us here?"

"It's possible, they are supposed to be friends."

"Close friends is the rumor," One Eye said. "The kind of friends who do favors for each other."

"This dungeon may not be as dark as I first thought," Bryn said.

"Ok, you got a reprieve," One Eye said.

Joel sighed and relaxed against the wall. He was in.

CHAPTER 31

"The king wishes to see you, my Lord," the servant said with a deep bow. "He awaits you in the library."

"Is he alone?" Eli asked.

"No, sire," the servant answered. "Is there a message?"

"Yes," Eli said. "Tell the king; I shall attend him presently."

"Yes, sire. Very well."

Eli recognized the man. He was one of his father's personal staff. The servant wiped beads of sweat from his forehead; bowed again and backed quickly out of the room. Eli wondered if the servant had been instructed to avoid questions. He thought it likely. The prince gave Luther a questioning glance.

"Care to wager who is with him?" Eli asked.

"I think not, my Lord," Luther said. The corners of his lips drew up. "Enjoy your visit."

"You're not coming?" the prince said.

"I was not invited, my Lord." Luther's smile grew.

Prince Eli paused outside the royal library. He painted a smile on his face; gave a light rap on the door and entered without waiting to be summoned. The Kings of Shiloh were known to kill sons that were less than completely subservient. Eli was not his father's favorite but had no fear of that. His father was about to relinquish the throne and would likely patiently bear a small breech of etiquette.

The servant was right; the king was not alone. He sat where Eli expected, behind a large writing desk near the open balcony. This was clearly not the company nor meeting he imagined. He was surprised to find Lord Zett was nowhere to be found. Rather than the Lord of the Army, the King was flanked by the Queen and Prince Melchiz. His father's arms were hooked across his chest. Melchiz looked like he just ate a green persimmon. Eli decided his best defense might be to take the offensive.

"Well, a family meeting," Eli said.

His jovial tone was a thin mask for his surprise. He would have much preferred an angry Zett to a family conclave. Family connections had their upside; the opposite was also true.

"So, it would seem," the king answered. "It also seems that I was a bit naive to hope my last fortnight on the throne might pass in peace and quiet."

"Is there trouble, father?" Eli feigned ignorance.

The Queen quickly hid a smile behind her hand. The King did not appear amused. The corners of his mouth strained to turn even further downward.

"Dammit Eli." His brother sprang to his feet.

The king stretched out his hand; his palm on Melchiz's chest. His sharp glare returned Melchiz to his seat. The King held his eldest son's eyes a moment longer before turning the look on Eli. The prince shifted in his seat.

"Dammit Eli," the king roared. "What am I going to do with you? Why do you delight in angering Zett? You seem to make a sport of it. Tell me what you have done this time to set the man off on one of his rages."

"Your Majesty," Eli stood, giving his father an exaggerated bow and sweep of his hand. "I have only acted with an eye to save the honor of your kingdom from injustice and embarrassment."

"Go on," the King said.

"I assume we are speaking of the young Valir taken captive by Lord Zett?" said Eli and hurried on without awaiting a reply. "This boy is the only son of an esteemed member of Valir's High Council. Byryn Bou of Vix is a warrior of renown in the Boubouja. I believe you are familiar with the Bou clan. Granted, a goodly name does not excuse the boy's crime. Neither does it serve to mitigate any deserved punishment. Nevertheless, I believe his execution calls for a modicum of evidence to be presented that he is actually guilty of anything. We would do well to at least go through the motions of a trial before we kill him and infuriate the Valir."

Melchiz was on his feet before the king could speak. "How is it you know so much about this Valir?"

"My brother," Eli said with a sneer. "How is it you do not?"

The anger that flashed in Melchiz's eyes made Eli mentally retreat a few steps. Giving in to displays of anger was not like Melchiz, though he generally greeted Eli's taunts with indifference as if he was above them. Something else was troubling his brother.

"Well," the king spoke up. "I am greatly interested in the answer to both of those questions."

His words evaporated Eli's hope the exchange would fade harmlessly away. A lecture was building like a storm upon the sea. There was no escape; nothing to do except to hang on tight and weather it the best he could. The King took a long look at Melchiz, then aimed his stare at Eli.

"Well, I'm waiting," the king said. "Who would like to start? What? No one has anything more to say? How about if I take a guess at what's going on here? Melchiz, you know so little because you have relied on Zett to do your thinking for you. He hands you reports, and you sign them without bothering about the truth. This is not the way of kings; not if they wish to reign for very long. Knowing this almost makes me afraid to step down. I am disappointed that at this late date you have not learned the first thing about being king.

"And as for you, Eli, you are more informed, but you have done no more thinking for yourself than your brother. I know the bird that whispers in your ear. Whose bidding have you really done? Perhaps you should rethink where your duty lies.

"Very well, if I am to be robbed of peace these last few days of my reign, hear my word. The Valir remains where he is in the palace dungeon. The next full moon, following the ceremony, he shall be taken to the Hall of Judgment. Melchiz, as king, you shall be his judge. Your man, Zett, may prosecute if that brings him pleasure. Eli, you shall have the task of defending the prisoner and dealing with the Valir's Council. When the trial is over, everyone will abide by the decision. Then, the two of you will publicly stand together before the world and pledge allegiance to Shiloh. Are we clear on this?"

"Yes father," they said in childlike unison.

"So let it be done."

***

The palace gardens were in transitional bloom. The quince, tulips and daffodils of early spring were giving way to iris and dianthus. A sweet fragrance of gardenias hung on air. The often fetid, air of the city seemed many miles away. A bee laden with pollen circled Eli's head before buzzing away to its hive.

Eli loved the gardens. He sometimes spent his mornings there in quiet meditation. Today, he had come for a much different reason. He sought the advice of the ranking gardener. The woman to whom the duty belonged was difficult to distinguish from the other workers. She preferred the simple overalls and cotton shirts of her crew to the flash of rank. He found her working on her knees among the lilies.

"Mother," he called and waved.

She beckoned him over and patted the ground beside her. Eli took his place by her side. He had resorted to this place beside her in the garden since childhood. It was his refuge from the worries lurking outside the lush greenery and bright colors. She smiled at him and continued to work her hands through the soil.

"Was he as angry as he seemed?" Eli asked.

"He'll get over it," she replied without looking up. "He knows you were right to intervene. It will just take him a while to get over how you came to be right."

"Yeah, that kind of slipped out."

"What is Eeryn's interest in this boy?" she asked.

"Something about the vision of a seer back in the Boubouja," Eli said. "Some disaster that is supposed to affect the whole world. The boy is to deliver details to Eeryn."

"You don't believe in that sort of thing, do you?"

"No, not really," he said. "But I believe in Eeryn."

"Yes, you may be right. But be careful," the queen warned. "Your plan to smuggle Eeryn in or the boy out, is going to cause more trouble than you imagine."

"I know nothing of any such plans," he said. "I mean to keep it that way."

"You're a good son." She gave his hand a soft pat.

CHAPTER 32

"What? Again?" Joel cried. "How's a man supposed to live on this crap?"

"You ain't," the guard told him with a chuckle. "You're supposed to starve so's we don't have to listen to your bellowing day and night."

"Yeah," said a second guard. "Be a good sort and hurry up about it."

Joel's bowl hit the bars of the inner door as the guards closed them. Greasy soup splattered across the guard's shoulders. Bits of soggy meal and onion stuck to their hair and clothes. They brushed at the dripping mess as they fumbled for the key.

Bryn and One Eye exchanged a glance and a shrug. Then sent their bowls sailing toward the bars. The guards saw the bowls coming and tried to dodge the flying soup, but caught between the two doors, there was no place to hide. The bowls hit the bars with a loud clang. Tepid liquid covered the guards. The guard worked the key in the lock and pushed the door open.

"Close that door and get out of there," a voice called through the window.

Wood scraped on stone as the outer door swung slowly open and a sergeant of the guard stepped inside. He grabbed his soup splattered comrades and dragged them out. The sergeant, a man named Hoskie, retrieved the key, and locked the inner door.

"That little stunt is going to cost you—dearly," Hoskie promised before exiting the cell and closing the outer door.

A little door closed over the window in the outer door cutting the feeble light in the cell. The light disappeared altogether a short time later as boards were nailed over the other window.

Seven days later, the outer cell door swung open again. Torchlight fanned across the cobblestone floor. Bryn Bou lifted an arm to shield his eyes from the light. The shrieking grate of the iron door's hinges raked across his brain. Somewhere above him a pry bar worked the boards from the cell window. Bryn's mind shouted the curses his lips were too dry and weak to form. One Eye stirred beside him. Footsteps pounded the stones.

"Well, who wants soup?" Hoskie's cheery voice asked.

A guard carrying a steaming bucket of dungeon stew followed the sergeant into the cell. The prisoners, weak with hunger and thirst, crawled forward to get the soup. The guard threw the hot contents of the bucket over them. The blistering liquid summoned a strength Bryn didn't know he possessed. He slapped at the hot bits of gruel and vegetables that stuck to his skin.

"On your feet you worthless dinks," Hoskie ordered.

A fist closed on Bryn's shirt, and he was jerked to his feet. A sharp slap sent his head swimming. Next to him, One Eye was propped upright by a pair of soldiers. The hand on Bryn's collar threw him toward the open door. Unsupported, he stumbled a few steps before crashing to the floor.

"Get up," the sergeant's order was punctuated by a boot in the ribs.

Bryn grunted against the pain; got his trembling arms under him and levered himself from the floor willing himself to stand. By some miracle, his body obeyed. Soldiers grabbed his arms, and he was pushed toward the cell door.

Bryn and One Eye found themselves herded into a small room furnished only with a small wooden table and two stools.

"Sit," the sergeant commanded and disappeared out the door.

They were only too glad to comply. Bryn didn't hear a key turn in the lock, but his limbs refused to carry him to check it. It was just as well; the door opened a moment later. Soldiers laid food and water on the table. Another threw a pile of clothes on the floor. This time when they left, the key turned in the lock.

Sudden strength surged into Bryn's arms. He lunged for a water pitcher. A hand closed on his and he found himself beak to beak with One Eye. The old smuggler shook his head.

"Slowly," One Eye said. "Tiny sips. Eat only a little bread."

He released Bryn and followed his own advice sipping slowly from a pitcher. The water was cool, soothing his tongue and parched throat. He was about to thank the Creator when the liquid hit his stomach. An iron fist squeezed his guts. Bryn gagged. He wretched once as the water tried to escape, but he held it down. He sat doubled over for a couple of minutes before daring to sit up and try again. The next sip was easier.

An hour later, the door was opened and a rotund Valir dressed in fine linen with a silk cape across his shoulders was ushered in by the sergeant of the guard. The Valir stood a step inside the door looking over the prisoners with unbridled disgust. He seemed to be waiting for something.

"Stand up, you dinks," the sergeant growled.

Bryn and One Eye exchanged quizzical looks.

"Now!"

Bryn rose slowly trying not to show the pain of a sudden muscle crap. One Eye stood glaring at the sergeant for forcing the sign of respect and inwardly promising himself that should opportunity appear during their escape he would kill this human. The Valir advanced to the table and sat. Bryn and One Eye did the same.

"I am Ambassador Dorryn."

Bryn and One Eye waited in silence for the ambassador to unwrap whatever it was he was here to sell. Neither expected it to be good news for them. After a few moments of growing silence, Dorryn decided he would wait no longer.

"As you wish," he huffed. "You both are to be tried for mass murder. There will be a public trial, but the verdict and the sentence are already decided. Our King wishes to be spared the spectacle of the trial and the continued tensions it will cause. We have worked out a deal with the humans."

"Do tell," One Eye sneered.

"I'm offering you an opportunity to redeem yourselves by doing your duty to your king and your people."

"And what is this great opportunity?" Bryn asked.

"You will confess your crimes to the new human king and there will be no trial and your execution will be done privately here in the prison. In return there will be no revenge against our people either here or in our homeland."

"Does anyone care that we are innocent?" Bryn asked.

A puzzled look swept over the ambassador's face. He rubbed his beak in thought for a moment before replying.

"No."

"Then, go screw yourself," One Eye said.

"Well," One Eye said when they were returned to their cell. "There you have the reward of doing your duty to the king. Kind of takes the shine off things, don't it?"

"Dorryn is not the Valir," Bryn countered.

"No," One Eye said. "He's just the Valir's official representative."

"And failing at it miserably."

"Makes it hard to put much faith in Eeryn."

"Do we have any other choice?" Bryn asked.

Before One Eye could answer, came the sound of a key turning in the outer cell door. The door grudgingly moved over the cobblestone. A pair of guards dragged in an unconscious prisoner. The tall prisoner was unlike anything Bryn had seen before. He had long pointed ears and was covered with hair. One Eye was less amazed.

"Have fun when this one wakes up," a guard called to them as he backed out of the cell.

"What is he?" Bryn asked.

"They are called Wolven," One Eye explained. "Wolf people from the northern forests."

"Vicious killers every damn one of them," Joel added. "Keep you distance and don't turn your back on him."

One Eye appeared not to hear. He got to his feet and went to examine the Wolven. He lifted the creature's head by the ears and softly chuckled.

"My, my," he said. "I've met this one before. Let's don't wake him."

***

Cross lifted his head from the floor; groaned and let his head drop. A few minutes later, he rolled onto his back and managed to lever himself into a sitting position. He squinted at his cell mates through half open eyes. Using his arms, he scooted over the stone. There he propped himself against the wall, dropped his head to his chest, and began to snore.

"Who is willing to waste a little water?" One Eye asked.

When no one protested, he scooped up the water bucket and threw its contents on Cross. The Wolven's eyes flew open, he gave his head a slow shake, but otherwise did not move.

"Wow," said One Eye. "What did they give you?"

"Hell if I know," Cross said, a slight slur in his voice. "You're the bird from the bar."

"That I am," One Eye said. "What brings you to my humble abode?"

Cross rose to his feet, stretched, and walked over to test the bars of the inner door. They had no give to them. He shook them again before retreating to his spot on the floor he had vacated. Focusing on One Eye, he slowly shook his head before answering.

"Some dink informed the police that I was making speeches about the king. There was a small scuffle when they raided the bar. I had this human's neck in my hands. I was about to snap his neck when everything went black."

Cross slumped back against the wall to study his cellmates.

"What's he doing here?" Cross pointed at Joel. "They don't put his kind in here."

Bryn and One Eye turned to look at Joel who seemed to shrink under their stares. Bryn stood but made no move toward Joel. Cross moved over to stand shoulder to shoulder with Bryn and stare down on the trembling human.

"Well?" Bryn said.

"He's right," Joel confessed. "Men are not usually kept with outlanders. Zett killed our captain, then made me kill the rest of my squad. Then he had me thrown in this dungeon."

Cross delivered a sharp kick to Joel's head, and he collapsed in a boneless heap. Cross straddled his body and stared down at him.

"He's a liar, a coward or both," Cross said.

***

Across town Eeryn joined Faryn and Vulryn at their temporary refuge.

"Eli says the king has ordered a reprieve of sorts," Eeryn said. "After the ceremony, Melchiz will try Bryn and One Eye before he passes sentence."

"So, we have seventeen days?" Faryn asked.

"Maybe," Eeryn told her. "Melchiz will officially be king seven days before the actual ceremony ends. Zett has a powerful influence on Melchiz. I can easily imagine him persuading the new king to kick off his reign with a play to the people."

"That leaves use ten days," Vulryn said. "Not very long."

"What are we going to do?" Faryn asked.

"I have a plan," Eeryn replied. "But first, we have to get a look inside the prison."

"What?" Faryn said. "Won't that give things away? What if you're caught?"

"I won't be caught." Eeryn laid a hand over hers. "You will have to trust me on this. We know they are alive, but I have to know what kind of shape they are in. Last we knew, Bryn couldn't stand on his own. On the first day of the festival there is a feast that will provide cover for us."

"I don't like it."

"Neither do I," Vulryn chimed in.

"I think we are all well beyond liking the direction things are going," Eeryn told them. "I advise you both to get used to it."

"What's that supposed to mean?" Faryn asked. "Are we to simply turn our lives over to you?"

"Haven't you done that already? But, to come to the point, yes. Until Bryn is free, yes. You two would not last a day in this city on your own. Because you have not seen army patrols chasing you does not mean Dorryn has called off his search. His investigators are constantly sniffing around our back trail. But it goes deeper than that. Did Bryn tell you his dream?"

"You mean Coryn," Vulryn corrected him. "He told his dream to the Council. I was there."

"No, my large friend," Eeryn said. "I mean Bryn's dream. Coryn did not pluck Bryn Bou's name out of the air. The message Bryn is to deliver is his own dream, not Coryn's."

"Bryn said nothing to me about a dream," Faryn said.

"He has revealed it to no one but Coryn," Eeryn assured her. "He told Coryn only because the seer witnessed part of his dream. Nevertheless, there is a dream inside him; a dream that will break through to our world. When it does, I promise, you won't like it."

"How will you get inside the prison?" Vulryn changed the

subject. “You are banned from the palace.”

“I was in the palace only a few days ago.” Eeryn said.

He turned toward the window; held out his arm and whistled. A small white owl flew into the room to land on the seer’s outstretched arm.

“Rest easy,” the seer said. “I am not going in person. I’m sending a friend.”

CHAPTER 33

Bryn woke to the sound of boots on cobblestone. Overhead, thousands of glittering bits of dust danced in the glow of the dying light that streamed through the only window. Joel and One Eye laid empty bowls near the iron door and moved away to allow the guards to exchange them for ones filled with the thin soup they knew and loathed. There was no soup. The guards carried in a dozen plates laden with colorful fruit, fresh bread, and roasted fowls. The smell of grilled fish rose from large platters and drifted on the air. These were followed by buckets of amber liquid.

"Holy Creator," One Eye shouted. "That smells like beer."

"It is beer," Joel cried.

"Gifts from the King," Sgt Hoskie announced. "In honor of his reign."

Hoskie left them to feast. When the inner door closed behind him and the heavy door opened, the sound of the guards holding a similar feast flooded in. Moments later, music floated in through the cell's single window.

"What's going on?" Bryn asked through a mouthful of fish.

"King Zedek," Joel said. "Is stepping down in favor of his oldest son. Melchiz becomes king in a week. Shiloh will celebrate for seven days before the ceremony in honor of the old king and seven days after to welcome the new one. It's tradition for the departing king to send a feast to everyone in the city."

"You mean we're going to eat like this for two weeks?" One Eye asked.

"No, just today. It's the first of the celebration," Joel said. "This feast is probably all we'll see. There's always a chance the cooks will toss a bone with a little meat on it in the soup once or twice though."

"Better than nothing," Bryn said. "Eat, drink and be merry for tomorrow, we die."

"There's a cheery thought," One Eye said.

"Speak for yourself," Cross said through a mouth full of chicken.

Shadows stretched across the cell as the sunlight leaking in through the window faded along with the feast. Outside, the music grew louder, and the crowds grew larger. The darkness that swallowed up the cell was interrupted by a series of loud booms and splashes of bright red, blue and green. The window was too small for them to see the fireworks, so they settled for listening to the crowd outside ooh and aah at the colorful blasts. The fireworks went on for several minutes before Bryn began to feel something was out of joint.

Slowly swiveling his head, Bryn scanned the cell. He drew a sudden sharp breath and punched One Eye in the shoulder.

"What?" One Eye groused, rubbing his shoulder.

He turned toward Bryn and his eyes narrowed straining to make out the figure standing in the corner.

"I hear you've been looking for me." Eeryn stepped from the deep shadows into the small shaft of moonlight. A red flower of light blossomed in the window over his right shoulder. "I am Eeryn, son of Enoryn."

"Bryn Bou, son of Byryn," Bryn rose to his feet, hand extended. "I'd like to say I've been looking for you, but mostly I've just been stumbling around trying to stay alive. As you can see, I'm not doing very well at that task either."

"I don't think he heard you," One Eye said with a jerk of his head in Eeryn's direction.

The seer stood unmoving; his hand still reaching in Bryn's direction and staring into the dark with unblinking eyes. Eeryn's face was as vacant as his eyes. The seer disappeared in a blinding flash. He was replaced by a small white owl that flew across the cell and landed on Bryn's shoulder.

"Oh, that's all we need," One Eye groaned.

"What the hell is that?" Joel asked. "What's going on?"

"You don't want to know," One Eye told him.

"Ssshhh," Bryn's voice dropped to a whisper. "What are you doing here? What happened to Eeryn?"

Oto touched a small band around his leg and the image of

Eeryn returned. Bryn glanced down at his fellow prisoners, smiled, and shrugged. Oto touched the band again and the seer vanished in a flash of light.

"I have a message," Oto whispered in his ear. "Be ready to go."

Bryn's cellmates looked on in stunned silence. He seemed to be talking to the owl, but it was a one-sided conversation. One Eye expected some kind of contact from the seer. But not this, Bryn was a kid.

"When?" Bryn asked.

"No time for questions," he said. "Do you know the third virtue?"

"I do," Bryn replied.

"Practice it and all will be well. Oh, one more thing." Oto plucked a crest feather from Bryn's head and launched himself out the window.

"How the hell did he do that?" One Eye asked. "What's going on here?"

"Patience." Bryn answered.

"Huh?" Joel said.

"We wait."

"Wait for what?" One Eye asked.

"Whatever happens next," Bryn assured him. "We are to leave that to Eeryn."

"You're in touch with Eeryn aren't you?" Cross said. "When is the break?"

"Shut up," One Eye hissed with a jerk of his head toward Joel.

Cross came to sit beside One Eye. "Does the kid always talk to birds?"

"No, only sometime," One Eyes whispered back. "That owl has been following us since we escaped Zett's soldiers."

"Take me with you," Cross said. "I have friends who can get us out of Shiloh."

Joel crawled to a corner away from the others. The rough stone bit at his knees and the palms of his hands, but Joel wore a smile. He finally had something to give Lord Zett in exchange for his life.

***

"Hoskie, take a look at this." A portly private handed the sergeant one of the prisoner's bowls.

A slender blue "x" was drawn on the underside of the bowl. Hoskie had no idea why it should be there. However, he had strict orders to report such an occurrence directly to Lord Zett. He fought a quick inner battle over whether to ignore the mark, decided against it, and fled the prison in search of Lord Zett.

He found the Minister of the Army on his third stop and was immediately ushered into Zett's presence. Hoskie's knees trembled as he approached. The Minister appeared to be holding court. Hoskie couldn't remember the last time he had seen so much brass in one room. Those not in uniform wore robes of office and not all of them were human.

"Sgt. Hoskie, your lordship," he said with a bow. "Of the palace guard."

"You found the mark?" Zett asked.

"Yes sir, this morning, sir. I came right away."

"Well done, sergeant," Zett replied with a flick of his hand. "You may go."

Zett leaned back into the plush upholstery of his chair and silently surveyed his audience. He could read the anxiety on their faces. Everyone in the room owed his station, at least in part, to Zett. However, only a select few knew that this was the moment when talk turned to action. Zett took special satisfaction seeing the bird, Dorryn, squirm. The Valirian Ambassador reeked of weakness. Dorryn only played at treason; he lacked the courage for the real thing. The time for such games was over.

"It is as I said," Zett assured them. "Eli and his pet seer are plotting against the king. The messenger has just confirmed Eli and Eeryn are, at this moment, planning a prison break to free the Valir that slaughtered our citizens. And he plans to kill Melchiz before he can ascend the throne.

"Prince Melchiz has long suspected his younger brother's designs on the throne and set watchmen within the palace. He has appointed me over the business of ensuring that his throne is secure. Prince Melchiz wants the royal family's hands to be free of blood in this matter.

But we are to wait for an overt act of treason before we move.

Eli must die and Eeryn with him. The new king must not to be involved in any way. All communications and actions are to be channeled through me. I hope that is well understood."

"I am relieved that the question is settled at last," General Nui spoke up. "No more speculation about who is involved or the lengths they are prepared to go."

"Thank you for your confidence, General," Zett said. "But silence and caution are still necessary. Melchiz and I have thoroughly examined his personal staff and they are loyal to the cause. However, there may be plotters within the palace who have, thus far, escaped detection."

The meeting was interrupted by an incessant pounding on the chamber door. Everyone inside the room braced for the Minister's explosion of rage. The rage didn't come. The doors flew open, and a mud caked messenger boldly stepped inside unannounced.

"My Lord," he said and bowed on one knee. "I bring news of the utmost importance from Marah."

"Proceed, Captain," Zett's voice was measured as if rehearsed.

"My Lord, it is my sad duty to inform you of the death of your uncle King Malcolm of Marah."

The news was greeted by the sound of gasps and subdued murmurs. All eyes were on Zett. The Minister stared straight ahead without speaking. There was a slight twitch of the muscles in his face that was rapidly wiped away. His voice wavered for a second, then continued calm and controlled.

"You will all excuse me please," he said. "We will reconvene tomorrow if I am able. Thank you all for coming."

Zett rose quickly and rushed from the room with Balfour bobbing in his wake. Inside his private office, Zett leaned against his desk, his face away from Balfour. His master's shoulders were shaking. It took Balfour a full minute to realize Zett was not weeping—he was laughing.

"My Lord, are you alright?" Balfour asked mystified by laughter.

"Oh, my dear, Balfour," Zett slapped him on the back. "Never better, never better. The entire world is about to come right at last."

"If you say so, sir." Balfour scratched his bald head.

"Come along," Zett waved for him to follow. "We must call on the new King of Marah and his mother."

"I don't understand, sir."

"No, of course you don't Balfour," Zett said. "Let me enlighten you. Young Prince Mali, the one and only son of Prince Melchiz and my cousin, Ada, is now the rightful King of Marah. He is also second in line to the throne of Shiloh. It is entirely possible he may become king of all mankind. In such an event the youth will need the guidance of a seasoned elder."

"You think the kingdoms will be united again?" Balfour said.

"Oh, I'm counting on it," Zett said with a dreamy smile.

CHAPTER 34

Eeryn released Oto and closed the window. The news was good, Bryn was fit to travel. There was another bit of good news.

The Wolven, named Cross shared Bryn's cell. It was an opportunity to form an alliance with the Wolven living in Shiloh. New friends would give them an advantage. The jailbreak was going to throw the city into chaos. He couldn't see how everything would unfold, but he could see enough. He went to join the others.

"Is he alright?" Faryn rushed to meet Eeryn at the door. "Tell me he is well."

"Yes, he is well" Eeryn said. "He's a bit battered but healing. He's a strong lad."

Elryn was doing a nervous little dance in the corner. He sighed, smiled, and shook his head.

Young love.

"Your one-eyed hero is also well," he told her. "Now, if we may, let's try and work out how we will free them."

Eeryn hung his cloak on a hook by the door. The glow of a few embers and four small candles gave the room a warm glow. A pair of sofas flanked a small wooden table covered with a linen cloth. The fading firelight danced in one corner of the room. Across the way a dozen chairs were tucked under a long table. The seer padded over a woven rug that covered most of the floor and took a seat in a rocking chair fashioned of unfinished birch. The little cadre assembled in the room gravitated toward him.

The room, hidden under a tavern, seemed strangely like home. Eeryn wasn't sure if that was a good thing or not. All of those gathered here should be far away living lives and chasing dreams. They should be high in the trees of the Boubouja toasting one another with mugs of ale, singing songs and laughing with their fellows. Instead, they were huddled in the light of a dying fire and plotting what might be their own deaths.

Except, he knew that wasn't quite true. Death awaited them all, that was true enough. One didn't need to be a seer to know that. But he was a seer and he had seen. Betrayal, blood, and war stood in line ahead of Death and by the time Death rode in on his pallid steed, the black robed shade just might be a welcomed visitor. That was the vision locked in a boy's dream. It was not a message he wanted to share just yet.

Eeryn pulled a leather pouch from his tunic and began to fill his pipe. The pipe was a gift from his old mentor. As he touched a match to the leaves, he tried in vain to recall Coryn's face. His vision was blurred, but he knew his old teacher had been arrested.

"I'd like a pint of ale with this smoke," he proclaimed as smoke began to swirl about his face. "Who will join me?"

It turned out everyone was of like mind. That allowed Eeryn a few more minutes to think about what he was going to say to them.

"Fortunately for us," Eeryn said after a sip. "The trial is to be a show. Melchiz is to preside so it will not be held in the prison. He will be king by then and it is taboo for the king to enter the dungeons of the palace. They will have to move Bryn and One Eye. That will be our best chance to rescue them. It is also where a rescue is the most expected. Zett will not lose him again for lack of guards."

"How are we going to overcome all those guards?" Elryn asked.

"We're not," Eeryn said. "I think our best chance is to grab them before the trial."

"From the prison?" Vulryn asked. "How do we manage that?"

"When nobody's looking." The seer leaned closer. "We snatch them during the coronation ceremony."

Murmurs of assent ran through the group. The issue was decided.

"That gives us six days," Eeryn said.

***

The cell's wooden door ground open, its slow arc punctuated by the grunting effort of the guards. The strained voices that drifted in through the iron grillwork sounded strange. Bryn knew all the guards and their voices were familiar. These voices did not belong to any of the guards he knew. He rose to his feet. The prison ran on routine, different was seldom good. Bryn turned to face it head on. One Eye appeared at his shoulder followed by Cross and Joel. A new guard entered and keyed the lock of the inner door.

As the iron door swung open, a streak of crimson burst into the cell with a high-pitched shriek of joy. Faryn hit him mid-chest carrying him off his feet. Bryn met the floor with a loud explosion of breath. Faryn landed atop him and peppered his face with kisses.

"Oh, Bryn," she said with a sigh between kisses.

"Faryn, what are you doing here?" he asked. "Let me up."

She made no move to comply. Bryn started to repeat himself, but she felt so good next to him escape lost its urgency.

"Get up." One Eye took over. He pulled Faryn to her feet.

"Let's get out of here," Vulryn called from the door. "Move it. Eeryn's creating a diversion, but we haven't got much time."

Vulryn distributed weapons as the prisoners filed out.

"Where is everybody?" Bryn asked. "Where are the guards?"

"At the coronation," Faryn said. "Now, hurry."

"I don't think so," Byrn said.

"What?" She pulled away from him.

"Something's wrong," he replied. "It's too easy."

Bryn's head swiveled left, then right taking in the empty hall. Two dead guards lay at their station. There were no other guards anywhere. It was more than easy.

"It's a trap." Bryn said.

He caught Faryn by the sleeve and pulled her into the hall after him. One Eye fell in behind, Vulryn brought up the rear. There was neither time nor opportunity to reverse course now. Bryn charged ahead. At the end of the first hall, he realized he didn't know the way and pushed Faryn ahead of him. Bryn struggled to keep up as she sprinted through the maze of halls without hesitation.

"Where's Eeryn?" he panted.

Faryn ignored his question. She plunged ahead toward a guard standing just inside a set of two large wooden doors like the one outside the cell. Bryn pushed by her raising his dagger to take out the guard. The guard heard them coming and he glanced over his shoulder. Rather than drawing a weapon, the guard left his back to them and pushed open the door. Faryn stepped between Bryn and the guard. She clapped a hand on the guard's shoulder and followed him through the door. They were outside at last.

Faryn slowed to a walk, falling into step behind the guard. Her hand patted up and down beside her signaling them to all to do the same. A second guard fell in behind them. They were transformed in a moment into prisoners being escorted.

"Keep in step," the guard leading them ordered.

"Wynn?" Bryn said.

"No talking," Wynn snapped out the order.

Bryn obeyed. He adopted the bowed head walk of the condemned that also served to hide the smile lighting up his face. They were not free yet. Why the trap was not sprung while they were inside the walls of the prison remained a mystery. Whatever the reason, it no longer mattered. They were out in the open now and their chances of success had multiplied.

The street outside the palace wall was jammed with revelers. Vendors filled the corners offering skewers of meat cooked alongside ears of corn roasted over glowing coals. Tables filled with pies and baked delights frosted in bright colors competed for buyers on the sidewalks. The cool, evening air was alive with the odors that tantalized the senses. Music played in the distance where crowds danced in the city square, and children played in the parks.

Just inside the gate, Wynn tossed aside his uniform. Faryn and Vulryn did the same. A pile of cloaks awaited them and were quickly passed to the prisoners.

"He won't need one," Cross said and pointed at Joel.

He followed the pointed finger with a steel blade. Cross pushed the dagger under Joel's ribs and twisted it before shoving him to the ground.

"By twos, let's go," Wynn said. "Cross with me."

The little group melted into the crowd, keeping each other in sight as they moved through the streets unmolested.

Far away from city center, a large black bird perched above an open door. Music carried on a cloud of smoke wafted out to the street. As Wynn turned into the pub, Bryn watched a small white owl silently descend from the rooftop to sit beside the raven. With a glance and a wink, he stepped inside.

A hand slapped Bryn's shoulder hard enough to stagger him.

He turned on his attacker, and crouched ready to strike. He found himself looking into One Eye's face. The old smuggler was beaming. He swept his hand over the crowded pub.

"We're home," he announced. "This place has it all."

"Sweetie," a voice screamed from across the bar. Elryn rushed across the room; threw her arms around One Eye's neck, planting a huge kiss on him.

"See what I mean?" he said.

Faryn grabbed Bryn by the collar and pulled him toward the back of the room. A Valir in a leaf cloak sat with his back to the wall; a pipe clenched in his beak. Eeryn waved to a chair beside him. Then signaled to the bar with a circling of his other hand. Bryn sat down with the prophet. Faryn kissed his cheek and wandered away leaving the two alone.

"Well, my boy," he greeted Bryn. "We meet at last."

"I wished for slightly more festive conditions," Bryn said as drinks arrived. "But I'm glad to be here. One Eye greatly approves of the place."

"And you?" Eeryn asked. "Do you approve of my congregation?"

"Not my place to approve or disapprove," Bryn lifted his glass toward the prophet. "Cheers."

"Ah, a diplomat." Eeryn grinned at him and raised a glass. "Cheers."

The two sipped dark brown beer and studied one another. It was an interesting study. The older prophet wore his leaf cloak in the relaxed manner of one who had faced the worst and lived to tell the tale. The warrior in him was evident in his back to the wall fearlessness. The tired lines about his eyes said the warrior no longer found war glorious.

The ragged youth's movements had a stiff newness about them. His expectant eyes constantly swept the room for approaching trouble though only a fool would take his wary manner for fear. There was no doubt he too was a warrior. Faryn had the uneasy feeling she was looking into a wrinkle in time; somehow seeing the past and future sharing a drink across the table.

"Tell me about your friend," Eeryn said.

"One Eye? I'm still trying to figure that one out."

"Oh, he's not complicated," Eeryn said with a wave of his hand. "But I was speaking of the small white fellow sitting outside the door."

"Judging by the company he's keeping I'd say you know more about him than I do."

"He speaks to you?"

"He does."

"Don't you think that rather strange?" Eeryn leaned closer. "Maybe you are losing your sanity."

"I've been thinking that since I left Vix." Bryn smiled.

Eeryn held out his hand. Bryn took it, and in his spirit, gears meshed, wheels turned, a rumbling stirred him.

"Good," Eeryn said. "Hold on to that. It will keep you from taking yourself too seriously. That, my friend, is the key to sanity."

Eeryn held up a finger and cocked his head toward the door. Bryn followed his gaze. In the distance something stirred; rising like a wave; building. A tall, ginger colored Wolven caught the door frame. His shirt was torn. He was panting. His eyes burned with anger as he stared at Eeryn. He heaved a huge breath and pushed through the crowd toward the seer. Bryn's hand fell to his belt. Eeryn laid a hand over Bryn's and shook his head.

"Cross, my friend," Eeryn called across the room. "What is it?"

"The King," Cross called back. "The king is dead. Soldiers are rounding up outlanders. Rioters are killing those the soldiers miss. They are blaming the murder on the escaped Valir."

"Which king?" Eeryn asked.

"The old one," Cross said. "Melchiz is king. Zett is on the loose and he has a free hand. We are getting out of the city."

Eeryn climbed atop his chair. Time and everyone in the bar froze.

"The old king is dead," he announced though all had heard. "Everyone make your way to the rendezvous. Go now. Wolven come with us."

CHAPTER 35

The door to Eli chambers exploded inward spilling the captain of his guard and six red-faced, panting, soldiers into his room. Luther, short sword drawn and ready, scanned the room eyes darting from corner to corner. His face wore the hard, cold look of battle.

"Are you alright?" Luther asked.

"Of course," Eli answered. "What is all of this? What's happened?"

"There's been a prison break. Guards are dead and your father was attacked in his chambers," Luther said. "I don't know more than that. I had to be sure you were safe."

"Where's Melchiz?" the prince asked.

"Still at the celebration," Luther said. "He has his guard with him, and more troops are on the way to bring him back to the palace."

"Take me to my father," Eli ordered.

The prince threw a cloak around his shoulders and fastened his sword to his waist. Luther made no protest. He led the way to the king's rooms at a cautious pace ignoring the prince's desire to hurry. A winding staircase led up to the next floor. They were met at the top of the stairs by the king's guard. The shock on the soldier's downcast faces was clear. The guards silently parted and let the prince pass. Luther remained at his side as they made their way down the hall to the group of men crowded into the king's door. Their hushed conversation came to an abrupt halt as Eli approached. A path opened for him, and Eli entered his father's room.

A fire burned on the hearth. A plume of steam curled from a mug of tea on his father's desk where papers were neatly stacked awaiting the king's attention. The only thing out of place was the blood beneath the desk and chair. The king, lying on his bed, appeared as peaceful as the room. A blanket was pulled up to cover his shoulders as though he were sleeping.

Lord Zett stood at the head of the bed hands folded in front of him; a long look of sorrow painted on his narrow face. Eli hated the man, but never as much as at that moment. Zett's mourning felt as false as his loyalty. Eli knelt beside his father and laid a hand over those of the dead king.

So cold, Eli thought. *Nothing remains but a cold, empty shell.*"

Eli and his father were so different. One would wonder whether they were father and son until the queen appeared beside them. Their unrestrained opinions had produced spectacular clashes.

Eli had no doubts that Melchiz was his father's favorite. Melchiz was the heir and unlike this older brother, Eli challenged his father's decisions. Nevertheless, there was no doubt they loved one another. Love that now squeezed at Eli's heart and brought tears to his eyes. He knelt holding his father's hands until the silence was shattered by wailing from across the room.

His mother ran in and threw herself over the king's body. She held a cheek pressed to his chest; hoping against hope for a heartbeat but found none. She had spent the evening with Melchiz and her grandson enjoying the coronation celebration that honored her husband not knowing she would never see him alive again.

"Why?" she sobbed. "He was stepping down. Why would someone do this?"

Zett laid a long pale hand on her shoulder. "A question we are all asking, Your Highness. I shall not rest until I have your answer. That is with the king's permission."

Zett looked at Melchiz who now stood at the foot of the bed. Without a word, he dropped to one knee and bowed to Melchiz. Everyone save his mother and brother did the same. The new king shifted uneasily from one foot to the other as he looked around the room. The moment Melchiz lived for took him by complete surprise. Zett rose and ushered all but the royal family from the room.

"I must speak to you alone," he whispered to Melchiz and quickly added, "Your Highness."

An hour later, the new king found his Minister of the Army waiting for him in the throne room.

"I took a chance you might come here," Zett said. He swept a hand over the room. "It's all yours now."

"This is not how I imagined it would be," Melchiz said.

"But you did imagine it," Zett told him. "You imagined being king and now you have achieved your dream. The kingdom is yours to shape as you will. That is, once you have secured it."

"Secured it?" Melchiz said. "I am the king. There is none who can deny it."

"Maybe," Zett said, drawing closer. "And maybe not."

"What do you mean?"

"I mean, this." Zett drew a bloody cloth from behind his back and slowly unwrapped the object inside it. "A Valirian dagger if I'm not mistaken. Taken this night from your father's back. Another was found not long after the Valir escaped from the dungeon. It too was found in this very palace."

"What? Where?"

"Someone called away the guards during the ceremonies," Zett said. "It was stupid of them to obey, I know, my humblest apologies. The proscribed punishment has been carried out."

"You executed them already?" Melchiz asked. "But why? They might have possessed information we needed."

"Information, readily given before their deaths," Zett assured him.

"Who called them away?"

Zett gave no answer as he studied the floor.

"Out with it," Melchiz ordered. "Who was it?"

"It was your brother."

"Eli."

***

Luther jumped from his chair wheeling on the intruder. Across the room lances dropped to the ready. Eeryn held his empty hands in the air. Luther returned his sword to its scabbard and signaled for his men to stand down.

"What are you doing here?" Luther demanded.

"I have come to warn the prince," Eeryn replied.

"Warn me?" Eli stepped closer. "About what? Do you know who killed my father?"

"You must flee the palace at once," Eeryn told him.

"Are we under attack?" Eli asked.

"Only from within," Eeryn said. "You must flee now."

"Men coming this way---a lot of them," said one of the guards by the door.

Luther pushed the prince behind him and drew his sword. The soldiers of the prince's guard formed a defensive line behind the closed door.

"Open in the name of King Melchiz," came the order from the other side. "Luther, do you hear me? Luther, you must lay down your arms at once and turn the prince over to me."

"Caleb, you know I can't do that," Luther said.

Caleb de Luna was the Marshall of the Army, and Luther's immediate superior. They joined the army together as boys and fought side by side in two wars. Luther knew as strong as their friendship might be, it was not as strong as Caleb's duty to their king.

"You can and you must," Caleb said. "Don't make me do this."

Luther felt movement behind him followed by a loud pop. He glanced over his shoulder unsure whether to be relieved by what he saw.

"What's this all about?" Luther said. "I need your assurance the prince will not be harmed."

"I can promise that my men will not hurt him," Caleb called back. "But no more than that. He is to be taken to the king."

"What of my men?"

"You are all relieved of duty. Go home."

Luther tossed his sword on the stone floor. "Did you hear, Caleb?"

"I did," he replied. "Now, open the door."

"You will let my men safely leave the palace before you enter. I must see them cross the grounds."

"What will stop me from coming in once they leave?"

"Honor."

"You know me too well Luther. Very well. Send them out."

Luther nodded at his men. They stowed their weapons and stood back as Luther slowly opened the door. Luther watched his troops cross the lawn before opening the door again. Caleb de

Luna stepped inside, and his men fanned out across the room.

The prince was gone.

"Where is he?" Caleb asked.

"He jumped from the balcony." Luther pointed at the open curtains. "Take a look."

Marshall de Luna stepped onto the balcony and peered over the edge. There was no sign of the prince, only a small bundle of silk at the base of the palace wall. There was a sudden commotion in the street, and he watched a small group run away from the palace. He couldn't make out which of them was the prince, but he was sure one of them was.

"That's going to cost you Luther," he said. "You should have played it straight with me."

CHAPTER 36

Eeryn led the rush out the pub's back door. Fleeing patrons streamed by him in a headlong dash for freedom. Eeryn came to a halt a block away to regroup. Of the Wolven, only Cross had joined their group.

"Do you have a plan?" he asked.

"Yes, as it seems, you do too," Eeryn answered. "We think alike."

"The humans were becoming dangerous," Cross said. "We have a meeting place in the hills to the northwest."

"We are heading in that general direction," Eeryn said. "We can be stronger together."

"Stronger than what?" Bryn interrupted.

"Stronger than the humans," Eeryn said. "Those with me cannot run to the Boubouja. That includes you, Bryn Bou as I suspect does Cross."

"Zett has traitors willing to sell their people in every land," Cross said. "When you say such things to the wrong people, you cannot go home again."

"What are you planning?" Bryn asked.

"To gather as many outlanders as we can," Eeryn said. "What happens after that we will learn as the future unfolds. Come with me or stay, the choice is yours."

Bryn nodded at Eeryn. He could hear the human mob advancing through the streets in their direction. The eight souls gathered around the seer merged into the rushing tide fleeing the city.

"Stay close," Eeryn cautioned.

Eeryn waved them on across streets; through buildings; and down alleys until the city wall loomed before them. They rounded a corner and the route suddenly opened up into a garden. Across the lawns and short hedges Bryn saw soldiers corralling outlanders into groups. A Valir with a dark green crest saw them and broke from the crowd. Bryn started in his direction, but Eeryn caught his sleeve and held him fast. The fleeing stranger's hands suddenly flew in the air. He lurched forward, stumbled, and fell on his face in the grass with a lance in his back.

Their escape cut off they turned left moving away from the gate. Weaving through the rows of shanties that littered the base of the wall and sliding along with his back against the hewn stone, Bryn still felt exposed. Eeryn brought them to a halt in a narrow passage. Twenty or thirty yards further down the wall a wooden lean-to blocked the way. It wasn't much of a shelter, just scrap slats staked to the ground and propped up against the wall. It was home to someone, smoke curled from a battered bit of stove pipe at one end. Eeryn ducked inside. A moment later, the seer's head reappeared.

"What are you waiting for?" he asked and waved for Bryn to follow.

Bryn lowered his head and stepped through the open end of the lean-to. He was met by a sharp pain in his right leg. His shin struck a square wooden door sticking up from the ground. He knelt and stuck his head into the opening where a torch lit what looked like a tunnel. Dirt walls stretched into the dark.

Below him Eeryn picked up a torch from a waiting stack of torches. The seer lit it from the torch on the wall and started down the tunnel. Bryn climbed into the passage and set out after the seer. Faryn dropped into the tunnel behind him. Further down the passageway, they came upon a second torch embedded in the wall. Eeryn lit it and hurried on.

Without landmarks it was hard for Bryn to gauge distance, but he felt certain they traveled at least a mile underground before coming to a dead end. Eeryn handed him a torch and retrieved a ladder from the floor. Eeryn used the top of the ladder to push open an overhead door. With a deep bow and sweep of his hand the seer invited Bryn to ascend.

Behind them, parts of the city were burning. The fire and the city lights painted the horizon with an orange glow. According to Eeryn they were two miles from the city. The tunnel entrance was shielded from the watch towers by a stand of thick oak trees. Using his body to block the light from the torch, Eeryn waited by the door for everyone to safely exit. Wynn was the last to exit the tunnel. He hauled the ladder up onto the grass and closed the door. Cross then spread leaves over the wooden entrance.

The Wolven's ears shot up; the hair on his neck bristled and his upper lip began to twitch revealing long, sharp canine teeth. A low growl rumbled up from his throat.

"It's okay," Eeryn told him. "I'm expecting someone."

The muscles in his face and arms uncoiled, but Cross kept his eyes on the nearby woods. Bryn picked up the sound of something large moving behind the trees and his head snapped toward Eeryn. The seer waved for him to calm down. It was easier said than done. An armored ceros carrying a human army officer in an elegant uniform pushed into the clearing. Eeryn seemed unperturbed by the human's arrival. He lowered the hood of his cloak to his shoulders.

"Your Highness," he said with a slight bow of his head in greeting. "Bryn Bou, may I present Prince Eli of Shiloh."

Bryn drew a dagger. Beside him One Eye did the same as a mounted escort of human soldiers slowly rode into the open and formed around the prince.

"What's going on here?" Bryn said backing away from the soldiers.

"Put that blade away," Eeryn snapped. "The prince is here for the same reason you are."

"He broke out of jail?" One Eye asked with a sneer.

"No, you dink," Eeryn said. "He's trying to escape the executioner."

Bryn and One Eye stared at him as if he had grown a second head.

"Prince Eli, should he be apprehended," Eeryn explained. "Is going to be charged with conspiring with me to free the two of you from prison. An escape which led to the two of you murdering the King of Shiloh on our orders."

"It's true," Eli assured them. "I had to escape through a window. Like it or not, we are all in this together."

"We meant no offense, Your Highness," Bryn said.

"Then no more calling me, 'Your Highness.'" Eli said. "I think those days are over for good. My name is Eli de Claire."

"This meeting is no accident," Bryn said. "Nor do I believe is this murder business."

"You are correct," Eeryn said. "I was warned ahead of time and plans have been in place for some time. That tunnel did not happen overnight."

"Warned, by whom?" Eli asked.

"By him." Eeryn pointed at Bryn. "He brought the final piece of Coryn's vision."

"You got all that from a single feather?" Bryn said.

"Sorry, I couldn't resist." Eeryn smiled at him. "The feather was just for show. You carried the vision in the safest place of all—in your spirit."

"What comes next?" Bryn wanted to know.

"We try to stay alive," Eeryn told him. "Beyond that, only the Creator knows. However, one thing is sure; we cannot stay here. Let us keep moving."

"Where are we going?" Bryn asked.

Eeryn looked around the clearing searching for something. Finally, he nodded twice and pointed. "That way."

***

Bryn stared into the red and gold flames dancing above the glowing bed of coals within a stone ring. The fire was reflected in his eyes, but he didn't see it. Nor did he notice the shadows on the overhanging branches that mimicked the rhythm of the flames. Faryn sat beside him, her arm wrapped around his, but he didn't feel her there.

"Where are you, Bryn Bou?" her whisper barely made a sound.

"I keep asking myself the same thing," he said.

Faryn, unsure he heard, jumped at the sound of his voice. His arm circled her shoulders and drew her closer. The eyes that left the fire to look into hers, had aged. They seemed old and out of place in his boyish face. She shuddered at the thoughts that aged them.

A smile seemed to rise from inside him. His beak moved along hers.

"Come to my bed," her breathless voice invited.

His fingers laced in hers, he lifted her to her feet. Hand in hand they left the fire for the soft bed of green leaves she had gathered earlier. Her head sought the hollow of his shoulder secure under the shelter of his arm.

"I love you, Faryn."

The beating of his heart against her ear told her it was true. Her beak locked in his, their breath became one. They moved together beneath the stars. Caress and touch; gasp and sigh; the ancient rhythm transformed two into one. Afterward he lay listening to her soft breathing; watching the gentle rise and fall of her breast.

Somehow sleep eluded him. Taking care not to wake her, he slipped away. The fire had settled into a smoldering bed of orange embers. By its dim light, Bryn slowly made his way toward the woods. The night was quiet around him. The denizens of the dark were silent.

Solitary meditation is harder to find than gold or glory.

He smiled at the thought. He climbed high into the boughs of a centuries old oak, leaned back against the sturdy trunk, and closed his eyes.

Where was he? It was a good question. He did not know how to answer it. He certainly could not conjure an answer Faryn would understand. He'd done no more than stumble from one crisis to another. He felt that he had not planned a move on his own since he decided to start on his journey. He felt he was being pushed along this path by lies, betrayal and unwarranted hatred rather than the duty he sought to do. He had begun talking to a bird. It made no sense. Yet, somehow, it seemed the most natural thing in the world. The thought sent a sudden chill down his spine. He shook it off. That kind of thinking was alright for the likes of Eeryn or Coryn, but not in his head, thank you kindly. He was a regular guy; nothing more.

Below him, a twig snapped. His eyes opened, but otherwise he did not move. Someone was moving through the litter below him. Pale skin flashed between the trees to his right moving off down the hill. Bryn pushed himself to his feet and followed the sounds gliding from tree to tree. The figure was too far away to make out details, but it was definitely a human. Size favored a man who made good use of cover, staying low and keeping out of the moonlight that occasionally broke through the clouds.

A man with training, Bryn thought. *A soldier.*

He had to get closer. Moving deeper into the trees he took up a parallel course hoping to anticipate the man's moves and get ahead of him. Gradually, Bryn narrowed the distance between them.

The man wasn't wearing a uniform, but that didn't change Bryn's mind about his training. What troubled Bryn was the direction in which the man was moving. He was headed away from the main body of refugees toward Zett's army. How had he slipped past the sentries Cross kept on their back trail? Was he a scout returning to base or was this a traitor from their ranks? Bryn intended to find out.

Bryn glided softly to the ground. As he stepped forward, the man dropped into a patch of ferns and disappeared from sight. His chance of surprising the man was gone. He charged toward the place he last saw the man. Bryn scoured the ground for a clue, but no trace of the man remained. Bryn turned to go back to the camp and collided with a pair of identical Wolven.

"What are you doing out here?" one asked.

Bryn looked up into the matching faces. It took a moment to realize they weren't identical after all. The one on the right smiled revealing a chipped tooth.

"Following a human," Bryn said.

"Where is he?" Chip Tooth asked. "We've been out here all night. Haven't seen any humans."

"Until a few seconds ago," Bryn said. "You didn't see me either."

Chip's smile widened. "But we got you, didn't we?"

"So it seems," Bryn replied.

Bryn sold them a look of resignation and surrender, then bolted by them. He ripped through the woods; jumped over a fallen tree trunk and launched himself toward the branches of a towering oak. A whooshing sound reached his ear a little less than a second before the stone hit the back of his head. Bryn crashed to the ground and rolled to a stop against the trunk of his would-be sanctuary.

He came to older and wiser. A blurry image swam before his eyes finally crystallizing into the face of Cross. The Wolven was leaning over him with an unhappy look on his face.

"You can't outrun a Wolven sling," he said.

Most of what he said was lost to the throbbing beat playing

between his ears, but Bryn nodded agreement.

"I know that now," he replied.

"Why didn't you just tell them who you are?" Cross asked, taking Bryn by the arm. "Come on, get up. What's this about a human?"

Bryn held his head in both hands waiting for the spinning to stop before answering.

"Serves you right for leaving me all alone," Faryn told him.

"I was coming back," Bryn said. "I just had some thinking to do."

"And you couldn't think next to me?" she asked.

"Absolutely not," Bryn said. "When you're with me I can think of nothing else."

Cross elbowed Chip in the ribs. "He's good."

"We didn't see a human," Chip said. "We did find human tracks after...er...well, after Bryn decided to come back with us."

"Everybody back to bed," Cross ordered. "And stay there. Not you two. You get back to your post."

The next morning instead of signaling to break camp Eeryn declared a day of rest and mourning for the fallen king. It soon became apparent Eeryn had another motive. Refugees began to stream into the camp by twos and threes. The surrounding woods were filling with newcomers joining themselves to the group. New camps sprang up. By evening the mass of fleeing outland species gathered beside the little stream took on the look of an army. Bryn was convinced an army was exactly what it was meant to be all along.

CHAPTER 37

The palace at Shiloh was abuzz with swarms of the great and not so great jostling one another for a chance to enter the royal chamber. Three human kings were dead. Every kingdom from the Northern Mist to the Southern Sea seemed convulsed with the change. The old world was dying, a new world was in the making, and everyone was scrambling to grab a piece of it. Oblivious to huddled ambassadors and mobilizing armies, the newly crowned king of Shiloh stirred in his cradle under the watchful eye of his uncle and regent, Zett, Lord of the Army of Shiloh.

Zett claimed no particular god, yet he was a man of vision. He was not a seer after the human fashion. Rather he was a sculptor chipping away the stone that hid the future of power and glory that lived in his mind's eye. Zett the Great, Emperor of Tettias, he liked the sound of it. A cold smile crossed his face. The title had a regal ring to it. He would have to wait a while longer to try it on, but it was good to be prepared.

"Bring my sister to me," he ordered.

"Lord Zett," the Captain of the Guard said. "Her Majesty left word she was not to be disturbed."

"Bring. Her." Zett's icy tone dripped malice. "I am not concerned with her wishes. Do it now."

"Yes, my Lord." The captain hurried from the room.

The Queen appeared alone in the doorway a few minutes later. She daubed at her red-rimmed eyes with a lace kerchief. To her growing sorrow, tears could not obscure the scene within her own rooms. Zett stood over her son wearing victory like a cloak of honor. When, at last, he looked at her, dread stabbed her heart. She pushed it aside. She was the daughter of a king. She squared her shoulders and lifted a defiant chin. But the hands neatly folded across her middle trembled.

"You wished to see me?" she said.

"Yes." He turned to face her. "Prepare for a journey. We are going home."

"To Marah? Whatever for?"

"To secure our father's crown for your son," Zett said.

"I won't do it," she replied. "He is king of Shiloh. Let Marah find a new one. You go be king of Marah."

Zett calmly crossed the room. He rolled a lock of her hair between his fingers and let it fall.

"My dear sister," he said. "It's really for the best that the young king goes to Marah. The persons who murdered your husband and father-in-law have yet to be captured. Who knows, they may still be in the city. I would hate to see anything tragic happen to you or your son."

"You bastard."

"Yes, well, that's always been the problem, hasn't it?" He lifted her chin so that her eyes met his. "Be that as it may, I will soon have the throne our father denied me. The question is, will your son live to share it? Well, will he?"

Cruel laughter chased her down the hall toward her bedrooms. Behind locked doors, the fear that paralyzed her moments ago melted into a new steel forged in the fires of rage ignited by her brother's threats.

She had been a young bride, much younger than Melchiz. Although their marriage was a political alliance, she loved him and had always leaned heavily on Melchiz for strength. Now, that strength was gone leaving only the dark void of her wounded heart.

For the moment, Zett commanded the nursery. She swore to take it back and free her son. Her tears haltingly gave way to a determined smile. A new thought occurred to her. Let Zett have his way. Let him build her son an enduring kingdom. Her brother's vanity could be trusted to lavish the throne with all the splendor the united kingdoms of mankind could produce. She would see to it that the same vanity would be his destruction. She summoned her maids and began preparations for the journey.

Except for the execution of Eeryn, Eli, and their little messenger, all was progressing as he planned. He had disposed of Melchiz as easily as he had the doddering old king. Leaving him dead on his new throne with yet another Valirian dagger in his heart.

There was no coronation ceremony held for young Mali, not yet. The deed was legally done, he was king, that was good enough for now. There was an empire to build. A coronation in Marah would show the world a new era had arrived. The generals of Marah must see the transition of power as complete. He would see them swear loyalty to their new king. He could buy their hearts later.

Zett led his entourage down the great staircase to ground level where the official business of ruling took place. He entered through the king's door, a new purple robe draped over his shoulders. His haughty look shone with newfound royalty. Silence fell like a curtain. Every eye turned to greet him; heads bowed, and Zett made his way to the throne.

Good, he thought with a nod to the crowd for their reverence. *Yes, very good.*

Zett settled against the high back of the golden throne of Shiloh. His regency had been declared. It was up to him to silence all opposition with the assumption of royal rule.

"General Winslow," he said.

A square jawed soldier with close cropped hair the color of cast iron pushed through a row of robed attendants to stand before the new Regent King of Shiloh.

"How is the city?" Zett asked.

"The palace is secure, my Lord," Winslow said. "The guard has been increased as you ordered. The walls of the city have been swept of rabble. The able bodied among them have been pressed into service and the rest expelled. The rebels are disorganized and fleeing. The gates are sealed."

"And the outlanders remaining in the city?" Zett asked.

"As you have instructed, my Lord," Winslow answered with a bow of his head.

"Very good," Zett said. "The safety of the government rests on your shoulders, General. Do not fail your people."

General Winslow backed away through the throng and disappeared.

"We assure the people of Shiloh there shall be no more deaths in this palace," Zett announced. "As all have heard, the responsibilities of King Mali extend beyond Shiloh. To secure a lasting peace among men, King Mali and the Queen Mother shall accompany me to Marah where he is to be crowned King of Marah. In our absence, Marshall de Luna will see to the day-to-day operation of Shiloh and direct military operations."

"Lord Zett," a rotund figure, nearly as wide as he was tall, with great sagging jowls waddled forward to assume the departed general's place before the throne. "You mean to say the child, Mali, will be laying claiming to the throne of Marah as well as Shiloh?"

"Ambassador Enroe," Zett strung out the name with a sneer. "How nice of you to pay your respects. There will be no 'laying claim' as you call it. King Mali is the King of Marah. He will officially wear the crown as soon as we arrive. I believe the King of Taurus and the King of Dagon are already on their way to the coronation."

"But there has been no coronation announced," Enroe sputtered.

"I believe I just announced it," Zett said. "You will pass the news along to your fellows, won't you?"

"You can't do this," the Ambassador protested. "There are protocols to be followed."

"Guards," anger blazed in Zett's voice. "Remove this man. He seems to have forgotten his place both as a guest here and as a servant of Marah. You are fortunate Enroe, I am feeling charitable. You may live, but you will vacate the embassy immediately."

Four palace guards hustled Enroe from the room on the points of their lances. They returned to their stations wiping sweat from their brows. Zett smiled his approval. He took a last look over his audience before rising and striding from the room. Balfour stepped forward to address the assembly.

"It is Lord Zett's wish that Ambassador Dorryn of Valir and Ambassador Magen of the Wolven meet with him in his chambers. All those without permanent duties inside the palace are to leave the grounds at once."

The assembled privileged persons filed from the room without protest. Passage through the halls packed with soldiers was difficult and only slightly less frightening than the scene they had just witnessed.

Outside, the palace grounds were lined with tents between

which soldiers scurried carrying weapons and food in preparation for the royal trek to Marah. The reason an army of this size was needed to transport a child and his family was clear. Zett would allow no protests from the generals of Marah.

The two ambassadors followed Balfour from the throne room through a door hidden behind the dais. The door opened onto a small anteroom and a spiral staircase of stone. A single sentry nodded at them as they passed. Two winding flights led them to a hall in the royal family's living quarters where tapestries of blue and gold decorated the walls. Balfour stopped before a heavy oak door and rapped gently for entrance.

Dorryn was surprised to find that they entered a bedroom. The large desk just inside the balcony said this doubled as an office of sorts, but the huge bed told him this was clearly not the king's apartment. Evidently Zett was looking after appearances. No doubt he controlled the infant king, but he had yet to set himself up in the royal chambers.

"Please, sit down." Zett motioned them to the big desk where a bottle of wine waited.

Dorryn knew Zett too well to be lulled into complacency by his cordial tone or sharing of wine with outlanders. Zett wanted something and he thought the ambassadors could get it for him. As he sat, Dorryn reminded himself once more to be careful.

"I apologize for the scene in there," Zett pointed at the wine and nodded to a servant. "That man is such a boor, and we are well to be done with him."

When the servant left them, Zett lifted his glass to his guests.

"To a historic new day," he said, and glasses clinked. "Destiny has made Mali king of both Shiloh and Marah. He's too young to appreciate the gift of fate, but his mother and I do. We are faced with an unprecedented opportunity for unity and peace for all Tettias.

"Unfortunately, there are short sighted, bigoted beings like Enroe among us who cannot see the possibilities the future affords. Shiloh and Marah will be one again. Taurus and Dagon have already joined us in an alliance to make it so. That's half the world, my friends. But what of the other half? What of Valir and Wolven?"

"I'm not sure I understand completely," Dorryn said.

"It's simple really," Zett explained. "Taurus and Dagon make up most of the world east of Marah. They have agreed to a united confederation of mankind. One united population under one rule of law without barriers to movement, trade, or prosperity for all."

"I sense there is a problem," Dorryn said. "In which Magen and I might be of assistance."

"You are absolutely right," Zett assured him. "There is resistance in your homelands. A vocal minority in both countries is threatening the world with war."

"I've heard nothing about this," Dorryn said.

"That's not entirely accurate," Zett said. "You know about the arrest of Byryn Bou and Coryn the seer. Unfortunately, their arrest failed to stop the murder of King Melchiz.

"Melchiz was working out an alliance with the King of the Valir to open our borders. That's why Eli and Eeryn arranged for Byryn's son to kill both kings. They hoped to make Eli king by force. Now, Councilor Raryn assures me Eeryn and Eli have raised an army of discontents to overthrow the rightful governments of Valir and Shiloh and install Eli as king. An army is gathering on the shared border of our countries."

"That can't be," Dorryn said. "The Council would have known if that many people were gathering."

"Exactly." Zett leaned closer. "Byryn not only knew, but he also engineered it on the Council's behalf. Then, he sent his son to see that Eli was made king. Byryn's arrest has stirred his supporters throughout the Boubouja. It is going to take a large force to dislodge them. Councilor Raryn has assured me that he is moving to take steps to provide for the security of the Valir. Are you ready to stand with us?"

"Of course," Dorryn assured him. "Raryn has always had my full support."

"And you Ambassador Magen," Zett said turning to the Wolven. "You have long been aware of the treason of Cross and his followers. It is confirmed Cross has joined the rebels. Are ready to persuade your king it is time to strike these murdering rebels?"

"My embassy guard is at your disposal," Magen answered. "I feel sure King Lon will further supply your need."

"Thank you both." Zett leaned back in his chair and sipped at his wine. "We live in perilous times. Maintaining the peace may require hard things of us. However, with the Creator's help, your homelands may yet be saved."

"How are we to communicate with you while you are in Marah?" Dorryn asked. "Valir has no embassy there."

"I was thinking you might join me and establish an embassy," Zett told him. "I can think of no one better qualified for the task. Councilor Raryn agrees. You have his blessing if you choose to go."

Dorryn floated from the room on dreams of future glory. At last, his genius was to be recognized and rewarded. He would see Eeryn's head tumble into the axe-man's basket. The seer's shame would be complete and the name of Dorryn venerated by generations of Valir.

He stepped from the palace. Overhead the sky was clear, the sun beamed down warmth made just for him. Dorryn waved away his carriage. He deserved a stroll through the palace gardens. Life was sweeter than the fragrance of the Queen's flowers that bloomed all around him. He wondered what had become of the Queen. The thought vanished swifter than it came. His life had been rekindled; this was no time to ponder such trivial notions. It had been years since he had walked from the palace to the embassy. Today was a day to restore old pleasures.

When he arrived home on aching legs, sweat pouring down his body and brow burned by the sun; he remembered why it had been so long. He dropped down on a stool in the gatehouse panting for breath and wishing he had not been so foolish. Moments later, one of the guards helped him complete the journey to his residence. He longed for the caress of his bed, but there was no time. He must make preparations for the trip to Marah. He would just close his eyes for a minute.

***

While Dorryn slept, Zett was busy with his own preparations for the journey. His walk to the dungeons was not as warm or colorful as the ambassador's trip through the gardens, but it was more productive. Two large guards pushed open the heavy outer cell door as he approached. The cell was dark and damp. Water dripped against the stone in a far corner.

That sound would get irritating quickly, he thought and shrugged it away.

"I hope the accommodations are not too inhospitable," he said adjusting his cloak as he sat at the small wooden table in the middle of the cell.

He pushed the candle across the table to get a better look at the prisoner. Dark crescents hung beneath her eyes in stark contrast to her pale skin. Her frayed hair mirrored the state of her nerves.

"I'm afraid there will be no jailhouse rescue for you," he said. "Not that your son or his friends had anything to do with the last one. A murderer was needed. How convenient one was so close at hand and clever enough to elude the guards. Although, it didn't work out so well for your husband."

"Does Eli live?" the dowager queen asked.

"Yes, he does," Zett admitted. "And that is why you live. He would come to avenge you but that would take too long. On the other hand, he will rush to your rescue and that will be his doom. Yours too, I'm afraid."

"Why did you come here?" she asked.

"Just to tell you that your trial begins and ends in three days. Perhaps, Eli will attend." Zett stood to go. "I cannot give you longer. I must be off to Marah to see young Mali crowned King of Marah. Don't worry, I will be with him to light the way."

CHAPTER 38

The cool breeze whispered in from the east. Smoke curling from a thousand campfires gathered in the treetops lending an acrid bite to the evening air. The camp vibrated with a multitude of conversations. Campers wandered among the makeshift shelters seeking loved ones lost in the rush from Shiloh. Scraps of black cloth hung from branches marked the fires of the mourning. Eeryn and Cross, after a day of directing traffic, huddled over a hastily thrown together meal. Faryn and some of the females set up an infirmary that morning. They were still bandaging wounds and shuttling families away from danger as the sun began to set.

Bryn watched it all from the branches of a giant banyan tree. His head still ached, but that was not the reason he avoided the growing masses. He couldn't quite bring himself to call it an army. A huge part of him hoped that time would never come. They were a headless mass headed for the slaughter. It seemed a strange attitude. He was trained to fight, but he was no warrior. Across the tent strewn camp, One Eye caught his attention with a wave. Bryn returned the gesture and motioned for One Eye to join him.

"Are you hiding from somebody?" One Eye asked.

"Not really," Bryn answered with a shake of his head. "Just watching all the activity down there."

"What do you see?"

"Not much that I care for, that's for sure."

"It is beginning to look like an army," One Eye said. "Makes me wonder how it all came together so quickly."

"Yeah." Bryn heaved a sigh. "It was far too quickly for my liking. I mean escape tunnels, supplies, tents, a rear guard of Wolven, everything but weapons."

"Those are in a ravine just the other side of the stream." One Eye pointed over his shoulder to the west.

"Oh, great."

"Mind if I ask a question?" One Eye said.

"Go ahead." Bryn shrugged.

"Does trouble naturally follow you, or do you simply manage to stay a step ahead of it?"

"I was beginning to wonder about that myself," Bryn replied.

They exchanged glances and burst into laughter. One Eye threw back his head nearly toppling off the branch. Bryn caught him, but a couple of uncertain moments passed before they regained their perch on the limb. The mishap set off another round of laughter. It had been a long time since either had laughed. They made the most of the opportunity, letting the moment fade of its own accord.

"*They* have plans," One Eye said with a sweep of his hand toward the camp. "What are *we* going to do?"

Bryn's brow lifted. His head cocked slightly. "Aren't *we* part of *them*?"

"I'd say your duty has been done," One Eye mimicked the gesture. "You delivered your message and nearly died doing it. Your debt's paid."

"I'm not sure Zett would see it that way. Or Eeryn for that matter."

"Not likely, but that doesn't mean we have to join in that." He nodded toward the camp.

"My father's in jail," Bryn said. "I have a feeling joining this is only way to save him and our home."

"I don't see how that can come about by joining these amateurs," One Eye replied. "But I'm sticking with you."

At the far edge of the clearing, two familiar Wolven sentries broke from the woods at a run. Like a stone breaking the water's surface waves of excitement rippled out from their path. Their news reached Bryn's ear before they could reach their leader's tent.

Soldiers are coming.

The words turned order to chaos in seconds. Mothers called for children and snatched up those at hand; unsure whether to run or hide. Would-be soldiers scrambled for any kind of weapon. Husbands pushed their wives into tents as others began to throw a few meager belongings into carts and packs.

One disruptor shot, Bryn said to himself. *Just one. The whole camp will bolt in a blind panic.*

Beside him, One Eye drew back his bow as mounted soldiers emerged from the trees. The air reeked of fear. The refugee army began to dissolve. By ones and twos, defenders retreated. Those who stood fast shared the same panic filled eyes. The riders advanced without fear at a gentle walk. Bryn held out a hand to stay One Eye's arrow. From the direction of Eeryn's tent came a sound that began with a rumble and built like a small earthquake into a single word.

"Hold!"

Eeryn stood beside his fire; hands raised to the sky. His shout rolled over the camp washing the terror from unsteady hearts and turning panic into stony resolve. The word rolled over Bryn with a physical presence. Power surged through his limbs. The physical and mental retreat of the crowd evaporated. The riders, halted for a moment by the force of Eeryn's order, started forward once again.

"What the hell was that?" One Eye whispered.

Bryn didn't answer except to drop from the branch. He beckoned One Eye to follow as he walked out to meet the mounted soldiers. The sight gave inspiration to hearts desperate to know what to do next. A wave of followers joined the march.

Eli, a wide smile on his face, left Eeryn and ran to meet the soldiers. The leader of the riders dismounted and hurried forward to the prince. Eli quickened his pace. The two met with the embrace of warriors separated in battle. After celebratory back slaps, Luther Silas knelt before his prince. The soldiers with him did the same. Eli pulled Luther to his feet, and they passed through the crowd to Eli's tent. Eeryn, Bryn and One Eye followed them inside.

Away from the eyes of the camp, Luther's countenance clouded. He refused to meet the eyes that looked at him. The anticipated explanation for his escape from Shiloh seemed to cause him physical pain. His companions waited in silence for Luther's study of his hands to end. He drew a deep breath and slowly released it.

"Much to my shame," Luther began. "I have won my life and freedom by becoming the messenger of Zett. It is that vile schemer's belief that you would accept this message from no other."

"Then, it's best you deliver it," Eli told him.

"Yes, my Lord." Luther's eyes rose to meet those of the prince. "He intends to try and execute your mother, the Queen, at the full moon. I am to assure your highness that you may spare her the indignity of the wheel and public execution by surrendering at once."

Rage rendered Eli incapable of speech. The muscles of his jaws knotted drawing his lips into a tight, thin line. The white knuckles of clenched fists shook with a barely contained fury that was mirrored in his blazing eyes.

"Hold it right there." Eeryn pointed a finger at the prince. "You stop and think. Rash action will do your mother no good."

"You would have her publicly disgraced?" Eli found his voice. "Is that how you repay her?"

"Sit down," Eeryn ordered. "You are acting like the fool Zett believes you to be."

Luther loomed over Eeryn sword in hand. "No one speaks—"

"What captain?" Eeryn cut him off. "You would kill me for speaking the truth?"

Eli stepped between them.

"You are an irritating, emotionless dink," Eli told the seer. His frown disappeared, replaced by a slight smile. "That's why you are so good at what you do. He's right, Luther. Charging into Shiloh is just what Zett wants us to do. Zett sent you to make me think attack is possible."

"What do we do?" Luther asked.

"We have an army," Eeryn said. "We use it."

"An army?" Luther waved his hand over the camp. "This is not an army. This is not even a good angry mob. It's a pack of whipped runaways."

"What they lack in training," Eeryn said. "They make up for in spirit."

"Forgive me, Your Highness." Luther looked at Eli. "Spirit doesn't win battles or breech city walls."

Eli laughed. "I hope Zett shares your opinion."

***

The sun set the eastern sky ablaze as reds, golds and yellows chased the night from the horizon and spread over the sea. An onshore breeze laced with the scent of brine blew through the towering coastal firs where an army of outcasts lay concealed among the laurel and jasmine. At the city gates, more of their number, dressed in ragged clothes joined themselves to the crowd waiting for entry to the marketplace. On the ramparts, the master gatekeeper watched the eastern sky. As the sun rose over the wall, he gave the signal to open the gates. The solar driven motors engaged, the gates parted, and the waiting throng pushed its way inside. The motley collection watching the city shared one trait with those crowding into the city. They were fiercely loyal to the Prince of Shiloh.

Eli was not among those watching. At the moment he was commanding disciplined ranks of his veterans and Wolven on the road to Marah. The mob entering the city followed the Valirian seer. Their task sounded simple when you said it out loud, but none of those trembling under the cover of laurel leaves believed it would be simple or easy.

Bryn Bou shivered at the thought of how many of them he was about to leave dead in the streets. He pushed away the thought. He had to see them through an assault on the city and deliver the Queen to safety. There was no turning back now. Bryn motioned for his troops to begin moving through the bushes.

The outlanders stayed concealed until the humans among them moved down the road to the gates. On the northern side of the city, One Eye and his troops did the same. They were to assault the palace from two sides. Neither would know whether the other succeeded until retreat was too late. The chances for things to go horribly wrong seemed infinite.

Under cover of the wall, the men Bryn sent forward threw off their beggar's cloaks. Dressed as guards, they infiltrated and quickly dispatched the gatekeepers and nearby soldiers on the wall. Wynn, from atop the gate, launched a flaming arrow into the sky. Bryn broke from cover with a shout. The masses behind him added their voices and charged down the hill headed for the open gates. The humans innocently going to market were suddenly caught up in a battle. They stampeded through the streets screaming for help. Bryn was counting on panic to add to the chaos inside the city. He was not disappointed. Wynn and those with him quickly disabled the gate.

The terror-stricken crowd ran into the soldiers rushing to the aid of their fellows. Attackers, disguised as panicked rope merchants, dispatched soldiers in the chaos that ensued and pressed on to the palace towers.

Bryn and the leading edge of the army hit the gates at a run. The soldiers were swept aside by the attackers who rushed forward to the palace gardens. Faryn sent a pair of defenders reeling, blood spraying from deadly wounds. Bryn threw his dagger into the chest of an oncoming soldier. He retrieved it as he ran over the fallen body.

Valirian archers gained the gate towers and rained arrows into Zett's forces. Bryn's advance slowed as the humans were reinforced and the gardens ran red.

"There's no king's guard," one of the men with Bryn shouted, grabbing Bryn's sleeve, and waving his hands. "No king's guard."

Bryn stopped on the upper steps of the palace to look around. Something wasn't right. He should have known sooner. The push into the city was easier than he anticipated, and he let dreams of victory cloud his judgment. Those detailed with rescuing the Queen ran by him on their way into the palace. Bryn let them go. He wandered back down the steps for a better look at the dead. They were regular army, but far from Zett's best. Older veterans lay bleeding beside young cadets. The attack was not only expected, but Zett also thought them no match for his cast offs and baited them. Bryn's heart sank as the realization dawned that the Queen was probably already dead.

"Eli is riding into a trap," he said aloud.

Of course, he thought. *The Queen was never at issue. It was Eli that Zett wanted.*

He was hit by another bit of bad news. Where was One Eye? He should have reached the palace by now. Bryn dashed up the steps and into the palace where he was met by a trio of men. To his surprise, the Queen was with them.

"We have to get out of here," Bryn said. "Back the way we came. Move."

Bryn emerged from the palace shouting orders for his troops to retreat. The plan had been to link up with One eye and escape through the north gate. That plan would have to be scrapped. The north gate might still be in enemy hands.

It took several minutes, but Bryn got their ragged army turned around in the face of a growing number of human soldiers. The Creator had smiled on him. The way to the west gate was still open. Bryn could make out his troops still atop the gate. As the number of dead mounted, the bravado of the attack evaporated. Bryn's men turned and ran for their lives toward the gate.

As Bryn retreated, One Eye wandered into the hillside rendezvous tired and bloody. The assault on the north gate had not gone well. They ran into a solid core of Zett's regular troops. The assault never gained control of the gate. It was not even close. One Eye stumbled away from the attack worn and bloodied. Less than half his original number was still with him, and the city gate remained closed. Fortunately, there was no pursuit of his beaten force. Once beyond the range of the archers and disrupters on the city walls, One Eye and the remnant of his troops fell down exhausted.

Their rest was short lived. The sound of battle erupted to either side of them. Then came word from the scouts. Cavalry was coming fast. One Eye got his weary fighters on their feet and began herding them towards the northwest. The forested hills would slow the cavalry and, perhaps, give them a chance to escape. One Eye scooped up a wounded Valir and threw him across his aching shoulders. As many as were able followed his lead and tried to carry off the wounded. There were too many. The ground behind them remained strewn with bodies of the dying and those too broken to travel any further.

The cavalry came at a run. One Eye urged his troops on, but he knew in his heart they were not going to make the safety of the woods. He lay the wounded Valir on the ground beside him and drew his sword. A few of the others did likewise. Thirty yards short of One Eye's position, the leader of the cavalry threw a hand in the air calling for a halt. Horses were reined in and wheeled about. The riders drew their weapons. The leader continued toward One Eye alone.

"Eli," One Eye exclaimed. "Thank the Creator, what are you doing here?"

"We were about to ride into a trap," he said. "Zett was lying in wait for us. We are not safe here. We had to ride through infantry to reach you and they are moving this way. Get your people moving. Once inside the tree line turn due west and try to meet up with Bryn. We will watch your backside."

"It's going to be slow going," One Eye told him. "We're pretty cut up."

"Do your best."

One Eye and the walking wounded slogged through the woods until twilight before stumbling into Bryn. He had made camp on a sheltered hilltop about ten miles west of Shiloh. A few tents were scattered among the trees, but most of the fighters lay on the ground. There were no fires burning. One Eye found his way to Eeryn's tent. He was surprised to find an agitated Bryn pacing before the Queen and the seer. Despite the presence of the Queen, Bryn did not look happy at all. They had their prize, but something must have gone terribly wrong.

"One Eye." Bryn stopped pacing. "Thank the Creator, what happened?"

"We got our tail feathers handed to us," One Eye said and plopped down on the ground.

"Looks like you did alright," One Eye said motioning toward the Queen.

"They were expecting us," Bryn said.

"Tell me about it," One Eye replied.

"No," Bryn corrected. "They anticipated that Eli would attack the force headed to Marah. We only ran into reserves. The prince is marching on the bulk of Zett's army. They will be slaughtered."

"No, they won't," One Eye said. "He's right behind us. He somehow sniffed out the trap and called off the attack. He saved us from an army Zett sent to finish us off. He should be here any time."

"We're going to need him," Bryn said. "There's another army waiting for us just over the next hill. We've been pulled into a giant box. We are either going to fight our way out or be crushed."

"Let's fight," Eli said from the open tent flap.

CHAPTER 39

Cross looked out into the darkness and sniffed the wind. Flickering campfires burned to the east and west. Ahead of him, nothing but wind in the branches of an oak forest. The possibility of yet another trap was foremost in his mind. Zett had made few mistakes that day. He had the rebels in a box.

Or did he? As near as Cross could tell there was a half mile wide gap between the left flank of the infantry to the west and the right flank of a legion of light horse and cannon east of him. Was it a mistake by the two commanders or an open door to disaster? The question tumbled over and over in his mind. If he guessed wrong, a great many people would die. He decided not to guess.

"Chip, Hann, with me," he ordered.

"Quit calling me that," Chip snapped.

"I like it. So, get used to it," Cross told him while his brother snickered.

"Damn bird."

Cross climbed down from the branch where they had taken up position to see the ground ahead. His Wolven companions followed him as they ran toward what they hoped was a gap in the enemy lines. Keeping to all fours they moved swiftly through an open area of tall grass to the cover of the woods. The breeze in their faces carried no human scents. Cross pointed left then right. The others split off toward the enemy camps while Cross continued forward. He worked his way through the trees stopping at intervals to listen and smell the air. A mile or two further on, the woods gave out into another meadow of tall grass. He found no trampled grass; no sign of anyone having passed that way for weeks. There was only one other thing to try. He stood up, an inviting target for any sniper. A minute later, he began to breathe again. Turning on his heels, he headed back the way he had come.

A short time later, Chip and Hann fell in beside him. It was about two miles back to the main camp. The Wolven were in a race they had to win. With the coming daylight, Zett's soldiers would begin to wonder why there was no one covering their flank and close the gap. Getting an army of tired and wounded through the breech before that happened was probably impossible. He knew that sometimes the impossible was all you had to work with.

They found the camp alive with activity. Entire families worked side by side digging defensive positions, stacking brush, and readying weapons. Cross bolted into Eeryn's tent.

"We found a hole," he panted.

In less than an hour the army was moving. Wolven scouts led the way while others of their kind moved to secure the gap. The Valir formed a rear guard that pushed the masses onward. The need to hurry was at the front of every mind. They would not be beaten by lack of effort. The big foe at the moment was noise. Thousands moving in haste made a great deal of noise; sounds that at any moment might be picked up by Zett's troops and give away their escape.

Faryn coaxed and prodded the stragglers to keep up. Those too exhausted to walk, she had piled into carts pulled by the rear guard. She was constantly on the move shuffling fresh backs and legs into cart duty, keeping the column moving straight ahead, and watching the flanks for signs of enemy troops. Bryn found her busy loading a mother and her young into a moving cart.

"How are you holding up?" he asked.

"Well enough." She handed the last of the young to its mother. "But I'll be glad when we're out of here."

"Another hour should see us through the gap," Bryn told her. "Are you sure you won't continue with Eli?"

She stopped and took his face in her hands. Her eyes drew him in. Their beaks hooked around one another. The kiss lingered long enough for him to join in. Then, she let him go.

"I'm going with you," she said just to be sure the message got through.

Bryn nodded, not trusting his voice. He slipped an arm around her shoulders and started forward. Faryn leaned against him. Her hand resting on his hip, her head touching his and for a moment they were lost in a world of their own. A world without troubles; without armies; and without constant cries for help. It was a world of two becoming one; an impossible world that lasts only for moments and flees away.

Desperate cries for help pulled them back to reality. Half their group were searching for a place to hide in the grass. The other half was stampeding over the searchers. A young human couple was bowled over by a terrified group of bovine-like Taurines. An infant was knocked from its mother's arms and trampled by sharp hooves. Faryn scooped the broken child up. Bryn pulled the father to his feet and pushed him onward. The mother was beyond help.

"Soldiers are coming," the fleeing human said.

To his left Bryn could see torches moving in the distance. The sound of the soldier's field equipment rattled above the rush ahead. The gap was being closed. Bryn dragged a ragged human to his feet.

"Stay here and you die," Bryn shouted. He threw the man forward. It was enough to get him moving again.

"Listen to me," Bryn yelled to the crowd. "Move ahead. There is no escape behind us. Move forward or you will die. One Eye, Vulryn, take our people into the gap and hold it."

Valirians surged forward to form a wall with the Wolven. Archers took to the trees guarding the flanks.

"It's dead," he said to Faryn. "Let's go."

She laid the limp little body on the ground. With a deep sigh, she stood and began pushing carts forward and breaking up groups hunkered down in the grass. Bryn formed a small group of refugees into an armed rear guard. They were almost through the gap.

The vanguard of Zett's troops hit the wall of Valir as the last of the refugees cleared the gap. The Valir held, but they could only delay the oncoming army. The gap was already closing like a swinging gate. The Valir formed against Zett's soldiers slowly gave ground. Eeryn was supposed to meet up with the Valir before the gap closed. Bryn had not seen the prophet for hours. The refugees were clear of the grass and into the woods and Eeryn was nowhere to be seen.

The soldiers entering the gap set fire to the woods and retreated a short distance. The rising flames drove the last of the Valir from the trees and forced them from the gap. The refugees who remained in hiding fled the fire and were cut down by Zett's soldiers. Fresh human troops streamed in from both sides, but the growing wall of flames prevented them from attacking. Bryn and the Valirian warriors pushed the crowd ahead of them to safety.

One Eye came up behind Bryn panting for breath. "Eeryn's that way. He says hurry; we have trouble."

"Oh, he noticed, did he?" Bryn said.

He motioned for those around him to follow and set off after One Eye to find the seer.

Eeryn stood atop a large stump surrounded by Valir. His back was to Bryn as he studied the area to the west of their position. Before Bryn could speak, the seer hopped down to the ground and turned to face him.

"If I told you to jump off a cliff, would you do it?" Eeryn asked.

"What the hell kind of question is that?" Bryn asked.

"The desperate kind that will save us all," Eeryn said. "Well, would you?"

"Do I have a choice?"

"Not really."

"Then, I'll do it," Bryn said.

Eeryn motioned everyone in as close as possible. His voice was slow and clear.

"There is a small band of Zett's troops just ahead," he said and pointed to the west. It's a small advance guard. We are going to run through them as quickly as we can. On the other side of them is an escape route. They will not be able to follow us down. Use your wings; do as I do; and for the Creator's sake, don't hesitate. I'll see you on the other side."

Eeryn drew his dagger, turned, and charged ahead. Bryn bolted after him and the Valir set off at a run.

CHAPTER 40

The sprint through Zett's lead elements was quick and relatively easy. The soldiers expected the Valir to turn tail and run away at the sight of human soldiers. A horde of screaming eagles charging their lines caught the soldiers by surprise. Many dropped their disrupters before firing a shot. The dagger wielding Valir slashed through them scattering the knot of soldiers to the four winds. By the time they regrouped, the Valir were gone—vanished into thin air.

Just beyond the line of human soldiers, they came to the edge of a narrow crevasse. Eeryn spread his wings and dropped into the opening. As promised, Bryn followed without hesitation.

Bryn floated down into the dark in tight circles on wings that served only to slow his fall. As he descended, he kept telling himself that this spiral into nothingness was better than dying. The opening in the ground above rapidly receded becoming a thin slit of light.

When his wings began to brush the walls without sight of the bottom he wondered if this was a good idea. There was little else he could do. Three hundred Valir were coming down on top of him when Bryn's feet finally touched down on the gravel strewn bottom. The slope was too steep to walk down. He had to keep his wings outstretched to maintain his balance and keep his feet from sliding out from under him. An eternity later, the ground leveled out into smooth, solid rock and darkness. Bryn's trepidation grew. A drop into hundreds of feet of darkness was one thing. The thought of entering an underground world went against everything he believed he was created to be, but he was short on options. He stepped forward and the far away dimly lit world he fell from disappeared.

"Take my hand," Eeryn's voice spoke from the inky nothing ahead. "Get hold of the person behind you."

The seer's hand brushed against Bryn's. His free hand found Faryn's and he repeated the instructions. A smile no one could see crossed Bryn's face. The thought of a group of winged creatures holding hands like school children and walking through a hole in the ground got the better of him. He couldn't suppress a chuckle.

"What's so damn funny?" Faryn asked.

"The blind leading the blind," he said.

"Not for long," Eeryn told him. "Have everybody sit down."

It was a welcome rest, but it wore off quickly. Bryn's curiosity overpowered his patience.

"What are we waiting for?" he asked.

"Sit," Eeryn spoke from the darkness. The command was repeated at intervals for new arrivals.

Bryn did as Eeryn instructed. Stirring only to accommodate those behind him.

"That wasn't fun," One Eye said. "Do we stumble around in the dark now?"

"Sit," Eeryn repeated. "Wait and watch."

To the amazement of all, the walls began to glow a bright green. The light was subdued but bright enough to allow Bryn to see the walls and those ahead and behind him.

"What makes them glow?" Bryn asked.

"It's caused by tiny creatures that live on the walls of the cave," Eeryn told them. "Just how they do it is their secret."

"Gives me the creeps," One Eye said to murmurs of agreement.

Faryn gasped and suddenly grabbed Bryn's arm. Her wide eyes were awash in reflected green light.

"The walls are moving," she said.

"They are called Eral," Eeryn told them. "They live on the walls. Quite the handy little creature, don't you think?"

Bryn touched a finger to the cave wall. The Eral streamed away from his touch leaving a black hole. He withdrew his finger and the dark gap filled with green light. Without further word, Eeryn got to his feet and started them moving again. The sound of dripping water kept a rhythmic back beat to the splash of footsteps through the pools that collected on the smooth cave floor. Hushed calls of "look at this" and "look at that" spread along the line. Eeryn didn't push them. He kept a steady pace. He had seen stalagmites and stalactites before. He'd seen other things too. Some of them things he prayed they'd not see.

Bryn thought the seer had a keen interest in the side tunnels. Was he unsure of the way? He knew Eeryn was uneasy about returning to the Boubouja, if that was what they were doing. The seer's unease seemed deeper than worries of home or a wrong turn.

"Everything okay?" He laid a friendly hand on the seer's shoulder.

Eeryn jumped away with a gasp. He took a couple of deep breaths before his hand dropped away from the hilt of his dagger.

"Anything I should know about?" Bryn asked.

"I don't like caves," he replied.

"You didn't seem to mind them when we left Shiloh," Bryn reminded him.

"That was a tunnel."

"What's the difference?"

"Tunnels are seldom homes," Eeryn said.

"Oh."

He did not ask Eeryn what might be living in the cave. Sometimes it's best not to know.

"If you can stand it," Eeryn replied. "This is the way home. Of course, you can always try to climb out the way we came."

"Lead on," Bryn said into the silence that followed the seer's words.

Bryn soon had cause to wonder if Eeryn operated in another world entirely. They spent a sleepless night getting their army of refugees through Zett's soldiers, fought a rearguard action, marched for miles before charging through yet more soldiers, dropped into a pit that turned into a cave and had been walking for miles. Weariness had turned Bryn's mind into a foggy swamp, he ached all over.

Does he ever get tired?

Eeryn came to a stop at a wide turn to make sure everyone was keeping up. Through the green glow, he looked into Bryn's face and smiled.

"There's a large room in the cave just ahead," he said. "We will stop there and sleep. Unless you would rather press on."

"I think we should stop," Bryn breathlessly whispered. "Some of the others may be tired."

Eeryn nodded and waved for Bryn to follow. The news lifted his spirits and Bryn passed the word of a halt to those further back. It was received with a joy equal to his own. Around yet another twist in the cave, the walls and ceiling flew away. Great columns of stone rose from the floor to a vaulted ceiling forty to fifty feet overhead. Three hundred weary Valir did not begin to fill the circular room. They spread themselves out drinking in the open space and stretching out tired muscles. Soon snores began to echo through the wide room.

"Come sit with me," Eeryn invited Bryn.

Bryn left Faryn with Vulryn, One Eye, and Elryn to follow the seer to a distant corner of the room. Eeryn seemed to study him as they sat without speaking.

"You have questions," Eeryn said at last.

"Many," Bryn replied.

"Foremost seems to be how all this fell into place so easily. The answer you have already surmised. It didn't. Nothing that has happened since you entered Shiloh has been by chance. The time has only been awaiting your arrival."

"Why me?"

"How were your studies at the Academy? Did you do well?"

"Yes, I believe so."

"And yet, son of a great warrior that you are, you were not happy."

"No."

"Have you ever considered why that should be so? Any other Valir would have accepted his station as fate and risen to the highest tradition of the army."

"But not on my own merits."

"Nonsense." Eeryn dismissed the thought with a wave of his hand. "You allowed the opinion of others to sway you. The truth is evident in your actions since your escape from the dungeon. You are a more than capable leader. But you were right to leave the Academy. You are not a warrior. You're more than a warrior."

"Huh? That doesn't make sense."

"You have a little friend who speaks only to you. You have had visions. You have experienced insights. What does that sound like to you?"

"It sounds like craziness to me," Bryn said.

"Come now, you are above childish denials. You are a seer. The seer who is a warrior and the Creator's sword raised against Zett. There is in you the power to deny men the mastery for which they hunger. Say not, I am a child. There is a time to break down and a time to build up and you shall know them both."

"To every thing there is a season."

"And a time to every purpose under the heaven," Eeryn finished the proverb. "When the time comes, seize it. And now, we sleep. There is still a long journey in this darkness before we get home."

"What did Eeryn want?" Faryn asked when he rejoined their little group.

"Oh, you know seers," Bryn said. "Who can tell what they are thinking?"

Bryn drew her to him wrapping her in his arms. He stroked her head soothing the feathers of her crest until she slept. His mind and spirit proved stronger than physical exhaustion. Sleep did not come so easily for Bryn. When sleep did claim him, it brought fitful dreams of spinning hour glasses, falling leaves, and distant thunder.

He was awakened by the murmur of voices and the stirring of those around him preparing to resume the march. Faryn kissed his head as he rubbed the remnants of sleep from his eyes. Breakfast was hard bread and a few dried berries eaten while donning packs and forming up for the march.

Eeryn lead the way through the serpentine cave whose floor alternatively rose and fell. The quiet conversations of those that followed him were suddenly stilled when the seer began to sing softly.

"When my heart knows fear, Creator be near.
When my light is almost gone,
Hear my cry, hold my hand…"

The haunting words of the old song were picked up and spread through the long line of marchers. Singing along, Bryn felt an unseen weight lifted from him. His steps grew lighter. Eeryn said this was the way home. For the first time Bryn believed it to be true and hope blossomed in his heart.

Time was different in the underground darkness. Bryn

estimated they had been walking for about half a day when Eeryn again called a halt. The room he chose was large enough for everyone to relax but was much smaller than the first one. As they settled in, the seer cautioned everyone to be as quiet as possible. Conversations were restricted to whispers and needless movement discouraged. The glow of the walls had grown fainter and Eeryn confirmed this was because the cave exit was close at hand. He urged them to rest as tomorrow promised to be trying.

Eeryn held a finger to his beak and waved Bryn over to a narrow cleft in the rock. Eeryn pointed for him to look into the opening in the wall. Bryn saw nothing but darkness. No Eral lived on the other side. He shrugged his shoulders and started to pull away when a large glowing, golden eye opened in the blackness. Bryn jumped away from the opening, his back to the wall and working hard to breathe again.

"Dragons," Eeryn whispered.

Bryn nodded understanding and followed Eeryn away from the opening.

"I don't think there is a connecting tunnel the rest of the way," Eeryn explained when they had moved away. "As long as everyone stays quiet, we should be safe."

"How many?" Bryn asked.

Eeryn shrugged and passed along another call for quiet.

They had been settled in the room for a couple of hours when the quiet was disturbed by a faraway rumble like thunder. The sound seemed to come from within the cave itself. It was not thunder. It was the sound of something enormous moving nearby. Judging by the uneasy faces looking back at him, Bryn realized others had reached the conclusion something was terribly wrong.

As the day wore on Eeryn answered their concerns with monosyllabic replies before he withdrew completely inside his cloak and spoke to no one. The change in the seer unleashed a deep dread that filled Bryn's heart. An ominous foreboding settled over the room. Bryn passed the night in fitful sporadic sleep.

He was not the only one who was uneasy. The moment Eeryn's cloak rustled with his rising, eyes around the room locked on him and preparations to move began. The rumbling in the cave walls had stopped sometime during the night. Eeryn held a finger to his beak, turned, and started forward. Less than an hour later, he brought the column to a halt. They had come to a fork in the passage. Eeryn walked a few paces down the right-hand fork. He paused to listen before returning and motioning for Bryn to follow.

"This way," he said pointing down the left-hand passage. "Move quick, move quiet, and keep everyone moving until you reach the trees."

Bryn searched the seer's face. The unrelenting resolve he read in Eeryn's eyes told him this was not the time for questions. He nodded in agreement and waved the column forward, signaling for them to keep silent.

They were warriors trained to move with little sound, but tiptoeing three hundred of them past a den of dragons without incurring their wrath was going to require a minor miracle.

A few yards down the passage, the water pools on the cave floor grew together and became deeper as they traveled along the path. The water lapped about his ankles. Bryn didn't seem to notice, his attention was drawn upward where a weak shaft of light pushed against the darkness. They were nearing the exit. Bryn stepped up the pace. He was ready to see the sun and feel its warmth again.

He passed through a rock archway and broke into daylight. Blinking against the intense light, Bryn stumbled blindly into a small creek.

"Keep moving," he told the others. "Keep moving, hurry. Get to the trees."

He heard the column splash by as he waved them on. Gradually, his vision cleared. He turned to watch his companions leaving the cave. The opening in the rock that led them out was flanked by a second much larger archway. The stream they were walking in originated somewhere inside the large entrance.

Bryn estimated that about half of their number were clear of the cave. A rumbling in the stone like the ones heard the day before was followed by a roar that shook the ground. Footing was treacherous on the mossy stones that covered the stream bed. Bryn and a few others rushed back to help those who had fallen and struggled to regain their feet.

The rumbling and roars grew louder. Bryn pushed the fleeing column toward the trees where One Eye was forming them into bands. At last, Eeryn appeared in the mouth of the cave chasing the end of the column out into the light.

"Run!" Eeryn shouted.

He could have saved his breath. The tail end of the column disintegrated. Three hundred Valir warriors who fearlessly charged Zett's army broke and ran for their lives. Bryn quickly realized that even fueled by fear, they were not going to outrun the danger.

"The trees," Bryn waved his arms and shouted at the fleeing warriors. "Into the trees."

Knee deep in the middle of the stream, Bryn began marshaling those who heeded his shouts, into the trees along either bank. One Eye rallied the rest of the Valir a short way further downstream. Weapons drawn, they waited for the coming attack.

Talons screeching on solid stone, the dragon exploded from the cave. Beams of sunlight shining between the trees reflected in bright flashes from the row of iridescent blue scales along the creature's back. The rumble of its footsteps did not do justice to the massive size of the body that now stood at the cave entrance.

Golden eyes burning with internal fire searched the stream and locked on a warrior scrambling to his feet in the stream. The monstrous neck coiled to strike. In a blur, the powerful neck propelled rows of teeth forward. The dragon's jaws closed around the Valir with a nauseating crunch of bone. A quick upward thrust of the dragon's head sent the broken body skyward. The dragon's jaws reclaimed the body as it fell and slid down the beast's throat.

The onlookers recoiled in revulsion. Fear was back threatening to destroy their resolve. Bryn shouted commands that steadied them. From the base of a tree, a warrior pointed over Bryn's shoulder to something behind him. He whirled to face the threat.

Eeryn waded toward the monster alone. The prophet drew the cloak from around his shoulders. His eyes never left the dragon as he rolled his cloak lengthwise and began to twirl it above his head while continuing to wade closer to the beast.

The spinning movement of the cloak caught the dragon's eye. It stopped chewing and spit out what remained of the dead Valir and roared a warning at the seer. Eeryn, not deterred by the display, kept advancing. The dragon answered with great lumbering strides that rapidly closed the gap between them.

"Ja Ryn." Eeryn shouted and snapped the cloak like a whip.

Electric blue fire crackled, snaking through the air trailing the scent of ozone. The bolt hit the dragon between the eyes, and it shrieked in pain. Its knees buckled. It staggered but kept coming. Eeryn retreated a few steps and snapped the cloak again. The blow took the dragon down in a heap that nearly splashed the stream dry. The wall of water knocked Eeryn off his feet leaving the two foes floundering in the stream. Eeryn lost his hold on the cloak of leaves. It floated away from him moving downstream.

The seer was the first to find his feet. He ran after the cloak and the cover of the weapons waiting in the trees, but he was not fast enough. The swing of one huge claw caught him in the back. Eeryn went down into the stream in a spray of blood.

"Fire!" Bryn ordered.

Those in the trees loosed a volley of arrows. Bryn, dagger drawn, rushed the beast. A hundred Valir followed him, their weapons driving deep into the dragon's hide. The dragon was able to do little more than bellow at the onslaught. The attack was swift and deadly. For a moment the dragon found his feet, but his legs would not hold him. He collapsed, bleeding and gasping for breath. More thrusts of the daggers made certain he would not rise again.

When the dragon was dead, there was no shout of victory, no rush for trophies. There was no sound but the breeze in the branches. The warriors gathered around the fallen prophet in stunned silence.

The stream carried away Eeryn's life in a fading flow of red. Blood oozed from his ears and the corners of his beak, but the light of life still shone in his eyes. He raised a trembling hand in a don't touch me gesture. Bryn sank to one knee near Eeryn's head, tears in his eyes.

"Take them home Bryn Bou," the seer said. He coughed and a fine pink mist shrouded his head. "It's up to you now. Give the cloak to Coryn. He will know what to do with it."

"But how—?" Bryn stopped short.

The seer could no longer hear him. Eeryn was dead and their hopes with him. Bryn looked down on the seer's face. The cold certainty of fragile mortality gripped his heart. He fell into the black abyss that opened in his mind. This was not possible. Eeryn could not be dead. He was to lead them home.

The seer's last words resounded in his head, "Take them home Bryn Bou."

ABOUT THE AUTHOR

Jack LaFountain is a chimera, with the arms of an aircraft mechanic, the head and heart of a minister, the body and back of an Emergency Room nurse, and the tales of a writer. Stepping from his peculiar comfort in horror, he is sallying forth into the realm of fantasy with Trails of Trouble.

www.jacklafountainauthor.com
www.facebook.com/authorjacklafountain
www.houseofhonorbooks.com
www.facebook.com/houseofhonorbooks

Be sure to sign up for the House of Honor monthly newsletter to keep up with all our latest releases.

PRAISE FOR THE AUTHOR

martha williams

5.0 out of 5 stars **Red River**
Reviewed in the United States on November 24, 2023
Verified Purchase

I accidentally started with the second book and it is so good that I now have to get the other 2 in the series. This book has scares, humor and history, an unbeatable combination in my opinion. Also the style of writing that Lafountain uses resonates with me. Very well done!

Melissa

5.0 out of 5 stars **Mr LaFountain's writing**
Reviewed in the United States on November 2, 2022
Verified Purchase

His writing is so detailed with emotions and environments that you feel as if you are in the story, not just reading it.
I am more and more impressed with his works the more I read by him. It's such a pleasure to be swept away into fantastical stories that I cannot put the book down. I have to find out what happens! I read a lot, so much so that I skip parts that to me, seem not important to the actual story. I have never skipped any parts of Mr LaFountain's stories. I soak up every word, every page and could recite them almost verbatim. I easily forget the novels I read the week before. He is a true master of his craft!

BOOKS BY THE AUTHOR

Ed Landry Novels
Bayou Moon
Blood Moon
Voodoo Moon
Lover's Moon
Wolf Moon
Hunter's Moon
Coming Spring 2024 the next Ed Landry novel

Red River Series
Death Rides the Red River
Death Haunts the Red River
Death Stalks the Red River

Short Story Collections
Tracks
Tokens of Perdition
Krampusnacht:
    An Ed Landry Christmas and Other Stories
Dead Man's Hand

Mann of God
Redemption
Judgment
Zion
Resurrection

Experimental Christianity

Made in the USA
Columbia, SC
06 March 2025

54737103R00150